# SHADOWS
## IN
# SUMMER

## *A Novel in Six Voices*

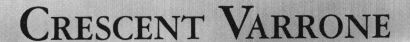

## CRESCENT VARRONE

ISBN: 1-4392-5196-7
ISBN-13: 9781439251966
Library of Congress Control Number: 2009907599

Visit www.booksurge.com to order additional copies.

BookSurge Publishing
7290 B. Investment Drive
Charleston, South Carolina 29418-8305

This is a work of fiction. All of the characters, organizations, and events portrayed in this novel are either products of the author's imagination or are used fictitiously.

Manufactured in the United States of America

For more information, please see www.shadowsinsummer.com

❖ ❖ ❖

*For Kirsten*

# ACKNOWLEDGEMENTS

First, I would like to thank my editor, Catherine Knepper, of Iowa Wordwrights. Sincere thanks also go to the patient, hawk-eyed readers of the many drafts of this work over several years, including but not limited to:

Kanika Bahadur
Norberto Barba
John Butter, M.D.
Philip Cacouris
Sébastien Doubinsky
Kathie East
Dominic Ferro, M.D.
Martita Fleming
C. Scott Lopez-Gelormino
Gus Haracopos
Julian King
Patricia Mooney
Linda Portnay
Frank Walsh
Peter Webster
Jonah Wittkamper

*And most especially*
Emilia Varrone

I would also like to thank Martita Fleming and Amy Swanson for their help with cover design. I thank the team at BookSurge (now CreateSpace).

Finally, heartfelt gratitude goes out to my parents, Camille and Chris Varrone, who have always been there to support me.

# CONTENTS

❖ ❖ ❖

A book must be the axe for the frozen sea inside us.

- Franz Kafka

# PROLOGUE
# Katrina Nielsen

Emergency lights glowed cobalt blue in the grainy atmosphere of the corridor. I crept toward a closed door. On the clouded glass, a freshly-painted name appeared below the familiar ones – an unexpected name, an undeserving name. My name.

Hunched over his work, a dark-suited figure stood with his back to me, scraping letters from the translucent pane with a flat-headed screwdriver.

*Hruskh-rhuskh.*

*Hruskh-rhuskh.*

Curls of auburn pigment lifted off the surface and splinters of glass rained down. Whole letters disappeared; already only "NIELS" remained. *I mustn't let him expunge that name.* But for what seemed like years, I was frozen.

The giant gouged harder, putting his weight behind the scraping tool. Glass squealed under the pressure of cruel metal. Wincing, I held my ears, but felt no relief. For the keening was inside me.

Finally I lashed out, striking the man's shoulder. As he turned, I gasped, recoiling from the veined and contorted face. It seemed familiar – but it couldn't be.

My father was dead, seven years dead.

The figure tried to speak, but only a gurgle and rivulet of crimson escaped the lips before the mouth and cheeks and throat began to swell. His skin turned an anoxic purple, as if he was suffocating in his Grandad collar. Pointing to his chest, he wanted me to undo the button – but when I looked down, I saw that inside his shirt, all was hollow and oozing blood.

I screamed and felt hands on me, jostling me awake.

Richard murmured in my ear, then snapped on the reading light. As his face materialized, I saw concern in his soft eyes of umber.

"What's the matter, Skat?" he asked.

Scattered snorts and grumbles arose from the delicate sleepers of Club Class, then subsided along with my cries.

I closed my eyes and tried to recapture the details of the dream, but the images melted and blurred. I reached out, but the multitude of bits eluded me, slipping like snowflakes through my fingers, falling like snow into the void below us.

Into the vast darkness above the North Atlantic.

The cure for anything is salt water – sweat, tears, or the sea.

- Karen Blixen

# SPRING
# 1. Katrina

The shadow of the 747 rippled over lifeless fields, patches of naked forest and the occasional frozen lake, a pastoral landscape still in the grip of the Snow Queen. Though I'd grown up in Denmark and knew how raw the month of March could be, the whiteness took me by surprise. We'd left New York green as Saint Patrick's Day, and while there had been a great deal of ice in my childhood, I did not remember snow.

The left side of my body felt dead, numbed by the draft from the window. I shivered and crawled deeper into my cocoon of blue blankets. *Who was the man in the dream?* I woke up thinking of my father, who'd died of heart failure in late 1988, when I was nineteen. I left home shortly after the funeral, and hadn't been back since.

Fa' was an intense man. Mor said his obsessions killed him in the end. He couldn't play bridge without becoming club champion, couldn't practice law without rising to partner in a leading firm, and he couldn't drink without reddening his cheeks and ours with the shame of his excesses.

In the rosy light of dawn, Copenhagen burned, a fiery whorl of crooked canals and serpentine passages. Through the crystals of frost on the glass, all seemed jagged, dog-legged, distorted. The only true shapes I could discern were the ice-skinned rectangles that we call "seas," gleaming like rear-view mirrors along the defenses of the old town.

*I was bred in this place. I was a girl here...*

The next afternoon, still jet-lagged, I bought a clutch of lady tulips and found a taxi stand on the city's west side. The driver stood and held the door for me. His flowing garments of shimmering white linen and starched skullcap contrasted sharply with the coffee color of his face and hands. I told him the address — Mor was still living up in Hellerup, a well-heeled, well-scrubbed suburb north of the city — and we set off.

The cabman introduced himself and started chatting away. As we drove down Vesterbrogade, I could see that "Jibril" was just one droplet in a wave of immigration from Asia and Africa. Long-bearded men stood scowling and gesticulating on the pavement outside halal butcher shops. Stocky women in headscarves of green, white, and gold walked flocks of children through open-air markets heavy with the smells of frying garlic and onions, falafel and döner kebabs.

The Copenhagen of my memory, a bland, depressed albino of the eighties, had been spiced up and invigorated by boom times. The year was 1996. New buildings were going up everywhere, and the older ones had gotten facelifts. As we drove north and east toward the better sections, we passed refurbished castles and the freshly sand-blasted Royal Theatre. The colorful New Harbor, across from our hotel, was bursting with tourists flush with cash.

Yet even in the presence of the city's glittering delights, one was never far from its doleful past. Stone battlements, melancholy as Elsinore, pondered their reflections in the glass and steel of newly-minted cafés and office blocks. At a construction site, mirthful inns and pubs emerged from the clayey soil, even as the dirge of a pile-driver rebounded off the stone monuments of what once had been a warlike state.

Jibril stopped at a traffic light in the shadow of the fortress Kastellet and asked in his South Asian lilt, "If you don't mind me asking, what is bringing you back to this kingdom of ice and snow?"

"I missed my family. My father passed away—"

"Oh, I am sorry to hear of it," he said as he turned and regarded me with deep-set bistre brown eyes. The crinkles and crow's feet told me he was older than I knew. The light changed and he accelerated northward onto the coast road.

"Thank you," I said. "But it was a long time ago."

"Yet," he said, glancing in the driving mirror, "it is not quite settled, I think."

*Was it that obvious?*

"Yes, that's just it," I said.

"So you are coming home to your mother?"

I nodded and said, "I left some things unfinished."

"You will come home for good?"

"Well, I don't know. I'm not sure whether I'm more comfortable here or in New York."

"Forgive me for saying so, but it's not about your comfort. Here you will be a comfort to your mother."

"Yes…" I said, hesitating. "I hope so. What about you? Do you ever think of going back to your homeland?"

"Oh, no, Mahm. You see, wherever I go, there I am home," he said, flashing a beatific smile.

"What about *your* mother? Don't you want to be a comfort to her?"

At this his face grew serious. "I'm afraid I have no mother, but I try to be a comfort to those around me wherever I go."

Jibril delivered me to my childhood home which lay at the end of a sea-scraping side street. Alighting from the cab, I preened a bit. I didn't want to show any ruffled feathers upon returning to the nest after so long. But it was difficult to appear anything but tousled on such a day. A wicked March gale blew in off the Sound, whipping my hair and biting the flesh about my eyes until the tears flowed.

Stepping into the lee of the naked trees that ringed the garden, I wiped my eyes with a gloved finger. There wasn't much to see. A leafless beech tree offered vacant birdhouses to a lifeless sky; the prize-winning rosebushes slept, still wrapped in the thorns of winter. Only a few tender shoots of green, overeager in the rush for life, emerged here and there from patches of frozen brown turf.

*Oh, was that a child's bootprint?* I could almost see miniature versions of Claus and myself playing soggy games of tag and hide-and-seek on the slippery surface of the side yard. How I loved to sing-song, *Du kan ikke fange mig!* while dodging my brother. Even though he was two years older, he never *could* catch me. I hadn't seen him in ages – just after the funeral, we bickered over something that seems unimportant now. We haven't spoken since.

From my vantage point at the end of the garden, through the bare branches, I had an excellent view of the Sound. The restless waters of Øresund licked at the thin edge of the coastal ice. The weakening sheet cracked and rumbled; a chunk the size of a small sailboat broke off and floated out into the deep.

I pictured Mor and my tiny self far out on the Sound, a mere dot on an in-finite slate of ultramarine. I must've been six or seven years old. We were so far out that day that I could barely see the dark strip behind us that was our island. As the fog closed in around us, I grew frightened and begged to turn back. But Mor just smiled and said, "A little farther, Skat." She always called me Skat. Later I learned that many parents call their children "dear" or "treasure," but in my elf-sized ears, it sounded like a shortening of my first name. I've always considered it my own.

As we sailed farther out into the Sound, the wind bellowing and the waves crashing over the bow, I shrieked with excitement. I pleaded to come about, but always on the knife-edge of wanting to test the extremes of wind and weather. I dreamed of us sailing in and out of weeks, exploring the crinkled coast of Sweden and the fjord-ripped fells of Norway, where in my imagination, one-eyed Odin and his followers still held sway.

Mor grasped my little hand in her strong sailor's grip, locked my eyes in her gaze and said, "There's nothing to be frightened of out here, Skat. Not out here."

The whitecaps toppled over us. The sloshing spray splashed my face. All around me was blue and green and sopping wet. I was thrilled, soaked, and as happy as I would ever be. Mor wrapped me tight in an oversized towel of white cotton, and hugged me until I was warm and dry and laughing.

"AHEM. Shall I take the bag for you, Mahm?" said Jibril, rousing me from my nautical reverie.

"Uh, no, that's all right. I'll get it," I said, extracting my purse from the back seat. I paid him the fare, and climbed the familiar stone steps. The engraved nameplate was new to me.

## Ingrid Margrethe Latour Nielsen

## Enke

Oh my God. I knew Fa's name would be gone by now, but to see *Enke* carved where other upstanding citizens would write "Doctor" or "Attorney"... It was really just too much. As if she were a *professional* widow.

I must've been standing some minutes in the gale, because my cheeks were hard as candy apples by the time I pressed the lighted rectangle and heard the chimes. The door opened and before me stood a thin, straight-backed woman.

"*Ach, kom ind, Skat,*" she said. "You're freezing to death out there."

"Hallo, Mor," I said. "It's good to see you." I handed her the flowers and pecked her on the cheek.

"Yes, well, it's good to see you too," she said, ushering me into the vestibule. "And good to have you back in Denmark. It's been too long."

I colored at the remark, and before I realized the words had passed my lips, I'd said, "I guess I just wasn't ready to come about until now."

"Come about?" Mor asked, her brows furrowed. Then her eyes widened; she nodded once and the corners of her mouth dipped as she made a quiet *mm* sound.

Mor went to put the white-and-yellow flowers in water. I took off my shoes by the front door – as one does in Danish homes to avoid tracking in snow or mud, depending on the season – and stepped directly into a puddle of meltwater.

"Eeyuch!"

"What's happened?" she asked.

"Oh nothing, I just stepped in something wet."

"Let me see. Oh, just take those stockings off. I'll put them on the radiator to dry and fetch you a new pair. I still have your—"

"No, Mor," I said, rubbing. "It's fine. You don't have to do that."

"You'll catch cold, Skat, let me—"

"No, Mor!" I said, more harshly than I'd intended.

She raised her eyebrows and regarded me silently.

"As you wish," she said. "Come into the kitchen, where it's warm."

But it wasn't.

In my memory, the kitchen was cozy, filled with the soft spices of childhood: cinnamon and cloves, vanilla and cardamom. But no cakes or cookies emerged from the oven on this day; no aroma of fresh-baked *klejner* or *kringler* hung in the air. My hands huddled round my tea cup, yet I remained chilled, wet feet dancing on the clammy tile floor.

We sat and chewed on store-bought *kransekage,* elegant, but cold. A tower of sugar-drizzled marzipan topped with the national flag, it was the quintessential Danish dessert. Each hardened ring independent, separate unto itself.

Mor sat stiffly, as if her limbs had become as brittle as the porcelain we drank from. The royal blue eyes were glossy now and the lamplight reflected in their liquid surface. Her face, lined and sere, reminded me of author Karen Blixen in her later years. She opened her purse and extracted a cigarette case in which a softpack of Prince lay snugly entombed. Removing a single cigarette with a deft flick of her wrist, she tapped the end and reddened its tip with her nickel-plated lighter. I winced as the smoke came between us.

"You really should give that up, Mor. It's poison, you know."

"At my age? Hmph! No point in giving it up now. Besides, I *enjoy* smoking. It's one of my few vices – and few pleasures."

"What do you do for fun nowadays? Do you sail any more?"

"Goodness, no. Not for years. I'm afraid my little boat is in its harbor for good. But I'm hardly a shut-in. I have my little circle of girlfriends. We meet for whist on Tuesdays and lunch on Thursdays."

"I'm glad to hear you're playing cards. Richard and I learned to play bridge in New York. Perhaps we could get a fourth sometime?"

"Perhaps," Mor said, and narrowed her eyes as she drew smoke into her lungs, then tilted her head back to expel it once more. "Tell me, how is your American?"

"Richard's fine, Mor. He sends his regards. He actually wanted to come today, but had to meet with his new boss. Perhaps we can all get together on the weekend."

"What is your husband doing here?"

*An ambiguous question.*

"Same thing he did in New York, more or less," I said, twisting my wedding ring.

"He's a banker of some sort, isn't he?"

"A financial consultant, with a firm called Fielding & Company. He worked out a transfer, you see."

"But what does he do, exactly?"

"He advises companies on, well, financial things – like big mergers and bond offerings and going public."

"I see. Per worked on matters like that."

"Yes, I know, Mor. But Fa' was a lawyer. This is the financial side. Richard's brilliant with maths, you know."

"And how's his Danish?" she said with a puff.

"He says he'll learn if he can find the time. But he'll be working in English anyway, so there really isn't a need."

"Oh, it isn't a question of the *need*! If I were living in London, I should speak English. If one lives in Copenhagen, one must speak Danish."

Mor managed to appear elderly and imperious at the same time. Her hair, blond in her youth and steel grey in my memory, was now tinged with white; it fluttered as she pronounced directive words like "need" and "must."

"Yes, well," I said, "I'm sure he'll learn." My hand trembled slightly as I sipped the cup of Lady Grey.

"Mm-hm," she said, nodding. Then she raised her eyebrows and added, "Oh, by the way, that Jespersen girl sends her greetings. I attended a luncheon with her mother not long ago."

"Oh, I haven't heard from Annika in ages!" I said, smiling as I recalled my best friend from high school.

"Was she one of your ballet-girlfriends?"

"No, but we were all in *gymnasium* together. You know she used to have the biggest crush on Claus…"

The room fell silent. We looked away from each other and sipped our tea. I pulled my feet up from the chilly tiles and hugged my knees. Mor finished her cigarette and crushed the stub in the silver ashtray.

Finally, I asked, "How is my brother? Still practicing law, I suppose?"

"Oh yes, he's specialized in tax."

"I'll bet he's a partner already."

"No, not yet, but I think it's coming. He certainly works hard enough. Agnete and the children don't see much of him."

"The apple doesn't fall far—"

"No, it doesn't," she said, looking away.

"You know I never did get the watch Fa' promised me."

"The *hvad-for-noget?*" she said, narrowing her eyes.

I reminded Mor about the pocket watch that Claus and I both coveted, but neither got, after the funeral. A few minutes later a deep blue velvet box sat on the table between us. She said she had no use for it. I opened the lid and beheld the golden orb. It seemed so much smaller than I remembered, felt tiny in my hand when I picked it up. But still it had weight to it, and the chain was heavy as Marley's.

I opened the case and revealed the face that had been hidden for so long. It was like seeing Fa' again. The watch felt electric in my hand. I wanted to press it to my cheek, but controlled the urge. The time, 4:38, seemed accurate enough, but even though it was afternoon, the little window that showed day and night was filled with darkness and the sliver of a crescent moon. Stuck, perhaps.

"Do you think Claus will want it?" I asked.

"You might check with him yourself. Meanwhile I can't see any harm in you taking it."

I covered the face with a satisfying click, settled the body of the watch in the form-fitted satin, and buried the box among the keys, compact, lip gloss and Tampax in my purse.

"Where are Claus and his family living nowadays?" I asked.

"Near the center of town, Overgaden oven Vandet. They have a lovely apartment overlooking the water – which reminds me, where will you be living?"

"We don't know yet."

"If you're in the market for real estate, you really should meet a spruce gentleman by the name of Niels Vier Dahl."

"I remember Herr Dahl, Fa's friend. He used to sneak me black licorice."

"Hm. I didn't know about that, but he is extremely well-connected in such matters, informed of properties *before* they go on the market. Shall I have him call your husband?"

I bristled at *your husband*, but took a deep breath and forced a smile.

"Richard was just saying he needed to find a realtor," I said. "We can't stay at the D'Angleterre forever."

"The D'Angleterre. My goodness, such luxury," she said with a little wave of her hand.

"The Firm is paying for everything."

"They must think well of your American."

"They do," I assured her.

The D'Angleterre was the grand dame of Copenhagen hotels. The royal blue carpets were of deep pile, the crystal chandeliers of French cut, and high tea was served promptly at the stroke of four each day. But something made me uneasy.

"Mor, is it true that the Germans used the D'Angleterre as their headquarters during the Occupation?"

"Yes, I think that's right. It's a grand, central venue with a commanding view of the port. Of course, the *Wehrmacht* took possession of whatever they desired."

A cold draft passed by my left ear and I shivered and reached for the warmth of the teapot. "Mor, what was it like?"

"What was *what* like? To be occupied?"

I nodded.

"Tja, I was just a girl, on the farm in Jutland. Sugar was hard to come by, I re-call. Coffee and cigarettes honestly impossible. One couldn't go anywhere, travel was restricted, and in any event, there was neither gasoline for the tank nor rubber for the tires. But first and foremost, one felt *invaded,* at the mercy of an alien power. It was ter-rifying," she said, buttoning her cardigan. "Why do you ask?"

"Oh, no reason." I examined my fingernails. "It's just that I passed a brass plaque in the lobby today, listing all the famous guests of the hotel."

"A long list, no doubt. The hotel is positively ancient."

"H.C. Andersen was there, Niels Bohr. Even Princess Diana visited last year. But when I got to the *G's,* I noticed…"

I stopped short and swallowed. Mor tilted her head. "Noticed what?"

I forced the name from my throat.

"Goebbels. The Nazi, you know, Joseph Goebbels."

"Hmph!" she said, flapping her palms as if to waft away the stench of the name itself. "I suppose he must have visited during the war."

"I couldn't believe it," I said, leaning forward in my chair. "There he was, a wolf in lambswool sweater, standing in the lobby among heroes and royals. I mean, isn't he the one—"

"Who killed his family, yes," she said, her head shaking. "In the bunker at the end of the war. Wife and six beautiful children. He was a monster, they all were."

"I couldn't get to sleep last night. I kept thinking of Nazis treading the floorboards. Do you think they kept an eye on the coast from those rooms?"

"I'm sure they did, Skat," she said with a distasteful expression. "All the more reason for you to get a place of your own as soon as possible."

Later that evening, as the taxi entered Kongens Nytorv, the lights of the D'Angleterre came into view across the darkened square like a huge ship upon the waters. Above the entrance, the Danish standard fluttered in the breeze as if on a prow. The spotlights cast shadows onto its red-and-white surface, reminding me of the swastika that once flew from the same staff.

Yes, even as one gazed at the city's glittering delights, one was never far from its doleful past.

# 2. Richard Marchese

Something smelled funny about it. We'd only been in the country for a week, for godsakes. How'd he find the place so fast?

Not that I wasn't due for some good news. We got in last Thursday. The next day I go in to meet my new, hyphenated boss, Frederick Brøns-Hansen, head of the Danish office. He's running late, so I go and wait by the door. Twenty minutes, I wait. Finally, he makes an entrance like a bishop on Palm Sunday. At the elevator he's met by one secretary, two managers and three assorted lackeys, all clamoring for his attention. He stands about six-foot-six, so I could see his long, narrow head and beaky nose hovering above the fray as he strolled down the carpeted hallway, handing out autographs and instructions to the faithful.

I felt privileged at first to be waved into his plush office overlooking the spires of Old Stock Exchange. But that feeling lasted about as long as a left-handed relief pitcher. He sat me down and told me, I don't know what kind of coddling you're used to, but you're over here now, so you're going to have to play by our rules. No car, no private secretary, no first-class air travel, no office (though you do get a lovely cube with plants). And by the way, the Americans are only paying for temporary housing through mid-April. After that, you're on your own.

Welcome to Denmark!

That's the way it's been, right from the icy blast of air that hit us when we stepped off the airplane. At 11:30 every day, the cook rang a bell – *what was this, the navy?* – and everybody dropped what they were doing and scrambled down to lunch. The Danes ate huddled together around long tables. But did anybody sit with me? Nah, give me a break, they don't even *talk* to me. There are people working in the same room with me that I don't know their names yet.

I felt weird, isolated, displaced. I hated sitting in the lunchroom alone. So today I ducked lunch. Noon found me sitting at my desk, surrounded by ferns and ficus, talking on the phone with a geriatric realtor.

Frederick had given me a deadline, three weeks. The clock was ticking, this I knew. But I felt like the guy was selling me a bill, so I said, "What's wrong with it?"

"Nothing, Richard, nothing," Dahl said. "Rosenborgs Allé is one of the best addresses in Copenhagen." His voice was low-pitched and breathy, his English fast and oily.

"Is it big enough?"

"It's 135 square meters, plus you get the cellar."

"So about 1,450 square feet," I said, calculating the metric conversion in my head. Twice the size of our apartment in the city. "Is there a backyard?"

"A lovely garden, you've just got to see it. And the sooner the better. The listing goes up tomorrow afternoon."

"Do we have to contact the owner to make an appointment?"

"Uh, no. The older gentleman who lived there died."

"In the house?" I asked – *hey, I'd seen my share of horror movies growing up.*

"No, nothing like that. The owner hasn't lived there since one year ago when he went into the nursing home. The Estate wants to sell the property as soon as possible – even the old furniture is available, if you have any interest in antiquities. There's a lovely piano, for example, and a Gustavian grandfather clock."

"Antiques? Absolutely. Katrina loves old stuff, and since we're moving from a Manhattan shoe-box, we won't have anywhere near enough furniture for a home of that size."

"Can you see it already this afternoon? I would be glad to show it to you personally."

We agreed that he would pick us up. I tried to reach Katrina, but couldn't get ahold of her, so the silver-haired, silver-tongued realtor and I went out, just the two of us. His BMW 325i convertible smelled of breath mints and Aqua Velva. The diamond-studded pinky ring on his right hand glittered against the black leather steering wheel as he twisted his way through rush-hour traffic. A nonstop talker he was, this Dahl. On the twenty-minute drive, he managed to explain the origin of his name (it means "valley"), how long he'd known Katrina's family (since the sixties), and how much he paid for the beamer (about three times what it was worth). A lawyer specializing in real estate – not your run-of-the-mill broker – the old chiseler got the inside track on selling the property because his firm was handling the Estate. Pretty slick.

Weaving and tailgating up the avenue like Mario Andretti, talking a mile a minute, he must've forgotten where to turn off, because all of a sudden we're whirling, twisting, squealing, honking. A right-hand turn from the left-hand lane! Brakes screamed, horns blasted, tempers flared. Hand gestures were made. We cut off two Volvos and a U-Haul before reaching the safety of a shady side-street.

As the boulevard receded behind us, the noise downshifted, and so did the driver. It was still a city street, but silent. It was amazing how muffled it was in there, as if we had entered another world.

Dahl slowed to a reverent crawl and almost whispered, "Welcome to Svanemølle."

I gave him a look like, What's up with the Driving-Miss-Daisy routine?

"Life passes slowly in here," he said.

A block in, gas-powered streetlamps appeared, marking our passage into the realm of Swan Mill, a buttoned-up neighborhood of trim lawns, high hedges and walled gardens. The first block was dominated by juniper and cypress, and then an arcade of plane and poplar trees grew up around us, their light-green spring foliage blocking out the sky. Even though it was still afternoon, the gaslights flickered like stars twinkling in a woody firmament.

Halfway down the last block before the coast road, Dahl pulled over and cut the engine. Raising his steel-wooly eyebrows, he bared his unnaturally-white upper teeth and announced, "We're here!"

The house was tall, with an intelligently-sloping roof decked in tiles of orange-red. Two dormer windows stood watch, their shades half-drawn like sleepy eyelids. Brick steps led up to a wooden door, painted vermilion. Katrina would like that, red is considered lucky in feng shui.

The house was older than the other homes in the area, and more exposed. While they were hidden, protected by ivy, hedges, walls, #18 was on display. No gates, not even a fence, just a few tall trees on the left-hand side and a handful of shrubs. Even its innards were laid bare in a huge picture window; though from where I was standing on the opposite sidewalk, all I could see were reflections of the gray clouds behind me.

The house disclosed nothing.

I went and stood next to Dahl on the stoop. On a marble slab mortared into the white wall, I saw one chiseled word, Sundhuset. I was going to ask about it, but as the door swung open, an exhalation of stale air hit my nostrils and I had to take a step back. I gave Dahl a look and he said, "I'm sorry, Richard. No one's come up to give the place air."

I was disappointed that he hadn't previewed the property – it served me right for using such a decrepit realtor, a guy his age should've been put out to pasture long ago. But the price per square foot was half what you'd pay in Murray Hill, so I stepped into the heavy atmosphere of the foyer. It was dusty and I sneezed. Dahl's mouth transmitted play-by-play nonstop, like the Mets' Lindsey Nelson. I caught the occasional sound bite as Dahl ran around opening windows: built ninety-odd years ago, maintained meticulously over the years, electrical and plumbing up-to-date. *A great day for baseball.*

It was the house of a smoker. The wallpaper was yellowed from the crown moldings down to about chest-height; the rancid memory of age-old cigarettes hovered close to my face, reminded me of endless car trips strapped into the back of Pop's old Buick-8. It's funny, when I was a kid, I loved the smell of tobacco. In Alexander's Department Store on Queens Boulevard, while my mother was shopping, I'd hang out in the tobacco aisle, breathing in the scent of snuff and cigars and pipe tobacco until the security guards would come and chase me. But I never smoked, never could figure out how something that smelled so alluring, so sweetly-delicious, can have such a vile, bitter taste.

A gray grandfather clock stood watch by the door. Its ticker silenced, face frozen in a perpetual scowl at twenty minutes to four. Well, at least it was right twice a day. Several old-fashioned but genteel pieces inhabited the living room – a green couch with clawed feet in teak wood that looked like it just came off the set of *Hedda Gabler*; a white ceramic stove, its black chimney disappearing up out of sight; and in the corner, an antique piano in a case of burnished cherry wood.

Katrina would be smitten by these things. I was pretty sure she played piano when she was a kid, though I couldn't remember ever hearing her play. The hand-carved dining room table and chairs were elegant, if not very comfortable-looking; the sideboard looked like it was made of polished oak. Everything was covered in a thick film of dust except for the piano, which looked like it had been polished yesterday, gleaming redly under its clear lacquer.

The backyard, I loved. Crocus was coming up through glops of snow; dark-green ivy climbed the walls. Birds cawed as Dahl showed me around, answered strangely by the squeaking of my three-hundred-dollar wingtips as they sank into the sodden turf. The antifreeze-green lawn was clipped short and flat as a putting green, shady on the west side under the trees, and sunny on the east side, where there was a patio.

Dahl described the landscaping as we walked. There were three or four oaks, a Norwegian spruce, a stunted elm. The elm was vulnerable, its root system exposed. Several roots had started to girdle. I asked about the towering tree on the west side.

"In Danish we call it *ask*." Struggling to find the English word, he said, "You make baseball bats out of it."

"Ash," I said, and we laughed at how similar the words were.

Back inside, we slogged through layers of dust, leaving footprints on the stairs. The back bedroom was large and bright, though there was a faint odor, that toejammy smell that lingers near the bodies of old people and cheeses. This was the master, I figured. The darker, front bedroom, small even by Manhattan standards, was set up as a study. Built-in bookshelves, now vacant, lined one wall; a butterfly collection slowly disintegrated in its frame above a roll-top desk, locked; a brass telescope trained its antique eye on naked poplars.

"Was your client an astronomer – or a Peeping Tom?" I said, only half-joking.

"Neither."

"What's with the telescope, then? Doesn't seem like you could see very far with it through these trees."

"I really couldn't say, but you can see how old it is. When I started in this business, the lots across the street were vacant, the *platan* trees were saplings. I expect the original owner had an excellent view of the Sound from here."

"The Sound?"

"Yes, you can still see it there at the end of the street," he said, pointing to a spot of blue, barely visible off to the left.

"Now you're not going tell me this is an ocean view, are you?" I asked, and we both laughed.

"But seriously, it does explain the name, Sundhuset," he said. "The Sound House. When it was built, it stood alone, and had a commanding view of the Sound."

This was foreign to me, this European habit of house-naming, I explained as we walked down the stairs. In the United States, only mansions had names. Fallingwater, Hearst Castle, Hill House, *Tara* for godsakes. But over here, even ordinary homes had titles. I liked the idea. "Sound House" did have a certain ring to it.

On the Long Island Sound, there was a club where my rich Uncle Carmine, the landscaper, was a member. In the summer, my mother and I used to go to this club, taking on new identities to get in. Mom became Rose Nunziante. I got to be my blubbery cousin Rocco. My mother assured me that unlike my cousin, I was not fat. I was *husky*. Though the point can be made that I was "husky" enough to pass for Fat Rocky at the pool.

The men's locker room stank of urine, mildew, and salt water. This inner sanctum of manhood was abandoned by the able-bodied during the week, relegated to a rear-guard of grotesquely hairy, bony and distended old men, who I could only assume went to the pool on a Thursday morning for one reason alone. The prospect of seeing my *piscio.*

"The laundry room is downstairs," Dahl said.

The second he opened the door, I caught a whiff of it. Dampness, mold, and a vague indication of rotting vegetables, like a garbage strike. I had an instinctive aversion to going down there. He pulled a short chain and a bare bulb flared into life. Beads of sweat clung to the roughcast walls. The old man descended slowly. I hesitated. He looked back at me, and I took the first step down into the tight stairwell. A blast of dank air greeted me. Another step, and the odors grew more distinct.

There was a deep, earthy smell like loam, the stink of green-mold like those French cheeses that nobody should ever eat, and the synthetic note of fuel oil. By the time I reached the bottommost step, the stench was really overwhelming. I had to cover my nose and mouth. It's hard to say what the hell smelled like that: sulfurous, like rotten eggs, and putrid, like something, an animal maybe, had *died* down there.

I turned on my Bally heels and left the lawyer droning on the slab at the bottom of the steps. Coughing and sputtering, I made a beeline for the nearest exit.

Dahl followed after, evidently panicking. "Richard, listen, there used to be an oil burner down there – please, wait!" I stopped in the front hall. "Look at it as an advantage," he said. "You're the first to see this property, you're in a great position. It just needs a thorough airing. The Estate is anxious to sell – if you make a reasonable offer, you can steal this place."

He was appealing to my greedy side – not necessarily a bad strategy, I admit – but I just shook my head and walked out through the China-red portal.

Back in the car, we didn't speak for several minutes. I was angry and disappointed, but I didn't want to jeopardize Katrina's position, Dahl being a family friend and all. So as we pulled out into the brightness of the coast road, I smiled and said, "Listen, I'm sure other things will come up."

He took his time answering. At the next traffic light, he touched my forearm and said with a soft, avuncular tone, "Richard, can I be totally honest with you?"

"Of course."

"I think your reaction was understandable, but not very rational."

"How do you mean?"

"The cellar has a certain odor. It happens. I've seen this kind of thing before. All we have to do is put a box fan down there for a few days and those evil-smelling vapors will disappear. That's all superficial, Richard. What you have to decide is whether you like the *fundamentals*."

This was a clever choice of words — a term from finance — and sure enough, it resonated with me. The light changed and he continued talking as we drove into the heart of the city.

"What are the three most important factors in valuing real property?" he asked.

"Location, location, location," I said, remembering the old saw.

"Sundhuset is just a few meters from the esplanade. It's just ten minutes to drive to Katrina's mother up in Hellerup, and your commute downtown would be a breeze."

"The location is great," I admitted. "I like that you can sit on the deck and smell the sea."

"And you can walk up to the boulevard shops and restaurants."

"Yeah, it's nice not to have to get in the car for everything. But I'm not in the market for a handyman special."

"Not at all. It's in fantastic shape, Richard. You should see the engineer's report."

"Really? No unpleasant surprises like rats in the basement or a huge crack in the foundation?"

Traffic snarled and we stopped dead in front of Kastellet. The wooden arms of a windmill extended over the tree tops like a basketball player guarding the net.

"Richard, I'll tell you the truth," he said, looking into my eyes without blinking. "You are a sophisticated purchaser and you know what *you want to buy. The house* is an excellent match for you and Katrina. I've known her since she was a little girl, and believe me when I tell you, this is the house for her. I don't know when you'll find another like it. When we first talked on the phone, I told you the market was really heating up. *From the beginning, you knew that. You and Katrina would be very happy together in Sound House.*"

I made no response, just stared at him, mesmerized. Stared into his lichen-green eyes.

"Listen, you don't have to *decide to buy today*," he said, lowering the stakes. "Just give me three days and I shall get the place ready for Katrina to see it. What do you say? Shall we make an appointment for say, two o'clock on Sunday afternoon?"

The light changed. Dahl depressed the accelerator and turned his attention back to the road. Hell, maybe I was being hasty. After all, I was in the catbird seat – the property had been empty for a year. Katrina could get the garden she always wanted, no more apartment-living, not to mention some beautiful antiques. And the location was perfect.

By the time we got to the hotel, I had nearly forgotten about the evil-smelling cellar.

"Who knows?" I said, as we said our goodbyes. "Maybe Katrina will fall in love with the place."

As I walked back into the regal, deep-carpeted hotel, I had a bounce in my step. I was really looking forward to the showing on Sunday. Truth be told, I was already hooked. A great address, and a bargain too! We could get out of the hotel before the deadline, and by the time my mother came for a visit in July, we would be thoroughly ensconced.

Of course Dahl was right. He's the expert after all. I knew it all along. From the minute I saw the place.

*From the beginning I knew that Katrina and I would be very happy together in Sound House.*

# 3. Søren Jensen

A real-life princess sauntered up the drive and into my life on the loveliest spring day I have ever known. The Gulf Stream had blessed my little kingdom with an early-April warm snap. I was sitting in the front room, savoring a cigarette and the Sunday edition of *Jyllands Posten*, when I glanced randomly out the window and beheld a vision of Nordic beauty that haunts me still.

White-armed and wheaten-haired, such a maiden would have made the proud wife of a Gothic chieftain or Norse jarl: high cheekbones, features clean as new-fallen snow. Her dress was blue – no, *azure,* "azure as the Northern Ocean," I should say – of a draped cut that flattered her height and lithe musculature. The navy-and-white scarf worn loose round her neck was adorned with tiny hand-sewn pom-poms like snowballs on a glacier-field.

But for all this, it was neither her face nor her raiment that made me put down my coffee cup. It was the way she moved. She moved with a grace that one normally observes only at the cinema: Audrey Hepburn, Grace Kelly, Ingrid Bergman, women of a previous era. Yet unlike the painted ladies of Hollywood, this maiden's beauty required no artifice, no tricks.

Her hands flowed like butterflies, tracing soft curves and figure-eights wherever they fluttered. Elbows at her sides, she held herself like a young duchess at a reception in Amalienborg: straight-backed, attentive, sensitive. No doubt she would be disturbed by a single pea under the mattress.

Of course the princess was not coming to see me. I knew that from the beginning. She was coming to see Old Man Damsgaard, the house next door. And she was attended not by a Danish prince, but by a loud, olive-skinned man, and that ancient property broker, Niels V, who had sold Mother and me our home so long ago. What was he doing, still working – still breathing – so many years after Mother was gone? I missed her—

*Auuh!* My fingers were burning. I shook the cigarette-hand, dropping the end on the sill. I must stop smoking these things.

Just then, the realtor spied me in the window and waved. It was a Come-out-and-say-hello-you-wretched-hermit wave. All my instincts told me to stay indoors, in safety – to watch this woman from a distance. But what could I do? There he was, waving again, cupping his hand towards himself and simpering. There was no choice now. I had to go out and meet these people.

"Good day, Herr Dahl," I said, nodding as I strode down the driveway.

"Good day, Herr Jensen. Let me introduce Mister Richard Marchese of New York." *Marchese,* that explained it. Italian. Mafia, no doubt. The greasy black hair betrayed his dark origins. I shook hands with him, showing him the crown of my head, but careful not to take my eyes off him.

"Mister Marchese worked on Wall Street…" Dahl said.

"Twenty Wall, that's right," the braggart said, chuckling.

"…and this is his lovely wife, Katrina Elizabeth Latour Nielsen."

Ah, at least she kept the Nielsen, didn't lose the maiden name – though she must have lost her "head," when she married this sot. I smirked at my own pun.

"Fru Nielsen has been living in New York these past seven years," Dahl said.

The beauty spoke. "Oh, please just call me Katrina."

"Charming," the old man said with a satyr's grin. "Katrina, this is Søren. Søren, Katrina."

I have never quite gotten used to the custom of calling people I've just met by their Christian names. But still, I supposed I should get used to the 20th Century before it became the 21st, so I smiled and said, "Katrina."

Color came to my cheek as I touched her warm, slightly moist hand, her blood heated by the sun. I drank in the heady draught of her nearness – the perfume of her, the smoothness of her hand against mine, the sweetness of her lips saying a single word.

"Søren."

My mouth ran dry and it was all I could do to say, "May I offer you something cool to drink?"

"That is very kind of you, Søren. Yes, thank you," she said, smiling.

It was certainly a gracious reply, but even then I suspected something more. Her smile revealed even the back teeth. Did she always grin like that? Or did she, perhaps, feel something too? I realized that I was older than she, but at 39, I was hardly ready for the knackers' yards, and I had a great deal to offer her. She had been out of the country for years; she would be happy just to meet a Dane. How she must long for her culture, her people, her true self...

But there was no time for reflection. I was soon dashing back to the kitchen. Was there lemonade? Beer? Perhaps foreigners would prefer gin and tonic on such a day? Hmph, no matter, as I had no gin. Surely, I couldn't offer tap water. Oh, we so rarely had guests. What was in that wretched refrigerator? Orange soda-water! There was a large bottle of Fanta. On ice, perhaps that would do.

I brought the refreshments to Old Damsgaard's sun porch, a lovely nook in the back garden that rarely lived up to the optimism of its name, but did so on this occasion. The ice tinkled merrily in the glass ewer. We simpered a great deal, as one does with new neighbors and the simple-minded.

"What brand of soda is that?" the Italian asked.

"It's called *Fanta*. *See* how it fizzes on ice?" I said to Katrina, speaking across the rest.

"I missed this in New York," she said.

"It's all I have to offer you," I said. Fantasy was indeed what I had to offer her – I looked at their faces, worried that I might have said too much.

No one noticed.

Then Mr. Wall Street barged in. "So, what's your line of work, Soren?" he said, pronouncing my name as if it rhymed with "torn."

Niels V. rescued me from embarrassment by saying, "It's pronounced *Søren*, like burn."

"Or yearn," Katrina said.

Ah! Now I had new reason to be embarrassed. Or did I? *Yearn*. Had she really read me that quickly? No, her face betrayed no hint. Her English was simply superior to Dahl's and she had found a word that rhymed more closely with my name. Still, such things gave me hope.

"Ohhh, I'm sorry," the Italian said. "It's like CERN, the nuclear research lab in Switzerland. I've never heard that as a name before."

*Only me and Kierkegaard, you unlettered puffball.*

"Søren," Katrina said gently, rousing me from my momentary pique, "What do you do for a living?"

"I'm a pharmacist," I said, looking only at her, my eyes wide open. I have grey eyes, and I've been told they are quite handsome. Even mesmerizing.

"Where do you work?" she asked.

"At Boulevard Apotek, not far from here," I replied, gazing into her cerulean eyes as if we were the only two people in the world.

But it wasn't to last. They showered me with questions, as if I were a local celebrity:

*Who lived in Sundhuset before?*

*How does District heating work?*

*Is it always this warm in early April?*

I relaxed into the role which I was nearly born to play. Peder Damsgaard lived there for many years. All by himself, I was sure. Yes, the place was cavernous for a man on his own. I explained about the remote heating and the Gulf Stream and double-paned windows and snow removal and gas-powered streetlamps and a dozen other things that really didn't matter. I tried not to show off too much, but I must have impressed Katrina as quite the expert. The three of them nodded and smiled like the Magi. I was very pleased with my performance. Mother would have been proud.

I hoped very much that Katrina would move in next door to me. I was feeling so confident that I asked about their intentions. They would move in on Saturday the 13th.

Outwardly, I was cool pleasantness and decorum, wishing them well. Inside, I was overjoyed, in ecstasy that I would bask daily in the light of my morning-star, already the goddess of my idolatry.

We said our goodbyes, and from the window I watched them walk down the driveway, manoeuver into Dahl's cramped German sports car, and pull away. I stood there some minutes with a glad heart.

It was the loveliest spring day I have ever known.

# 4. Edvard I. Frankl

Of course I was overjoyed when Richie called to tell me he was moving to Copenhagen with his young Danish bride. Though I was born on the German side of the border, I have always been a fan of the sensible Danes, and I was very fond of his father, Vincent, when he was alive. I owed him a great debt from many years ago, the sort one can never repay. So I looked forward to helping Richie settle in to his – and my – adopted country.

I arrived at the Housewarming feeling a little guilty for not having found the time to stop by earlier. I had been in Croatia for most of the month of April, counseling rescue workers and the families of victims of a high-profile plane crash.

A tall woman, her hair up for the occasion, opened the door. We had met once before, in New York. She was even lovelier than I remembered.

"Velkommen, Edvard," she said, extending a hand and a smile. "You're early."

As I stepped into the lovely, antique-filled room, I said with a little shrug of the shoulders, "I thought I might make myself useful."

"Like hell you will – you're a guest!" Richie said, bounding out from the kitchen and giving me a bear hug, as the Americans do.

"Argh! Thank you so much," I said. "Now I don't have to visit the chiropractor this month."

A grown man, Richie was taller than me now, but in the boyish grin I could still see the precocious, energetic lad who liked to challenge authority. The couple was well-matched. Katrina slender and refined, Richie built like the American footballer he'd been in college. What he lacked in the social graces, he made up for in intelligence and drive.

"You've done a wonderful job decorating, Katrina. When did you move in?" I asked.

"Just over a month ago," Richie said.

"Listen, I would love to stand here chatting with you both, but we've got work to do," Katrina said.

I was assigned to peel and slice vegetables in the kitchen, where I stood alongside my host, who pursued the alchemy of mixed drinks.

"What are you making?" I asked.

"Margaritas. I got ahold of tequila and Rose's lime juice easy enough, but you can't get ice cubes in this town for love or money," Richie said, "and I had to go to three liquor stores before could find triple sec."

"Hmm, I won't pretend that I know what triple sec is – but it sounds very dry," I quipped.

Ignoring my riposte, he continued, "We've found that the best way to hold a party, especially when you've got people coming who don't know each other very well, is to start off with margaritas. Then everybody loosens up and talks to each other, and things can get rolling."

"Good recipe. We Northern Europeans have a lot of – oh, what is the word in English? In Danish it's *hæmninger.*"

"Inhibitions," said Katrina, scooting in from the dining room.

"Oh, *those,*" he said laughing, "Yeah, we've got those in America too. Especially us Catholics."

"I thought it was *guilt* Catholics specialized in," I said, playing along.

"Yeah, that too. But seriously, I thought Danes were wild. In New York, the Scandinavians were always the life of the party. Drinking, messing around, and very free—"

I raised my palm. "You may find them different at home."

"Well, then I'll put enough Cuervo in these margaritas to make everybody feel like they've just landed in Cancun."

At the stroke of seven, the soirée filled rapidly with dozens of prompt Danes: friends and family, business associates, and neighbors. I was on my own – I lost my wife to cancer several years ago – but hardly alone. I knew quite a few of the guests: some from the neighborhood, several from the University Hospital where I still hold a position in the Psychiatric Department, and one or two from my private practice.

Katrina managed everything herself: no catering. Of course, the guests helped: her mother brought homemade *sild* in the various Danish flavors of herring: mustard, sherry, curry; Niels V. Dahl and his wife, Helle, brought a glazed ham;

Richie's lanky colleague Christian – he topped two meters – brought wine from his trip to Italy. The next-door neighbor, who introduced himself rather formally as Søren Sigurd Jensen, brought a collection of blue cheeses – Roquefort, Stilton, Saga. I particularly gorged myself on a piece of St. Clemens, stopping only when some crumbles fell onto my belly and I was reminded of how it had overgrown my belt. I myself had brought some cream-filled pastries from the French patisserie on Nørregade, but tasted not-a-one, having been chastened by the cheese crumbles.

Someone put on background music, Frank Sinatra. Richie manned the blender and the frozen margaritas began to work their magic. Soon everyone was buzzing about this and that: how early the roses, how warm the weather, how refreshing the drinks.

I removed my tweed jacket and put it on the back of a chair in the dining room. An older gentleman with a shock of white hair, rosy countenance and twinkling blue eyes introduced himself as the Reverend George Pearson. An Englishman long-resident in Denmark, he had been the chaplain down at St. Alban's, the stone church down by the statue of the Little Mermaid, until his retirement several years ago.

"How did there come to be an Anglican Church here in this Lutheran country?" I asked.

"Ah, well you see it all started when Princess Alexandra of Denmark married—" he started to explain when he was interrupted by Niels Dahl, who by this point had drunk more than his share.

"Herr Doktor Frankl! *Mein Freund*, good to see you again!" he said loudly.

Nodding a quick apology to the Reverend, I turned to the real estate man and said, "Good to see you again, Herr Dahl."

"How are things in Kronborgs Gate 21?" he asked, as if to remind me that he knew exactly where I lived.

"Just fine, thanks."

"Are you enjoying your retirement yet?"

"No, not at all. The rumors of my demise have been greatly exaggerated. I'm working harder than ever, and traveling extensively as well."

"Traveling? I thought you were a headshrinker?"

"Yes, that's right. I specialize in trauma counseling, so I am often called to the scene of a tragedy. I've just come back from Croatia. You may have heard about that plane crash."

"Ach, *ja!* That's right! Some American Secretary of Something was killed. Bad business, bad business. But let me ask you something, Edvard – I can call you Edvard, can't I? – with all the travel you do, how do you find the time to keep up that big place of yours?"

*Click.* I saw where this was going.

"Oh, I'm sorry. Have you noticed the grass getting too long?" I asked, raising my eyebrows.

"Oh, no, not at all. Nothing like that. It's just. Well, I thought I would of-fer – after all it is my profession – to come by and give you a free evaluation some time. You don't really need all that space, now do you?"

"How do you know my 25-year-old girlfriend and I aren't going to have a baby one of these days?"

"You have a 25-year-old girlfriend?"

"No, as a matter of fact I don't. But how did you know?" I asked, and we both laughed.

Just then the lights flickered a bit. Dahl looked around, scanned the ceiling as if for cobwebs.

"You know," he said, leaning in. "Sundhuset has seen a lot over the years. I'm glad it has strong young people to take care of it." I looked at him. He lowered his voice. "You see, after Gerda, I mean, after Fru Jensen died—"

*Ting, ding, ding.* Our host was tapping his fork against his wineglass. Someone turned "The Summer Wind" down to a zephyr, and Richie began to speak.

"Ladies and gentlemen, welcome to Sound House! Katrina and I are very happy you could all be with us here tonight. I'm just a kid from the streets of New York..." he said, pronouncing it *Noo Yawk*, as Vincent did.

After several well-chosen sentences, he raised his glass to the lady of the house. We all said *skål*, sipped, brought our glasses down to the level of our jacket-buttons and looked our companions in the eye, as is tradition.

Since Richie's parents could not be present, I stepped forward, ahem'd a few times and said, "I don't know about everyone else, but I am having a great time. Isn't this a fine party?"

"Yes!" sounded the predictable response.

"Yes indeed, and I can remember when Richie was a little boy—"

"*Please* call me Richard," he said with mock-annoyance.

"Yes, well, all I can say is that if the measure of a man is in his choice of mate, then you have done well. I think I speak for all of us in saying that Katrina has really outdone herself tonight!"

Cheers and applause – I was on a roll.

"Like you, my boy, I am also an immigrant to the Danish lands, an outlander, though I have lived here most of my life. In the half-century since the war, I am happy to say the world has grown smaller and more peaceful. Perhaps we have finally learned to get along with one other. Look around you at how many different types of people are here, all eating and drinking and getting along: Lutherans, Catholics, even some Jews like myself," I said, nodding to a Jewish acquaintance.

"And a wall came tumbling down in Berlin a few years back." A wave of hear-hears rippled through the crowd. "I wouldn't have thought even Gabriel himself could have brought down *that* wall!" A flutter of chuckles meant I was ready for a big finish. "So let's raise our glasses to the New World Order in which global peace and international understanding reign. No one shall disagree with me—"

I was interrupted by the lights flickering once and going dark. We must have overloaded the vintage wiring what with the halogens flaring, the stereo playing, the oven baking and the blender whirring. It was ten o'clock already and the windows gave no more light than if they had been tarred over. There was a good deal of confusion as people scurried about turning off various appliances, bumping into one another, and asking each other where the fuse box was. Two or three butane lighters cast an eerie glow.

I raised my voice. "Please, everyone stay where you are."

After a minute or so, Richie said to me, "I found a flashlight. Let's go downstairs and see about the fuses."

As we moved through the crowd toward the truncated door that led to the cellar, Richie's colleague Christian said, "I'd be happy to come down with you."

Richie put the torch under Christian's face and shadows shot upward across his features, like children telling ghost stories around a campfire.

"No thanks, I need you to stay up here and keep everybody calm," Richie said, and opened the door to the underworld. I followed at his heels.

Creeping down the narrow stairwell, he bumped his head on the overhanging masonry and said, *"Helvede!"*

"Ah, good for you, my boy – here just a month and already swearing in Danish!"

"Hey, in any language that hurt," he said, holding his forehead. "Look, I'm bleeding."

*"Richie,"* I intoned, remembering the little boy who reveled in the maternal attention that comes of cuts and bruises. "I am a medical doctor, and I can assure you the wound is but skin-deep."

Continuing down the stair, he grumbled a bit more about how I mustn't call him "Richie." As we reached stepped out onto the concrete slab of the cellar, he asked, "Now where are those damned fuses?"

I was about to encourage him to look behind a pillar, when I felt a chill breeze go not so much by me as *through* me. I shivered at the sudden downdraft, must've been damp with sweat from the warmth of the living room. I consider myself a man of science and do not spook easily, but I must admit it made my scalp prickle.

"Did you feel that?" Richie asked.

"The draft? Yes. These older homes are very drafty," I replied, not entirely convinced myself.

"And cold."

"Yes, as if it's still the dead of winter down here."

Moving deeper into the vault, he stumbled behind an outcropping and said, "Yeah, well, we can discuss the four seasons another – ah, shit in plain English!"

I heard the clunk of metal on stone and the darkness closed in around me. No, not darkness, *blackness.* It was dark upstairs, the cellar was black as pitch. No windows, no vents, no openings at all, so far as I could see. The chamber was sealed, airless as a crypt. I marked my breaths. Soon they started to come more quickly.

"Did you drop the flashlight?" I asked.

"Yeah. Oh, for crying out loud," came the distant reply. Then for a long time I heard nothing but occasional shuffling sounds far off, echoes in a cave or mine shaft.

I rifled through my pockets. *Where was that lighter?* Ach, upstairs in my tweed jacket, hanging on the back of the dining room chair. Damn.

Cold, but still sweating, my breaths came but shallowly. I tried to breathe more deeply, but it was stifling down there, like being smothered in black curtains.

Seconds trudged by like minutes.

Finally, I heard, "Here it is. Oh Jeez, I hope it's not busted."

I held my breath, but no light emerged.

*Tramp-tramp-tramp-tromp.*

Footsteps, footsteps on the stair. One hears more acutely when sight is extinguished. The tread was rough, heavy, athletic. At first, this was reassuring. Whoever-it-was was making himself obvious. But who could it be? I knew right away that it wasn't the lithe Katrina or the slow Dahl. I called out, "Christian, is that you?"

No answer. The footsteps continued, softer now.

*"Who's there?"* I called again, and the sound came to an abrupt halt.

"I'm back of this column," Richie replied, though he voice seemed awfully far away. He was fumbling with something.

My heart was racing, beating in my ears. Madly, I thought of rushing up the stairs, the darkness be damned. But I couldn't leave the boy down here alone, could I? Or was I just afraid of meeting whoever it was on the staircase?

I backed soundlessly against the damp stone, felt droplets on the back of my neck. Richie stopped his puttering. No doubt he too was listening in the dark. Without lifting my back from the wall, I craned my neck toward the stairs, strained my eyes. No one was there. Yet I was paralyzed. I dared not shiver, dared not breathe.

*It was November, so it must've been cold, but I don't remember that. I was four years old, and all I remember was the darkness. Roused from my bed, I was frightened in the black hole. It was the cellar that time, too. Was the noise coming from the apartment upstairs? No, never. I could hear them outside, banging around, yelling, smashing things, cudgeling dogs who dared bark at them, shattering store windows. I still wince at the sound of broken glass. What more? Singing. Songs of the fatherland, fight songs for the devil's own side.*

For a moment I thought I could hear the ancient singing, see the hateful standard. *Die Fahne hoch.* Then exploding glass. Surely I was dreaming, reliving that night in 1938. But then the noise resumed. This was no flashback. Soft shuffling, closer now. A sweeping noise on the very stone under my feet.

Afraid it would touch me, I cried out, "Richie, is that *you*?"

Then the sound of a latch opening and a door closing and perhaps – or did I imagine it? – a small groan farther off.

I said harshly, in a voice quite unlike my own, "Richie, what the devil are you doing back there?"

And just then he must have flipped the mains, because the chamber was suddenly engulfed in white light, blinding me. I blinked repeatedly, to rid myself of the afterimage on my retina. Of the unshaded lightbulb, I suppose.

"I found the light," he said, unruffled.

When my eyes adjusted, we were standing alone in an ordinary basement. Yet my hands were palsied; my brow was soaked. I took out my handkerchief and patted my forehead. I put my hands on my knees and took deep breaths.

I'd had a panic attack, my first. Yes, surely that's what it must've been: elevated pulse, shortness of breath, paranoia. Connected to a traumatic memory, this was classic PTSD.

*But why here, why now, after so many years?*

As shaken as I was, my host was calm. With the confidence of his father in his eye, he strode across the floor and said, "And call me Richard."

I did from then on.

We agreed to return to the party. As we moved toward the foot of the stair, he asked, "Did you hear footsteps?"

"Yes, distinctly."

"Did you see anybody come down here?"

"No, I didn't see anyone. Perhaps the footfalls came from upstairs."

"It sounded just like somebody came down here."

"I thought so too, Richard. But – but it can't be."

*"Ghosts?"* Richard asked, managing a laugh.

I turned away and headed up the stairs. "Hmn, swearing in Danish and believing in ghosts," I said more jovially than I felt. "Why Richard, we'll make a European out of you yet!"

As we emerged from underground and entered the living room, a din and commotion flowed over us. A maelstrom of partygoers was sweeping up hats, jackets and handbags, and streaming out the portals into the night air. Richard walked to the front door to play host; I went over to Christian, who stood in the dining room with his coat over his arm.

"Surely you're not leaving so soon?" I asked, looking up at his gaunt face that was full of worry-lines.

"Yes, I'm afraid Annika was quite disturbed by the whole thing."

"By the lights going out?"

Just then Annika herself, an attractive little sparkplug with curly blond locks and a pug nose, stepped up and said, "The glass *exploded* less than a meter—"

"Ouch!" I felt a sharp pain in my right hand, which I had placed on the back of the chair where I'd left my jacket. The collar was covered in tiny fragments of broken glass. The hand was bleeding in several places. I plucked out a few of the larger splinters as discreetly as possible, and wrapped my fingers in a cloth napkin.

"Oh my goodness, are you all right?" Christian asked.

"There. You see?" Annika said.

"Yes, I'll be fine. See what?" I asked.

"The wineglass – it exploded!" she said.

"You mean someone knocked it over?" I asked.

"Hardly," Christian said, pointing. The stem of a wineglass sat on the table, unmoved. Its bowl was utterly absent, evidently disintegrated.

"I saw the whole thing. I was standing right there," Annika said, pointing to a spot near the antique sideboard. "The lights came back up, and all of a sudden, *boom!* The glass shattered into a thousand million pieces, for no reason at all. No one touched it!"

*So I did hear glass breaking.*

"Hmm, that is strange. Perhaps one of the halogen bulbs burst," I said, glancing at the light fixtures over the dining room table. "What with the current coming back on so suddenly—"

"But the lights are fine, Doctor," Christian pointed out.

Just then Katrina came walking toward us, her face drawn and ashen. She whispered something, took Annika's hands in hers and led her away.

I asked Christian whether he'd come downstairs, but he said, "No, Doctor, I never left my wife's side. She was a bit jittery even before the wineglass incident, to tell you the truth."

"You were standing near the cellar door. Perhaps you noticed someone else follow us downstairs?"

"No. I can't think of who that would be. We were all stuck in this room during the blackout. No one moved."

As the music came back on, I recognized an old Sinatra tune, one I hadn't heard in years:

"Ghost of a Chance."

# 5. Katrina

In the seven years of my self-imposed exile, I had not forged a single friendship like the ones I'd known in *gymnasium,* the academy I'd attended in Copenhagen. And of my schoolmates, Annika Jespersen was my all-time favorite. They used to call us bookends: short where I was tall, giggly where I was serious, flirty where I was cool, we seemed like opposites. But we shared more important things in common: a love of art and music, a certain sense of style, and most of all, shopping.

So it was no surprise that our first get-togethers this spring have been on Strøget, the world's longest "walking street," where one can buy just about anything, as long as one has the kroner. I was well into the process of redecorating, and on the lookout for wallpaper for the front bedroom, so we nipped into Larsen's Color Emporium.

The shop was filled with original designer furniture from the entire 20th Century. The male staff dressed in jacket-and-tie, and the women clopped around in high heels. Herr Larsen was himself a designer, one of the first celebrity designers in Denmark, long before Jacobsen and the others. At one time, his home furnishings boutique offered everything from chairs to lighting, but in the wake of his death, Larsen's had focused increasingly on fabrics and pigments. It was still *the* place to go to get that special tinge – but was not good for much else.

As Annika and I surveyed the hundreds of wallpaper samples hanging from brackets on the wall, I started to get a burning feeling in the back of my neck. As if someone were staring at me.

I clapped my hand to the nape, turned and said, *"Søren, hvad laver du her?"* What was my erudite neighbor, who spent most of his time at home reading or gardening, doing in a fabric store downtown?

"Recovering Mother's chairs," he replied with a grin. "They've been blue for decades and they need cheering up. Mint green, I'm thinking."

I introduced him to Annika, and went off to find a "color consultant" to see if we could page through books of antique hues. I was looking for something more 19ᵗʰ Century, to match the provenance of Sundhuset. By the time I got back with the bulky folio, Søren and Annika were already sitting together in comfortable chairs of black leather, chatting about gardening as if they'd known each other for years. They had already found a late Victorian swatch book.

"What do you think of this one, Katrina?" asked Annika, holding up an ornate Watkins Glen frieze.

"I like the creamy one Søren's holding better, it's simpler," I said, admiring a rectangle of chintz. "For the front bedroom, I wouldn't want to overdo it. Bright colors can make it hard to sleep – too much energy."

"Oh, Katrina, one can never have too much energy in the bedroom!" Annika said with a giggle.

"Have you been having trouble sleeping too, Katrina?" Søren asked.

*Perceptive.* Ever since the night of the Housewarming, things did seem a little askew, out-of-balance. I sat down and poured myself a coffee from the goose-necked Georg Jensen thermos.

"We were just talking about insomnia – I'm a chronic insomniac," Annika said. "Søren was telling me about an herbal remedy. He's a veritable encyclopedia of alternative medicine."

"Well, Annika, if you're not sleeping well, the first step is probably to stop drinking so much coffee," I said, looking down at the black liquid in her cup.

Søren laughed and said, "That's true. But an infusion of vervain just before bed can do wonders as well."

"Have you tried valerian?" I asked.

Søren raised one eyebrow and cocked his head. "Valerian? That's pretty strong stuff. You'd best be careful with that. How do you even know about valerian?"

"I worked at a natural food store in Tompkins Square, not far from where I was living in the East Village. We had a whole section devoted to herbal remedies, homeopathy, Chinese medicine. That's where I first learned about the art of feng shui. I fell in love with the harmony of Eastern interiors."

Annika leaned forward.

"Did you become an interior decorator?" Søren asked.

"No, I was in New York to dance ballet, but it took two years to find a position, with the Joffrey. I had four solid years with the touring company – before I wrecked my knee last summer."

"Oh, I'm so sorry," Annika said, putting her hand on mine.

"Hmm, I didn't notice a limp," Søren said. "Perhaps you'll return to the stage?"

"Oh, no," I said. "Ballet is a young person's career. I'm ready for the next challenge." I smiled, but it was forced. Truth was, I didn't know what I was ready for.

An officious "hue expert" strode up to Søren and informed him his paperwork was ready to be signed.

"Farewell, ladies," Søren said with a half-bow. "What a pleasure to meet you, Annika. I do hope we'll meet again. See you back home, Katrina."

Once he'd left, we went back to the swatches for a while but couldn't find anything we liked. After a while, Annika said, "Isn't Søren a sweetheart! You're lucky to live next door to him."

"He's all right, I guess."

"Oh, the man is pleasure to talk to: intelligent, with a sense of elegance, attentive – he really listens, you know. And he's incredibly good-looking, too," she said, her eyes wide.

"Annika, I think you fancy him! And you, a married woman. What would Christian say?"

She blushed and looked away.

"What's wrong?" I said.

"No, it's just that I – well, I've just had an affair, you see," she said in a low voice.

"Really?"

"A younger man, it was never going to work."

"Younger?"

"Okay, nineteen."

"Oh my goodness, Annika—"

"Now don't judge," she said, lifting a hand.

"I wasn't. But you love Christian, don't you?"

"Yes. I suppose so. But marriage got old in a hurry – Christian can be so, well, predictable. Jesper was young and exciting. We met in secret," she said, with a furtive movement of her eyebrows. "At the Falconér. But it's over, I ended it."

I fished for more details, but she didn't want to talk about it any more, so we went back to the bland swatches.

A woman with half-moon glasses came over and asked to trade books with us. Unfortunately, we got more modern tones, strong shapes and primary colors, a range between Mondrian and Miró. The vibrant shades unsettled me.

"There's just too much energy in these colors," I said, remembering what my Chinese friend Hester used to say in New York. *Go with the flow.*

"That's why you're having trouble sleeping," Annika said. "There's just too much energy. The events at the party last week prove that."

"You mean excess energy can short-circuit the lights and make a wineglass explode?"

She smiled and said, "As my teacher says, as long as your life is not in balance, Qi will not be able to flow evenly."

I was startled. This was the girl who owned fifty pairs of shoes in high school. "What would you know about Qi?"

"All Buddhists know Qi."

"Since when did *you* become a Buddhist?"

"At university. As you may recall, my family had never been much of anything. We went to church for baptisms and funerals and not much in between. I never even made my confirmation – you remember that!"

I recalled an embarrassing scene at a fish restaurant long ago in connection with Annika's "non-firmation."

"You said you started studying comparative religion."

"I'm still working on the Master's. Buddhism gives me the spirituality, the touch of the divine that I never had growing up – without the children's stories. Which school of feng shui did you study?"

"Black Hat," I said and saw her face cloud over. "What's wrong?"

"Nothing," she said, placing a taupe rectangle next to plum. "It's just, from what I've heard, it's a pop spiritual movement that reduces Qi – the life force of the universe – to an organizing principle for interior decorating."

"I know that Qi is more than just placing furniture. Acupuncturists use Qi to reduce pain—"

"Qi is an unfathomable power that can cure dread diseases. Or indeed, cause them." She took a deep breath and said, "Tell me, what interventions have you attempted so far?"

"I've tried to fill out the Ba-gua by placing bamboo wind chimes in the ash tree and hanging crystals at nodal points. But I must've done something wrong."

"*Ach,* gaps in the Ba-gua are the least of your problems. The tuning is far too high. That's why the goblet exploded. Glass shatters when struck by a high-frequency vibration."

"Like when a soprano shatters a champagne glass by singing High C?"

"Precisely. The place is a spiritual powderkeg – anything could happen! I get nightmares thinking of that doctor, Edvard, standing there with his hand dripping blood. All the while pretending that nothing had happened," she said, shaking her head.

I nodded and made out a little mm-hm sound.

"Katrina, I believe the situation is dangerous." The word she used was *døds-farlig,* literally, "deathly dangerous."

"What should I do?"

"The first step would be to put in cooler colors, heavy fabrics. That sort of thing."

Holding up a purplish swatch, I asked, "How do you feel about auber-gine?"

Late for Sunday dinner on Mother's Day, Richard and I were fighting in the car. We had already debated the merits of Danish store opening hours, taxes, and gas prices, picked apart the government's asylum policy, and analyzed whose fault it was that we were late (it was his). So I wasn't surprised when he dredged up an argument from years ago.

"Your mother still wishes I was German, I suppose."

"She does not. Mor doesn't even like Germans."

"Well, Lutheran then."

The day before our wedding in New York, we took a car service out to JFK, picked up Mor at the arrivals building. It was the first time she'd met Richard. On the way back into Manhattan, he sat up front with the driver; I sat next to her in the back seat. On the Belt Parkway, she started sniffling, shading her face in her hands. I asked if she was okay, and at first she didn't answer, just kept sobbing into her white linen handkerchief.

Finally, in Danish so Richard wouldn't understand, she asked, *"Er han katolik?"*

"Yes, of course he's Catholic, Mor," I whispered.

"Oh, couldn't he at least have been Lutheran?" she said with a gentle roll of her eyes. "German, yes, but Protestant at least."

"No, not German, Mor, Italian. *Marchese,* very Italian. What made you think he was German?"

"Mark Käse," she said, her face melting into a grimace. "I thought you said his name was *Mark Käse!*" And she started bawling, right there in the car.

It was a story that would be repeated many times.

"Remember that?" Richard said. "She'd heard my name on the telephone and somehow got the idea that I was German."

I knew that if I let him, Richard would rehearse the whole scene, complete with exaggerated accents and weeping. So I didn't let him get started.

"Well, even if Mor does prefer Danish men, *I* don't," I said, giving his hand a squeeze. "I'll take you just the way you are." And that, as they say, was the end of that.

We arrived 18 minutes late.

"Good *after*noon," Mor said at the door. She likes to have dinner on the table at the stroke of twelve. If Fa' were alive, they would have started without us.

"Hi, Missus N. Happy Mother's Day!" Richard said. Incongruously, he grabbed Mor's bony shoulders and kissed her full on the left cheek. Stumbling back a step, she reached out both her hands for Richard's right palm and held onto it like a fire hose.

"Sorry we're so late, Mor," I said, brushing her cheek with mine and handing her the blue irises we'd bought on the way.

"Yes, well, you're here now, so let's put the food on the table," she replied, nodding us into the immaculate home.

In a few minutes, we sat down to meat loaf, mashed potatoes and white asparagus, at the silver-clad dining room table.

"Meat loaf! My favorite," Richard said, rubbing his hands together and digging into the food like a trencherman. After a single bite, he put down his fork and declared, "Wow. It's delicious, Mrs. N – buttery. Melts in your mouth."

Mor smiled, flattered despite herself at the obvious compliment, and said, "Thank you, but it really isn't anything special. And as I think I've said before, *please* call me Ingrid, or I shall be forced to call you Mister Marchese."

"Yeah, sure – I keep forgetting, uh, Ingrid. Say, what do you call meatloaf in Danish?"

"*Farsbrød*," I said. He took it in, then raised his eyes and lifted his head back. "Ah, I get it! Father's bread – it was Dad's bread – Dad's *loaf*. Just like meatloaf in English."

Mor broke out in laughter. Though my jaws opened slightly, I pressed my lips together and nearly swallowed them, as I stifled a guffaw.

"What? What's so funny?" he said, his face suddenly sun-burnt.

Richard received no response – Mor was laughing too hard to speak and I was holding my breath. Then, unable to hold back any more, I started giggling too. Richard drank a glass of water. We laughed a long time. Finally recovered, we explained that while *far* does mean father, it has nothing to do with the meatloaf, which is named for *fars*, Danish for chopped meat.

"Well, it was a good guess for someone who doesn't speak the language," he said.

"Aren't you taking lessons?" Mor asked.

"I've had a couple, but it's really hard," Richard said. "It seems like everybody mumbles all the time. Honestly, I don't know how you people understand each other – all the words run into each other. A sentence is like one long smear of gargled vowels and swallowed consonants."

"There is a great deal of elision in Danish," Mor said, her language degree showing.

"Elision?" Richard asked.

"Yes, I believe that's what they call it when it's difficult for the listener to tell where one word starts and the next begins," she said. "But I assure you, we Danes have no trouble understanding each other. We just have our own little code that keeps foreigners on their toes. It baffled the German spies during the war, you know."

"It did?" he asked.

"Danish has many unique sounds. The Resistance people would have someone say, '*rød grød med fløde*' – 'redberry porridge with cream' – and if they couldn't say it correctly, well, let's just say they didn't always live past dessert."

"Well, nobody's shot me yet, but I have to say people haven't exactly been friendly either," Richard said.

I shot him a look that seemed to miss the mark.

"Is that so?" Mor asked through thin lips.

"Yeah, it's like people are polite and all, but not friendly. I'm not the type to be self-conscious, but sometimes I think the guys at the office are laughing at me," Richard said.

"Just because you're paranoid doesn't mean they're not out to get you," I said.

Richard turned to me, reddened and closed his mouth tight. Mor raised her eyebrows at me – I suppose it was a cruel remark, but this was the same thing he was whining about in the car, stranger in a strange land, blah-blah-blah. *Oh, grow up!* I wanted to say. *Do you think everyone was friendly to me in New York?*

"Perhaps Danes aren't necessarily the friendliest people," Mor said, taking his side.

"What do you mean? Danes are the decentest people I know," I said.

"Decent is not the same as friendly," Richard said. "If I was bleeding to death on the street, somebody would probably call an ambulance. From a safe distance."

"Well, you're not likely to *be* bleeding to death on the street," I said. "There's no poverty or crime here. And we don't have to round up the homeless people every night."

"Of course not," Richard replied. "The homeless are dirty, they've got body odor, they block the sidewalk. *So* unpleasant. Ew, the dainty Danes would have to step over them."

"What's wrong with wanting to make things pleasant?" I asked. "You could do with being a bit more pleasant – and less whiny."

Now I shouldn't have said that, especially in front of Mor – Richard hates to be embarrassed – but by this point I was tired of the discussion, and if nothing else, the remark put an end to it. Richard made polite conversation with Mor, but didn't say another word to me. When we got home, he changed and went straight out for a run.

Of course, he'd left his clothes on the bed. Again. I shook my head as I picked up the laundry. *Annika was right about one thing…* Then I caught myself, halfway down the stairs. That way madness lies – or possibly divorce. I couldn't believe Annika had an affair. How long had they been married? Four years, just like us.

Perhaps I was being too hard on poor Richard. After all, he couldn't speak the language, didn't know a soul here. He was sweet, really, moving all this way for me. The move had been harder on him than I'd imagined. He was so worldly and well-traveled that I thought he'd adapt. It was one of the things that attracted me to him in the first place.

Five years older, Richard always seemed more than that. He was a native New Yorker; I was the new kid in town. I had a part-time job; he was already on the fast track at the renowned Fielding & Co. I was dazzled by champagne-and-caviar brunches. Not that I was a hick, exactly – I was educated in one of the finest academies in Denmark after all, the same one the Princesses had attended – but I was so young when we met, he just overwhelmed me. He looked directly into my eyes when he spoke, always posed the question that I wanted to ask but wouldn't dare, and he knew the difference between Cognac and Armagnac. All this combined to make him, let's just say, very interesting to me. And physically, well, we just clicked right away. First on the dance-floor – Richard is a natural dancer. And soon enough in the bedroom.

Setting the bundle down on the washing machine, I yielded to temptation and buried my face in his things. *Mmm.* I breathed in. When Annika asked me what made me fall for him, I said – without missing a beat – *han duftede dejligt.* He smelled good.

Back upstairs, curled up on the vintage sofa in the front room, I dived deep into the world of my book, the shadowy fjordlands of Western Norway at the close of the last century. I'd been reading voraciously – *fin de siècle* pieces mostly – Henry James and Edith Wharton, Oscar Wilde and Charlotte Perkins Gilman. Perhaps I was inspired by the house, or was it because we were coming to the *fin* of our own *siècle?* What ever the reason, I was ensnared by the 1890s.

It seemed like people grew paranoid at the end of a century, as if it were the End of the World. At the moment, the newspapers were full of Y2k, the science fiction that on the morning of January 1, 2000, all of our faithful computers would turn against us. I was sure there was an H. G. Wells story like that, only with robots. Technology as our servant, but one that could turn and destroy us.

The truth was that inventions could bring people together – think of Bell – or lead to unspeakable carnage – think of Nobel. The Swedish inventor of dynamite, Alfred Nobel, established his high-minded Prizes as an aged man, as Death stalked him. Perhaps out of guilt for having grown rich on the corpses of millions.

Knut Hamsun, the author of the book I was reading, won the Prize for Literature in 1920. Many years later, as Death stalked *him,* he gave away the precious medallion. But not to charity. It was a gift to Joseph Goebbels, the author not of books but of *Kristallnacht*, the night of broken glass.

And so it goes. For actions taken in their dotage, Nobel, the war-profiteer, is remembered as a humanitarian; Hamsun, the peaceful writer, as a Nazi. For every Bell there is a Nobel. And Old Hamsun is dancing with Goebbels.

I shook my head.

The sun slumped in the sky, shadows lengthened, and the story was starting to make me nervous. I came to the part where the protagonist is reading alone at night and feels someone breathing next to him. In frustration, he says, "Damn," and a tiny, pale man with a red beard appears. Just then, the clock struck eight and I startled.

*Where could he be?* He'd been gone more than four hours. I was anxious and annoyed. It was dinner time. Hungry, but not in the mood for cooking, I went to the kitchen and set out a plate with some Roquefort that Søren had brought over. I poured a glass of Fumé Blanc and inhaled the smoke of the wine, which tickled my nose. I bit into the living cheese, making it separate into smeary curds and wafer-like, crumbling mould. The sugar and alcohol hit my bloodstream, dulling my senses. My anxiety ebbed away.

The wine also blurred the words on the page. I put the Midget down on the table. I wasn't sleepy, just had a headache. Sleep was such a problem these days. Ever since the Housewarming, it was increasingly difficult to focus on things during the day. Even if I was tired by three o'clock in the afternoon, I fought the urge to take a nap, thinking it would make it harder to sleep at night. But my condition was devilish: even on days when I longed for the couch during the heat of the afternoon, I would struggle to find sleep at night. Chamomile tea, vervain, even valerian failed to help. I took to port wine, but remembered Fa's "little problem," and sought another solution. I knew Richard sometimes took a sleeping pill on long flights, something called Ambien. I hated to take drugs, but what could I do? Within a few weeks, the bottle was nearly empty.

When Richard failed to appear by ten o'clock, I secured the doors and went upstairs, slid under the duvet and wrestled with Old Hamsun. I couldn't figure it out: he was a pioneer, the most modern writer of his generation. Ernest Hemingway later said that he'd "learned to write" from Hamsun.

I pictured the aging Norwegian gentleman-writer as he stood at the depot in Larvik: he held the box containing the medallion close to his heart, his ink-stained fingers quavering as he wrote out the paperwork. Would Goebbels' name appear on the package or that of an underling? Would the Norwegian clerk – a patriot, surely – flinch, perhaps even make a remark? It was a slow process. All seams had to be taped, stamped and dated for the registered mail to Berlin; the package would travel under lock-and-key.

*Did he regret at the last instant?*

I could not imagine what the old man was thinking, what he could hope to gain from such a gesture. Did he even detect the irony of sending the world's noblest award for expression to *Joseph Goebbels,* Minister of Propaganda for the Third Reich, the man who stamped out creative expression, who pioneered techniques of manipulation and mass delusion?

My thoughts raced. Our suite at the D'Angleterre had a commanding view of the harbor. Had I stayed in Goebbels's room? Slept in his bed? *Ewhhh.*

I imagined him as he paced up and down the wooden floors. Obsessed with watching the coast for Allied shipping, but most of all for the Jews, to make sure the Jews would not escape him. His club foot banged against the heart-of-pine floorboards. *Shuffle-clunk, shuffle-clunk.*

I shivered and crawled deeper under the covers, forced myself to focus on the words on the page, and the protagonist said:

"A Turk cries 'Allah is great' and dies for his convictions; to this day, a Norwegian kneels at the altar and drinks the blood of Christ. There are even places where people believe they can attain salvation through cowbells! But what really matters is not *what* you believe but the faith and conviction with which you believe."

I fell back into the world of the book. Four or five pages later, the protagonist was criticizing Ibsen for failing to be a Man of Action, when I heard tramping on the stairs. There was an extra-hard footfall on the landing, halfway up. Was he still angry after all this time? I was just relieved that he was home. I lifted my head and gazed towards the door. When it failed to open, I rose and peered into the corridor, expecting to see him adjusting the radiator or browsing through the bookshelves. But the hallway was filled only with the reddish glow of sunset.

No one was there.

I moved into the hallway, called out Richard's name, but the only response I received was the banging on the stairs again. I jumped, ran back into my bedroom, stood with my back to the door, panting.

*I was standing right there, it can't be!*

No one was in the house. The doors were locked. My entire body was quivering. I sat down on the bed, couldn't stop shaking. What was wrong with me? I needed something to soothe my jangled nerves, so — the ghost of Fa's alcoholism be damned — I decided to go downstairs and make myself a drink. I stood up, but became light-headed immediately. Must've gotten up too quickly. I sat back down on the bed. A stripe of pain throbbed from my right eye to the back of my head. The world was sparkling in front of me. I closed my eyes for a few minutes.

When finally the stars stopped flashing before my eyes, I saw that the last of the sun's rays had sunk beneath the horizon, and the grey and indigo of dusk settled over the garden. I moved cautiously toward the bedroom door. The air felt heavy, electric against my skin, as it does before a thunderstorm. I cracked the door open a hand's width. In the hallway, an eerie bluish light streamed in through the skylight. I crept toward the closed door at the end of the corridor, the door to the front bedroom.

A feeling of déjà vu ripped through me. I was in my dream, where a tall man scratches at a glass door. For an instant I thought I could see him at the door to the front bedroom. I froze and covered my face with my hands. When I removed them, I saw nothing in the darkened hallway, but turned and ran down the stairs. I flipped on the overhead lights, sat down at the dining room table, breathing hard.

The rooms were empty, quiet. The windows were open and a breeze brought in the smell of cut grass and the sound of a sprinkler. My breathing slowed, my head stopped pounding. I went to the liquor cabinet and made myself a tall, cool Tom Collins; drank it down. Then made a second, and soon forgot all about the incident on the stairs.

At eleven o'clock, Richard found me slumped in a chair in the front room. I had drifted off in the middle of a scene where the Midget is asked whether he drank the prussic acid the protagonist keeps in his hip flask – an odd question, since it seemed to be some kind of poison. In my dream, I sipped fiery green liquor in a Paris night club with a deformed little man wearing an imperial goatee and tails. I awoke to a blurry image of Richard fiddling with the Collins mix.

"You want one, Sweetheart?" he asked with a smile.

"Sweetheart?" I asked, as I blinked awake. "I thought we were fighting."

"I'm done fighting," he said, ambling over with the drink.

"I'm sorry for the way I behaved," he said, inclining his head and handing me a cool fresh Collins. Then he leaned down and kissed me.

"I'm sorry too," I said, too sleepy to fight. "But where *were* you? I was getting anxious."

"I took a long run down around the castle and then over to Eddé's. I showered over there," he said with a smirk. He was wearing a miniature-sized Argyle sweater with matching socks and plaid pants that were definitely not his.

I gave him a look. He gave a little Italian shrug and said, "Yeah, well, what was I going to do? He offered. I guess fashion was never his strong suit," and we both laughed.

This broke the ice, and we sat on either end of the camelback settee and talked easily. He asked about the mysteries of the book I was reading; I told him about the tea shop I'd found.

"Tea shop, eh? Where?"

"On Kronprinsensgade – it's called Perch, claims to be the oldest in Europe. I bought this wonderful house-blend called Pushkin Earl Grey – it's flavored with citrus."

Richard nudged over till we were side by side. He kept coming closer until his nose was just inches from mine. After three Tom Collinses, at a distance of four centimeters his nose was the size of a baking apple, and I laughed. When he asked why I was giggling, the laughter became hysterical. He grabbed me behind the knees, tickling. We ended up on the floor with him on top of me, and he kissed me, full on the mouth. I kissed him back, pressing my mouth hard against his. He moved up to my cheek, and then to my left earlobe, biting the flesh there. Normally this would light me up, but all I felt was an overwhelming feeling of nausea.

"Uhhhhhgh!" came up from my throat as I ran toward the toilet.

Richard jumped up. "What's the matter?"

I continued my run to the powder room, threw open the door, knelt and vomited repeatedly. It was putrid. I flushed, rested my forehead on the cold porcelain, glad that I'd managed to get it all in the bowl.

He leaned against the doorjamb and said, "Gee, I've been told I'm a lousy kisser before, but I've never gotten that reaction."

"No, it has nothing to do with you. Must've been something I ate." I stood up, rinsed out my mouth and spat. As I walked back into the living room, I said, "I'm sorry. I guess that really spoils the mood, huh? Not that this evening was exactly sexy to begin with."

"You mean with us fighting?"

"That too."

Richard gave me a puzzled look. "Did anything happen while I was gone, Skat?"

"No. I mean yes. Well, it's just – I had the strangest experience tonight. I was in the bedroom reading when I heard footsteps coming up the stairs."

"Aw, I'm sure it was just the beams creaking or a branch beating against the downspout. That ash tree—"

"No, Richard, I heard the sound distinctly. These were footsteps – tramping on the stairs. I thought you'd come home. But when I got to the head of the stairs, the hallway was empty."

Richard froze. "You heard banging on the stairs?"

"Yes. Or – at least I thought so. But I could be mistaken—"

"No," he said, stopping me. "I heard it too."

"What, tonight? That's not possible, Richard. You weren't even home yet."

"No, not tonight. At the Housewarming," he said in a lower voice. "Downstairs while I was looking for fuses with Eddé."

"Did he hear it too?"

"Yes. Then when the lights came on—"

"No one was there," I finished for him. "Why didn't you tell me?"

"You were upset enough as it was, remember? What with the lights going out, glasses exploding, and the guests tearing out of here like the house was on fire."

I bit my lower lip. Was there such a thing as a ghost?

Later that night, Richard was in bed with a book, a depression-era novel about union organizers, and a cup of coffee.

"How can you drink that and then sleep?" I asked.

"Warm drinks always relax me, especially if they're filled with milk and sugar."

I got under the covers next to him and tried to read. But I had trouble concentrating, kept reading the same paragraph over and over. The deformed Midget fell in love again and again with the heroine he was destined never to have. Finally, just after midnight, Richard's head fell forward onto his chest. Half-awake, my thoughts dwelt on the world of my book, the world of a century ago.

The late Victorians were fond of séances and spirit-writing, and invented the Ouija board, not as a parlor game but as a communication device to take its place beside the Bell telephone. I wasn't sure what Hamsun meant by "salvation through cowbells," but people of that era believed in, desperately *wanted* to believe in things they couldn't see. Science was reducing us to robots. So everything spiritual thrived: theosophy, Mesmerism, animal magnetism, ghosts.

If ghosts were real, death was not final. If ghosts were real, we could communicate with the departed. Every family had felt the touch of Death. Images flew into my mind – 35 mm slides from dark Art History classes, all those morbid paintings by Edvard Munch – *The Sick Child, Death in the Sickroom, The Dead Mother.*

I imagined a baby sister, named something like Sophie or Emma. Her doll's body mutilated by a disease whose name was familiar then, but sounds outlandish, even impossible now: whooping cough, scarlet fever, tuberculosis, smallpox. The emaciated remains were prepared and placed snugly in a toy coffin, a four-footer. They set her up by the window in the front room, a candle at her head, and I would sit by her, keeping watch all night, guarding the tiny corpse.

This was the tradition, yes, to guard the corpse.

*But from what?*

A ghost is a vibration, the physical memory of a personage that no longer exists. A shadow, like the primitive moving pictures in a hand-cranked penny arcade. A bit of breath flickering whitely on the dark screen of night. Surely such an ethereal thing must be harmless.

*But then why was I so scared?*

It was after one. A blast of wind shook the trees. Branches of the grasping ash clawed at the window. My heart jumped, Richard snorted in his sleep. I removed the dubious Steinbeck from his breast and placed it on the nightstand. He settled in under the covers. I doused my lamp and climbed back into bed.

But I could not sleep.

Such tricks hath strong imagination,

That... in the night, imagining some fear,

How easy is a bush supposed a bear!

> \- William Shakespeare
>
> *A Midsummer Night's Dream*

# MIDSUMMER
# 6. Søren

Clad in a white cotton shirt with long sleeves and navy-blue trousers, I emerged from the darkness of Number 16 into the bright afternoon sunshine. I walked up to the bus stop on the boulevard, rolling behind me a cooler filled with summer-ale; the others were bringing the food. The satchel slung over my shoulder contained the customary protections for a day in the field: sunblock, floppy hat, no, *captain's* hat, light jacket, umbrella. Not that it looked like rain: the sky was so solid one could break off a piece and bite right into it. Oh, and I brought chocolate too, a brick of Tom's Dark, bittersweet.

The bus was crowded. Thrown together with random beachgoers, I was shaken and jostled as the bus ground its way up the winding coast road. The atmosphere was festive, even euphoric. It was the longest day of the year, the day missionaries baptized "Saint John's Day," but the unrestrained parties of the modern holiday owed more to the heathen solstice festival than to anything Christian. Several teenaged boys, already intoxicated though they and the afternoon were still young, started singing a football chorus; the girls were nearly naked under their cover-ups, so as the bus leaned and careered up the winding coast road, one could spy the winter-pale skin of a deep cleavage or quivering thigh. The midsummer holiday, "Sankt Hans" as we call it, can be a bit tawdry, what with all the wild bonfires, exposed flesh, beery teenagers and casual encounters. But it is quintessentially Danish, like Bastille Day is French and Fourth-of-July is American. And I am nothing if not a loyal Dane. So every year, I have endured the crowds and marched to the beach for luncheon on the dunes, washed down with a wave of watery summer-ale.

Mother took me as a child. My all-time favorite food was her *snobrød*. She prepared the wheaten dough at home, kneading the wet mass with her tired hands. Poor thing, she was never well, and I was too much for her. Even after she died, taking the recipe with her, I was never able to replicate it, filled as it was with so many secrets from our herb garden.

I must have been three or four years old the first time. The lump of dough plastered on the branch resembled a weird cocoon. I held it near the flame, as Mother instructed, but perhaps not close enough, because the process took ages, at least according to the quick pulse of a toddler. I had nearly given up in frustration when, to my utter amazement, the white blob began to transform, to expand, turn colors, and make exciting crackling noises. My eyes wide, the open fire baked the bread to a crisp and roasted the wiener inside to whistling-hot, all without the benefit of the four walls and roof of an oven.

The oven in our kitchen was orange-hot. I knew the heat of it, as I'd already been burned. It would teach me a lesson, Mother said. Later I heard the story of *Hans and Grete* and came to believe that the witch was killed in *our* oven. Oh, how I bawled when I heard; I was inconsolable.

*How could a child shut the door on that nice old lady? She gave them candy, didn't she? Oh, let her out – she'll burn up in there; she looks like Mormor; children shouldn't run off into the woods like that, now you'll have to be punished. Oh, it's all your fault!*

The bus lurched. Off-balance, I was thrown into the shriveled crone who was standing next to me, sweating and stinking of garlic. Dark underarm hair protruded obscenely from the oversized armholes of her denim dress. I'd stepped on her foot – it was a mistake – and said, "Oh, I'm sorry." She tightened the muscles of her leathery face, poked me with the stiffened tips of her fingers, and grunted some words in her own inscrutable tongue. I had just been cursed or forgiven, I couldn't tell which.

Finally we arrived at Charlottenlund Strand. I was meeting Katrina there, along with the Italian and his headshrinker friend. Wanting to impress her, I'd researched the national holiday and committed the notes to memory:

*Which Saint John?* John the Baptist, six months older than Jesus, whose birthday comes in late December – so it's his birthday;

*Why the bonfire?* Ancient pagan ritual;

*Why the witch on top?* Germanic tradition where a doll symbolized Winter;

*When was the last "heks" burnt in Denmark?* Anne Palles, beheaded and burnt as a witch in 1693, simultaneous with the trials in Salem in Massachusetts Bay;

*Burning the witch sends her to Hell, also known as Bloksbjerg, is that a real place?* Yes, very real – the Brocken peak in the Hartz, where witches gather on *Walpurgisnacht* and other black solemnities, often flying in for the occasion;

*Where does the term "St. John's wort" come from?* The Danish *urt* meaning herb; the "wise folk" knew that gathering this plant on the longest day of the year yielded the most potent potion.

When I stepped off the bus, it was like opening the oven door. The heat of the day promised to break all records. As I trudged toward the promise of a breezy shoreline, following my shadow, sharp on the sand, the sun's fire singed my neck and earlobes. The bag dug into my shoulder and the cooler dragged in the fine beige powder and caught on exposed roots. Exhausted and dizzy, I collapsed in a shaky lawn chair within sight of the sea.

A few minutes later, Katrina arrived wearing a light-blue summer-dress and a strand of off-white pearls which matched the untanned skin of her throat. I had never seen anyone wear pearls to the beach, would have found it over-the-top on most, but on Katrina they were charming. Gliding effortlessly across the burning sand, she bade me *God Sankt Hans.* I did my best to respond in kind, but as cool as she seemed, I was feverish.

It was Africa-hot. I was parched. My tongue swollen, my teeth felt like loose Chiclets in my mouth. As I took a Tuborg from the cooler, I felt as hot and dusty as the man on the label. Holding the stubby green bottle to my forehead and cheek, I felt the cold perspiration run down my face. I popped it open and drank, but simply couldn't slake my thirst.

To tell the truth, I don't remember much about the afternoon, a golden blur of sun and beer. I know we ate a meal; I remember seeing the German darken the weisswurst and his shirt in the heat of the open grill. But when the sun sank in the sky and the air cooled, I recovered a bit and recognized myself again. By then I had accumulated a small regiment of Tuborg men. I had to drink all the beer myself, as the others were uncorking long-throated bottles of Bernkastler Doktor and I wanted no part of that. Such cloying Germans always make me sick.

As Katrina was setting out the dessert, she asked me to go fetch the doctor, who had wandered down to the water's edge. He stood with his back to us as he peered out over the waves in the gloaming. I crossed forty meters of beach, careful to avoid the smouldering remains of bonfires and clusters of Sankt Hans worshippers.

Up and down the coast, countless hoods of flame flickered through the clouds of smoke, casting an eerie light. Sooty billows drifted out over the water, forming a violet haze through which little could be seen. *What could he be staring at?*

"Have you spotted something, Herr Doktor Frankl?" I asked the back of his head.

"What?"

"Out there – do you see something?"

He said, turning now, "No, just shadows on the water."

I told him it was time for coffee cakes. He nodded and we started back up the beach, but as we crossed through a crowded area, the man seemed to lose his bearings and walked directly across the hot coals of a bonfire – in his bare feet.

"Watch out, you'll burn yourself!" I said, but it was too late.

As I caught up to him on the other side of the crowd, he tried to make light of it, saying, "Oh, don't worry about me."

I was impressed with his stoic mettle. In what started as an effort to stop smoking, I was studying hypnosis, mind-control. Belief overcomes pain. Adepts can control their heart beat and blood pressure, even walk across hot coals without burns. But surely this man of science was not one for such beliefs? Perhaps there was more to this lump of German potato salad than met the eye.

As we got back to the picnic table, he asked Katrina for some coffee.

"I think Richard has some in the car."

"Oh, was I supposed to pick that up?" Richard said. "Oh Jeez, I completely forgot. I'll drive back to the main road and get some. There was a Baresso a ways back."

"I don't mind going with you," the doctor offered, and off they went.

Katrina and I looked at one another.

It was the first time that we were alone.

# 7. Katrina

We were alone.

Shadows danced across the dunes as Søren and I sat among the stunted trees that congregated in the loamy soil between asphalt and sand. Halfway across the beach, the insatiable bonfire had burned lower, having consumed heaps of driftwood, scrap lumber, broken furniture, wastepaper and cardboard boxes. The rag-doll witches had long-since been executed, but pale moths perished by the dozen, making soft popping noises in the evening air. Once in a while, a bottle rocket or "witch-howler" would shriek by, but the big fireworks display was yet to come.

Around the dwindling pyre, bands of merrymakers drank and caroused; women flirted and men sang drinking songs. I looked across at Søren's face, ruddy in the firelight. I smiled, and he smiled back, shyly, as if we were on a first date in high school. He was as different from Richard as north is from south. Søren was an angular man with pointed nose and thin lips; Richard had soft features and a sensual mouth. While Richard was as friendly and forward as a golden retriever, Søren played the cool professor-type. He dressed like an academic, too, forever wearing cravats and corduroy jackets over turtlenecks. Today he wore a long-sleeved shirt – in this heat! – and a *captain's* hat. But there was something attractive, vulnerable, underneath the thick shell. Something that made me want to hold his hand and comfort him.

Although he had been drinking – that much was clear – he spoke lucidly and with warmth about his mother, who died when he was a boy. His stories, always about just the two of them, revealed him as a lonely child, isolated with only his mother for company. This must've been why he was so old-fashioned, the type of man who stands up when a woman enters the room. He said *De* to me when we first met, and he often sounded more like a fine lady of seventy than a man in his thirties. For example, he said, *"Dog det er en sjældent sjæl som—"*

"Excuse me?" I said.

"*Sjældent sjæl,* it means 'unusual person.' I was saying that today it's an unusual person who can explain the origins of Sankt Hans."

I agreed, and he proceeded to tell the story fluidly, calmly but with drama too.

"As you know, our Germanic ancestors burnt their dead. Special oxygen-fed fires had to be made if they were to be hot enough to melt bone, thus the English term *bonfire,* literally 'bone-fire.' At the midsummer solemnities, it was natural to place an effigy on top in place of the corpse. A symbol of winter, of death, the rag doll is burnt away in cleansing fire."

As if to illustrate, Søren struck a match and lit his filterless cigarette. He put on quite a show, describing pagan rituals and witch hunts, making them come alive. His eyes wide as a witness, he concluded the account of the last witch-burning in Denmark, saying, "Finally the ladder fell into the flames which consumed both wood and body, by now just a headless corpse that was already long-since dead."

"How gruesome!"

He nodded, paused for effect. "Thus was the sin expurgated and the community allowed to resume its life of piety." As he finished speaking, he closed his eyes and nodded like a Shakespearean actor concluding a soliloquy.

"You're not serious."

"I was being sarcastic," he admitted, changing his tone. "The community was *pious* neither before nor after the crazed witch-burnings. The trials came in waves, usually started by some petit jealousy: one girl desired another's beau; a yeoman farmer coveted his neighbor's land."

"Oh, I never thought of that. Imagine accusing someone of a capital crime just to get at their land or their husband – how horrible!"

"You'd be surprised at what a man will do when he covets his neighbor's wife," he replied. He sucked too deeply on his cigarette and coughed.

There was an awkward pause, and I tried to get the conversation back on track by saying, "I've always thought that these so-called wise women who were accused of witchcraft were nothing more than old-time healers using herbs that we are just now coming to appreciate – like Echinacea, saw palmetto, even St. John's wort."

"Katrina, your knowledge of plants is impressive!" he said, beaming.

I was glad the firelight would mask my blushing.

"As a licensed pharmacist and avid gardener, I am well aware of the healing power of plants. But you must appreciate that these women were not just herbalists, nor were they merely scapegoats. No, you see, in places where people believe in witches," he said, sitting forward and wagging his finger, "there will be witches. And *witchcraft will work*."

I had never heard anyone talk like this, in provocative riddles. I was mesmerized. "I don't understand what you mean by 'witchcraft will work,'" I said. "You can't seriously believe these women flew to Bloksbjerg on their broomsticks? Or got men to fall in love with them using potions and charms?"

He took a dramatic breath and asked rhetorically, "Who's to say what 'Bloksbjerg' was? Yes, I know geographically it's in Germany, the highest peak in the Hartz – but during a more modest time, it may have been a way of describing a different sort of peak. Perhaps it was a metaphor, for *sexual* heights."

Despite myself, I blushed again and looked down.

"As for charms and spells," he continued, "Anyone who has been in love knows the intoxicating power of a look, a scent, a touch."

As he said this, Søren looked fixedly into my eyes, and I thought he was going to grab my wrist, but I pulled away and asked, "So you're saying that witchcraft works, metaphorically?"

"No – well, yes, but no, not *just* metaphorically. I mean if you believe in something, really believe it, you grant it power over you."

"You mean like money or science or religion—"

"Yes, but also folk beliefs. If you believe there are witches in your village, and someone gets sick or has an accident—"

"You'll attribute the bad luck to the witch's malice. Kind of a self-fulfilling prophecy," I concluded, happy finally to be following his logic.

"Precisely," he said, and smiled. "The *suggestible* victim becomes convinced that someone is out to get them. Then the paranoia itself makes them vulnerable. Ultimately they fall ill to a mysterious disease," he said, crushing his cigarette against the throat of the empty beer bottle. Then he looked up and dropped the nub into the void where it sizzled for a moment before being extinguished.

"Wouldn't such an illness expose the witch to prosecution?"

"Sometimes. Especially when the witch was foolish enough to curse the victim in a public square. But over thousands of years of folk medicine, witch hunts occurred rarely, mostly in the 1600s, a unique time in which Religion, Science and Magick vied for supremacy in our part of the world."

"So it's a small risk for the practitioner, you'd say?"

"Yes, I suppose you could say that," he said with a smirk.

"But what about the victim?" I asked. "If what you say is true, then belief is very risky for the victim."

"Belief carries with it great risk, it's true. But great reward as well: if you believe someone can cure you, even be your salvation, then this also becomes true."

There was that look again. *Was he trying to say that I was his salvation? Or that he was mine?* I shook off the thought and said, "Thinking something is true doesn't make it true, does it?"

Then he moved in, touched my forearm, gazed into my eyes without blinking, and spoke in a staccato cloudburst of words. "Katrina, if I tried to break a brick in half with my bare hand I would crush bones – if I walked across ten meters of burning coals in my bare feet I would get third-degree burns – if I stuck a needle through the palm of my hand right now this sand would be showered with blood – isn't that right, Katrina?"

"Why – yes, yes of course."

"Yet I tell you, one can do such things."

"Hot coals?" I asked, watching the embers fly up into the night sky.

"Yes, we could walk across hot coals together, overcome any obstacle. No one could stop us. We just have to *believe*. We could do it together. Let me hear you say it."

"We could do it," I repeated.

*"We could do it!"* he repeated, his eyes ablaze.

When he said this, I was totally convinced. I had complete faith in him. There were hot coals not twenty meters away. If he had asked, I would've untied my sandals and followed him without a second thought.

"I would gladly walk across hot coals for you, Katrina!" he swore, gripping my forearm and staring into my eyes in a way that seemed sincere, ardent, compelling.

Søren put his hands around my waist and pulled me close. He kissed me full on the mouth: a sweaty, passionate, summer-beery kiss. Of course, I should have pulled away. I don't know why I didn't. I felt his passion, the all-out desperation of love usually reserved for teenagers. I kissed him back. It was good, honest. His mouth felt strong on mine and the taste of tobacco tingled on my tongue, pleasantly naughty. I allowed him to pull me closer. We were both sweaty. The hot day, the cotton summer dress, his hard leanness so close against me. I felt my body respond to his passion.

*We could do it.*

But the moment of weakness, if that's what it was, didn't last long. I pulled away and said, "Søren!"

"My love! Oh, how I've dreamed of this moment."

"What are you saying?" I said in a hoarse whisper.

"Katrina, the best part of my day is seeing you. I wake in the morning hoping we'll meet; I go to work hoping you'll come into the shop; at night, I gaze at your curtains, imagining you."

"Have you gone mad?" I asked, standing. "I am a married woman and my husband could be here at any moment! What if he walked in on us just now?"

Søren stepped back a pace. "I'm sorry. I got carried away. It was the beer." He threw the bottle away from himself as if it were a snake. "And the sun." He put his hand to his head and said, "I'm feverish. Of course you're right, we shouldn't have risked it here."

"Please let's not tell anyone about this, Søren," I said, getting control of myself again. "I'm flattered by your feelings, but—"

"Katrina, listen. If it's your husband, don't worry about him—"

"Søren—"

"I can be the picture of discretion."

"I'm *married*, Søren," I said gently, stepping up to him and taking his hands in mine.

"If you *believe*, Katrina, we could do it," he said, almost pleading now. "Your husband is gone most of the time – I live just across the drive. I'm not a proud man. No one needs to know. The world's opinion is nothing to me. Your opinion is everything." He started to kiss me once more. I put up my hand and caught his face. It was burning-hot.

"SØREN!" I called out.

Just then Edvard cleared his throat loudly and said, "Ah, look, they've just started setting off the fireworks."

The whistles, shrieks and reports of rockets out over the water drowned out any further conversation. Scarlet, I turned to Edvard, looked at him for a moment as if to say, How long have *you* been standing there? Then walked right past him and back to the car.

We never drank the coffee.

# 8. Edvard

My back soaking in the heat of the bonfire, I stood and watched what appeared to be ghost craft scudding through the Sound under cover of night and fog. This beach, like so many others along the coast from Copenhagen to Elsinore, harbored refugees in the autumn of 1943. Thousands of Danish Jews, their young anaesthetized to keep them from crying, were stowed away as living ballast in fishing boats, rowboats and skiffs of all sizes.

I imagined the makeshift wooden armada creaking as it flouted the steel of the Nazi cutters that patrolled the channel. The Swedes had promised that all Jews would be granted asylum on humanitarian grounds, neutrality be damned, and I smiled in the face of the darkness as I pictured the exodus making its way toward the icy shore of the unlikely Promised Land.

"Have you spotted something?" said Søren's voice.

I turned round and said, "Just shadows on the water."

"It's time to go back up for dessert," he said, and we walked back up the beach to the others.

Richard had forgotten to bring the coffee, so the two of us drove off to fetch some. As the Mercedes crackled onto the gravel side-road, I asked, "Do you think they'll be open this late?"

"What time is it?" he asked.

"The sun is down, it must be ten or eleven o'clock."

"Damn. Baresso'll be closed for sure. Do you think there's a 7-Eleven around here?"

"We can look. Drive south along the main road and you're sure to come to something."

A few minutes later, we passed the darkened coffee bar on the right and kept heading south. "To tell you the truth, I'm glad to get a few minutes alone with you," Richard said. "I'm worried about Katrina."

"Yes? What's the matter?"

I had been concerned about Katrina myself ever since the party when she seemed so distraught. But I kept this to myself and listened.

"She's not been sleeping well. Insomnia, you know? She's tried all the old tricks like herbal tea and reading – one night she read till dawn. A few times she had a Tom Collins or two before going to bed, but you know that's not the answer."

"I agree with you there."

"So then yesterday I find my bottle of Ambien. I got it for when I went out to India last year, but I've only used it once or twice. Now the bottle's almost empty. I don't mind that Katrina's been taking it, of course, but could it be dangerous, maybe habit-forming? And it's weird that she didn't ask me."

I thought for a moment and said, "She was probably embarrassed. I wouldn't be overly concerned, Richard. Ambien really is a wonder-drug – safe and not habit-forming."

"So it's *not* addictive?"

"Not in the least. Still, a healthy young woman like Katrina shouldn't *need* to take sleeping pills on a regular basis. The real question is why she's having trouble sleeping to begin with."

"There we go!" Richard blurted as we saw the lights of a gas station convenience store; we went inside and bought a thermos of coffee.

Sleeplessness is a classic sign of depression. Not wanting to make Richard more nervous than he already was, I tiptoed around the issue. "Have you two been settling in all right? Are you thriving here in Denmark?"

"Yes. Well, yeah sort of. I mean, there's a lot of things to get used to, and the working environment is a lot different than in New York."

"Have you been facing the challenges together, as a team, would you say?"

"We have our disagreements if that's what you mean."

"Disagreements?"

"You could say we've been fighting."

"Fighting? About what?"

"Nothing. I mean, little things. Like she's very defensive about Denmark – the least little thing I say gets blown out of proportion."

"Such as?" I asked, fishing for specifics. The examples a person chooses often reveal more than they intend.

"Like the other day I mentioned about the Olympics. I asked her why Denmark never wins any medals."

"What did she say?"

"Aw, she got all in a huff and said that they did, that Danes were good at sailing and badminton and team handball, things I would never pay attention to."

"Mm-hm, so what did you say?"

"Well, I said it had more to do with things being too easy over here – no competitive spirit. Everybody's taken care of from cradle to grave, so there's just no spark in most people. I said maybe Denmark should become the travel agent to the world, because the one thing they seem to get excited about is vacation."

I had to laugh at that. It occurred to me that the example he chose, about competitiveness, may refer to him feeling more competitive, more cutthroat to put it negatively, than his colleagues. But the subject at hand was Katrina, so I asked, "Why do you think she's so sensitive right now?"

"I don't know. I think maybe after living in New York for so long, she's not so happy with Denmark herself, but she doesn't want to admit it."

I let this hang in the air a moment and then said, "You're no doubt familiar with the expression, 'You can't go home again.'"

"Yeah, sure."

"Denmark today is not the same place Katrina left as a 19-year-old. The nation has moved sharply to the right politically. Danes feel threatened by the new Europe, especially the eastern part, and they're afraid of the growing Muslim population."

"I've noticed that. It's been hard for me too, as a foreigner."

"Yes, I'm sure. Meanwhile, Katrina's friends and family have aged and changed. Some of them have drifted away and may not even want to see her anymore."

"That's true – look at her brother Claus. Hasn't said 'Boo' to her since we arrived. So you think she's depressed because she's home but she's still not happy. Gee, I never thought of that. Maybe it's like the 'holiday blues.'"

"The Holiday Blues?" I asked, thinking it might be a jazz band, something to do with Billie Holiday.

"Yeah, like people who are sad at Christmastime – they feel like they're *supposed* to be happy. So when they're not, it makes them even more depressed."

"Yes, perhaps it's something like that," I said, smiling at this homespun definition of seasonal affective disorder or "SAD."

As we rolled onto the asphalt of the parking lot back at the beach, Richard made a final comment. "Oh, yeah, and one more thing: she has bad dreams."

As a therapist, I know that such a "parting shot" is often the most important thing a person will say.

"What kind of dreams?" I asked.

"I don't know exactly – about her father, I think. She doesn't remember them clearly. But she keeps saying there's something 'unfinished' about his death. What do you think—"

He was interrupted by a loud BOOM! The fireworks display had started, so we agreed to continue the conversation some other time.

I took one step out of the car and my shoe sank a centimeter into the tarred surface, still soft from the heat of the day. Explosions buffeted my ears and the night sky was illuminated with rockets shooting sparks of Danish crimson-and-white. It was so bright that when I looked out over the water, the amorphous "ghost craft" I had been watching earlier could be readily identified as nothing more than launching barges and fireboats that were supporting the fireworks display.

I walked on ahead as Richard got the coffee out of the back seat. From behind a clump of dwarf pines, I heard voices: Katrina and Søren were exchanging words hotly. If I didn't know better, I would have sworn I had interrupted a lovers' quarrel. I ahem'd loudly, and their squabble, whatever it was, came to an abrupt halt. Katrina glared at me and almost mowed me down as she huffed back to the car. It was a very quiet ride back to town.

It's hard to imagine that there's anything between them – what an unlikely couple! – but then again, Søren is a handsome man, and Katrina is an attractive young woman. Given what Richard had just told me, she may be a bit depressed, vulnerable right now, and her husband is away a lot. So I decided to pay her a call. I had a duty to the memory of Vincent Marchese to keep an eye on his son – but right now it was Katrina who needed looking after.

Two Wednesdays later, while Richard was in London on business, I called Katrina and invited myself over for coffee. Though it was July, the evening was cool and threatening, so I put on my rain jacket for the walk up to Rosenborgs Allé. Along the way, I stopped at the boulevard bakery and bought some pastry.

I arrived just as the sun was setting fire to the edges of the trees in the west and deep shadows filled the lawns.

*"Noget er anderledes her* – something is different," I said, as we sat together in the kitchen. "Tell me, is it a new color scheme?"

"Yes, my friend Annika and I worked on it together. We felt the décor was too bright," Katrina said.

"Is it burgundy?"

"Yes, and in the dining room, aubergine. It really tones down the energy."

"That it does."

The colors were dark to the point of being depressing. Her choices worried me. Worse still was the tell-tale puffiness under her eyes – from lack of sleep, crying, or both.

As we unpacked the layered-dough pastry, which in Danish is called "Vienna bread," Katrina suggested, "As long as we are having Viennese pastry, let's make Austrian *jaegertee* as well!"

"Fine with me," I said, thinking the rum-laced tea might calm her down.

As the water boiled, we kept to safe subjects like Richard's travels and the Olympic Games which would begin in Atlanta in a few days' time. Katrina poured out the ruby-colored tea. As we sipped the tea and cut into the layers of the Danish, her smile was weak. She seemed on edge. It occurred to me that she might be uncomfortable about my walking in on her and Søren on the beach, but I couldn't say anything about it directly. So I tried to draw her out by asking, "Are you thriving, being home? I suppose it has been a long time."

"It *has*, nearly eight years. Since Fa', um, died, you know?" she said, looking down into the depths of her teacup.

"Was it a great shock, your father's death?"

"Oh my God, yes. At least it was for me. I don't know about Mor. She seemed to take everything so stoically. Claus, too. I was a complete wreck at the funeral, shed enough tears for the three of us, I suppose. I felt so alone. I don't know, after that, I just had to get out of there, out of everything. My whole world was shattered. I guess some families come together in a crisis – ours flew apart."

"It sounds like you had different ways of dealing with your grief. You were all trying to make meaning as best you could."

"To find meaning in Fa's death?"

"To *make* meaning in your own lives."

Katrina seemed to drink this in with her tea. She sat for quite a while looking out the window – at the yard or her own reflection, I couldn't tell.

Finally she said, "You're right. Each of us finds meaning in different things – my brother in his work, Mor in her home, and I—"

She hesitated. I saw a tear rolling down her cheek.

"And you?"

"I don't know, Edvard. I went to New York to escape, a refugee."

"No, you were not a refugee," I countered. "You went to New York as an adventurer, a dancer, an artist, and you came back—"

"A *hausfrau*," she said, smirking.

"I was going to say 'conquistadora' – you conquered New York, and returned a celebrated success."

"Why? Because I married a rich man?"

"You came back a wife, yes, but you are no ordinary *hausfrau*. Never."

"Oh, what else am I good for? I never finished my education. I'm washed up as a dancer," she said, tears flowing now.

"I am surprised at your sudden loss of confidence, Katrina. There, there," I said, putting my hand on hers. The skin was incredibly soft, like an infant's. "What about your business idea – the natural foods store?"

"Oh, that's just posing. I'm no businesswoman."

"Nobody is anything until they *become* something," I said a bit too glibly, as if reading from the Existentialist Handbook. She turned away and started crying outright. I got up and crouched next to her, so as to be on her level, and took her face in my hands. "My dear, I mean it sincerely. One can choose one's attitude to any situation. No matter how bleak it may appear. That's what this century has taught us, Katrina."

"I feel so – alien," she said, looking into my eyes.

"You mean the Denmark you remember is no longer here?"

"Everything has changed, and it's just like – I hate to say it, but sometimes it seems like they've all forgotten me."

"Forgotten you? Who?"

"Oh, I don't know, everyone. At least in New York I had my own friends, my own life. I was an adult, a dancer with the Joffrey Ballet. An accomplished person. No one takes me seriously here. Mor and my friends—"

"Remember the person you were at nineteen," I said.

"What do you mean?"

"You were so very young when you left. In the interim, you've matured, but the people here haven't seen that. So they treat you as the teen, the naïf you were. Here, now, blow your nose, will you?" I offered her my handkerchief and smiled, conscious of the irony.

After a tiny nose-laugh, she said, "Well, maybe that's it. I was so naïve. But what can I do? Gather everyone together and announce that I'm all grown up now?"

"I think that's the right message, especially for your mother."

Brightening, Katrina said, "You mean I could actually sit down and say, 'Mor, it has been nearly eight years since I've lived in Denmark, and I've changed a lot in the between-time. You haven't noticed, but it's about time you did.'"

"Why not? It would do a lot to clear the air between you. Your mother is a refined, intelligent woman. Intellectually she knows you're an adult, but emotionally, it seems she is still treating you like a teenager."

"Yes, she still wants to pack my lunchbox."

"And what about your brother, Claus? You had some sort of a falling-out with him?"

"Yes, right after the funeral."

"If you don't mind me asking, what happened?"

She looked away, suddenly felt the need to get more honey, went over to the counter and said with her back to me, spooning away, "Oh, I don't even know anymore. Something about Fa's pocket watch."

"His pocket watch?"

"Yes, I wanted to keep it because – oh, it doesn't matter!"

"Have you tried to reach out to him?"

"I called him just after we arrived in the country. I left a voice mail, but never heard back."

"You didn't try again?"

"No. I felt I had already made the first move. And anyway, I've been so absorbed by the house."

"Claus may not have gotten the message. And after so many years, frankly you need to make more of an effort."

We talked about this for awhile, and she agreed that she would reach out to her brother. But she still seemed troubled, so I decided to follow up on Richard's comments on the insomnia. "Forgive me for saying so, but you look a bit tired, Katrina, are you sleeping all right?"

"No, I'm not," she said, getting up and pacing to the counter.

"Is this your first bout with insomnia?"

"No, but it's the worst."

"What's different this time, what makes it worse?"

"I'm *afraid* to go to sleep at night – afraid the dreams will come back. I don't have the dreams in the hours after dawn, you see. Only in the night, in the dark."

"Is there a recurring dream?"

"Yes. For the longest time I couldn't remember—" she started, then stopped, came over and sat at the table again. "I haven't told anyone about what I've remembered. Please don't tell Richard."

"I consider this entire conversation privileged. I am a doctor, you know," I said with a wink. "How does the dream start?"

"Scraping sounds, always *scrape-scrape, scrape-scrape,*" she said, contorting her features in disgust.

"Can you see who or what is making the noise?"

"Yes, it's a man – he's scraping the name 'Nielsen' off a door."

"The man is removing your name from the door?"

"I thought so at first, but—" she said, her face melting, mouth quivering.

I waited for it, but nothing came. My thoughts raced ahead. *If he's scraping off "Nielsen," and it's not her name, then...*

"Is the man your father?"

Then she nodded and broke down entirely. Between sobs she said, "I see him and I don't know why he's erasing his own name, and then he starts to choke and his face turns this horrible bluish purple, oh it's horrible!"

"There, there," I said, holding her hand.

"Then he points to his chest, and I think he wants me to undo a button, to relieve the pressure he's under, but inside the shirt he's completely *hollow* – blood is oozing everywhere, the white linen stained with blood!"

I embraced her then and told her not to speak any more. While the interpretation of dreams holds an honored place in my profession, I myself have never believed in it. Dreams are odd bits of information in the brain that haven't been filed properly. A Freudian would start interpreting a dream like this as an expression of latent sexual desire for her father – the blood on the "linen" could be seen as menstrual blood. To me, this is no more scientific than the Pharaoh planning for famine because a slave named Joseph interpreted his dream of seven skinny cows. On the other hand, sleep deprivation was a real problem; she needed to stop obsessing about this dream. So once she'd calmed down, I asked for her own interpretation.

"Sometimes," she said, "I think that there's something *unfinished* about Fa', about his death. He was only fifty-three, and he never had a heart condition."

"You're suggesting foul play?" I said, raising my eyebrows.

"His body was found in a conference room at the firm. His partners found him: what if they found him because they were the ones who killed him? That would explain why Fa's spirit is not at rest."

She was getting all worked up again. I tried to calm her down by saying, "Katrina, now I want you to be a good detective for me, all right? A good detective needs a theory and evidence. Your theory is that your father was murdered by his partners – but why? There's no motive, no evidence."

"But the dreams!"

"Are coming from your own subconscious. Your father's name was expunged from the Book of Life, from *your* life, and your brain has constructed this dream showing him removing his name from the door."

"But his chest—"

"Is hollow because you know he had a heart attack."

Then she grew pensive, nodded a couple of times, and said, "I see what you mean, Edvard. But – as a good detective – I think I need to gather some more facts."

I hadn't expected this, but nodded.

"I'm going to sniff around, talk to Mor. If I can't find any hard evidence, I promise I'll drop the whole thing."

"Good girl," I said.

Her face broadened into a beautiful smile, the first real smile of the evening. That was the first time I noticed that her teeth were yellow, like a smoker's.

"Well, I'm glad that's settled. Say, would you care for a cigarette?" I asked, getting a pack of Prince Lights out of my breast pocket.

"No, you know I don't smoke."

I paused, then said, "I ask out of politeness. Do you mind if I light up?"

"Let's sit outside then. I try not to have smoke in the house. I guess it's an American thing," she said. "You go on out and I'll fix us a little midnight snack. Would you like some coffee?"

"Yes, I could use an eye-opener just about now," I replied with a smile.

I went out into the yard and sat at the patio table, facing the kitchen. Lighting a cigarette, I took a long drag. A case I'd had in Croatia was still scratching at the back of my mind: a black woman named Angela, who'd worked for a high-profile victim, claimed that he'd been murdered. She insisted he'd been shot through the head *before* the plane crashed. The shot, at altitude, made the plane go down, she claimed. It's amazing what the grief-stricken mind will—

Just then I looked in the kitchen window. There was Katrina, making coffee as expected. *But who the devil was that standing behind her?* I watched as she cleaned the strawberries, set out cups and plates, took spoons from the drawer, all the while ignoring her guest. But I was perplexed: it must have been midnight. No one would call at such an hour.

The figure, perhaps distorted in the glass, was preternaturally tall and thin. No one I knew had such a face, gaunt and stolid. There was a dead stillness about him as he stood there calmly smoking a cigarette. This caught my eye – frankly it annoyed me – because Katrina had just sent me outside to smoke, and here was this other fellow puffing away right under her nose, and she wasn't saying a thing.

"Hmmpf," I said and stumped out my cigarette. Striding back into the kitchen, I was all set to speak my piece, but to my surprise, the room was empty.

For a brief moment I wondered if the mysterious "smoking man" was none other than my own reflection in the glass. But this was not possible: I'd been sitting at the patio table, the man I saw was standing; he was wearing an old-fashioned suit with an ascot, while I had on my nylon rain jacket. I don't even own an ascot.

But I didn't have time to ponder the matter for long. For through the doorway into the dining room, I saw Katrina teetering at the head of stairs leading down to the cellar.

# 9. Katrina

*"Du er ikke Hamlet."*

"What?"

"You are not Hamlet."

"I am not Hamlet," I repeated, not understanding what he meant.

Edvard sighed and said, "It's fiction, Katrina. Shakepeare's Prince of Denmark was indeed haunted by his father's Ghost, but in real life, such things simply don't happen."

He wanted me to view my dreams as products of my own subconscious, but he wasn't there when I identified the body with Mor; he wasn't at the funeral; he doesn't know.

Edvard said later that he saw something in the window. I don't know what it was. The night was dark; there was no moon. We had been drinking rum. Perhaps he just saw his own reflection distorted by the glass, the lighting, the drink. Who knows?

No one was in the kitchen with me, that's for sure. I remember exactly what I did: I put the kettle on and took dessert plates out of the cupboard, the delft ones. I got the strawberries out of the refrigerator, rinsed them and cut the tops off, so I could serve them with the vanilla ice cream. I brought the plates and spoons out to the dining room and set them on the table. They were still sitting there afterwards, after the incident, I mean. If there had been a man standing behind me in the kitchen, I would have seen him when I turned round to go into the dining room. I would have walked right through him.

I opened the door to the cellar. The ice cream was in the freezer down there. The light was already on, but I didn't think anything of it at the time. I heard a whooshing noise, like a gust of wind, rush past my ear. Then I must've stumbled on the door saddle, and I fell. To be honest, it felt as if I stubbed my toe on the saddle and then got a hard push to the lower back.

My right arm lashed out to grab hold of something, anything, as I began to pitch forward. I crushed my hand against the stone wall, breaking the little finger, but there was no stopping the momentum. I was just falling and falling, like in a dream. I thumped my right knee on one step, knocked my left elbow on a second, and banged my head just above the temple on a third. I wrenched my back trying to stop myself, rolled head over heels onto the cold stone of the landing. I lay with my head down and my legs pressed up against the wall and arms splayed out like a broken doll. I cried like a child. A trickle of blood made its way from my temple to the foot of the steps and onto the cellar floor. I shrieked and Edvard ran in from the kitchen and hurried down the stairs. Poor thing, while he tried his best to minister to my wounds, I screamed at him as if he was trying to kill me. Finally I remembered it was just Edvard – he was a doctor after all – and I let him touch me. I was a complete mess; there was blood everywhere. There was a deep cut over my right eye; my knee, elbow, hand and ankle were throbbing with pain and starting to swell; my back was thrown out.

"Someone pushed me – he's trying to kill me, Edvard! Did you see who it was?"

"Calm down, Katrina. You just took a spill is all, banged your head. I saw you fall. No one pushed you. No one is trying to kill you."

Edvard examined my injuries and got me upstairs to the living room. He made a joke about how long it had been since medical school, and explained that my wounds, while dramatic, were probably not serious. My pride was hurt more than anything else. A dancer is not used to being clumsy. And I'd just gotten over blowing out my *left* knee. Now I lay flat on the green sofa as he iced the right one; we talked about going to the emergency room, but decided against it in the end. I would see my GP in the morning; meanwhile, Edvard agreed to stay the night in the front bedroom. The next day, he told me about seeing the man in a morning suit smoking a cigarette.

When we got back upstairs after the incident, I smelled smoke. I assumed that Edvard had brought his cigarette back inside with him, but he denied it.

"I put out my cigarette in the ashtray on the patio table. And besides, this smoke is definitely not mine. I smoke Prince Light, a mild blend. This is a dark tobacco, can't you tell?"

It did have a strong, distinct smell, a little like burning tar.

Sniffing the air again, he said, "Hmm, it smells Turkish. Camel perhaps or, no, rather more French, like Gauloises. Gauloises, that's it. Like the Queen."

A few days later, after I had been x-rayed and bandaged up, Annika came by to see how I was doing. I ached everywhere, but the cuts on my face had already started to heal, and I was able to hobble around despite a swollen knee and ankle. She was kind enough to run around making tea and a snack as we chatted on the sun porch. I told her about the smell of harsh tobacco, asked if the Queen really smoked French cigarettes.

She laughed behind her Dior sunglasses and said, *"Dronningen kan godt lide franske ting i munden,"* referring to the fact that our Queen had married a Frenchman and the royal family spoke French at home.

"How can you make jokes at a time like this?" I said, "I'm really scared—"

"Yes, you're right," she replied. "The tuning of the house is so high that—"

"Annika, you're still talking about feng shui, but 'tuning' can't push a person down a flight of steps."

"You lost your balance at the head of the stairs, Katrina. If an imbalance of Qi can cause heart disease and brain tumors, it can certainly throw off your middle ear."

Her pat explanation didn't satisfy me. Qi was too abstract. These phenomena seemed directed, personal.

"We changed the color scheme," I said. "The atmosphere is more subdued, more relaxed, and I've been sleeping better. But the walking on the stairs, the man in the window, my accident..." I trailed off. I didn't want to say it, but her silence forced me. "Do you think it's possible that we have... I mean is there such a thing as a *ghost?*"

"Oh," she said, nodding as if she hadn't thought of that one. "Yes, that makes sense."

"You believe in ghosts?" I was surprised.

"Of *course*. Katrina, billions of people believe in spirits. Only the hyper-rational Western intelligentsia denies the existence of the human soul."

"So you think ghosts are the souls of the dead?"

"What else would they be? I'm not an expert, but it seems there are several different varieties. There's the obsessive type that repeats the same action again and again – pace the floor, open and shut the window. Very tedious. Then there are poltergeists, who are mischievous and destructive. They haunt anyone who moves in. Other spectres are the spirits of our forefathers."

"Forefathers?"

"Yes, Chinese culture is filled with stories of ancestors who come back to wreak vengeance on someone or other, often their own descendents."

"So the ghost could be one of my ancestors?" I asked, screwing up my face.

"It's possible."

*Was the man in the window Fa's ghost, angry that I abandoned the family so soon after the funeral? Or did he want to warn me about something?*

"I don't think it's Fa'—" I sputtered.

"Your father? Who said anything about your father?"

"Well, you remember he died just before I left for the States."

"Yes, but the dead do not number the years as we do. It could just as easily be the founder of the House of Nielsen from hundreds of years ago as your father so recently dead."

"But there's something else, something that I haven't told you – I've been having bad dreams."

"What kind of dreams?" she asked.

I told her what I could remember about them. "Sometimes I'm afraid to close my eyes. I told Edvard – I could tell he thinks I'm nuts."

"The psychiatrist? Oh, puh-lease! That's the *last* person you should be talking to about a thing like this."

"Why?"

"Because I'm sure he's just like all the allopathic practitioners – caught in that rationalist trap I was talking about before. 'There are more things between heaven and earth,' you know. Listen, you seem perfectly normal to me. Why don't we assume that you're *not* nuts, and go from there, shall we?"

That made me feel better, and I smiled and touched her hand.

"I remember that you had a really hard time after your father died," she said, stroking my hand gently.

"It was terrible – I really loved him, you know."

"You couldn't stop crying at the funeral – I think you sobbed the entire time."

"I was the only one."

"Your mother was very strong."

"Or maybe she just didn't care."

"Oh, you shouldn't say that," she said, removing her hand and wrinkling her brow.

"I never forgave them those dry eyes," I said, remembering the resentment I felt. After the ceremony, I just counted the days till I could get away. I was supposed to start studying that fall, but gave up my place in Art History at the University of Copenhagen. I fled as far as I could think of, and didn't look back – much.

"How did your father die, anyway?" Annika asked.

"He had a heart attack at the office and was dead on arrival at Rigshospital. I had to identify the body with Mor because Claus was still on holiday, and I didn't want her to go alone."

"How terrible! That was lot for a nineteen-year-old."

"Something, the heart attack I guess, had left his face badly disfigured. Sometimes I wonder whether – well, poison can do that to a face too, can't it?"

"Or shock," Annika said. Then she removed her shades and sat forward. "Are you saying you think he was murdered?"

"I don't know."

"Was there anyone who profited from his death?"

"I have no idea," I said.

"Perhaps you should ask your mother. It could be that your father's spirit is restless – that he's trying to communicate with you."

"Do you think that's what's really going on?"

"You should contact a Master," she said, and then brightened, adding, "How lucky it is that you live in Svanemølle!"

"Lucky?"

"You're so close to the Buddhistic Center of Copenhagen, on Svanemøllevej."

I gave her a perplexed look.

"You didn't know?" she asked. "Oh, yes, you can walk there from here! There's a holy-man there called Master Li-Pin. I don't know if you'd be able to see him, he travels so much, but I think you should try. I met him last year. He's the most amazing man, gifted with 'far sight.'"

"What's that?"

"The Master can see things remotely – he was able to describe our apartment to me without ever having set foot in it."

This reminded me of something I'd read about – how the CIA used people to "see" into enemy bunkers. Or was that in a film?

"What's he like? What did he tell you?" I asked.

"A small man with a great round head, bald as an egg. I touched my fingertips with his and felt electricity flow through us. He closed his eyes and entered a Tantric state, breathing slowly. First he began to describe our street. You know we live on a hill; he said he was entering a home where the doorway was straight but the street was crooked, which describes our front door perfectly. Then he said he saw a dark green stairwell with black and white tile and went up, up, up to the top floor – we live on the top floor, you know that – and he entered a wooden door. And inside he said he saw water right away – we have a huge aquarium in the sitting room. Then he said, 'All I see is books, books, books' – you know what my place looks like, there are bookcases everywhere. He was even able to identify several of the volumes, right down to which shelf they stood on."

"That's amazing," I said. "I would love to have him survey the house. Do you think you could introduce me?"

# 10. Angelina Marchese

So I get this phone call from my son the night before I leave. Now when you're a widow and you're in your sixties, Friday night is not a big deal, but flying to Denmark is a very big deal. Of course I was nervous. It's not every day I go to a different country.

The first words out of his mouth are, "Katrina fell down the stairs."

"Wha-a-at? Is she all right?"

"Banged up a bit, but she's okay. Thank God Eddé was there."

"Vinnie's friend from Germany, the doctor? What was he doing there?"

"He was keeping Katrina company while I was in London. She was going down to get some ice cream from the freezer in the basement when she tripped over the threshold."

"Oh my God. Did she break anything?"

"I don't think so. Mostly she's just shaken up, but she had some x-rays done, just in case." I was about to say this was a wise precaution, but my son talked over me. "Ma, I hate to tell you this, but – there's something else."

As if I hadn't gotten enough news for one phone call! I waited for him to tell me what it was, but there was static on the line. I thought we were going to be cut off, and we hello'd back and forth a few times before we were sure we still had a connection.

"I think we have a ghost," he said softly, almost whispering.

"A *ghost*?"

"Yeah, I know it sounds crazy, but it's like we have a ghost in the house, and we've got to get rid of it."

At that point, I heard Katrina's voice calling from the other room. Richard excused himself and went away from the telephone. When he came back on the line, he said, "You'll never believe this."

"What happened?"

"The minute I said we had a ghost – this is the first time I've verbalized it – Katrina calls to me from the other room and says her document disappeared."

"What document? What do you mean, *disappeared*?"

"The business plan for the natural food store, she's been working on it all day. The minute I said the word 'ghost,' the document blanked out, vanished from the screen for some reason."

"It was just gone, all of a sudden?"

"All but one letter."

"Well, it's a computer, she must've just pressed the wrong button."

"I figured the same thing. But when I went to recover the saved version, it was erased too. All but one letter, the letter *D*. Now it's possible to erase the saved file, but it takes a heck of a lot of keystrokes. And she swears she didn't make them."

That was weird. Then he started telling me about all the things that have been happening – running on the stairs, wineglasses exploding, and an apparition, a "ghostly man in mourning" he called it. Of course, none of this was what I needed to hear the night before my flight. I was almost ready to cancel the whole thing. But what was I supposed to say? I promised to say a prayer for them. I wasn't looking forward to sleeping in such an unsettled place. At my age, such adventures I don't need.

After I hung up the phone, I kept thinking about the ghost. Now I'm a Catholic, and the Church does not officially condone belief in ghosts. But on the other hand, I am a spiritual person, so I decided to keep an open mind. Maybe all souls do go to heaven or hell, but not right away.

I got myself ready for bed. Who should I pray to? St. Anthony is for lost objects, St. Jude for lost causes. St. Christopher protects travelers, St. Blaise the throat. But who takes care of ghosts? I said a prayer to St. Michael, asking for his intercession to help a soul that maybe got lost between the two worlds, to help that little butterfly find peace.

The next day, on the way to JFK, I got a sign that I made the right choice. The cabbie took a wrong turn on Woodhaven Boulevard, and we ended up stopped dead in traffic. There was some kind of an accident on Queens Boulevard, a tractor-trailer jackknifed. And of all places, where were we stopped but in front of St. Michael's parish in Briarwood. There's a huge statue of the Archangel; we sat there for maybe ten-fifteen minutes. I looked closely at the stone sculpture. The artist must have been an Irishman, because he had given his subject the blazing eyes, beetle brows and chiseled features of Celtic good looks – stamped the "map of Ireland" on his face, like we used to say. The scene showed Michael in full battle dress – plates of armor, chain mail, broadsword – as he slayed the dragon in Revelation.

Now *that's* a sign.

I felt well-protected, and I had just started to say the Angelis in thanks, when I heard *thwack! thwack!* Two young guys, skinny as telephone poles and their skin black as coal, were washing the windshield of the cab. Their heads were sticking up out of oversized white tee shirts that blew in the breeze like laundry on a line. The taller one smiled at me through the window. His shirt proclaimed "Frick" and at first I thought this was a curse word, but then I saw his partner's shirt said "Frack," and I realized they were Frick and Frack. Each was missing an arm, but together they were a well-oiled window-washing machine. Frick, a righty, held the bucket while Frack, a lefty, squeegeed the windows.

The driver, a real caveman who looked like he'd been fighting a five o'clock shadow since kindergarten, started to shoo them away in heated Greek, but I told him I'd pay for the wash.

"Why should you pay for these no-good-black-sons-of-bitches to clean my windshield when I don't ask them and it ain't even dirty?"

I was tempted to make a smart reply like "because of the Sermon on the Mount," but I controlled myself and said, "Because they're good friends of mine."

Grinning, I waved to them as they worked. They finished before the light changed. I took a few bills out of my purse, and handed the money to them through the window. The two of them put up their hands as if to a crowd, smiled with what teeth they had, and bowed repeatedly, like they'd just completed a grand performance of Madame Butterfly.

When the cabbie saw the money, he said, "So what are you rich or something, Lady?"

"Yes, in a way I am, loaded."

"And a rich lady like you, these are your friends, this rabble?"

I smiled and said, "They are now."


The day after I arrived, Eddé came by in the morning, and we set off for the bus stop. Like in New York, you really don't need a car in Copenhagen. We could see everything from the bus: canals like Venice, windmills like Holland, castles like England, gardens like France. There were flowers everywhere. The cute little city-houses were dolled up in children's colors of goldenrod, butternut squash and blueberry cream. The snow-white window frames gleamed and the national pennants streamed in the summer breeze.

Copenhagen is a fairy tale city, and we visited the Little Mermaid, who sits on her rock in the harbor for the benefit of tourists and seagulls alike; toured the gardens of Frederiksberg Castle; ate lunch in the New Harbor, and did some window shopping in the longest pedestrian mall in the world, a thing Eddé called the "Walking Street." We certainly did our share of walking, and by the time we climbed aboard the Number 18 bus going back uptown, I was totally exhausted.

Eddé left me at the door. I rang the bell, then let myself in with the key Richard gave me. Walking into the living room, I called, "Katrina!" No answer. I wanted to talk about my adventures, but it seemed I was alone in the house. It had been a long day, so I went upstairs to extract my swollen feet from my shoes and climb into a nice, hot bath.

I went to change in the front bedroom, where I was staying. The day had been hot; the upper rooms were stuffy. I opened up one of the dormer windows, and the fresh air wafted in over me. The wind in the poplar trees made a riffling noise. To get to the other window, I had to move the handsome surveyor's scope that was standing in front of it. It was an antique instrument, reminded me of the ones Vinnie used to have at job sites in the old days. The tube, which was made of heavy brass and had stood in the sun all afternoon, was warm to the touch and felt good in my hands. What wonderful craftsmanship.

I opened the second window, lowered the shades, and changed into my robe for the walk down the hallway to the bathroom. The white porcelain tub reminded me of the one Nonna had in Corona, with feet. The taps, they were a mystery. Through pure trial and error, I figured out that *V* was warm and *K* was cold. At least I wouldn't forget: *V* was for Vinnie, because my Vinnie was warm. *K* was... well, *K* was the other one.

When I got the temperature just right – some like it hot, and God help me, I'm one of them – I lowered myself into the steaming water. One end of the tub was higher than the other, so it was very comfortable. The warm, soapy water embraced my body. My muscles unwound. The grime and stress of the day slid off my skin. I put my feet up and relaxed.

It was so kind of Eddé to show me around. He reminds me of Vinnie, he really does. And I can't get over how young he looks. After all he must be nearly my age, but he looks ten-fifteen years younger. His teeth are beautiful. He doesn't even wear glasses. Of course, he would look even better without that beard, but he is a psychiatrist. It does make him look professional. And he's such a gentleman. Thinking of others all the time. *What would you like to see?* he would say. *Which would you prefer?* and *This is your day.*

Thinking of him, and other men of that era like my Vinnie, and Harold Morgenbloom who gave me my first kiss in high school, and Pappa, gone so many years now, I drifted off. The dream I had was remarkable, so realistic. We were at a carnival or bazaar of some kind. There was a hurdy-gurdy man with a monkey, and a merry-go-round where they played that honky-tonk song, "Listen to the Mockingbird." I wanted a ride on the carousel, but was too old for that, though I must've been very young in the dream, because I was still in a plaid school uniform. We walked by wheels of fortune where people were betting on numbers. The spinner stopped at 18 again and again. There was a taffy-pulling machine – maybe we were at the Steel Pier at Atlantic City – and the smell of cotton candy was in the air. Then we came upon a seller's cart filled with candied and caramel apples. I eyed a ruby-red one.

It was then I saw who I was with. It was a man, a handsome man, middle-aged. Eyebrows bushy, piercing green eyes, pointed goatee, he looked like a czar. His forehead was high, and his thin hair was slicked back with redolent pomade. He smiled as he handed me the stick; I felt the sticky coating of the apple on my skin between my thumb and forefinger. I bit into the sugary surface. I could tell he liked me. In the dream I guess he was my boyfriend, although he was older. He looked out at me from under the shade of his eyebrows, as if he knew something he couldn't tell me. It was the look of a man with a secret.

Striking a kitchen match, he lit up a cigar, sucking and puffing on it to start the burning process, like cigar-smokers do. But the harsh smoke bothered me, and I coughed. Seeing my distress, he put it out, not saying anything – I never heard his voice – but nodding and smirking as if to say, *Anything to oblige a lady.*

We saw a white orchid on the ground. Apparently I had lost my corsage; it was the kind that we used to keep in the icebox and wear to affairs years ago, when there were still iceboxes. And affairs, for that matter. Bending his long frame, he picked up the flower, and pinned it on the lapel of my uniform dress. He touched my left cheek. His hand felt wonderful on my skin – it felt so warm.

But the rest of my body was growing cold, perilously cold. Slowly I became aware of an icy feeling, starting in the legs and then moving up my body. My face remained warm, and I was held in the man's gaze. I couldn't move. Finally, shaking my head so violently that bath water spilled on the wall and floor, I willed myself awake.

The bath was nearly overflowing. Up to my chin in ice-cold water, I slipped and went under, my arms flailing and splashing. I struggled for breath and shook my head wildly, but it was of no use. It was as if my legs were being pulled up and out of the bath. I was as helpless as a turtle on its back.

*Jesus, Mary and Joseph protect us.*

Then a great shiver went through me, and the tension in my legs relaxed. My arms found the sides of the tub, and I sat up.

I caught my breath. Then I started shaking, my teeth were chattering. I'd never been so frozen. Like I was paralyzed, it was so hard to move. Slowly, I reached over with palsied hands to turn off the cold water that was still dribbling into the tub, pulled the plug, and got out as best I could. I wrapped myself in the maroon towel that hung on the rack.

*What had happened?*

I'd fallen asleep and the *K* tap had gotten turned on somehow, maybe my foot hit it. If I'd stayed in there I would have drowned, or froze to death. In the middle of July, that would have made some headline for the local papers.

The details of the dream came to me right away, like the scent of flowers from the garden. Not orchids, but calla lilies, the kind you can use for anything from weddings to funerals. Also the smell of smoke, it must've wafted in from outside. Or maybe Katrina was home. I had the idea that she must be a closet smoker, since her teeth had gotten awfully yellow-looking since the last time I'd seen her.

Sitting on the commode, I massaged the feeling back into my feet and legs. The skin on my left cheek was tingling, and in the mirror, I could see it was a rash of some kind, looked like poison ivy. But it didn't itch or anything, so I left it alone.

*The man in my dream touched my left cheek.*

I went back to the bedroom and dressed. Katrina had come home, and I called out to her as I came down the steps. There on the wall above the sideboard in the dining room was a portrait of a man. I stopped mid-stair.

Beetle-browed, balding, goatee – there he was, the man from my dream!

I gasped, and Katrina turned and asked, "Are you all right, Angelina?"

"Why, yes. It's just – that photograph. Where'd you get it?"

"Oh, him. He came with the house. I just brought him home from the frame shop. But I meant your face."

"The rash," I said nodding, trying to hide how shaken I was. "Yeah, I saw it in the mirror upstairs – it looks all red and angry-looking, but it doesn't bother me. I was trying on perfume in the store. I must be allergic."

"Why were you asking about the photo?"

"Oh, nothing," I said, masking my feelings with a smile. "Handsome devil, isn't he?"

# 11. Richard

"Italian sounds smooth, romantic, even when they're saying you can't visit the museum today. *Non é possibile visitare il museo oggi.* Ah! Beauty-full," my mother said as we sat in the dining room having dessert and coffee with Katrina.

"I'm impressed with how well you're holding up, Ma," I said.

"Well, I'm all off-schedule," she said. "It's nine o'clock here, but it's only three o'clock for me."

"Yes, but you've been all over Copenhagen today," Katrina said.

"Yeah, it was a long day," my mother said, pouring cream in her coffee.

"Didn't you take a nap when you got home?" I asked.

She flinched and spilled cream on the tablecloth.

"Oh, dear," she said and started to get up, but Katrina was faster and got a cloth to clean up the spill.

"No problem, Ma, don't worry about it," I said.

Looking across at the daguerreotype of Old Damsgaard that hung on the wall above the sideboard, she asked, "Do you know who that is?"

"The original owner of the house," I said.

"The man who died last year?" she asked.

"No, that was his son, Peder," I explained. "When I met with Dahl, the real estate man, he told me the whole story. This gentleman, Karl Damsgaard, was a lawyer here in town."

"*Damns-God* was his name?" she asked.

"In Danish, it's pronounced more like *Dams-gaw*," Katrina said.

"Well, this *Dams-gaw*," I said, imitating her pronunciation as best I could, "bought the raw land in the 1890s. The neighborhood was just being built up around that time. Sound House was completed in 1904."

"That would explain the scope in my room," Ma said.

"What do you mean?" I asked. "Isn't it just a telescope?"

"Really, Richard, and you with your father in construction. It's a surveyor's tool. I think they call it a 'transit.' It's an old one; they probably used it during the construction."

She was right — it wasn't the kind of telescope you'd use for the stars. I had seen modern versions of them a million times around Pop's job sites. I blushed a little and said, "Yeah, well, now that you mention it, that makes a lot of sense. Damsgaard picked the site, developed the property, and his son lived here until he went into a nursing home about a year ago."

"So it really is the House of Damsgaard," Ma said.

Just then the Pac-Man theme song rang out, my cell phone. I walked into the kitchen to take the call. It was Christian.

"What can I do you for?" I asked.

"It's ditsy. Frederik called me at home. There's a problem with the financing." I was managing a project for Danish Information Technology Systems, affectionately known as DITS or "ditsy."

"For goodness' sake, it's after nine on a Friday night — can't we handle this on Monday?"

"No, Richard. He's very worried. I've never seen him like this. We have to come in tomorrow."

"Well why didn't *he* call me?"

After a pause, Christian said, "You'd have to ask him that yourself." But I already knew the answer, just as surely as I knew it would be a mistake to ask my boss the question.

"Okay. I'll see you at nine. I'll stop at Baresso and pick up some coffee and pastries, all right?"

"Seven."

"What?"

"Frederik wants us all there at seven."

"Okay," I said, and sighed as I hit the red button.

I went to put the phone back in the alcove that served as my "office," and heard raised voices in the dining room. It sounded like an argument about religion.

"… if he really wants to help the poor in the southern countries," Katrina was saying, "he should promote literacy, clean water, contraception — things that will improve people's lives in *this* world."

"The Church does take an active role in fighting poverty," Ma said. "But it's not a social welfare organization. It's in the business of saving souls. Prayer is a big part of that. Richard, you went to Catholic School..."

My mother had never gone to Catholic school — her family couldn't afford it — so she had a somewhat idealized picture of it, as if the brothers spoon-fed me the answers to all life's mysteries once the gates were shut. What I remembered most was finding out the real reason why the brothers wore those ropes.

"...you were an altar boy. Tell her there's room for prayer in our lives."

Now this put me in an awkward spot. On the one hand, I had always kept to the straight and narrow. I even convinced Katrina to get married in a Catholic Church. But on the other hand, I hadn't gone to Mass in years, hadn't given religion much thought since freshman year of college. It just didn't seem all that relevant.

"I felt close to God when I was a boy," I said. "I would pray to the Holy Spirit for clarity of mind just before a test. I did that when I was six years old, and it worked. So I kept doing that, especially before big tests."

"Did it work?" Katrina asked.

"For the most part. I think it helped me think more clearly, yeah."

"I bet it worked better when you studied," Katrina said, with an edge to her voice.

"Maybe it did. I never said it was scientific," I admitted.

"But they've done studies on the power of prayer," Ma said. "Sick people who get prayed for get better faster."

"Then you two had better start praying because we have a problem in the house and it's not going away on its own!" Katrina said, eyes flashing. Then she stormed out of the room.

"Maybe you should go after her," Ma said.

"Nah, better let her cool down a little first."

"What did she mean, 'a problem in the house?'"

I figured Ma meant *Was she referring to me?* My mother tended to take things personally.

"She meant the *ghost,* Ma," I said, putting my hands over my eyes. My head was throbbing.

"Are you okay, Richard?" she asked.

"I'm tired, is all. I've just been swamped at work, and now my boss wants me to come in with the whole team tomorrow morning at seven o'clock..."

"On a Saturday?"

"Yeah, he's one of those macho guys – the earlier you come to work, the more of a man you are. What's worse, he didn't even call me, he called Christian, who works for me. That's a bad sign."

"What do you think it means?"

"He's lost confidence in me."

"Oh, Richard, he probably just couldn't get ahold of you. You probably have a voice mail…"

"No, I don't think so!" I said, too roughly, then softened. "Aw, gee, Ma, I'm sorry. I'm just mentally and physically exhausted; I've been traveling for weeks. It's like I'm fighting a monster here. As soon as I lop off one head, two more take its place. Down at work, nobody wants to see me succeed – they'd just love to see the American taken down a peg. Then when I get home, I've got to deal with Katrina's mood swings, insomnia. She's a wreck. And it's starting to affect me. I couldn't get to sleep myself last night."

"That's not like you – you always slept like a baby. What happened?"

"Well, it was very strange. I'd been asleep for maybe half an hour. Then I woke up and realized the bed's moving back and forth. Katrina's reading light is still on, but her book is closed on her chest. She's just lying there, eyes wide open. I ask her if she's shaking the bed. 'No,' she whispers."

"It must've been a truck."

"That's what I thought – like when a semi would hit a bump on Woodhaven Boulevard. But this was something else, a sustained rocking," I said, making a shaking motion with my hands, fingers spread apart. "It must've lasted thirty-forty seconds."

"Maybe it was an earth-tremor of some kind."

"After all that's happened, I think we have to face the fact that we have a ghost in the house," I said, lowering my voice.

"Well, I don't know," came her wishy-washy reply.

"I thought you believed in spirits."

"I believe in our immortal soul, in the spiritual world," she said, raising her eyebrows.

Now I knew my mother believed in everything from St. Anthony finding your car keys to the Bermuda Triangle, but I tried to focus the conversation.

"What about near-death experiences?" I asked. "People say they see a light. They've got to walk into the light, right? Then Jesus meets them on the other side and they're reunited with their loved ones. Do you think that's what really happens?"

"Maybe – you see a lot of stories like that on television."

"Yeah, well, I've been thinking – what happens if they *don't* follow the light?"

"You mean, get stuck on this side," she said, nodding her head.

"Exactly."

My mother closed her eyes for a few moments. Then opened them and said, "Why don't you say a prayer when you go to bed tonight? Do you pray anymore, Richard?"

"No, not really," I said, avoiding her eyes.

"When was the last time you said the Rosary?" she asked.

"I don't know – high school, maybe."

"What made you give it up, Richie? You were such a good boy, an altar boy."

"I don't know, I went to a college run by Quakers, remember? Then I started working, and there wasn't a lot of time for church. And then I met Katrina, and while she is a spiritual person, she's certainly not Catholic."

"Far from it."

"Well, we did try to find a parish in New York where we could feel comfortable, but it just never worked."

"I understand," Ma said, to my surprise. "You have to compromise in a marriage. But you can still have a prayer life even if you don't go to church every Sunday. It's your relationship with God that I'm talking about. Just promise me you'll say a little prayer once a day. You'll be surprised at how much better you'll feel. About everything."

"You mean just talk to God every day?"

"Yes, just talking is fine, or say the Our Father, the words Our Savior gave us. But the most powerful prayer there is, is the Rosary. Why do you think the Berlin Wall came down, and the Soviet Bloc fell apart?"

"I thought it was because of MTV."

"No, not MTV," she said with a *tsk* and a shake of the head. "It's because Our Blessed Mother promised the children at Fatima that if we kept saying the Rosary, Russia would be converted. And it's going to happen, just you watch."

I did not want to enter into a debate on geopolitics with my mother, so I said, "You know, I don't own a set of Rosary beads. I don't even remember how to say the prayers any more, Ma."

"That's not a problem. I brought you these beads. They were your father's," she said, reaching into her pocketbook. "We each got a set when we were in Italy years ago. There's a card inside with the prayers on it."

"Gee, if they were Pop's, maybe you want to keep them."

"Nah, I've got other things of his. You take them – and use them."

"Okay, thanks, Ma. I'll try."


Even though it was Friday night, I went upstairs at ten o'clock – it was going to be an early morning – and I was glad to see that Katrina was already asleep. As I brushed my teeth and got ready for bed, I thought about why religion had faded from my life these past ten-fifteen years. I hadn't gone to Mass regularly since I was 19 years old. It's not like I quit believing all of a sudden. It just slipped away bit by bit. I don't know what I believe any more.

Katrina and I went to Mass together a couple of times, but for her, the stone cathedral was cavernous. She felt small, lost. And like her mother, she didn't care much for incense: my mother-in-law attended our wedding in the same dress she'd worn to her husband's funeral. Holding a perfumed lace handkerchief, she coughed dramatically every time the Monsignor lifted the thurifer.

Next we tried a chatty German Lutheran church up in Yorkville. We started off in the church basement with funnel cakes and peach cobbler, coffee and hot apple cider. Like a Midwestern barn-raising. But from the minute the waves of organ music washed over the nave, it was all Bach and business. The sermon droned on about sin and death; I had to take a shower afterwards. And there was a lady-priest. I whispered whether the correct term was "priestess." It didn't go over too well, and we never went back.

Then we found this church in Murray Hill, High Anglican. It seemed like a good compromise: incense and holy water for me; female clergy and thumbing-their-noses-at-the-Pope for her. The stained glass windows and holy water fonts were comforting, but it had a style all its own. Catholic churches are serious and silent as school libraries – you drop a book, everybody turns around. The Anglicans were having a cocktail party. Husbands in monogrammed Brooks Brothers shirts shuttled back and forth fetching drinks for the fashionable women who stood clustered together in their flowery print dresses like human bouquets. Vivaldi's *The Four Seasons* played softly in the background. Instead of somber ushers handing out missalettes, I was greeted by a silver-haired man with a golfer's build wearing a blue blazer and a toothy grin.

"Good *morrning, Frriend,*" he said in exaggerated tones, like the Quaker Man, on speed.

"Good morning."

"Would you like a *drrink?*" he asked, indicating the refreshment table behind him. "The *orrange* juice is excellent. *Frresh* squeezed."

He spoke with an underbite so his front teeth came together in an artificial way, as if he were FDR smiling for a wire photograph. His accentuated *R's* seemed to say, "I may be from New *Yorrk,* but I do not 'tock' that way."

I went and got two glasses of the "frresh-squeezed" OJ, and by the time I got back, the man's healthy-looking wife had joined in, and the couple and Katrina were deep in conversation about the ballet. The gentleman turned to me, stuck out his hand and said, "My name is Cotton Williams, and this is my wife Sarah Williams."

"Hi, uh, Cotton," I said. *He was named for a cash crop?* "I'm Richard, and I suppose you've met Katrina – it's our first time here."

"It's *won-derr-ful* see two fine, *fresh*-faced young people coming into our *churrch* on a sunny Sunday *morrning.* Tell me Richard, what is your *surrname?*"

"My what?" I was thirty years old. My entire life I had never been asked this question.

"Your *surrname,*" he repeated, raising his voice slightly, as if I were hard of hearing.

"Uh, Marchese. I'm Richard Marchese, and this is my wife Katrina Nielsen, from Denmark."

They looked at each other as if I had responded in Swahili. Finally Cotton repeated, "*Marr*-kay-zay. Hmm, that name sounds *familiarr.* What kind of a name is that?"

"Is it French?" tried Sarah, wrinkling her little ski-jump nose.

"No, it's Italian," I explained.

There was a slight pause.

"Yes, of *courrse,*" Cotton drawled, waggling his finger. "I thought there was something about that name."

"We were at Lake Como last *summerr*," Sarah said.

"I'm fourth generation," I said.

"*Intrresting*," Cotton said. "So what brings you to our little *churrch* today? You *arre* Anglican?"

"No, I grew up Catholic, and Katrina is Danish Lutheran. So, we thought we'd meet in the middle." The smiles melted off their plasticine faces like Ken and Barbie in the microwave.

Cotton nodded, then inhaled and said, "I see. Well. The *serrvice* is about to *starrt*. *Pleasurre* meeting you both."

As soon as they had scurried into the sanctuary, Katrina and I looked at each other, clasped hands, and dashed out the side door and up Park Avenue. We didn't stop running till we were back at our building on Thirty-Sixth Street.

Katrina wasn't comfortable with the Catholics, I wasn't comfortable with the Lutherans, and neither of us was acceptable to the Anglicans. So we gave up trying to find a church, and began to drift into cultural Christianity. We slept late on Sundays, read the paper, ambled to brunch at one of the local places.

But now I was feeling really at sea, with this whole ghost thing. So when I went to bed, I knelt and tried a little prayer, an easy one. I didn't want to *strain* anything. At first it was very awkward, like an adult playing Twister, but I managed to get through the Hail Mary, must be the shortest prayer ever written. Then I said out loud, to myself or Whoever was listening, "Dear God, Please help me and Katrina adapt to our new home, and if there *is* some kind of entity walking these halls, please take this soul to Yourself. Amen."

I slept soundly all night, without dreaming. I didn't even change position.

# 12. Katrina

Søren and I hadn't spoken since the incident on the beach a month ago – so I was surprised to see him in my kitchen on a Saturday morning.

"Oh, I hope it's all right," Angelina said. "I invited Søren over. We were in the backyard talking about all the beautiful flowers, so I thought we could just as well sit in here, out of the sun."

Søren stood up when I entered the room and said, "I'll go if it's – inconvenient, Katrina."

I looked at him. Four weeks in the summer sun had turned him golden-brown – he was working in the garden every day. He looked – well, I have to say he looked good.

"No, not at all," I said, as neutrally as I could.

I wasn't quite *ready* for Søren, but it wasn't as if he'd attacked me or anything. He'd expressed his feelings for me, and I'd rebuffed him. Now it was time to put it in the past. We were, after all, neighbors; we would have to be adults about this. Seeing him again now, I realized that I had missed him. I sat down and joined them.

Pouring myself a cup from the thermos on the table, I sipped the steaming, black liquid. "What's in the coffee?" I asked.

"Chicory," Søren replied.

"From Søren's garden, isn't it wonderful?" Angelina said. "Some of the old-time brands used to be flavored with chicory, the New Orleans style."

I glanced down at the newspaper that was lying on the table. Not much was happening this time of year – it was the "cucumber-times" – and the headline was an article on smoking.

Søren noticed and asked, "Have you read that article?" I shook my head. My pulse seemed to beat faster, perhaps it was the coffee.

"More than fifty percent of Danish adults smoke, and the figure is still rising every year," he said. "The costs are enormous."

"I think it's true all over Europe," I said, though I knew Denmark was one of the worst for smoking. "What about you – it's seldom I see you without a cigarette."

"I'm trying to quit using hypnosis."

"Hypnosis – does it work?" Angelina asked.

"I'll tell you in six weeks," Søren said. "It's a course in self-hypnosis, not as powerful as the real thing, but I've always been a do-it-yourselfer. Hypnosis is said to work on lots of habits – smoking, chewing gum, biting nails – not to mention helping people remember things."

"You mean like in a murder trial. I saw that on TV," Angelina said. "This woman was witness to a murder, and under hypnosis, she discovers who the real killer is."

"Who was it?" I asked.

"It turned out she did it herself, but in self-defense."

"That's a dramatic example, Angelina, but real people use practical hypnosis every day to remember their great aunt's children's names or find their car keys," Søren said. "You see the mind records everything as we go through our day. It's all in there," he said, tapping his temple.

"Do you think someone could use hypnosis to remember the details of a recurring dream?" I asked.

"Why yes, I'm sure they could," he said.


*Plink. Plink. Plunk!*
*Oh, for Satan!*
*Helvede!*

It was like that all Monday morning. The piano tuner spent three hours banging and cursing the upright in the front room before calling me in around midday.

"So are you finished?" I asked, careful not to say "yet."

"Ohh, yes, the old girl's ready for her close-up," he said, wiping his brow.

"It certainly is a lovely piano," I said.

"Yeah, she's a pretty one – but temperamental. She gave me a lot of trouble this morning."

"Is there anything wrong with it, I mean *her?*"

He gave me a look and said, "Nothing that some tender loving care won't fix. She's high-strung is all. Like so many of these Continentals." He patted and stroked the back of the piano as if it were a thoroughbred race horse.

"Petrof – made in the Czech Republic, no?" I asked, repeating what Dahl had told us.

"Aye, that's what they call it now, yeah. It was Czechoslovakia before that, and back in the day when this fine instrument was crafted, the Petrof family were purveyors to the Imperial Court. The Habsburgs."

"Austria-Hungary?"

He nodded and said, "This instrument is the product of colonial empire. You'll not find anything like this made today. Your black keys are crafted from ebony wood hewn in British Hindoostan; your whites are genuine elephant-tusk, probably harvested from beasts slaughtered in German East Africa."

"It's pre-War then?"

"Oh, yeah – you can see the inscription clearly on the back, nineteen-ought-four," he said, leading me over to the brass plaque that bore the writing.

"Is it in good condition?"

"The soundboard, hammers and felting are all in terrific shape, and you can hear she's been played regularly over the years – though perhaps less so in the recent past," he said with a sidelong glance.

"How can you tell that?"

"Well, for one thing, she hasn't been tuned in an age. It was a bugger to get her equilibrium back. It's a good thing I went down to Germany a few years ago and picked up some special hammer techniques. She purrs like a kitten now, though." He petted her again and said, "Listen here." Then he played two octaves of a C-major scale, up and down. The tone was like Brazil nuts in dark chocolate.

"That's lovely," I said. "Is it a good sound, in your professional opinion, I mean?"

"Good? Miss, this piano has the richest tone of any upright I've ever tuned. It's positively uncanny. Go on, play it!"

I hadn't sat down at a piano in years. We'd kept the piano more for the glistening cherry-wood finish than anything else.

"Oh, no, I couldn't."

His face turned sour and he muttered, "Ach, the finest instruments are always wasted on the unappreciative – don't you even play?"

I didn't want him to think I was just a spoiled little rich girl – we have an expression in Danish, *She grew up with a piano at home* – so I said with a toss of my head, "Why yes, of course I play, but I haven't any music."

"Oh, is that all?" he said, brightening. "Here, I found this in the bench." And he handed me a piece by Maurice Ravel, the French composer, best known for *Bolero.* I looked it over – six pages of complex music, well above my level. And I hadn't played seriously since *gymnasium.*

"See if you can bang out the first eight bars for us, go on," he said with a wink.

I sat down at the piano as nervous as a schoolgirl at her first recital, and addressed the first few measures quietly, tentatively, as if asking whether we could be on a first-name basis. The tempo was marked *très lent,* which gave me time to get my bearings. Tension and discord were evident from the beginning, but also muted passion, the slow heat of a wood stove. The soft clusters of notes drew me into their black circles; the repetitious chords were hypnotic.

As I turned the first page, I don't know what came over me. The music crept inside my fingers. I didn't have to think, the phrasing just flowed. I could feel the eyes of the tuner boring into the back of my neck, but paid no attention, absorbed as I was in the layers of thirds and sixths and ninths. On the third page, the music drifted away as on the wind, only to return to prominence on the next, but *sans expression.* The musical themes were repeated obsessively, like the piteous self-soothing of an autistic child. The B-flat octave rang out again and again, tolling as if for one dead, giving me a lonely feeling. A gallows feeling.

The key changed from the somber G-flat to a bright C-major in march tempo for a time, then returned to G-flat in *pianissimo,* just before building to a crest, then another, and finally a subtle climax in *piano.* The discord that the piece began with never really resolved, even as the music died away to a distantly audible denouement. The final chord, accented by yet another B-flat octave in the treble clef, echoed through the rooms of the Sound House like a cannon shot over marble stones.

Then all was silence.

In the aftermath, I sat stunned, as if I had just witnessed an execution. I reached up and felt my cheeks were wet.

The tuner stood for a few moments with his mouth open, and then started to clap, right there in the front room. Faster and faster he brought his cupped hands together.

"Miss, I sure am sorry I doubted you. That was wonderful. Eerie as Hell, but bloody brilliant. Must be a piece you know well, yeah?"

"I've never encountered it before."

He stared at me for a moment, then burst into belly laughs, shaking his head as he packed up his tools. "Ach, you had me going for a minute there, miss!"

After he'd left, I sat back down at the piano, turned to the final page. There was a quotation from Faust and verse by a man called Aloysius Bertrand. Ravel composed the piece as a "tone poem," based on Bertrand's poem by about a death by hanging.

Sunset in a small French village. The town is quiet. In the distance a church bell tolls. As the rest of the villagers go about their daily business, the hanged man raises his eyes for one final glimpse of the setting sun, and listens to his death knell.

Like one transfixed, I played *Le Gibet* again.

And again.

# 13. Søren

I was thirteen the first time. I knew it was wrong.

I was sitting at the dining room table doing my Latin homework. Uncle Peder's tweed jacket hung on the coat tree in the front parlor after supper on a sultry summer evening. The windows were open, the air heavy with humidity and the greasy smell of roasted meat. My uncle himself, having imbibed two martinis and a decanter of claret, lay unconscious on the chaise longue in the garden. The steady clatter of dishes emerged from the kitchen where someone, the housekeeper no doubt, was washing up.

I stood up from my Vergil, caught the scent and stalked the coat rack like a carnivore. I petted the sleeve. The hand of the cloth was rough and hairy against my own. Shyly, my fingers touched the inner lining. Silk. My quarry was lodged inside an inner pocket, but which one? My arm deep inside the garment, I groped blindly until I came upon the box. The cellophane crinkled in my hand, startling me. My head whipped round, sure I would see a stout matron marching in from the kitchen. But the mild clatter just continued and all was as before. I extracted two cylinders from the heraldic blue package and stuffed them in my pants.

It wasn't until I was fifteen that he found me out, and by that time it was too late.

Smoking is a vile habit, but try as I might, I've never been able to quit. So when I stumbled across a book on self-hypnosis some time ago, I took it home with me. Through the power of suggestion, the author claimed, one could control virtually any habit: oversleeping, chewing nails, smoking cigarettes, self-abuse, alcohol.

I tried, *Tomorrow morning you will wake up at six o'clock.*

And I did, on the dot.

But the simple suggestions worked, the hard ones didn't. So I began to prowl the antiquarian shops and lending libraries for something stronger. Slowly the books began to pile up around me. I found worn volumes with crumbling pages and occultist titles like *The Secret of Mesmer.* Bearded men in white lab coats stood on the glossy covers of other books, filled with faux-medical terms like "Neuro-Linguistic Programming."

My bedroom became a canyon of books. I sat on a stool, practicing. I cross my legs, he crosses his legs. I raise my eyebrows, so does he. Mirroring to establish rapport, you see. When the subject orders chicken, I do the same.

I spoke to the mirror with the practiced, fluid tone of announcers and ad men. Following a script, like an actor lost in the real world, I unleashed a waterfall of words, overwhelming my poor flat-brained partner with criteria and considerations, facts and figures.

*"Do you realize that we use only 10% of the power of the human brain and as the chicken in your stomach right now begins to digest, it draws all the available blood away from the neurological system, removing the brain's ability to think clearly? It makes a person utterly light-headed, unable to process what he's being presented with."*

Speaking across the rest was the hardest technique. I said, *"You, like me,* must be thirsty. I'll get you a drink."

I smiled, it was working. *You like me* came across. But when I tried some of these things on Katrina that night on the beach, I got the timing wrong. I'd been drinking, and the day was too damn hot.

But then she told me about her dream, and I knew I would have a golden opportunity. Katrina is highly artistic, verbal; as a subject, extremely suggestible. I've been trying conversational hypnosis with its wrist-grabbing and plays on words, like when the shops announce there are ten *stopping* days till Christmas, to make the ladies stop in their tracks. But now I would be able to get her on a couch, give her suggestions while she's under completely. I almost twitched at the prospect. No need for a swinging pocket watch either. Just talk her down, use the voice, see the staircase.

Still, it was best to be prepared. I looked at myself in the mirror and said, "Søren, there are so many things *you don't like. Smoking* is a habit that you can break."

My sparring partner shot me a look that said, It's hopeless.

I tried again. "You've barely touched your chicken. If you aren't hungry now, by *tonight you will be. Afraid* I can't say exactly when."

Better. It sounded natural. My partner did look a bit afraid, or was he just tired, as if he'd been up all night? I suppose he had been.

Finally, I said, in a voice as fluent as the call of a nightingale, "Close the shades when *you want to sleep. With me,* it's darkness that enables me to relax."

I was ready.

The front room was stuffy, the curtains closed. No one was home. We were alone for the first time since the day on the beach. I removed my corduroy jacket but was still sweating, trapped as I was in my French cuffs. As Katrina reclined on the green camelback in her diaphanous cream-colored blouse, a ruffle snaked across her skin. I looked away and crossed to the stereo.

Her brow wrinkled when I asked about the fiendish dream. *"Hvornår begyndte drømmene?"*

"About a year ago," she said as I put a tape in the player. "It was in the spring, I remember – Richard was at a baseball game, opening day I think."

"This was spring 1995, then?" I asked as I sat in the chair next to her. She nodded.

That was a hard spring for me, when Uncle Peder finally vacated Sundhuset. Not that he was much company for me; his mind had been declining for years. By the time he left for the home, he'd become unhinged, didn't even know who I was. But still, it was the end of an era.

"I think it has something to do with my father." Her eyes opened wide and she lifted her back off the fabric. I touched her shoulder, said *naa-naa* and *saa-saa.* She lay back and closed her eyes. As I began my introduction, clicking noises emerged from the stereo, an artificial soundtrack that sounded like water dripping or someone walking down an endless flight of stairs.

I asked her to imagine descending a black spiral staircase. Into her subconscious, you see. Her shoulders relaxed. I watched the constant rise and fall of her chest. Her breasts, round under the ruffle, distracted me only for a moment.

Pulling the chair closer, I sat by her head and spoke softly. "To benefit from today's sessions, you'll want to share everything with me. Withhold nothing. You understand that, don't you?"

"Yes. Yes, of course." Her voice was distant, she was completely under. This excited me.

I shifted on the chair and continued, "Good, very good. You're going to tell me all about the dreams you've been having. Then after you tell me everything, you will feel relieved, fully relaxed, and you'll never have these dreams again. Do you understand?"

"Yes."

"Good. How does the dream begin?"

"I'm in a long corridor, or maybe it's a tunnel. The lighting is dim. There's cold blue all around me. It flares up sometimes. I'm holding something, a flashlight, I think."

"What do you see?"

"A door, a closed door. I'm in a law office, my father's. I can see the names on the door. Justesen, Svindborg, Nielsen."

"Your name is on the door?"

"No, silly." She giggled. "It's Fa's name. He finally got his name on the door!"

"The front door?"

"Yes. No, no it's a conference room. Oh, my God, this is the room where my father died."

"Are you sure?"

"There's a name. I can't see it clearly, the man is in the way."

"What man?"

"His back is toward me. He's scraping."

"What's the name of the room?"

"Wannsee – oh God, what's he doing? He's scraping Fa's name off! Stop that!"

"What's the man doing, Katrina?"

Her face grimaced and she started to tear up. "Oh, the noise, he's got to stop!"

"The noise does not bother you now," I said with confidence. Immediately, she grew quieter.

"I've got to stop him. Several of the letters are gone already. Only 'Niels' is left!"

"Who is the man, can you see?"

The features of shock came over her face, even with her eyes closed. She cried out.

"No one will hurt you, Katrina. Tell me what you see."

"The face is terrible, disfigured..."

She was sitting up and bawling by this point. I was moved to pity, but controlled myself, and said as smoothly as I could, "Katrina, the dream is over. The man is gone. You are in no danger."

She stopped shrieking and began to breathe easier. I touched her on the chest, just below the clavicle, to check the heartbeat. I felt an electric charge run through my fingers. She lay back down and returned to the slow, even breaths of alpha level. I allowed my hand to remain where it was, resting on the golden skin, so soft, so fair, so warm. I should have removed it. But I didn't.

I allowed my hand to caress her there, just below the clavicle. I rubbed along the collarbone in both directions. I smoothed the ruffle on the front of her blouse, but it would not stay down. My fingers felt the seam, the neatly stitched seam of the bodice that lay against her perfectly formed breasts. I looked up at her face: utterly at peace. I crossed my hands, the fingers of my left hand finding the softness of her right breast; the right hand stroked her left breast and felt the life force beating there. Gently, I plucked the slack, tender nipples. I made little circles. To my delight, they stood forth. So she *could* feel what was happening!

But just as my ardor started to grow, the grandfather clock loudly struck the hour. I sat up as if slapped, my hand going to my face. She remained quite calm, but I was rattled by the sudden gonging. The session was over for today.

Verbally, I led her back up the staircase, giving her post-hypnotic suggestions along the way – she would be alert upon waking, she would not remember what we had discussed, she would never have the dream again, if she gets afraid at night, she will look to me for comfort. I snapped my fingers, and she woke, unaware of what had transpired.

She made a pot of tea, and we moved to the kitchen to discuss the meaning of the dream.

We agreed that the man in the dream was her father, who appeared to her outside the room where he died because in fact it was not a natural death.

"You think he was murdered?" she asked.

"It's possible. Poison sometimes has the effect of contorting features post mortem."

"But Fa' couldn't have been poisoned—"

"How do you know? Was there an autopsy?"

"No, but—"

"What if someone did kill him, one of his partners, perhaps. Then he appears to you, pounding and scraping on the door of the room where he died, to lead you to the killers."

She nodded.

As I took my leave of her, she thanked me.

She actually thanked *me.*

# 14. Ingrid Latour Nielsen

My spirits were as dampened as my chapeau as I emerged from the taxi onto the slick paving-stones of Smallegade, a narrow passage on the west side of the city. I was not familiar with this grimy workmen's quarter, and my initial impression was not positive: soot-stained, broken-windowed factories in both directions. The dour manufactory of Royal Copenhagen, home to generations of artisans – going back to the time before the French Revolution – was no exception. It looked more like a textile mill than a structure designed for artists.

Katrina suggested a rendezvous here on this Thursday afternoon. She knew I was a devotee of the elegant blue china, both tableware and the Christmas plates. Her mother-in-law was in from New York, and wanted to make a girls' day of it. I had never toured the facility before, and I was curious about both the porcelain-making process and my son-in-law's mother.

The cabman was kind enough to accompany me to the entrance with his umbrella, ushering me through the misty rain that hung like draperies over the grey pavement. Katrina met me at the entrance and introduced me to a sprightly little woman of my own age.

"I am *so* pleased to see you again, Ingrid," Angelina said, taking my chilled hand in both of her warm ones. "We had so little time to talk at the wedding!"

"The pleasure is mine, Angelina. So good of you to arrange this little excursion," I said, widening my lips into a smile.

"Well, now we have the perfect opportunity to get to know each other," she said, and with that, took my arm in hers and marched me through the preliminaries of vestibule, turnstiles and brochures, and escorted me down the grand promenade.

As we parleyed, my ennui evaporated. Replete with *joie de vivre*, her brown eyes expressed a great deal of emotion as she talked. Which she did a lot of, and quite charmingly: fluttering her arms and gesticulating with her hands and fingers as if she were conducting an orchestra.

The expertly-renovated edifice was as impressive on the inside as it was dilapidated on the exterior. We assembled, along with a dozen other women and *their* daughters, in a baroque salon reminiscent of Versailles: ornate mirrors lined the walls; enormous crystal chandeliers illuminated the proceedings.

As soon as we were installed comfortably on the Louis Quatorze reproductions, Angelina asked, "What's that lovely scent you're wearing?"

"Ah, my companion these many years," I said with a smile. "It's called Fracas."

"Isn't that the one Baroness Blixen wore? How on earth do you get it?" Katrina asked.

"By post, from a distributor in Paris," I said. "There will never be another Robert Piguet, you know."

Just then an officious madame entered and proclaimed in French-accented English, "Unfortunately, I must announce that our audiovisual equipment is at the moment non-functional. This is why we don't exhibit the prepared video, but I will lecture at you for some minutes, after which I will entertain your questions before we advance to the remainder of the visit."

The lecture was educational, and more engaging than any video could have been. We learned that the porcelain technique was developed in China – that's why it's called "china" – and was first achieved in Europe some three hundred years ago by an alchemist in Dresden. The original prototype was Blue Fluted, the pattern I have at home. All porcelain at that time had to be blue because only cobalt could withstand the very high temperatures of the glazing process.

Several questions were put to the speaker: one woman asked about the origin of the collectible Christmas plates, another asked how to order replacement pieces. Angelina posed a different type of question:

"You mentioned that the porcelain was made by an alchemist and nicknamed White Gold. Can you tell us more about that?"

"Of course it was not literally made of gold, but hard porcelain was at that time extremely rare – and producing such pieces for the royal family was a lucrative enterprise, thus the expression."

"But why would an alchemist get involved in making porcelain? Alchemy is turning lead into gold, isn't it?" Angelina asked.

"Yes, indeed, and the alchemists never achieved that, did they? But did you know that the raw material for porcelain is simply earth?"

Murmuring from the crowd.

"We have an expression here at Royal Copenhagen, 'From earth to art.' So you may consider it an *alchemique* transformation, if you like. The dark body loaded with platy clay metamorphoses into ethereal, white, translucent, resonant porcelain."

As the group began to hum toward the next phase of the tour, Angelina turned to me and said, "My goodness, the way she put it, it sounds like something religious, like the Resurrection — *the clay of the body is transformed into a substance translucent and ethereal.*"

I wasn't sure what to say.

"Yes, indeed," was all I could muster, and we moved on with the group, heels reverberating on the hardwood floors of the corridor.

The next room was filled with unique porcelains of antique vintage — a selection of Flora Danica made for Catherine the Great, a Heron dinner service fired for H.C. Andersen, a vase of Blue Flowers that adorned the boudoir of Her Majesty Queen Victoria.

Finally, we embarked on the most interesting part of the visit: observing the artists as they demonstrated their painting techniques. Each produced a finished plate which was "the same as all the others," but when you looked closely, it was a unique work of art, the singular result of more than a thousand brushstrokes. *Danes are like this: all the same until you look closely.*

I observed a grand dame, her mind and brush sharp for over fifty years in the atelier, whose oeuvre was the delicate faïence, a fragile first cousin of porcelain. A fabulous polychrome blue pheasant exploded into life as I gazed.

"Tell me, do you try to imitate Nature?" I asked her.

"Nature yes, but stylized — given a form beyond the natural."

"Doesn't that yield a product that's artificial?"

"Nobody would mistake one of my birds for one that flies, and yet," she said, smiling and holding up the nearly-finished plate, "isn't she beautiful?"

Angelina was deep in conversation with a handsome, beefy American sculptor who seemed to specialize in crouching kittens and pouting puppies, so Katrina and I walked on ahead to the boutique.

*"Tak for at du kom, Mor,"* Katrina said, thanking me. "I hope Angelina hasn't been too much of a plague."

"Not at all. On the contrary, she really lifted my spirits today with her enthusiasm."

"Her constant talking drives me to distraction sometimes."

"She does blather a bit, but she also says some of the most interesting things, like when she asked that question about transformation—"

"Well, I'm glad you're having a good time."

"Yes, dear," I replied, overlooking the interruption as I touched a richly embellished volume on the history of Blue Fluted.

"That's a beautiful book, Mor. Isn't this the pattern you have at home?"

"Yes, I've always been partial to it. The cobalt gives it a magical look, but muted in the white of the porcelain."

"Oh, let me buy it for you," she said, trying to take it from my hands.

"No, it's not necessary," I said, holding on to it. It cost a thousand kroner.

"Please let me do this."

"It isn't necessary – you don't have to spend your money on me."

Katrina made a sour face and exhaled. "Mor, we really have to talk about our relationship."

"Whatever do you mean?"

"It's been nearly eight years since I've lived in Denmark and I've changed. I've grown up. I'm not a teenager any more!"

*Where was all this coming from?*

"Of course not," I agreed, nodding and pursing my lips.

"I came back because I love you, but you still treat me like a child – wanting to wash my socks and take care of me."

This was a surprise – I had never coddled my children; quite the opposite, I always focused on preparing them for independence. Perhaps my little girl just needed my support right now.

"Katrina," I said, looking in the eyes of my beautiful, grown-up daughter, "I know you're a woman now, a married woman with a husband. I hope you'll start your own family some time soon. I'm nothing but pleased that you've chosen to settle in Denmark. I'll support you in any way I can."

"And not baby me?"

"No," I said with a smile. "No more babying, I promise."

"Good," she said, and smiled broadly. "Because I need your help."

"With what?"

She inhaled and said, "I want to make up with Claus, but I don't know how. I've been calling him and leaving messages, but he doesn't call back."

I pursed my lips. I did not want to get between the two of them. Ponderous and stubborn, like his father, Claus thinks about things deeply. If he was not responding to Katrina's advances, it was because he did not want to.

Still, I had just promised to support her in any way I could, so I said, "I'm not sure he'll listen to me."

"Oh, but he will – he's got to," she said. "Just help me get him to the dinner party Saturday night. He's just *got* to forgive me."

"I'll try, but I can't make any promises," I said, and just then Angelina marched up waving a little figurine of a boy and a girl reading.

"Oh, wouldn't this be just darling in Katrina's living room?" she asked.

I nodded, amazed at the likeness to my own children. "It certainly would be."

Katrina followed up with a phone call two days later. I took the phone in the kitchen; I was just starting supper. Expecting that she would ask about Claus, she surprised me again.

"*Mor, jeg har—*" she started, and then paused. "Listen, Mor, I have a question for you," she said, and paused again.

"Go ahead, what's this about?"

"It's about Fa's death."

"What about it, Skat?" I couldn't imagine.

"Well, for the past year I've been having a recurring dream. Then just the other day – well, I've been able to remember it in detail."

"You've been dreaming about your father's death?"

"Uh-huh."

"About identifying the body? Oh, I should never have taken you down there!" The heart attack had left Per's face horribly disfigured.

"There's only one way to say this: Mor, do you think Fa' could have been murdered?" My knees went a bit weak and I sat down at the kitchen table.

"Murdered? Good heavens, no," I said. "What would make you say a thing like that?"

"He wasn't very old, just fifty-three. Tell me, did he have a heart condition?"

"No, he didn't."

"And he was a successful man, a rich man – one of his partners might have benefited from getting him out of the way?"

"I suppose that's possible—"

"And there was no autopsy performed, was there?"

"We didn't need an autopsy, Skat. Your father was killed by his obsessions: alcohol, tobacco and overwork," I said, repeating something that I'd said many times over the years.

"In my dream, I see him scraping his name off the door at Justesen & Svindborg."

This struck a nerve, and I paused. *How could she...*

"How did you know about that?" I asked.

"Know about what?"

"A week before he died, the Board voted unanimously to make Per a 'name partner' – that is, to change the name of the Firm officially to 'Justesen, Svindborg & Nielsen.' Who told you?"

"No one told me."

Per had been the top-earning partner for years. But the Firm's bylaws stated that the partnership would be called "Justesen & Svindborg" in perpetuity, and specified that only a unanimous vote of partners could change this provision. A competing firm had offered Per a very attractive situation, and he announced his intention to leave the Firm. His partners asked what it would take to get him to stay; he wanted his name on the door.

The partners – there were nearly twenty at the time – voted to change the Bylaws on a Saturday afternoon. Overjoyed, Per called me from the office and we went out on that town that night – the first time in years. I had never seen him so happy. He didn't care so much about the money by that point, but oh, how he relished the idea of seeing his name on that wall!

It would make him part of history, he said.

Well, by Wednesday, he was dead, and the Firm never has changed its name.

"Was there anyone who would have murdered him rather than see his name on the door?" she asked.

"No, I don't think so, Skat."

"Perhaps another partner felt passed over? Someone more senior than he was?"

"There were more senior men, but Per had been the lead partner and top earner for years. No one felt slighted."

"Did the partners resent being forced to change the Bylaws? It's easy to make a murder look like a heart attack, you know – one could use common foxglove from the garden to do that!"

This didn't sound like Katrina.

"Since when do you know about foxglove?" I asked.

"Well, Søren mentioned it."

"Your neighbor, is that where all this is coming from?"

"No, Mor. It's my idea – I've been haunted by that face in my dreams. What about Justesen and Svindborg themselves?"

"Those two old goats? I'm sure they would have hated to share the Firm's name with an upstart like Per."

"That's it, then! The old misers didn't want to see a third name on the masthead, so they killed Fa' by putting something in his morning coffee. Before lunch, he fell over dead in a conference room, and his Ghost has come to me in my dreams."

I shook my head and said, "You really should write crime stories, Skat. It's an engaging theory, really, very creative. But there's just one problem: Justesen and Svindborg had already been dead for years. Dead as doornails."

# 15. Angelina

Saturday was my last day in Copenhagen and boy, was it a doozy. I slept soundly and awoke refreshed. When I went down to breakfast, the kitchen table was laden with local delicacies. Creamery butter, wild strawberry preserves and cheeses: Danish Havarti and Norwegian goat-cheese the color of peanut butter, shaved thin with a cheese-razor. Katrina had gone out already and she came back from the bakery with piping-hot rolls loaded with poppy, sunflower and caraway seeds. All washed down with strong coffee, there's nothing better.

I was focused on the food because this was the day of the Dinner Party that Richard and Katrina were holding in my honor. Even though it was Saturday, my son had to work again, so I spent the most of the day with Katrina, preparing. She'd slept well, and seemed in fine spirits. We visited several markets along the boulevard to get the freshest ingredients for the evening meal. If it was me, I would've got a caterer, or else picked things up already made, but not Katrina. Everything had to be made from scratch, so naturally this took all day.

First, we boiled the ham, then added spices and glaze and put it in the oven. The smoky smell of cloves reminded me of Mamma's kitchen. Then there were Danish new-potatoes to be scrubbed and peeled. Katrina made lots of thin halfway-slices through the potatoes so pats of butter and grated cheese would melt in. "Hasselback Potatoes," she called it.

As the afternoon wore on, their next-door neighbor Søren walked in wearing a green velvet jacket with a jaunty burgundy ascot. I was standing by the sink, opening a bag of potatoes.

"Aah, Læsø potatoes," he crooned. "Experts say they are the best in the world."

"I didn't know there was such a difference between one potato and another. What makes them so special?" I asked.

"Læsø is just a dot of land off the coast of northern Jutland, just a few thousand souls living in half-timbered homes thatched with seaweed—"

"Seaweed?" I asked, grimacing.

"Yes, it's very special," he said. "You see, the island is too small to form its own clouds—"

"What?" I asked.

He explained, "A great land mass forms its own clouds..."

*Maybe that's the way it is with people: the great also form their own clouds, their own unhappiness.*

"...so Læsø is the sunniest spot in all Denmark. Every spring the first new-potatoes of the year emerge from its sandy, salty soil. That's front page news here."

"The front page, for potatoes?" This seemed even less likely than roofs made of seaweed.

"I have Læsø salt for them as well," said Katrina. "You're joking," Søren said.

"No, I picked it up at the specialty market down on Grønnegade," she said.

"That must cost 2,500 kroner per kilo!" he exclaimed.

"That sounds very expensive," I said. "What's that a pound?"

"Oh, I hate conversions," Katrina said.

"It's $150 a pound," said an unexpected voice.

"Richard, when did you get here?" I asked, as I turned and saw my handsome son in the doorway.

"Just now. I gave Christian a lift," he said, producing two bouquets. "Roses for roses," he said, handing them to me and Katrina and kissing us in turn. We thanked him and she stopped what she was doing to put them in water.

"What's for dinner?" he asked.

"I asked Katrina to include as many local  Danish ingredients as possible, so we're having ham, potatoes and white asparagus," I said.

"Ah, the appetizers will be foreigners, I'm afraid," Søren noted, pursing his lips. "Still, I think you'll like them all the same. I picked up a wonderful chorizo sausage and a full-bodied Bull's Blood from Spain, enough to tantalize and enchant any tongue."

"My goodness, this meal is going to be overwhelming," I said. "Like that Danish movie, what was it, *Babette's Feast.*"

Richard went into the living room and made a drink for Christian, while Katrina, Søren and I continued working in the kitchen. Katrina washed and snapped the pale asparagus and set it aside, to be steamed at the last minute. I always felt a little sorry for the white kind of asparagus, raised without sunlight, like a child kept in a closet. Søren opened the wine and arranged the appetizers on platters. I made my famous tiramisu – it was my mother's recipe – you have to use raw eggs, and it's the port wine in the zabaglione filling that really makes all the difference.

Katrina started setting the table for eight, and I asked, "Who's not coming?"

"My brother Claus and his wife couldn't find a baby-sitter."

As she placed the last piece of stemware, she added, "Or so he said on the answering machine."

"Oh, I'm sorry."

"Me too."

"So you never really got to talk to him."

"No, I never did," she said, her lips pulled tight together.

The doorbell rang and guests started to arrive around seven o'clock. Eddé strolled in bearing a little bottle and a big grin. Annika walked in holding Ingrid by the elbow; she'd picked her up in Hellerup. Such a nice girl, that Annika. Soon the rooms were buzzing with talk and laughter. Eddé told a funny story about a German tourist in lederhosen that he'd seen at the Little Mermaid, and was laughing the loudest at his own joke. Søren put out the appetizers on a small table in the living room, and Katrina made sure there were enough napkins and glasses for everybody. Richard poured the wine, and once everybody was served, he cleared his throat a couple of times, tapped the side of his glass with his fork and the room grew quiet.

"Thank you all for coming," he said. "As you know this little get-together is in honor of my mother, Angelina Marchese. She's come all the way from New York to be with us here tonight. It's amazing to think about how far that is. Not all that long ago, the trip would've taken *eight days* by ocean liner."

Some murmurs of recognition confirmed this.

"Nowadays we hop on a plane and arrive just a few hours later," he continued. "Yes, so much has changed just in the past few years. Now I don't remember the telegraph—"

"I do!" Eddé called out.

"Eddé, you remember smoke signals," Richard said without missing a beat. He waited for the laugh like a pro, and then continued. "But seriously, we've gone from telex to fax to email in a very short period of time. And typewriters are just for envelopes now.

"Well, I've spent the last year financing the next wave, and let me tell you it's exciting. Your telephone is going to be obsolete, your TV is going to be obsolete. The Internet is about to change everything once again. I can't even keep up with the vocabulary: email, chat rooms, search engines, uploading, downloading. The World Wide Web is transforming the entire globe into an enormous brain, what they call a 'neural network,' and each of us is like a node, a neuron in that brain. This international get-together tonight is a small way in which we can forge connections between people, to build out our own networks. So let's get forging! I raise my glass to my mother, Angelina Maria Marchese, the Baroness of Bloomingdale's, the Queen of Queens, long may she reign over us," my son said, bowing his head.

For a moment I was not sure if I was being made fun of, but then I saw how Richard's friends were taking it in good fun, and I didn't want to spoil the mood. So I smiled, waved like the Queen, and said, "Thank you for being here today," in a wee voice, and they all roared with laughter.

Everybody looked at me, but I hadn't prepared anything, so I said, "Thank you, Richard, and thank *you* especially, Katrina, for arranging this lovely evening. I've really been looking forward to this dinner – the food, the wine, and especially to the conversation."

Now I should have stopped there, but I felt I should say something about the Internet, to show that I'd been listening. So I said, "I appreciate what you're doing, Richard, helping all these little companies pursue their dreams. But I think we have to keep in mind that technology is a mixed blessing. Technology is neither good nor evil – it can always be bent to the will of our fallible leaders, who one day build a bridge and the next day bomb it back to the Stone Age."

I saw that they were looking at me a little funny, so I tried to link it to computers, but my tires were spinning and I was just digging myself in deeper: "Say a good government uses computers to keep track of children who need to be vaccinated. Those same computers could be used by the next government to track down those children…" I was going to say, "for deportation to concentration camps," but I caught Eddé's eye, and let the sentence die. In a final hopeless effort to save myself, I turned to the Good Book: "What I'm trying to say is that swords can be 'beaten into plowshares,' but plowshares can also be beaten back into swords."

You could've heard a pin drop. After a long minute, Søren came to my rescue by standing, dinging his glass, and holding up his salad fork.

"Wise words, Angelina, and tonight, the plowshares have been beaten into *forks*," – at this everyone breathed out and said, "Ah!" – "as well as knives and spoons for our feast! Our conversations will no doubt be arduous, and so we have some delicious appetizers to sustain us..."

Søren launched into a description of the appetizers and wines; everybody started drinking and loosening up again, and the awkward moment was forgotten.

After awhile, Katrina called us all into the dining room and Eddé said, "How festive your table looks, Katrina!" Several nods of approval and "uh-huhs" were uttered around the table.

"I had a lot of help," Katrina said, her face blooming into a big smile; she looked radiant tonight as she scuttled to and fro bearing platters of food.

Christian, a quiet man with tousled hair and a boyish grin, poured out the wine, and explained about the Italian vintages.

"...and here is the *pièce de resistance*. When Annika and I were in Tuscany last summer, we had the pleasure of touring the vineyards of one, Marchese Frescobaldi."

"Marchese," I said. "Gee, I didn't know there was a winery with that name."

"One of the leading vintners in all Italy," he noted. "We had the pleasure of meeting with the resident oenologist and dining at his home at Castiglione, one of the nine estates of the Marchese. The *specialità della casa* is the Brunello di Montalcino, a Reserve bottle of which I hold in my hand."

As he poured a sample into my glass, he read from the *Wine Spectator*, "We award 99 points to the 1985 vintage, a 'super-Tuscan' that deserves the name..."

As he continued, I closed my eyes and drank deeply. *Oh my.* I was transported, could see the lemony Italian sun, the clayey hillsides of burnt sienna and umber.

"...ripe plum and blueberry character, this wine soon turns to mint and freshly cut flowers...'"

I could feel the dusty soil in my teeth and the dryness of the Mediterranean summer on my lips.

"*Magnifico! Delizioso!*" I exclaimed.

Then, opening my eyes, I was suddenly embarrassed again. I had interrupted Christian's connoisseurship. Luckily, he took it well.

"Oh, to hell with talking about the wine, let's drink the damned thing!" he said, and they all laughed and took to sniffing, swirling and sipping the big Brunello.

Richard, seated to my left at the head of the table, sliced the ham. The table was dazzling, groaning with an array of platters, pitchers, stemware and flatware. I recognized the Royal Copenhagen pattern, which provided a blue and white canvas for the culinary artwork. The candlelight glistened on the outer layer of hogfat; the scent of cloves and cinnamon filled the air.

"Pardon me, but what is that on the potatoes – it looks like flakes of mica," Eddé said.

"It's Læsø salt," said a brittle voice. It was Ingrid, who had hardly said a word all evening.

"I'm sorry?" Eddé said.

"Have you never heard of Læsø salt?" Ingrid replied.

"No, I'm afraid not."

"Well, it's said to be the best salt in the world. It is in any event the most expensive."

"Really?" Eddé asked.

"Yes," I inserted. "Søren was telling us all about it earlier." He beamed. I had a feeling he wanted a bit of the spotlight, and after how he had helped me out earlier, it was the least I could do.

"So what makes this Læsø salt so special?" Eddé asked.

This was the opening Søren was waiting for. Søren held forth for several minutes on the authentic Viking methods of production using seawater and rain-water, the size of the resulting flakes, and the debate over using seaweed in production. Then he started reminiscing about his boyhood summers on the island of Læsø; he told a story about how he once managed to get a fishhook through his big toe.

Eddé leaned over and said to me quietly, "Søren's a bit of an island himself, if you ask me – and a queer one at that."

"Oh, he seems nice enough," I whispered back. "Don't be such an old sour-puss." And he laughed.

After the fishhook story, the conversation flowed freely. At my end of the table, Annika mentioned that the Danish men had won a gold medal in rowing at the Olympics in Atlanta. People were getting silly on the wine – when Eddé said that the Danish men were "coxless," Richard snorted and laughed so hard that he had to leave the table. We learned later that this was the day of the Centennial Park bombing, but of course as we sat there enjoying ourselves, we had no way of knowing.

*Maybe it's always like this – whenever we sit down to a feast, somewhere else there's a famine; at every wedding party, somebody's just coming from a funeral.*

We all relished the meal, praising the salt as much as the meat, the butter as much as the potatoes. No one was shy – all the guests filled their plates and drained their glasses repeatedly.

"Where did you get these beautiful wineglasses?" I asked my son.

"They're from Saint Louis," he replied.

"Missouri?" I asked, bewildered.

"France," Richard replied. "Last summer, Katrina and I visited the factory in Alsace-Lorraine – it's the oldest leaded-crystal factory in Europe. It's in a town called, get this, Saint-Louis-les-Bitche."

"Sounds like my kind of place!" Annika said outrageously, and everyone laughed.

"You can't make this stuff up," Richard assured us, imitating a car commercial.

"I love the blue. It's cobalt, right?" I asked.

"Yes, all the colors are made from pure minerals; no dyes are used. The red-dish hues are the most expensive, because they have to put 24-carat gold in the glazier's mixture," Richard explained.

"You don't see colored glass on tabletops in America much any more – only in stained glass windows in church," I said.

"Most people nowadays think of colored stemware as garish. They prefer the clean, sharp lines of transparent crystal," Annika said.

"Ma, have you had the chance to take a look at the Danish school of design – furniture, architecture?" Richard asked.

"Yeah, very practical, but I find it a little bloodless. I think people need a little drama, some color in their lives."

"I also appreciate the traditional designs, Angelina," Eddé chimed in. "I love the stained glass windows in St. Patrick's Cathedral. But you have to understand that in the north of Europe, painted glass is seen as false, a distracting carnival of color to hide the hypocrisy of corrupt churchmen."

"Transparent glass lets the cleansing light of the Lord stream in," Katrina said

I wasn't sure if I'd heard a touch of sarcasm, so I asked, "Is that what you think, Katrina, that the trappings of Catholicism hinder people from seeing the light?"

"For me, it's purely a matter of aesthetics," Eddé intervened diplomatically. "It's like having a favorite color – there's no wrong answer."

"Well, I have a favorite color – cobalt blue," I said, admiring my dinner plate and bluish goblet.

"You know, a *kobold* in German is a kind of underground gnome or elf," Eddé said. "This is how cobalt got its name – people believed that the presence of the glowing blue mineral was a sign that *kobolds* were in the area."

"It's funny what people will believe in. But nobody believes in elves anymore, do they?" I asked.

"In Iceland they do," Christian said.

"Oh, they do not!" Katrina said, laughing.

"Yes, they *do*," Christian insisted. "My hairdresser is from Iceland, and she assures me that ninety percent of Icelanders believe firmly in the little people. There are empty lots right in downtown Reykjavik where it is not allowed to build."

"Why not?" asked Richard.

"Because someone already lives there!" Christian said.

And everybody laughed again.

Before I knew it, Katrina was asking us to go into the living room, where we would have coffee and dessert. As I got up I noticed that eight wine bottles stood empty on the sideboard.

"Look at all those bottles," I said to Annika.

"We always plan on one bottle per person – but don't worry, I'm driving home, and I had only one glass."

Eddé had gone out to the kitchen to fetch a small bottle from the freezer and was just coming back in when Christian asked, "Say, Edvard, you hedonist, what have you got there?"

"Ice-wine, of course, for afters," Eddé replied, opening the bottle.

"What's ice-wine?" Annika asked.

"*Eiswein* is the ultimate expression of the fermented grape," Eddé pronounced. "Only in perhaps one or two years out of ten will the 'noble rot' affect enough grapes and a frost occur at just the right time so that *eiswein* can be made at all. And even then an entire vine will only produce enough juice to result in a single glass of *eiswein*. For this bottle, the miracle occurred on December 7, 1990, on Egon Müller's estate on the river Saar," he concluded, reading the information off the bottle.

"Vanity, gentlemen – all is vanity," Søren said.

"That sounds familiar – it's from the Bible, right?" I asked.

"What's your point?" Eddé said.

"All due respect, but they could leave those grapes to rot on the vine for all I care," Søren said, his cheeks flaring from the alcohol. "No offense intended."

"No offense taken, my good man," Eddé said. "Most palates today fail to appreciate the nectar of a *sauternes* or *eiswein*. It's because we're gorging ourselves on refined sugar all day long. So we find a sweet wine merely cloying. But it may interest you to know that in the 1700s, the most highly regarded wine in the world, the most sought-after wine in the court of the King Louis the Sixteenth, was not the dry Bordeaux but the *sauternes*."

"Well, I hope he didn't lose his head when he drank too much of it!" Søren joked. It seemed to me that Søren was the one who had been drinking too much. I was glad when he got up from the table and ambled to the living room and collapsed on the green couch.

Christian appeared with his jacket on, and I asked, "Where are you going?"

"Evidently Katrina's mother is not feeling well. Annika and I are going to give her a lift home," he replied in low tones.

So I went over to Ingrid. Her face was pale; when I took her right hand between my palms, it was like ice. I smiled at her and said, "Good night, Ingrid."

"Farewell," she said, her head bobbing up and down a little like Katherine Hepburn. "And *bon voyage*. It has been a pleasure meeting you." As Christian and Annika led her down the walk, she appeared quite frail for a woman my own age. The death of her husband must've hit her awfully hard. I waved from the front stoop, then as I walked back inside, I heard the piano.

*Who was that?*

At first it was barely audible, like a bell ringing on a far-off mountaintop. A certain tone rang out again and again above the music. The pulse grew slightly louder as the music started to build. But the pace remained slow, ethereal, haunting. And still a high note clanged out again and again. I sat down in the blue chair, transfixed.

No one so much as breathed as we watched Katrina entranced at the spinet. I knew they had a lovely instrument, but Richard never even mentioned she played. She knew the music by heart. No one turned the pages for her. The booklet stayed open to the first page.

Later Richard said she played like a woman possessed, which was true, but she didn't sway or loll in her seat. On the contrary, she barely moved. She played completely without expression, which ironically made the music seem even more emotional. Her eyes had a faraway look in them, and by the end of the piece I saw they were glassy with tears. As the final peal rang out, she remained sitting there in silence. There was an uncomfortable feeling in the room, like when someone brings up a dead relative that nobody ever liked. Finally, not knowing what to do, I started clapping; we gave her a standing ovation.

"Katrina, that was wonderful," Søren said, walking over to her and touching her on the shoulder in congratulations.

"I had no idea you could play like that," Eddé said.

"Neither did I," said Richard. "You've been practicing, I see."

They crowded around her like doctors around a wounded child. She shook her head, as if trying to clear it, then she smiled as if waking from a dream and said, "It's a beautiful piece, isn't it? It's all I seem to want to play these days."

"What is it?" I asked, getting up and standing next to the upright.

Richard had already picked up the sheet music. "Ravel," he said.

"Ah, it's from *Gaspard de la Nuit*," Eddé said. "That's a very advanced piece."

"Yes, I've never played anything like it before. But the pace is monstrously slow, so I can manage," Katrina said.

"It's a tone poem. Here are the words, written by Aloysius Bertrand, a French Romantic poet," Eddé said, reading the back of the booklet. "Say, this is a first edition, 1909."

I took Katrina's hand and suggested we go get the dessert ready and leave the men in the sitting room. Like me, they also seemed troubled by Katrina's playing. Just before the kitchen door swung closed behind me, I heard Richard say, "Yeah, but Eddé, we just got the thing tuned this week – and her playing…"

The tiramisu was all ready; I just had to get the tray out of the refrigerator. Katrina seemed completely recovered as she fiddled with the urn. As I came out of the kitchen carrying the dessert tray, I noticed the smell of smoke in the room and asked, "My goodness, have you been smoking cigars in here?"

"No, but we could, what brand do you prefer?" Eddé joked.

"Actually, many a Danish woman over the years has enjoyed a fine Cuban," Søren noted.

"I'm sure," said Eddé, "but let's hope she hasn't cut his tip off and put a match to him!"

As the laughter died down, Richard said, "No one has been smoking, Ma. Katrina won't have it."

On cue, Katrina entered with the coffee urn. "That's right, I won't have it."

"Well, you don't mind if I go out back for a smoke, do you?" Eddé asked.

"Not at all," replied Katrina.

"I think I'll join you," said Søren.

"I thought you were quitting," Katrina said to him.

"Tapering off, my dear," he replied with an apologetic grin.

"But we just brought out the tiramisu!" I said.

"We won't be but a minute," said Eddé over his shoulder, and they were gone, leaving Richard, Katrina and me sitting together in the living room.

"Well, we can at least pour the coffee," Richard said, helping himself to a cup. "I don't understand how this tobacco smell gets in here. Katrina, you're not smoking, are you?"

"Of course not. I haven't smoked in years," she assured us.

"Maybe it drifts in from the street," I said.

"Sometimes it does seem like that. But this is a quiet street, so we don't get that many people passing." He paused and then asked hesitantly, "You don't think it has anything to do with the ghost, do you?"

He had said the G-word, and it suddenly got uncomfortable in the room.

"I don't think you have any ghosts here, Richard," I said.

"Maybe it comes and goes. I've been sleeping well myself for the past week or two," Katrina added.

"I've never encountered anything like a ghost before," Richard said. "But it's starting to become difficult to explain all these phenomena – and Eddé said he saw a ghostly man in the kitchen window the night you fell down the stairs."

"And the man he saw was smoking," Katrina said.

"No one was there in the kitchen with you, Katrina?" I asked.

She shook her head.

"But you smelled smoke," Richard said. "So maybe this 'smoking ghost' is here again tonight."

This reminded me of the man in my dream. I didn't want to worry everybody, but it seemed wrong to keep it from them any longer.

"Richard," I said. "I never told you. I didn't think it was important, but…"

"What? What didn't you tell me?"

"I had a dream a few days ago – it was when I got back from sight-seeing with Eddé."

"A dream? What kind of dream?" Richard asked.

"It was about the man in the picture, the original owner."

"Damsgaard?"

"Yes. It wasn't a nightmare or anything – it was a very nice dream. He was a real gentleman. I wouldn't even have mentioned it, but…"

"But what?" Richard asked.

"I remember he was smoking," I said.

"Well, a lot of people smoke," Richard said.

"Yeah, but I had that dream without ever having seen his picture. How did I even know what he looked like?"

"You'd seen it on your way up."

"No, I'd have remembered that. I was shocked to see it there when I came down the stairs," I said.

"Maybe you saw it from the corner of your eye," Richard suggested.

"No," Katrina said flatly. We both looked at her. "Your mother couldn't have seen the picture before she went upstairs because it wasn't there. It was at the framing shop. I picked it up Monday afternoon, and hung it in the dining room – *after* Angelina had gone upstairs to take her bath."

# 16. Edvard

I didn't trust Søren.

As we walked into the backyard for a smoke, I thought it would be a good opportunity for me to probe him a bit. He sat down across from me at the patio table, and we lit up. The set-up reminded me of years ago when I used to play in chess tournaments.

I opened with the neutral, *"Fin middag, ikke sandt?"*

"A fine dinner, yes indeed," he replied, nodding. "And the wine was especially good: a big, red-blooded beauty that fills the mouth with dry, complex flavor."

I took this as a slight dig at German wines, which he'd criticized earlier for being too sweet. He may have "made the first move," so to speak, but I was ready with mine.

"As a bachelor, I suppose you don't dine like this every night?"

"Hardly," he admitted, giving ground. "Same for you, I suppose?"

"I get some interesting meals on the road. There were some tantalizing dishes in Croatia – venison stew, hot-pepper sausages, and something called *paprika haendl*. I got the recipe."

I took a drag on my cigarette and waited for his next foray. It wasn't long in coming.

"I wanted to tell you that I was impressed with your hot-coal walking on the beach," he said. "Tell me, how did you do it? Was it a trick, or are you just a man of steel?"

"No, not at all," I said, barely remembering the incident from Sankt-Hans. "I saw the coals only at the last instant, but it didn't concern me. You see, only stationary heat burns – one can run a match up and down one's arm all day without injury. It's only when one holds the flame *still* that it gets the chance to damage the skin."

"So if one keeps moving, one won't get burned," he concluded. Saying this seemed to disturb him and a tic flickered across his right cheek.

"Yes," I said. "Yes indeed."

Now it was his turn to take a long drag on his cigarette as the clock ticked. I decided to probe his background. "Tell me, did you grow up on this street?"

"Yes, Mother and I came here when I was just an infant," he replied immediately.

"You were an only child, then?" I asked.

This time his answer was not so lightning-fast. "No... as a matter of fact I had an older brother."

*Had.* I'd found a weakness and was determined to exploit it.

"But you don't any longer?" I asked, pressing on the weak spot.

"No, unfortunately not. He died in a playground accident when he was nine years old," he replied, not looking away at all.

"Oh that's terrible," I said, showing concern for my opponent, but I pursued the line without mercy. "How old were you at the time?"

*Check.*

Even in the pale moonlight, Søren's face was ruddy, and his lips were clamped down tight. His head shuddered slightly and he said, almost through his teeth, "I was five – listen, Doctor, you must understand, I don't like talking about this, it's all very painful for me, so unless this is going somewhere, I'd really rather change the subject."

I noticed that when he said it was painful for him, he grabbed his left triceps muscle with his right hand, hugging himself. Whether he did this to comfort himself in a tense situation or whether his upper arm was actually injured in some way, I couldn't tell. But I recalled that I'd never seen him in short sleeves.

I had not achieved checkmate, but I'd made progress, and he had been forced to put up an awkward defense. I sat back, somewhat pleased with myself. "Oh, of course I understand," I said. "My apologies." I blew a smoke ring lazily into the evening air. *I could afford to wait.*

It was his turn and he made a gambit, coming forward with, "I noticed that you like word games – puns and the like."

"Oh, yes – highest form of humor, you know."

"You seem to be able to manipulate Danish as well as English, and I daresay you could manage it in German as well. You must be a real language-genius, yes?"

"Oh, I don't like that term, but I've always been good with languages – I speak a reasonable French as well," I countered, not knowing where this salvo was leading.

"Yes, your language ability has really enabled you to integrate into Danish society unusually well – after all, you're a doctor, traveling everywhere. I've really got to hand it to you. Well done, for an *immigrant*."

Ah, now I understood – he was attacking my foreign-ness.

"Søren, I've lived in Denmark most of my life. I did my medical training here. I'm a Danish citizen—"

"But you are, Doctor, you are – you've integrated, assimilated. That's what these so-called New Danes don't understand. They want to settle here but continue to behave as if they still lived in *Farawayistan*."

Now it was my turn to let the clock tick. On the one hand, immigrants do have to recognize that they are in a new context. Expecting everything to be as it was in the old country will only lead to disappointment, even depression. On the other hand, I felt that my generation overdid it, stamping out diversity entirely in the name of fitting in. The ham I'd just consumed rolled over in my stomach.

"I agree that newcomers should learn about the Rule of Law," I said. "Also core Western values like freedom of expression. Certain customs like the burkha, female circumcision..."

"What about *honor killing*?" he asked. I hadn't heard of it. "When the men of a family band together to murder someone who has dishonored the house," he explained.

"Well, such customs are—" I was about to say "unacceptable," but he cut me off.

"*Barbaric,*" he said, pushing me.

"Well, they do seem a bit medieval," I admitted, ceding him that square.

"My thought exactly," he said, putting his forearms on the table and leaning forward. His cigarette was burning down to the nub now – there was no filter – and he grew thoughtful as he sucked the last few puffs out of it.

"Say, I can speak freely with you, correct? Doctors are like priests, right? Everything is completely confidential?" I nodded. "So I'll tell you, I've thought of making a map of the world, showing the intellectual and cultural development of the various lands. I'd say the Muslim countries – almost all of Africa and Asia really – would be in about the 11th century."

*Check.*

I didn't reply at first. The clock ticked relentlessly. I didn't want to agree with such a bald statement – a racist statement really – but I'd just admitted their practices were medieval, and I didn't want to contradict myself. So I temporized, responding with a question. "What makes you say that?"

"You just said yourself they were barbaric. Most of them can barely read; they treat women like beasts. And when they come here, all they bring with them is a list of *demands* – halal meat in our school cafeterias, girls in head-scarves. They won't be satisfied until we adopt their heinous Shariah Law and place minarets atop the Round Tower!"

"I hardly think—"

"You mark my words," he said, really going now. "Our little kingdom can't digest so many castaways. We take in these potato-peelings, the waifs that nobody else wants. They arrive here, make their demands, cash their support cheques, and screw like rabbits. It's just a matter of time before they take over, cover the land like locusts, like a *myggesværm!*"

*Double check.*

Mosquito-swarm, the combination showed evil genius. "Swarm" suggests uncountable black hordes, and they're "mosquitoes," that is, blood-sucking parasites on Danish society. This was an image worthy of the Nazi propaganda machine, and I resented it. Still, I tried to keep my cool and said, "I think you're blowing the threat far out of proportion."

"What? Should we wait till we're outnumbered? The average French family has two children – the average Muslim family in France has *eight*. But at least France is fighting back! Le Pen, that's what we need: a Man of Action. Someone who's man enough to raise the barricades against the crush of illiterate peasants."

"Not all immigrants are illiterate peasants," I countered. "Some contribute greatly to Danish society – look at Richard. He's also a recent immigrant."

His wide smile told me immediately I'd made a tactical error.

"What, our host? The man hasn't learned one word of the language. It's pathetic: he hasn't made the slightest effort to fit in here – he wants everyone around him to fit into his language, his culture, his agenda."

*Discovered check.*

This caught me unawares. It was true that Richard hadn't made much of an effort – and that stung – but I was proud of his accomplishments, and I would defend him.

"Americans do tend to see the rest of the world as their backyard, I'll admit that," I said, leaning back as I retreated to my own side of the board. "But he's a good man, and Denmark is lucky to have him. Nothing will ever change that."

"Nothing will change the fact that he doesn't *belong* here. He is an outsider. A Papist and an Italian, he will *never* fit in here. And his brood of dark little Marcheses will never be Danes – not now, not in a thousand generations!"

*Checkmate.*

Like a back-rank mate, his tirade shocked and embarrassed me. I turned nearly blue with rage. If we had been playing chess, I would have overturned the board.

"Now see here," I said, standing up and raising my voice. "I will not have you talk that way. I'm very fond of Richard. I know where he comes from, how he has struggled to get where he is today. He's like the plant that grows up between the cracks in the sidewalk."

"Yes. He's... a... *weed*," Søren said with a sneer, then stood, turned on his heel, and walked off.

I'd lost. I sat there quivering in defeat and disbelief. This was not an old man. Søren was a child of the new Europe, born after World War II. He never stood in line for ration cards, never listened to Hitler or Goebbels on the radio Yet his was the dehumanizing rhetoric of the 1930s, all over again; describing people as locusts, insects, weeds. Weeds to be burned in the incinerators.

Tawny fingers of vegetation, the weeds have overgrown the camps. *Night and Fog.* Grainy images of bulldozers amidst the bodies in the endless mass graves. Fifty years have passed, yet Evil will not stay buried.

Shaking my head, I slunk back into the kitchen and almost stumbled into Richard.

"Whoa, big fellah!" he said.

"Oh, Richard, you're just the man I wanted to talk to," I said.

I had to tell him the awful things – but wait! I couldn't. The rogue had just sworn me to secrecy.

"About what?" he asked.

"Oh, I just wanted to commend you on holding this dinner party for your mother – I'm sure she really appreciates it."

"Well, thanks for saying that. I hope you're enjoying it. Did you have a good smoke?"

"Yes, nothing like smoke to clear a man's head."

"Maybe I should try it," he said, putting down the dishes and sitting in the kitchen chair. "I don't feel like my head is very clear right now. There's just so many weird things happening. Do you think there could be such a thing as a ghost, Eddé?"

"Certainly not. How can you even say such a thing?"

"All these strange incidents…"

"Strange things happen and you look for a rational explanation. Ghosts are strictly the symbolic representation of our darkest fears."

"How can you be so sure?"

"I'm not like most people. Most people have beliefs, many beliefs – they believe in God, in the power of prayer, in leprechauns and *korrigans* that dance in the meadow under a full Midsummer moon. But I myself believe in very few things. I do *not* believe in hauntings. If there are unexplained footfalls during the night, one may consider the possibility of a prowler, animals on the roof, water in the pipes, inconsiderate neighbors…" I paused for effect, thinking of Søren. "… or floor joists settling in for a cool summer night. But one must never jump to irrational conclusions like *spooks*."

"What about the bed shaking? What do you make of that?" he asked, looking at his hands as he rubbed them.

"A passing S-train. Maybe even a strong electrical current nearby."

"Electrical current?"

"Yes, it's possible. Power lines, or even a storm cloud passing directly overhead. The ions in the ground passing through the foundations can create static electricity—"

"Hey, I'll bet they don't teach *that* in medical school. Have you been doing research on this, Edvard?"

I laughed. "All right, I admit it. I asked a physicist friend of mine."

Richard snickered, and just then Katrina poked her head into the kitchen and asked us to join them in the front room. We had forgotten all about the tiramisu.

As we entered the drawing room, Angie started doling out fingers of the espresso-creamy dessert. I bit into the soft layers and said, "The tiramisu is luscious, Katrina. Rich, yet light and fluffy. As good as any I've had in Italy!"

"It is fantastic, but I had nothing to do with making it – you should compliment Angelina," Katrina said.

"It's my mother's recipe," Angie explained. "She came from Treviso, north of Venice, you know. That's where tiramisu comes from too, so making it reminds me of her."

As the room went silent to allow for ooh-ing and chewing, Richard said, "I respect your skepticism about the ghost, Eddé, but I wonder what you would say about my mother's dream."

"What dream was that?" I asked.

"Well, we were talking about it just before," Angie said, looking down. "You know the portrait in the dining room? It's the original owner. I had a dream about him, Eddé – *before* I ever saw a picture of him."

"I'm sure you interpreted it that way at the time, Angie. But couldn't it be – isn't it possible that you had a dream about a *similar* man, a gentleman of a certain age, from a certain era? And then when you came downstairs and saw the daguerreotype, your mind latched on to precisely this man, concluding it was the man in your dream?"

All eyes turned to her, except for Søren who had stood up and was languidly perusing the bookshelf.

"Well, I suppose it's *possible*," she said.

"What about the wineglass?" Katrina asked.

This one I was confident about. I said, "Oh, I forgot to tell you, I read an article. It seems that there's a lot of Eastern European crystal coming into the market nowadays. It's of an inferior quality, and if one puts it in the dishwasher—"

"Eddé, I am not in the habit of buying cheap crystal," Katrina said.

Oh, I should have thought of that. I didn't wish to offend.

"I'm sorry if I insulted your crystal, Katrina, but extraordinary claims require extraordinary evidence," I said. "Science does not allow us to—"

"Science!" Katrina exclaimed. "It's just like when the allopathic doctors give a person only two options: take a pill or we'll cut you open. Tell me, is the only truth *Western*? What about the East?"

"The East?" I asked, not understanding where she was going with this.

"The Chinese use *herbs* to heal, they work with the body's own natural defenses, instead of attacking the body with artificial drugs. They relieve pain using acupuncture, which is based on Qi, the energy that flows through the human body. Perhaps it's a massive imbalance of Qi that's causing all these incidents."

"Ghosts, imbalance of Qi," I said, making a sour face. "Is this what it's come to? Are we reduced to superstition and shamanism? This is the end of the 20th Century, *for-Søren.*"

From the book corner came Søren's voice. "Did I hear my name?"

I had not meant to summon him; I was just uttering a mild oath in Danish, a euphemism for the potent curse, *"for Satan."*

"No, Søren, I didn't mean to disturb you. Go back to your books."

"Actually, now that you've roused me, perhaps you would find this passage interesting," he said, and started reading aloud:

*"What we call real estate – the solid ground to build the house on – is the broad foundation on which nearly all the guilt of this world rests. A man will commit almost any wrong – he will pile up an immense pile of wickedness, as hard as granite, and which will weigh as heavily upon his soul, to eternal ages – only to build a great, gloomy, dark-chambered mansion, for himself to die in, and for his posterity to be miserable in. He lays his own dead corpse beneath the underpinning, as one might say, and hangs his frowning picture on the wall…"*

"Who wrote that – Edgar Allen Poe?" Richard asked.

"Nathaniel Hawthorne," Katrina said.

Everyone turned to her. I cocked my head.

"Don't look so surprised," she said. "It is my book, after all – from literature class in *gymnasium.*"

*"The House of the Seven Gables,"* said Søren. "I spied the book on the shelf and thought it might be amusing. Perhaps relevant."

"How could that dour, tenebrous passage, written more than a century ago, possibly be *relevant?*" I asked. "Do you mean to compare the 'frowning picture' with the photo of Damsgaard?"

Søren ignored my question, and looking at Richard, posed one of his own. "How much do you know about the story of the house?"

"Not much," Richard said. "It was built in 1904, at the behest of Karl Damsgaard, a Copenhagen lawyer. A son, Peder, was born in 1920, lived here most of his life."

"He died shortly before we bought the property," Katrina said.

"Yes, well, perhaps I could perform a service by telling you a few additional things," Søren said quietly, looking down.

"Katrina and I came to see you with Dahl before we bought the damned thing – why didn't you tell us then?" Richard asked with thin lips.

"Details of the Damsgaard family history, what little I know, hardly seemed germane at the time," Søren replied coolly.

"Well, that's true enough," Richard admitted. "We were more focused on the remote heating system."

"So tell us," I joined in, chuckling. "Did Old Damsgaard harbor an insane wife in the attic or dig his vegetable garden in an ancient Teutonic graveyard?"

"Neither," Søren said. "Karl Friedrich Damsgaard was a libertine as a youth, and an obdurate old sinner in his dotage."

"Tell us about him," Angie asked.

"Old Damsgaard was born in 1872, the third son of a farmer in Jutland. A brilliant schoolboy, he surpassed even his masters by the time he was twelve years old. His pastor taught him Latin and Greek, and encouraged him to study theology in Copenhagen. Karl jumped at the chance to leave the muck of Jutland behind, and matriculated at the University of Copenhagen at the age of sixteen."

All eyes were riveted on Søren now. He was obviously enjoying being the center of attention.

"I don't understand," Richard said. "Dahl said he was a lawyer, not a priest."

"Oh, he was no priest!" Søren said with a dull laugh. "Karl lasted six months in Divinity School. He petitioned to change his studies to Law, and given his excellent record, the petition was granted. He received his *Juris Doctoris* at the tender age of twenty. Unheard of, then or now."

"Where did he get the money to continue his studies?" Katrina asked, sensibly.

"I don't know," Søren replied, "but from some of his later exploits, we may form our own suspicions – he was known as an avid card player, cigar-smoker, and womanizer. At university, he ran with a crowd that called themselves the Sons of Dionysus and were known for their drunken revelries."

"Damsgaard is starting to sound like a great guy at parties," Richard said.

"That he was," Søren said. "Ruthless at cards as he was in business, often accused of finagling at both. Never caught."

"When did he get married?" Angie asked.

"He married one Mrs. Fabricius, a widow from a fine Copenhagen family. She was nearly twenty years his senior and died in 1914, of tuberculosis. She left everything to Karl, despite the fact that he cheated on her scandalously."

"Did they live here?" Katrina asked.

"Yes, they did," Søren replied.

"And she died within these walls, I suppose?" Richard asked with a smirk.

"No. As a matter of fact she died in Switzerland, in a sanitarium there. In, uh, Davos, I believe. Why do you ask?" Søren asked.

"No reason. I was just expecting you to tell us scary stuff, like kids at summer camp," Richard said, taking a glass of the frigid ice-wine.

"Are you making this up?" I asked. "Telling ghost stories around the fire?"

"Of course not. Why would I make up stories?" Søren replied, apparently hurt by the accusation.

"I don't know – perhaps to tease us, play a joke," I said.

*How could he possibly know all this?*

"Don't listen to them. We believe you, Søren," Katrina said. "What happens next? How does he have a son, Peder, born in 1920 if his wife dies in 1914?"

"You have to understand his financial situation," Søren continued. "His own business dealings, primarily in commercial real estate, went very well. Then he added the considerable Fabricius fortune to his own. The Great War came, and he speculated successfully. By Armistice Day, Damsgaard was a millionaire. But he was also lonely."

"So he found himself a second wife?" Richard asked.

"Just after the War, he married a young woman, Camilla Bendixen, who had been born in 1902."

"She was just seventeen?" Angie asked.

"Yes. And he was forty-six," he said.

"That's hard to believe," Katrina said.

"Camilla came from modest circumstances," he explained. "At the time, her family probably saw the opportunity to marry her off to a rich lawyer as an incredible stroke of luck. But he was a monster – insanely jealous. They say he beat her, engaged in 'unnatural acts.' No doubt just rumor. In any case, soon after giving birth to Peder, she died."

"So the little boy grew up without a mother?" Angie asked.

"Peder had nursemaids, governesses, private tutors. But no mother. His father had many women, but never another wife. Mother said Peder often spoke of his father, but never with tenderness. Karl was stern, and as strict with Peder as he was indulgent with himself."

"Wait a minute. Mother... *your* Mother?" I asked. "Is that where you got all this information?"

"Yes. Mother was... a close friend of Peder Damsgaard. She even met Karl, though only when he was as decrepit on the outside as he was dissolute inwardly. You see, unlike the portrait of Dorian Gray, Karl's picture did not bear the burden of his iniquity," he said, indicating the photograph on the wall.

"How can that be?" I asked, thinking I might have caught Søren in a lie. "Your family didn't move here till the sixties – Karl must've been—"

"Dead by then, yes," Søren said, nodding. "But Mother grew up in the neighborhood. She and Peder were in school together."

"Did your mother say what Karl was like?" Angie asked.

"Oh, Karl was the dapper, articulate gentleman so typical of his generation."

"How did he die?" Katrina asked.

"Didn't you know?" Søren replied. "Oh, I suppose I've never mentioned it. Karl Damsgaard fell down the cellar steps. Never recovered from the fall."

"Everything can be interpreted one way and
then again interpreted in the opposite sense."

- Hermann Hesse
*Magister Ludi*

# HIGH SUMMER
# 17. Edvard

Even up against the halogen, the amber liquid remained cloudy, tainted as it was
with the ancient impurities, the congeners of the Scottish Highlands. I swirled
the ice at the bottom of Loch Morar, the 18-year-old single malt in my glass, and
my thoughts went round and round with it.

Richard and I sat alone in the living room; it was the first time I'd been back
since that awful dinner party. I had begun to make case notes on Katrina – bad
dreams, insomnia, anxiety, possible incipient alcoholism (it ran in her family),
likely depression.

Yet this was no ordinary case – too many strange things had happened, several witnessed by persons other than the subject. Richard and I both heard footsteps; I saw someone in the window that night; and then there was the recurring
smell of smoke. Since I didn't admit the possibility of ghosts, this left only mis-
perception – or willful misdirection. What was Søren's role in all this?

"I'm worried about Katrina," Richard said quietly.

"I think she should get a full medical exam," I said, bringing my lips together tightly.

"What do you think's the matter with her?"

"It's hard to say. She may be suffering from any number of things: hormonal
imbalance, depression, bipolar disorder."

"Bipolar – you mean manic-depression?" he said, narrowing his eyes. "It can't be that – she's not manic."

"Sometimes the manic phase is latent."

"Well, it'll have to wait till we get back from vacation, I'm afraid. We leave Saturday."

"Oh, I'm glad to hear that. A vacation," I said with a wry smile. "You're becoming a real Scandinavian, Richard. Where are you going?"

"We rented a place up in Skagen."

"Ah, fantastic, the sunlight will do her good," I said. "Has she been getting some sleep?"

We heard the back door open and shut.

"That sounds like her now," Richard said, cutting off the discussion. "Katrina, is that you?"

Katrina, who had cycled home, emerged from the kitchen apple-cheeked. "Yes. Hallo, Edvard!"

"Hallo, my dear," I said, getting up. "How have you been?"

"Good – better."

"Wonderful to hear," I said, smiling. "Tell me, have you been sleeping better? Richard told me you've been taking Ambien, which is perfectly safe. If you want a prescription—"

"Perhaps it would help to have a bottle with me," she said, looking at her husband. "Just in case."

"All right, I'll call it in tomorrow. You use Boulevard Apotek, don't you?"

"Yes – thanks, Edvard," she said. "And thanks for coming to the dinner party last week – *tak for sidst*, as we say."

"*Selv tak*," I returned. "It was a really unforgettable evening, and I wanted to compliment you again on your playing. I had no idea you were such a virtuoso pianist."

"That was incredible, Skat. Was that something you played as a girl?" Richard asked.

"No, the tuner found it in the piano bench."

"But he was just here – what, did you sight-read it?" Richard said with a nervous chuckle.

Katrina just nodded.

"Do you mean to say that you played *Le Gibet* on first sight?" I asked, amazed. The piece by Ravel was brief, no more than five minutes or so, but complex; written at the height of French Impressionism, it was a tone poem as rich and subtle as a beach scene by Monet.

"Yes, more or less. I've gotten better at it through practice, but I played it correctly on first sight, yes," she said. Then she cocked her head and said, "Somehow I feel it was Destiny that brought me to this piece."

I nearly cringed. My patients often used such words to shift responsibility away from themselves. "Destiny?"

"Yes, I feel so wonderful when I play it," she said with a dreamy look in her eyes. "Transported."

"Ach, I do not believe in such things," I said with a small wave. "My experience tells me that men who believe in Destiny or Fate are generally deluded and often dangerous."

"What about Luck then?" she asked. "Surely you have experienced good fortune in your life."

"I'm skeptical of Luck too," I said.

"People can make their own luck, I think," said Richard. "But what about *coincidence*, chance meetings that can change a person's life? Like when you met my father?"

I took a deep breath. I'd expected this subject to come up at some point. I didn't know how much Richard knew about that story, so I proceeded cautiously.

"It was of course a happy coincidence for me. If I hadn't met your father, I would probably not be sitting here today. But surely you've heard the story many times – there's nothing to it but an American serviceman's desire for fresh eggs and a young boy's adoration of chocolate."

"I've never heard the story, Edvard," Katrina said. "Please tell me – how did you meet Mr. Marchese?"

"Well, he was Private First Class Marchese at the time," I said.

In my mind's eye I could see him still, a young GI striding toward me confidently, with a big grin on his face and the dark brown wrapper of a Hershey bar in his outstretched hand. It was the way I preferred to remember him, not the cancer-shriveled version I encountered the last time I saw him.

"Pop was stationed in Germany in the Occupational Forces," Richard explained.

"And you met him there, since you're German," Katrina said.

"Eddé is Jewish, Katrina," Richard admonished.

"No, it's all right, Richard," I said, waving him off. "My family *was* German. That is to say, we were Jews who *thought* we were German."

"You mean they didn't give you passports?" Katrina asked.

"I mean that a Jew could no more be German at that time than the Muslims in Denmark today can ever be Danes. They will speak Danish, they will go to Danish schools, they will begin to dress and act like Danes. But they will not be Danes," I said, and with some discomfort, recalled Søren's words, "not in a thousand generations."

"Don't you think eventually?" Richard said. "I mean, the Irish and Italians and all the others became Americans, didn't they?"

"This is not America," I said simply.

"It seems unfair. After all, nobody chooses their nationality," Richard protested.

"Interesting you say that, because almost uniquely in the history of Mankind, a few years before I was born, my family did have a choice in their nationality."

"What do you mean?" Richard asked.

"Living in the border province of Schleswig during the Referendum of 1920, the Frankls could have chosen to be German-Jews or Danish-Jews. Turns out, we chose wrong," I said with a shrug.

"Why'd they choose Germany do you think?" Richard asked.

"My family voted to stay part of the newly-democratic Germany, the nation of Goethe and Beethoven. My parents were contemporaries of Thomas Mann and Hermann Hesse. Germany was arguably the most advanced nation on earth at the time, the most enlightened."

"But all that changed," Richard said.

"Well, for a while it seemed like the Frankls had made a wise choice. The twenties brought the Weimar Republic, a flowering of art and culture – the Bauhaus, Expressionism. But alas, it was to be as fleeting as the German summer."

"What made them stay in Germany in the thirties, after Hitler rose to power?" Richard asked.

"Our family lived in a trim little city-house in the middle of Flensburg; my father had a successful business. We spoke German. People said it would get better – or at least it could not get any worse." I sipped at the whisky. "Finally, I suppose, they stayed until it was too late."

"What happened to them?" Katrina asked.

"It was the fall of 1942," I said, remembering the day as if it were last year instead of more than half a century ago. The air was chill, bright with the golden light of autumn. I had been helping with the harvest, even though I was just a boy of eight years. I was so tired my bones ached.

"I was trudging back from the fields, when a classmate of mine, Hans Müller, came up to me and knocked me down. For no reason at all. Now Hans and I were friends, and there was no cause for him to knock me down. So I got up and pushed him back. A shoving match ensued, as happens between small boys. Then all of a sudden Frau Müller was there, angrily telling the work-boss that she would take care of it, not to worry, she would beat both of us severely. The next thing I knew I was at the Müllers, and Herr and Frau Müller were discussing something in hoarse whispers. I was frightened, convinced that I would be beaten with the switch. I sat alone by the hearth preparing a defense – they had to know it wasn't my fault! – but when Frau Müller finally came in to me, she smiled and held my hand. I was taken aback, because I expected her to be cross. She explained to me that my family had been taken away."

I drained the last of the whisky, exposing the deformed lumps of ice, monsters of the deep emerging from a dried-up lake bed. Pouring out another two fingers of Loch Morar, I downed them in one. When ancient Greek heroes visited their dead, they poured out libations of wine. Mine evidently preferred Scotch.

"Frau Müller told me," I continued, "that my family was chosen to participate in a new program for workers across Germany. 'You are the youngest, so they couldn't take you,' she told me. Of course, later I found out that it was only because I was not at home that the Nazis didn't take me. It was a clerical error that delayed their looking for me, and that gave Grete Müller the chance to send Hans off to find and slug me."

Richard asked, "So what happened to you? Did they take you in?"

"Yes, I went to live with the Müllers in their home on Bertrandstrasse. They were very kind to me. Grete told me stories and sang to me at night. *Sterne Ste-*

*hen.*" Seeing incomprehension in their faces, I sang softly, *"Weisst Du wie viel Sterne stehen an dem blauen Himmelszelt…"*

Then Richard asked, "What about the neighbors, what did they think of all this?"

"That's a good question," I said, nodding. "Often I've wondered the same thing. Flensburg is not a huge city, not then and not now. So people must have known. But perhaps this was one way in which my father's close relations with the Gentiles paid off.

"No one told. For nearly three years any number of people could have told, been rewarded for telling. I have always held this to the credit of the people of Flensburg: they never told."

"When did you realize that your family was not coming home again?" Katrina asked.

"I wondered why they never wrote. I suppose I always knew someplace deep inside that I would never see them again. I wrote to them as best I could – that is to say Frau Müller and I sat down and wrote letters and drew pictures that never went anywhere. She burnt them in the fireplace. I caught her once. I was so angry with her. She apologized and said it was a mistake and that we could write another one. But then I knew there was nowhere for my letters to go. Only up in smoke. Later I learned that they all perished in the camps – Muti, Pappa, my grandparents, my small sister Steffi."

After saying my sister's name, a name I had not spoken in many years, my eyes became moist and my mouth dry, a dryness not quenched even by the smoothest single malt. I could not bring myself to say the word. *Buchenwald.* A hell on earth where human beings were harvested for their wedding rings, gold fillings, hair, shoes; even the skin itself was used for soap, lamp shades. *The legendary German efficiency.*

We sat there a long time not speaking.

Finally, Richard said, "I'm sorry for making you go through this, Eddé. If you want to stop…" I shook my head slowly. Then he asked, "So how did you meet Pop?"

"Ah, yes, that's how this conversation started, isn't it?" I said, forcing a smile. "Well, the war in Europe finally ended – and things got decidedly worse."

"Surely you mean things got better?" Katrina asked.

"No, not for us. Of course all the Flensburgers were relieved that the war was over and the boys would be coming home – some of them at least – but there was no work. Physically, the country was devastated. The shortages – food, fuel, rubber, paper – got worse every week. But worst of all was the sense of shame that hung over everyone. The nation, *das Volk,* was disgraced. Again."

"The Germans would always be known as the people who started two world wars," Katrina said.

"Yes," I said. "Psychologically, what the Third Reich had done was even harder to accept than the military defeat of the First World War. The evil that had been committed in the name of the German people was beyond anything we could have guessed at. We were crushed, desolate.

"The first bright spot was when the American troops rolled in to take control of Flensburg as the regional hub. We kids ran up to the GI's, hoping for chocolates. It was a warm summer day, it must have been August, I suppose. This one soldier – your father, Richard – walked up to me flashing a big grin and handed me a Hershey bar – a WHOLE one. I would have polished his boots for a month. But all he wanted was to know where he could get some eggs."

"Pop talked to you in German?"

"He couldn't say a proper sentence, but he managed the ungrammatical: *Wo ist Eieren?* I understood. I told him *Mitt Haus*, and he followed me there.

"Frau Müller screamed and ran around like a decapitated chicken when she saw me bringing a soldier up the walk. Vincent put up his hands and smiled like Humphrey Bogart with a cigarette dangling from the side of his mouth. He said *Pax vobiscum* and *Eieren, Eieren*, and I explained that he had given me a WHOLE Hershey bar and was therefore obviously to be trusted. All he wanted was a couple of eggs.

"Grete gave him the eggs – and milk and bread and butter (a luxury then and for a long time afterwards), and somehow managed a hunk of salami, which even Herr Müller didn't get. Vincent, used to tack rations, told me later that he was very impressed. She told him about me and at some point he must have asked her something like, 'What do you expect me to do about it?'

"What she expected was that he would take me to her cousin Gretchen in Christiansfeld, a German-speaking hamlet on the northern side of the border – they got outvoted in 1920 and ended up in Denmark, lucky for them. She wasn't in touch with Gretchen, but she would write a letter and say that I was her youngest son and that she didn't have enough food for both Hans and me, so could she take me in, at least for a while. She didn't want to risk writing down that I was a Jew.

"Vincent took me to Christiansfeld – a hundred kilometers in an open Jeep – an incredible adventure for a twelve-year-old boy. The rock-strewn roads were rutted and dangerous, but we made it there all right. Gretchen didn't flinch when she heard I was a Jew. She just said, 'You poor boy,' and took me in her arms – I remember it well, as she was an ample woman, and I *was* a twelve-year-old boy after all," I said with a grin.

They laughed and I stopped a moment to remember the scene: the stout farmwife taking me to her bosom, yet another woman protecting me from unseen threats in a world hostile beyond my reckoning, beyond all reckoning.

"So that's why you're so fond of Christiansfeld honey-cakes," Katrina said.

"Yes, I stayed in North Schleswig until I finished *gymnasium*. Later on I went to University in Copenhagen and fell in love with the city. To this day, I still go back and visit my Danish siblings in Jutland. Over time, I have come to think of myself as a Dane, or at least a Danish Jew. So it's as if finally the Referendum of 1920 has been reversed, at least for me."

"You're traveling a lot, Eddé," Katrina said. "Do you get back to Germany often?"

I breathed out and said, "Of course I expected to return to Flensburg, to the people who never told. But I never did. In fifty years I have never once set foot in Germany."

"Didn't you want to visit the Müllers?" Richard asked.

"I'm afraid that part of the story doesn't end well, and this is why I credit your father with saving my life. It turns out that Grete was not getting me out of Germany 'for safety's sake,' much less to save on food. You see there were some locals who had been away during the War, and now they were back. She thought they might cause trouble for me. There were threats."

"Oh my God, what happened?" Katrina asked.

There was no way to say it, no way to soften the blow.

"Three young thugs, apparently known but never charged, firebombed the house on Bertrandstrasse on Christmas Eve, 1945. No one survived the blast."

# 18. Katrina

The mood in the house changed after that dinner party. The air was chill and every day brought with it more clouds and rain. Fog washed in from the Sound. It was the dreariest July I could remember. And the drear without matched the gloom within. Shadows lengthened quickly in late afternoon, and I swear they *moved.* I would see a shadow run by me, or flash along the windows just outside, but when I would look...

No one was there.

I became nervous, edgy. Ever since the accident, I dreaded going down to the cellar. I started to ask Richard to fetch things for me, as if I were a frail Victorian lady. But at least once a week I had to do the laundry, and this meant going down those steps. Richard was a man of many talents, but capable of doing the laundry without female supervision, he was not.

By Thursday of this week, the hamper upstairs was filled to overflowing. So I bundled up all the bras and bedclothes, stockings, sweaters and towels, and trundled down to the laundrette on Svanemøllevej. I was mortified that I had to take my dirty laundry to a public coin-op – it was the first palpable sign that Fear was getting the best of me – but what choice did I have?

An hour of watching washers chug and dryers spin left me with an empty, blank-headed feeling. *Zen and the Art of Laundry.* I shambled home, zombie-like.

For the past few weeks, I've been trying to work out the details of a business plan for a natural foods store, but haven't made great progress. I was obsessed with the piano, studied the Ravel for hours: every chord, every accidental, every quaver. Compulsive, I'd worked out that the B-flat octave sounded exactly 141 times.

So today I took control – no more piano. I forced myself to sit at the dining-room table and focus on the design of the shop, which I'd imagined in Østerbro, a trendy quarter on the east side of Copenhagen. I'd agreed with Richard that the business plan should specify the size of the store, the number of items in each category, how much floor space should be devoted to fresh food, dry food, naturopathic medicines, vitamins. There was a certain "grocer's margin" required per square meter. But the numbers kept coming out wrong – it had been ages since I'd done maths.

My thoughts darted this way and that. Then I would meet the eye of Karl Damsgaard in his frame. I changed seats, made myself tea. I went off on intellectual side-trips – what should the name of the store be? What color scheme? I doodled in the margins, sketching fat logos in block letters like a fifth-grader. I stopped myself only by getting up to make tea again; then I had to pee. It was hopeless.

With the passing of each quarter hour, the grandfather clock would toll mockingly. I even made up words to the chimes:

*It's another quarter hour,*
*And you have got nothing done.*
*Forget about the business planning;*
*Just go out and have some fun.*

Damsgaard leered at me from his frame. I simply couldn't take it anymore, so I got up and ripped his face off the wall, sending the picture-hook flying with a *ping!* I wrapped him in brown kraft paper and buried him in the back of the hall closet.

"Rest in peace," I said out loud. Cold comfort.

As I was closing the closet door, I caught a look in the long mirror. My teeth were yellowed, like the Queen's. I opened my mouth and tilted my head so I could see the inside the lower front teeth. Stains the color of licorice. I picked at them with my fingernail and chips flaked off.

*Oh my God, were my teeth falling apart?* No, it was just flakes of the tartar buildup or whatever-it-was. Could it be calcium deposits? No, calcium would be white, chalky.

*What would cause such dark stains?*

Centuries ago, the nobility believed sugar was a poison that turned the teeth black. Responsible hosts banned sugar from the main course, relegating it to an optional "dessert" course in which guests could indulge at their own risk. Even separate kitchens with specialized chefs were set up to deal with the *matériels dangereuses.* This is how we got pastry chefs, dessert kitchens. But other than honey in my tea, I didn't consume much in the way of sweets.

I went to the telephone and called Dr. Borgen, the dentist, and then I decided to follow Edvard's advice and schedule a checkup with Dr. Madsen, a male obstetrician who had been Mor's OB forever. I couldn't get in to see either of them the week of the 14th (the week we get back from Skagen), but made appointments for the week of August 21st.

Secretly, I was hoping that the vacation would be a cure in itself. I was really looking forward to getting away. When Richard got home, I told him that the house was stifling me. I expected him to pooh-pooh the whole thing, but he didn't.

"You know," he said in a low voice, "I don't like to be down here alone late at night either. I keep watching the shadows and sometimes it feels like that portrait is staring at me – say, where is the old boy?"

"I took him down today," I replied softly

"Took him down? You just spent a hundred dollars framing him."

"I just couldn't keep him there anymore after what we heard last Friday night."

"What, that he died in the house? Listen, most every home in Denmark has experienced a death at some point. It doesn't mean anything."

"You don't find it strange that he fell down the basement stairs to his death, and then shortly after moving in, I fell down the same steps?"

"Well, steps can be dangerous: I hit my head that time, you fell. We'll have to be extra careful—"

I started to tear up. Richard's expression softened.

"What's wrong?" he asked.

"I wasn't being careless. I wasn't even in a hurry that night. I was *pushed*, Richard!"

No glib answer to that. Richard took a moment, looked directly into my eyes and said quietly, "Don't you think it might be your imagination working overtime?"

Now he was patronizing me. I was hurt, angry. So I said, calmly but firmly, "I am *not* going crazy, Richard."

"Whoa, who said anything about going crazy?"

"You just said—"

"I didn't say anything," he said, showing me his palms. "I think you're sleep-deprived. Maybe you could use some more minerals or something."

"I just made an appointment with Doctor Madsen. Maybe a blood test could show a deficiency – mineral, or maybe hormonal."

"You think your hormones could be off?"

"I don't know. I feel anxious, I can't sleep. Today I couldn't concentrate. My thoughts kept darting this way and that."

"Just today?"

"All week, actually. I've gotten nothing done on the business plan."

"Listen," Richard said, coming over and putting his arms around me. "We're leaving for Skagen in two days. Just try to relax till then."

Tonight before going to bed, I removed the pocket watch from its case and sat in the bedroom examining it. I had barely looked at it since Mor gave it to me. By pushing a button, I could easily reveal the dull face, the color of Ivory soap. But the back was shut tight. Had Fa' ever opened it? I took the Swiss Army knife from Richard's drawer and with an effort, forced it open. There was an inscription, *Für Karl.* Then at the bottom, *Ein auf Zwei,* and a date, 1942.

I turned the watch over and stared at the face. The second hand, thin as an eyelash, swept across the white surface, time marching forward but always in darkness. The spidery hands never strong enough to turn the indicator over to day.

Putting the watch down on the dresser, I felt my heart racing. I was filled with anxiety – I'd never be able to sleep like this. Richard was still downstairs watching the television, so I sneaked to the bathroom and opened his medicine cabinet. One pill left. Well, I really needed it. I would get some more Ambien from Edvard for the trip, and then get Madsen to prescribe something more permanent in a couple of weeks. The problem was it didn't seem to be working. It used to work right away – perhaps the effect wears out or something?

I popped the pill anyway, crawled into bed and doused the light. But no sandman came to call. An hour later, I was still awake, but pretended to be asleep when Richard came to bed. He started to nibble at my ear. *Mmm,* I was sort of interested. I stretched, cat-like, and turned toward him, put my arm around him. We kissed, but I just couldn't keep my mind on it. Images kept flashing through my head, like a TV with a broken tuner – Damsgaard's portrait buried beneath the stairs, Søren on the beach at Sankt Hans, the laundrette woman with her flabby arms and skeptical looks, what my mother would say about me being afraid to go to the cellar.

"Stop," I said.

"What, did I do something wrong? Was it too hard? I can be more gentle."

"No, no it's not that. My mind is racing. I'm everywhere but here."

Richard was silent for a moment and then his lower lip softened and he said, "Maybe you're just not interested in me anymore."

"No, that's not it," I said, and held his hand.

I didn't blame him for trying – we hadn't made love in weeks. Perhaps there *was* something wrong with my hormones?

"I don't know – I'm just distracted," I said with a weak smile. "We can try again when we get to Skagen."

Richard didn't say anything, just gave me a kiss and rolled over. Soon I was lying there – as I had every night this week – envious even of his nasal bluster. The man slept like a washing machine, but at least he slept. I would only fall asleep, exhausted, in the small hours – three, four o'clock in the morning.

At the moment, I was double-espresso wide-awake. I jumped at every noise that drifted in through the open windows: every car, every bike, every drunk rolling home. At 11:30, the wind started singing in the trees. Just after midnight, the bed quivered for a minute or so. This had happened before, I was almost used to it. What would cause a thing like that? I didn't hear a train. *Could it be a tremblor, like a mini-earthquake?* Nonsense, we don't have faults in Denmark. I put my fingertips close to the wall, to see if the swaying would cause them to touch. It didn't. *Could whatever-it-is be inside me, my imagination?*

I felt like every nerve ending was frayed, open. What was *that?* Oh, it must be a cat or an owl. *Did that shadow move?* Oh, God, what's happening to me? I started to cry softly.

Then I heard a distinct *clunk.* The sound seemed to come from the front bedroom. Richard did not stir, so I put on my robe and got out of bed. The pocket watch winked at me from the bureau. I tiptoed into the hallway to investigate. I hesitated, remembering the incident on the stairs, but steeled myself and walked to the little bedroom. The room was cold. I turned on the light. The windows were open and the curtains were blowing; the brass telescope had fallen over and was leaning up against the left dormer. I shut the windows and went to right the scope. I found it was warm to the touch, as if – as if someone had just been holding it. The transit had evidently flipped over in the fall. On the underside of the barrel, I saw, just under the inscription *Carl Zeiss AG,* the eagle and swastika.

I threw the cylinder from me as if it were red-hot. The telescope crashed again. I sat on the guest bed and started shaking. My mind began racing, making connections and discerning patterns where before there had only been white noise:

Construction at the end of the street had caused the removal of several large trees;

without the trees – as it would have been fifty years ago – the harbor was in plain view;

looking through the glass, one could easily monitor the coast;

Karl Damsgaard could have been monitoring the coast from this very room, just like the Nazis who were pacing the floorboards of our rooms at the D'Angleterre;

the owner of Sundhuset had been a collaborator, helping the *Wehrmacht* monitor the long Danish coastline;

there were German spies who lived past dessert, ones who could say *"rød grød med fløde"* because they were natives, and Damsgaard was one of them.

I imagined him sipping tea with his club-footed master at the D'Angleterre – Damsgaard, who moved silently, like a ghost, who was someone and yet... No one.

Tonight, who shook the bed, opened the windows and overturned the telescope?

Who was in the kitchen with me?

Who pushed me down the cellar steps?

Always the same answer.

*No one.*

It was as if I'd passed by a variegated tapestry every day, but never seen what held it all together. Finally, I had found the red thread.

Oh my God. Edvard said the Flensborgers never told. He repeated several times, "No one told." But then how did the thugs found out where he was hiding?

*No one told!*

I screamed and ran from the room, hysterical. I told Richard I couldn't spend another night in this godforsaken house. I begged him to leave for Skagen tomorrow, a day earlier than we'd planned.

And so we did.

The verdant hill-country of Jutland was as alive as Copenhagen had been dead. Everything was covered with growing things – tawny stands of August grain, wildflowers, heather; even the dwellings were topped with turf and thatch and moss.

"Gee, the fertility goddess sure blessed this place – there's stuff growing everywhere," Richard said.

"This was the farthest south the glaciers came in the last ice age. The rolling landscape is made from all the rocks and earth they pushed ahead of them on their trip southward and then deposited here."

"So it's like a prehistoric garbage dump."

"They call it a 'terminal moraine,' I think. We learned about it in *folkeskole*. The teacher told us we had the glaciers to thank for our rich farmland. I always liked that image. Life coming out of those mountains of death – as if our crops were watered by a trickle from that ancient ice."

"I love it when you say stuff like that."

We motored relentlessly northward. My eyes became sandy and narrowed as the towns became fewer and farther between. The orange light of sunset shone in the windowpanes. Somewhere around Aalborg, town of aquavit, I drifted off, and so when we entered into the extreme county of Vendsyssel, I was unaware of the crossing.

Hours later, I awoke to a strange landscape as the scrubby pines of the north cape came into view, shadowy in the failing light. On our left, what appeared to be black towers were silhouetted against the western sky of deep indigo. But these were in fact even more fantastical than towers: they were dunes, enormous creatures of sand that had swallowed entire villages in their time.

It was midnight by the time we reached the seaside village of Old Skagen. This outpost of humanity at the northern tip of Denmark was nothing more than a ramble of upstreets and downstreets thrown haphazardly against the wave-worn coast. So it wasn't difficult to find our haven, a golden-yellow edifice wedged up against the sea.

The Sea House was our refuge at the end of the world, standing stoutly on a spit of land that jutted into the waves of the rowdy North Sea. In such an exposed spot, a lesser building would have blown away long ago. But the doughty Sea House, rooted to its foundations of exposed rock, seemed to lean into the wind and had stood the test of time, swaying in the salty gale as it melted slowly into the earth and elements.

The upstairs consisted solely of a sparsely-furnished bedroom with enormous, naked windows looking out on three sides to the endless sea and sky. These portholes were perched high above the water, so unless they minded the gaping of the gulls, a couple could dance in the nude or make love in the sunlight without the need for curtains.

I lay on the broad featherbed in the starlight. Richard opened the windows, and amidst the smells of salt water and freshly-laundered bedclothes, we fell asleep to the lapping of the waves.

The next morning, the creeping fingers of dawn felt more like a slap across the face. Pools of white light splashed across the down comforter. I grimaced; squinched my eyes, then opened them wide. Even at five o'clock in the morning, the light of Skagen was dazzling.

I'd slept well and felt terrific. Richard, exhausted from the drive, lay motionless, his face buried in an oversized pillow. Allowing him to sleep in, I dressed quickly and walked outside.

Ambling along the cobblestones to the main street, I followed the scent of fresh bread. A bakery was open and I managed to buy a loaf of ciabatta with a twenty-kroner piece I'd forgotten in my culottes. I pressed the paper sack to my blouse and felt the warmth of the baker's oven against my tummy.

Ripping off a hunk, I chewed the bread as I strolled. It took awhile, but eventually, the art dealers started airing their shops and setting up their sandwich boards. In one window, there were contemporary pieces: dramatic seascapes of rocks, puffins and waves of turquoise; and superrealistic landscapes of sedge, insects and graceful wind turbines.

But the dusty shop I entered, the Hirschsprung Gallery, specialized in high-end reproductions — at least, I assumed they were reproductions — of the famous Skagen painters: Michael Ancher, Peder Krøyer, Christian Krohg. Luminaries of the art world of a century ago.

In the spirit of *La Belle Epoque*, the Skagen artists painted each other and their wives enjoying wine and music and the Good Life. Ancher painted rowboats, sailboats and fisherfolk dragging their dinghies to the sea through the harsh dunes. Krogh was known for his striking portraits, this one of his wife

Oda in a floppy hat and blouse of vermilion with Prussian blue skirts, standing frankly with arms akimbo. The colors were bold, the clothes bohemian, and her attitude briskly modern. As if she were saying, *Aren't you done yet, Christian?*

But the best of all was a strandscape in which Peder and Marie Krøyer strolled along the beach with their faithful English pointer under the light of a half moon. Peder himself seemed overdressed, foppish. Typical Victorian walking in Nature, sporting a bowtie, cummerbund and pocket watch with gold fob.

By placing the figures to one side, Krøyer makes the moonlight a major player in the piece. Lovingly, he follows the light as it bounces among the waves and reflects in the wet sand. With great skill, he traps the elusive light of Skagen, "freeze-dries" the liquid of the ocean and captures the moment in oils on canvas.

I saw some of myself in Marie, clad in a full-length gown for a walk on the beach. It made me sad to look at the painting. Peder's hand clings to Marie's arm, but her eyes are far away, hypnotized by the light. He is losing her. A dark ship sits on the horizon, ominous.

The gilt-edged placard on the wall told me how it would end: soon after this final trip to Skagen, the couple divorced. Marie moved in with a composer; Peder, suffering from depression and hallucinations induced by mercury treatments for syphilis, died not long after.

# 19. Richard

In the Queens of my boyhood, nobody's windows looked out on anything but other people's windows. No wonder why all the shades were drawn. And to keep out burglars, the residents put up black, wrought-iron bars on the windows, which effectively imprisoned them in their own homes.

I'll never forget this one time I met a limo driver down in South Carolina, a fellow who used to live in Ozone Park. I couldn't believe it. Down there, among all the *yawls* and *mayams*, there was this guy who "tawked duh tawk," and remembered the old Mets – that Ed Kranepool's name spelled backwards was "Loopenark," and why Tug McGraw liked grass better than Astroturf – he had never *smoked* Astroturf.

So I asked him how he survived in a place where you can't get a decent pizza, nobody even knows what a bagel is. He said he loved it: in New York, he lived in a basement apartment; down in Carolina, he was the owner of *real estate.*

"When I tinka duh guys I useta know back in duh ol' neighbuhhood," he said in a voice like DeNiro in *Taxi Driver.* "I tink o'dem like dey're in jail, y'know? Iz like we wuh awl in freakin' prison, and I was duh only one dat noticed and got duh hell outta deah."

At the time, I was living in Manhattan, the self-proclaimed center of the universe. So naturally, I scoffed. But that first morning in Skagen, as I stood buck naked in the clean sunlight that was streaming in the open window, there was nobody to see me for miles in any direction. The mild sea breeze flowed over my body, and it occurred to me:

*The man had a point.*

The bed was empty; it was Saturday morning. Katrina must've gone out for rolls or something. So I found my blue nylon running shorts, and eased into a pair of Tevas the color and consistency of forest mold. Walking out into the dazzling sunlight, I blinked. Then I went to get my Ray-Bans out of the car.

A lot had happened the past week. Ma left on Sunday. I was in-town for a change, and the atmosphere in the office on Monday was weird. Frederik didn't show his beaky face. The pressure was low – like just before a tornado hits. Then he called a meeting of all his direct reports on Wednesday and told us that there would be a blockbuster announcement the next day – illustrious Fielding & Co. had been bought by AmeriBancorp, a financial supermarket that was looking for a jewel in its otherwise tin-plated crown.

By Thursday night, Katrina's condition had taken a turn for the worse – she couldn't concentrate, didn't want to make love, and then woke me up in the middle of the night saying we had to leave right away; she couldn't spend another night in the house. Luckily, we were able to get the rental property a day early. So I came home from work on Friday at noon, and we packed up. But Katrina had forgotten to pick up the Ambien, so we called the drug store. Søren was nice enough to rush through the order, and we picked it up on our way out of town.

Standing on the rock jetty that connected the Sea House to the mainland of Europe, my eyes followed the famous light of Skagen as it bounced between land and sea. The sunlight hit the white shell of the beaches, where it was tossed out into the unruly waves of Skaggerak. There the whitecaps volleyed it back onto the glasslike quartz and mica of the tall dunes which smashed it into the mirror-like surface of the inland sea, filling the atmosphere with the ethereal golden haze of Apollo's fire. So this was the secret of the light. The brilliant, lemon-yellow effulgence of Skagen was the result of a series of reflections.

Just then I saw Katrina coming back with a loaf of bread. We kissed and walked back into the Sea House. As we sat down in the breakfast nook, I ripped into the chewy ciabatta with gusto – I didn't realize how hungry I was.

"You slept well?" I asked.

She nodded. "And I didn't even take a sleeping pill."

"You were really frantic to leave Copenhagen."

"I felt the walls were closing in on me. I was becoming the woman with the *yellow wallpaper*," she almost whispered.

"You seem fine now," I said, avoiding any discussion of interior decorating.

"I am. Perhaps it's the fresh air." And she smiled and held my hand across the breakfast table. We were good again.

After breakfast, I changed into my running shoes and we took a long walk up to the end of the peninsula, called *Grenen* in Danish. We strolled hand in hand along the wild, deserted stretch of beach. The wind blasted us with sand and the surf pounded the rocks along the shore.

"I wish I could snatch and preserve the mood, the splendor of life here," she said.

"Yeah, the weather's been unbearable in Copenhagen. I swear it rained every day in July. Where was the summer?"

"It's like another country. Another world."

It was true. The minute we set foot in Skagen, it was like a dream. Everything dissolved – the stress of Fielding, the haunting atmosphere of Sound House, the hectic pace of city life. Like schoolkids on the last day of classes, we hit the panic bars, the doors opened, and we stepped out into the reality of nature, beauty, and each other. Sea foam lapped at our toes and the briny wash sloshed over our ankles and up to our knees. We splashed and played tag along the water's edge like a couple of kids. She was good at dodging me, and got my competitive juices flowing. We ran seaweed and jellyfish hurdles along a beach of sun-bleached shells.

We talked quietly about why we came to Denmark, this kingdom of rock and sand. I had resisted the move. The winters are long; it rains like 300 days a year; income taxes are a backbreaking sixty percent; and I don't speak the language, a guttural morass so unintelligible that even Danish children have trouble learning it. (There was a study.)

But then again, I figured, there were two of us. The move was important to Katrina, she was not happy in New York toward the end. A lame dancer, she really needed to get back to her home, her roots. It was time for us to live in *her* country for awhile, even if it was hard on me.

As we approached the end of Europe, there was a large gray sign with black bold letters informing us in *three* languages that this was an area of DANGEROUS UNDERTOW. Nervously regarding this northerly Rosetta Stone, I said, "Well, I guess this is as far as we can go."

"What do you mean? It's out *there*," she said, pointing to a sand bar on the horizon.

"Nah, I think we should look at it from here."

Battery Park, this was not. There was no distinct boundary between solid and liquid; little streams and rivulets crisscrossed the sand; and the tongue of land sloped, creating a series of progressively deeper tidal pools. Ahead of us, a trickle of tourists made its way out into the waves. A few souls had already reached the final sand bar – from this distance, they appeared to be in a bark of the damned, foundering amidst the waves.

Katrina, of course, wanted to test the limits, venture out to the point where the eastern and western seas came together confusedly, water not knowing which way to flow. She looked at me over her designer sunglasses and said, "Look, everyone is going out there, even the children."

I shook my head. "It's not safe out there," I said. "What if the tide comes in? We'll be trapped!"

"Oh, we don't have *tides* in Denmark."

"What do you mean? There's tides everywhere."

"Well, I'm going," she laughed.

I wasn't just going to stand there waiting for her like a big chicken, so I stepped out into the wet. I hated the feeling of soggy athletic socks, but the first pool was tame, not bad at all really. The water had been warmed by the sun, and it only came up to mid-calf. After splashing for ten yards, we came out onto a salt-water flat about fifty yards across. The next pool was deeper. The water was cold, and sloshed up around our knees. As we came up again, we stepped onto unsteady ground, my feet sinking in a bit with each step.

As wet as it was out there, I felt like I was in the desert. This extreme world was barren, lifeless. Not a wilted leaf of seaweed or a creeping mollusk survived; only sand and brine and glaring sun. *Water, water everywhere, but not a...* damn, we should have brought a canteen or something. I licked my lips. The wind started whistling in my ear, and I started to get anxious, looking back continually. The Rosetta Sign, its warning unheeded, had shrunk to a pinprick. The late afternoon stream of tourists was moving away from us now, their baseball caps and fanny packs receding into the shimmering distance as they waddled toward dinners of langoustines, salmon and potato salad.

Land's end was visible, a pathetic bar of sand no more than two or three yards across. To get there, you had to cross a channel. I hesitated. Then for a third time, we submerged, this time down to the waist. Katrina was ahead of me and thought nothing of drenching herself. The water swirled, freezing around my thighs and I felt an uncomfortable constriction between my legs. The powerful current swelled up to my chest. It was all I could do to clamber onto the soft shoulders of the islet.

The sea surrounded us now, wild in all directions. Looking back, I could see we were alone, the last tourists of the day. I was a cat on a live wire. Walking upon the waters on faith alone, we could fall in at any moment. At the first doubt.

In front of us was nothing but water as far as the eye could see, really deep water. The peaks of Norway were somewhere out there, incalculably far for a human swimmer. The home of gods and frost giants. Rationally, I knew that this was the end. I stared into the blue, squinting – not knowing what I expected to see, but desperately wanting to see something, *anything*. Yet there was nothing. All that moved upon the face of the waters were our own shadows, rippling below us.

A big wave broke over our kingdom of mush, washing us over into the drink. Sticking my knee into the pillow of ooze, I dug my fingers into the sand and crawled back above the water line, breathing hard. Then the sea receded again, and all was as before. I peered back into the glare behind us. We were seriously far from dry land now. I couldn't even see the warning sign any more. I was sweating, scared. I'd heard of people getting trapped out in bays while digging for clams or cockles or some goddamn thing. What if the water level rose? What the hell were we going to do? I didn't swim so great to begin with, and even strong swimmers could drown in a place like this. The currents were wicked.

I looked at the swirling waters all around us. The Gulf Stream, orderly and confident as American troops, streamed in from the west: columns of crests marching in a continuous pattern. But as the warm water met the chilly fingers of the eastern sea, all hell broke loose. The waves broke ranks like soldiers in a rout, fleeing chaotically in all directions. A fell maelstrom of churning vortexes. I followed the swirls and eddies with my eyes until I became dizzy, wobbly, woozy. I tried to move my legs to steady myself but found they were trapped, held fast in the wet cement of the sand bar. I looked down – my feet had disappeared. I pulled my right foot up with a *squerch*; my foot came up rough and clotted as if cast in adobe. But then all my weight shifted to the left leg, and my left foot sank deeper into the ooze.

"Help, I'm sinking!" I cried.

Katrina grabbed my arm, but it was no use. I couldn't get my balance; I went down hard, denting the bank solidly. I twisted my ankle, banged my knee, and got thoroughly soaked again by the hellacious waves. The shock of the water must've snapped me out of whatever funk I was in, but I don't even remember how I got back to dry land.

I was exhausted. We had been walking for hours. The backs of my calves were sunburnt and tender. My lips were salty, mouth moistureless. I was glad to see the dune bus they call the "sand-worm," and we rode back to town.

We walked the couple of blocks to the jetty, and I was thrilled to see the Sea House, shining the color of Gulden's mustard in the evening sun.

Katrina said, "Beat you back!" and was off like a shot.

"Will not!" I shouted, and with a burst of adrenaline, took off after her, grinding the sand with my roughcast hooves. Her scarlet swimsuit moved gracefully up and down as she ran. I was careful not to ruin the view by running *too* fast.

"I won!" she beamed as she held onto the door handle.

"Hey, you really get an old man's heart started." I smiled and kissed her.

She laughed, pulled away, and walked inside.

"I'm going to have a nice cup of tea and a shower," she said, raising her eyebrows as she walked into the kitchen.

As she reached for Earl Grey, I grabbed her from behind, caressing her breasts. Turning, she kissed me and the moisture of her mouth replenished my arid gums and tongue. I let my hands drift down to cup the roundness of her buttocks and she twisted away, running upstairs in a shower of giggles. I took the stairs two at a time, then got lightheaded in the heat of the close upper room. I opened the windows and allowed the sea breeze to flow in.

Surrounded by pine and glass, before bare windows, we took off each others' clothing in the lemony light. I kissed her golden hair and we came together. On our knees facing each other in the middle of the bed, we embraced: the soft, smooth drama of her body melding with the hard, hairy comedy of mine. I felt a pleasant pain as the sand between us abraded my naked chest and arms. Katrina lay back on the pillows in the sunlight, motioned for me to join her. I lunged for the duvet and made a spring roll of her, wrapping her in the fluffy eiderdown that smelled of lavender, sunshine and laundry soap. I flipped around, pinning her beneath me; I had her feet and lower legs to myself, and went to tickle her feet, which were still wet with seawater and encrusted with pebbles from Skaggerak. She squealed in anticipation, knowing she was completely at my mercy. But I didn't have the heart to torture her. Brushing my lips against her moist ankles and feet, I tasted sea salt. She relaxed and let out a small sigh. I caressed her calves and instep, took her delicate toes into my mouth like some exotic shellfish. *Percebes... Mmm,* I drank in the flavor of brine... seaweed... Blue Points... the Long Island Sound of my memory.

We made love and lay together afterwards listening to the surf and the gulls. I put my ear between her breasts and listened to the rhythms of her body and the sea.

We were at peace.

# 20. Katrina

I could finally breathe again. Trapped behind closed doors in the rain-drenched city for weeks, I'd been a shut-in, an invalid. Here in Skagen, it wasn't just city air I expelled from my tormented lungs, but tobacco smoke and exhaust fumes, dreams and ghosts and Nazis. When I breathed in again, I was fortified by salt air, heather and honeysuckle, and the seaweedy tang of the sea.

This afternoon, Richard and I made love in the pools of sunlight that were splashed across the queen bed in the upper room. The first time in weeks, it was a surpise to both of us. There was nothing wrong with my hormones today! Afterwards, I lay amongst the fluffy duvets and pillows and listened to the *whoosh* of the surf, loud yet quiet. The cyclical rhythm of our first few days in Skagen had brought balance to our lives and harmony to our relationship.

We decided to go out for dinner. As we strolled to the village, I hummed a new song by Shawn Colvin. *Sunny came home to her favorite room, Sunny sat down in the kitchen...* We feasted on halibut steaks, then settled on a bench near the coin-operated telescopes at the "sundown place" to watch the sun slide into Skagerrak.

There was a fine mist in the air, and few tourists on the promenade. No whirr of sirens or rumble of trucks disturbed us. The only sounds were the eternal rolling of the sea and the gentle peeping of sandpipers, terns and golden plovers, as they hopped in and out of the waves along the wet, sanddab-colored strand.

The telescopes on the embankment reminded me of the incident in the front bedroom. What had made so much sense in the night, in the dark, was gibberish to me now. No doubt there were thousands of Nazi-era transits in garages across Europe. Mere bric-a-brac. It meant nothing.

As the sun lit up our faces, Richard said, "It was a great idea to come out a day early."

"It wasn't just an idea, Richard. I felt like an animal in a trap."

"You seem fine now."

"I *am* fine now," I said, giving him a smile. "I slept, and I don't know, being here, I just feel like a different person. Alive again, awake after weeks of sleep-walking.

"You look great. You look just like you did the day we met and walked along the beach on Long Island, remember?"

"Ach, you're just turning on the charm."

"No, I mean it," he insisted. "You're still the most beautiful woman in the room, in every room you're in."

"I don't feel beautiful. Most of the time, I feel like a zombie. You know the song I keep humming? *The days go by, and I'm hypnotized…*"

I'd never told Richard. I stopped abruptly and looked away.

"Something wrong, Skat?"

"I let Søren hypnotize me."

*"What?"* he said, making a face.

"You know he's been trying to quit smoking by using hypnosis."

"Yeah, he mentioned that – doesn't seem to be working."

"Well, I asked him if it could help me remember the parts of my dream that I've been blocking out. So he came over one day and hypnotized me on the sofa in the front room."

"And what happened?"

"I don't remember, exactly. I closed my eyes and breathed deeply. I counted backward. When I awoke again – it seemed like just a minute later, but I saw by the clock that an hour had passed – I could remember everything about the dream."

"But nothing about the session."

"Uh, no."

Richard smirked. "What hadn't you been able to remember?"

"The names on the door were the partners of the law firm where Fa' worked. The man with his back to me is Fa', and he's scratching his own name off the door, as if to dissociate himself from the Firm. Mor says that the week before he died, he was made a name-partner. So I started to think—"

"That somebody killed him rather than see his name on the door."

"Exactly. But when I told Mor, she said there wasn't anybody alive at the time who would have had a motive to kill him – Justesen and Svendborg were already dead years before."

"So you've put the whole Sherlock-Holmes thing out of your mind?"

"I have. No one killed Fa', I accept that, but—"

"But what?"

I choked up. The sun was below the horizon now, and we were alone on the shore. The tears flowed silently. Richard sat next to me and encircled my shoulders easily with his long arms.

"You miss your dad, is that it?" he asked.

"*No.* I mean yes, of course I do," I stammered back. "But mostly I miss the family we used to be. I'm back now. And I want to put it all together again—"

"Sometimes you just can't put Humpty Dumpty together again," he said, putting up his hand.

"Humpty Dumpty?"

"Like the nursery rhyme. *All the king's horses and all the king's men couldn't put Humpty together again.* When the egg hits the floor, all you can do is clean up the mess. You're not going to get your egg back."

"Thanks, that's a nice thought," I said with a wry smile.

"I'm sorry, maybe it's not the best analogy," he said. "But listen, I lost my dad too, remember? Lung cancer, a terrible way to go. I miss him. And I miss the family unit that we used to have."

"Of course you do, you were the Prince."

"I was. But it's not just that. I used to have the feeling that no matter what else happens in my life, in my career, whatever, I always have a home to go back to, a place where I belong. I don't have that any more. I miss that – and I can't get it back."

"Yes, but you *have* a career, a résumé, something you've been building out in the real world for years. What do I have? I've become a woman who decorates, who lunches."

"Like your mother," Richard said, drawing the same conclusion I had. "But what's so bad about that? Ingrid is a strong woman, independent."

I looked out on the half-moon rising, low and orange in the northwestern skies.

"Mor is an intelligent woman, but she never had her own life. She was a decoration. She was the pretty gilt frame. It was Fa's portrait that filled out that frame. When he died, all we were left with was the scaffolding, the carcass of what used to be our family."

"Carcass? That's kind of severe, isn't it?"

"A carcass is what's left when something has been hollowed out."

"Maybe what's missing in your family is communication."

"I did speak with Mor about how she's always treating me like a child."

"Oh, all mothers do that to a certain extent."

"Well, I really told her off, told her I wasn't going to let her baby me any more."

"You did?" he asked, his eyes wide. "What did she say?"

"She agreed. And then I asked her to help me make contact with Claus."

While I tried to put a good face on it, my lower lip started to protrude and quiver as I said this. I turned away and started sobbing, right there on the beach.

"That sounds great... Hey, what are you crying for?"

"I told her I loved her..."

He looked at me and then raised his eyebrows.

"You never told her that before?"

"Not since I was little."

"Well," he said, and took a deep breath, "I'm sure she appreciated hearing it. What did she say?"

"She said she would *support* me." I bit my lip.

"Ah, she didn't say she loved you?"

"No, she didn't mention that."

Richard came behind the bench and held me. "Your mother's not very expressive, Katrina," he said. "I'm sure she loves you – it's just, uhm, she doesn't use that word, you know?"

I stopped crying, and we sat there like that, me resting in his arms, in a silence almost reverent. The moon was high in the sky by the time we started back to the Sea House.

"Your mom never really got over losing your dad, did she?" Richard asked.

"None of us got over Fa's death," I said. "He cheated all of us."

"You sound like you blame him, like you're angry with him for dying."

"Why shouldn't I be angry?" I said, my voice rising. "He went and worked himself to death..."

"I'm sure he did his best for you..."

"You mean I should be grateful for the money he left us?"

"Well, that," he said, "and don't forget your horse, Nickers."

He was teasing, but I was nettled now and talked over him, "Yes, that's right. Let's remember Fa' for all the things he left us: the starter-castle in the first row overlooking the Sound, the sailboat, the grand piano. It's not *what* he left us that's important, it's *that* he left us. And once he was gone there wasn't an 'us' anymore."

By this point, I was wild with rage, screaming, "He had no *right* to go off and die – I wasn't *ready* to lose him! I was nineteen years old. I was cheated! There wasn't anyone to walk me down the aisle. He always said it would be different, that he would be there for me. And he never was."

I broke down, sobbing. Richard held me.

After a long time, I sucked back my tears and said, "Fa' could be so kind and warm when we were together, just the two of us. I would sit on his lap in the big leather armchair in his office sometimes right before I went to bed. He would read me a goodnight story – I laughed at Pippi Longstocking, cried for the Little Match Girl. Sometimes the stories were too long, and I would struggle to hold my eyes open. I would pinch myself or press my fingers into the burgundy wing, feeling the coldness of the studs to keep myself awake. But then finally I'd weaken and put my head on his shoulder. Smell the pipe tobacco on his soft cardigan. And then he'd carry me off to bed and kiss me goodnight. Or we'd sit together and read the newspapers – he would explain everything to me – politics, world events, history, finance, even the comic strips. He was a masterful man, Richard. I wish you'd met him."

"I wish I'd met him too. I would have told him what a wonderful daughter he had," Richard said, and kissed me on the cheek. "Katrina you are not just a decoration. You can do anything you want. You're smart and creative and beautiful and sophisticated. And I love you."

I smiled and knew then why I was with Richard Marchese, why I'd married a foreigner. I had never met a Dane who could say things like that without getting self-conscious or undermining it with a joke. Richard could give compliments and say he loved me without any hindrances inside.

It was getting cold. Enfolding me in his heavy, ecru cable-knit sweater, he held me for a long time. He handed me his handkerchief and I blew my nose stridently through the fog that was rolling in.

Then he said in a low voice, "Listen, you lost your dad eight years ago, but I don't think you ever really processed it. You put your emotions – your anger, your love, your grief – in a deep-freeze. I think maybe you all did. You, your mother, your brother Claus. As long as you were thousands of miles away, your emotions stayed frozen, like Frankenstein's monster. Now that you're back, it's like they're thawing out, breaking out of their icy tomb."

Through the bleariness, somehow this made sense.

"You mean it's time to make peace with my family?" I asked.

"I mean it's time for you to grieve, together with your family. You buried your dad, but you never really recognized what it was that you loved about him, and why you miss him. And you never let yourself be angry with him either. You just threw dirt over everything and tamped it down. Now, after all these years, it's time to dig it out."

"You think that's why I had the dreams?"

He nodded.

"You're right," I said. "None of us ever let ourselves scream like I did tonight. Mor didn't even cry at the funeral. It was all buried deep inside. We didn't say negative things about Fa' because it would have been disrespectful, and we didn't say positive things because we resented him so much for leaving us. So we just didn't say much of anything at all."

As we strolled back home, the full moon had risen white and high in the sky, and our shadows danced on the sand. I felt warmer as we walked and gave Richard back his sweater. He put his arm around me and I put my head on his shoulder.

I was no longer crying. But I had started to grieve.


Wednesday night I took a sleeping pill, and the next morning, I had trouble getting up. I felt queasy and still drowsy, even after eight hours' sleep. By contrast, Richard was chipper and suggested breakfast in town, about five kilometers away. Brøndums, the gingerbread hotel that had been the gathering place for the Skagen painters a hundred years ago, beckoned with a lovely breakfast buffet of smoked salmon, halibut, herring and trout, accompanied by crisp-rolls and black coffee.

After breakfast, Richard proposed we take a walkabout in town, and off we went. As we passed the apothecary shop, a lurid poster in the style of Toulouse-Lautrec caught my eye. I examined the horrific scene done up in garish colors. A woman in a plain dress and white bonnet was lashed to a ladder beside a raging orange bonfire. The goodwife gazed down into the flames, her eyes wide with fear, her mouth gaping. I could almost hear the screaming.

"Look at this, Richard."

"What's that?"

"An exhibition at the Bangsbo Museum. *Hekse i Vendsyssel.*"

"*Hekse* – doesn't that mean witches?"

"Mm-hm. And Vendsyssel is the name of the county we're standing in."

I took up a brochure from the caddy beside the entrance, read the Danish and explained to Richard. "The flyer talks about the persecution of witches in Denmark, mostly in the 1600s. About a thousand witches were executed, including many in this area."

"One thousand, wow, that's a lot."

"Even after witch-burning was outlawed in the 1700s, peasant-beliefs continued strong here. Women were persecuted for witchcraft well into the 19th Century – a woman was lynched by a mob in Vendsyssel as late as 1897."

"What, that can't be right. Maybe it says 1697, let's see."

I handed him the glossy trifold.

"Yeah, well, the print is all smudgy, hard to tell. But at the turn of the century, they had electric lights and phonographs and moving pictures – I wouldn't have thought anyone was burning witches at that stage."

"They didn't burn her. They hanged her. And is hanging a poor folk-healer so different from lynching Negroes in the Jim Crow South?"

"Yeah, well, I guess the world loves scapegoats," he admitted. "You don't actually want to *see* this exhibition do you, Skat?"

"Well, it would be a chance to take a little drive."

"Aw, it's just so beautiful here. And you wanted to see the Buried Church today, right?"

"We could do that tomorrow."

"Well, how far is this place?"

"Frederikshavn, about thirty kilometers away."

"Okay, that's not so far. Is it open today?"

"Yes, till five o'clock."


The road to the Bangsbo Museum took us through the inhospitable "Raabjerg Mile," a vast wasteland of alkali flats, silicon dunes and sulphurous springs.

A wild, alien stretch of country, it's completely unlike the rest of Denmark, which is a sheltered, hunter-green land of rolling hills and orderly fields. The copses and groves between the fields are wolf-less nowadays, harboring nothing more dangerous than roe deer and the occasional fox.

The towering sand-drifts cast menacing black shadows across our path. A single dune can grow to a mile wide and over three hundred feet tall, and at times, it was like we were surrounded by them, like we were being suffocated, baked in a box-canyon of sand. This is the white space on the map of Denmark, the territory marked *Here There Be Dragons*. The undulating dunes even looked like ridgeback dragons, humped as they were and littered with patchy vegetation that grew on their backs. The intense sunlight glinted off the quartz and mica of their surfaces, as if off a dragon's scales. Like dragons, too, these sand-creatures have destroyed whole towns in their time. Only a handful of settlements remain in this region, hugging the eastern, leeward coast; they were rescued at the eleventh hour by regiments dispatched by a wise Danish government some hundred years ago.

Indeed, they were still in place, for the regiments were not soldiers but *trees.* Legions of conifers, planted in straight lines, bravely dug their heels into the sandy soil and faced down the beastly dunes. I was relieved to see these militiamen, scraggly and tired-looking as they were. I was even happier as we rolled into Frederikshavn, the spick-and-span sea-town that harbors Norwegian ferries and a local museum, called Bangsbo.

"This is it? It looks like a private home," Richard said.

"Yes, the Museum is housed in an estate. That's what the brochure said."

"Bangsbo, that's an interesting name. Let me try my Danish," Richard said as we walked up the gravel path. "*Bange* means to be afraid, and *bo* means to live. So this place is where people live in fear – of the dunes, I guess?"

"Don't be silly," I said with a nervous laugh. I didn't know where the name came from, but I knew it wasn't that. I associated it vaguely with Herman Bang, an Impressionist writer of the late 19th Century whom I'd never read. I made a mental note to put him on my reading list.

The familiar poster was hanging on a sandwich board in front of a stately old residence. We paid 100 kroner for two tickets and crept inside the darkened building. As my eyes adjusted to the sudden gloom, waxen figures began to emerge from the darkness of the chamber. The effect was surreal. Distressed women – pilloried, tortured, hanged, pressed with stones, beheaded, and burnt alive on huge bonfires – came at me from every angle. Madame Tussaud herself could not have created a more ghastly waxworks.

"What the hell is this?" Richard whispered. "It looks like scenes from the Spanish Inquisition."

"On the contrary," said an unfamiliar voice, startling me.

I turned to see a dapper, dwarfish gentleman with dark hair slicked back and thick glasses that magnified his eyes grotesquely. Dressed in a short frock-coat, he might have been in "period" clothing, but for his paisley necktie, which was quite modern.

"Excuse me?" Richard said.

"Pardon me for overhearing. I couldn't help but notice your use of the word *Inquisition*. Permit me to introduce myself. My name is Halfdan Bangsgaard, I am *cueraytah heah*," he said in a nearly flawless upper-class British accent.

"I merely wished to point out that what you see here is most unlike the Spanish Inquisition, which was most active in the 1400s under the infamous Tomás de Torquemada and had pretty much run its course by 1610. That is to say, about the same time as the Danish witch trials got going."

"So the Danes were late to the witch-roasting party?" Richard said.

"One could say that. More precisely, I would point out that while the two movements employed similar methods – mock-trials, torture and public executions – they had divergent goals and were totally different historical phenomena."

"How so?" I asked.

He had a ready answer: "The Inquisition was a centrally-organized attempt to rid the Catholic lands of heretics and political threats to the supremacy of the Pope. The charge of witchcraft was rarely employed. Primarily, the Inquisition targeted and executed religious offenders: Jews, Mohammedans, Cathars, and later Lutherans and other Protestants.

"By contrast, witch trials in Denmark, like those in Germany, Scotland, and the Massachusetts Bay Colony, were 'grass roots' affairs in Protestant communities that relied heavily on folk beliefs in Magick, and which died out as such superstitions faded."

"If the goal of the Inquisition was to purify the Catholic countries of heretics, what was the goal of the witch trials?" Richard asked. "Did they even have a goal?"

"Oh, they most certainly did."

We both looked at him with anticipation. He looked from the one to the other of us, as if the answer were obvious. Finally, he said, "To fight Satan."

"Satan?" I asked.

"You see, for thousands of years, people had believed in a distant God. Benevolent, but dangerous. Could smite you if you give Him the chance. So the Faithful were not encouraged to become all-too-familiar with Him. Rather, they should appeal to the long chain of ecclesiastical hierarchy, pray to saints not God directly, et cetera. Then along came Luther and Calvin proclaiming the idea of a *personal* God, a *personal* Savior..."

"I recognize that phrase from contemporary American Bible-thumpers," Richard said.

"Yes, it's fundamentally the same notion. And along with a personal God comes a personal Satan. And this would have been fine too, except that Luther and Calvin took away all means of fighting personal evil: incense, holy water, exorcism, relics all went right out the stained-glass window. It was *unilateral disarmament on a cosmic scale.*"

"So people felt – or imagined – the presence of Evil more than ever, but had no way to defend themselves against it," I concluded.

"Precisely," the Curator said with a self-satisfied smile.

The Museum was nearly deserted, so I ventured to ask him, "Would you mind showing us around a bit, I mean, if you have time?"

"I'd be delighted," he replied.

"What's this scene, for instance?" I asked, stepping up to one of the dioramas.

"Ah, this is the case of an accused witch not far from here, in Jerup, one Mette Jensdatter, who was called 'Hose Mette' – presumably she mended stockings or something. She was condemned to the fire on the 20th of December 1623 in the Viborg Assembly."

"Jerup – didn't we just drive through Jerup on the way down here?" Richard whispered.

"Yes," I replied.

"This is a depiction of how she would have been put to death," Mr. Bangsgaard continued, matter-of-factly.

"Someone once told me that many people were accused of being witches because others coveted their land or spouses," I said, recalling Søren's tales from Sankt Hans.

"Oh, I shouldn't think that would've been a common occurrence," the Curator replied. "You must understand that witches, like most persons accused of crime, are low-status individuals. Elderly, poor, no formal education. It's not likely that Hose Mette had much to be envious of."

"So why were they accused?" Richard asked.

"Many of them claimed to be so-called *kloge koner*, that is to say, 'wise women' or medicine-women."

"They healed people using herbal medicines?" I asked.

"Yes, sometimes they did. But you must remember that neither doctors nor naturalists in the 1600s really had much knowledge of how the human body actually works – people still believed in the Four Humours, the Four Elements, and so on. So the results were erratic. No doubt they cured some; they made others ill."

"You mean on purpose?" I asked.

"I meant by accident," he said quickly, but then paused and continued, "but I suppose that a *klog kone*, if she didn't like someone or were offended by them, could, perhaps, make them ill on purpose."

"How could they do that?" Richard asked sharply.

"In several ways," the Curator claimed. "Psychological, for one. You know, natives who believe in voodoo dolls will feel physical pain at seeing their doll stuck with a pin. Then there are the botanicals. These women would have had a good working knowledge of plants, including poisons and their antidotes.

*"History is littered with poisonings, even from ancient times. The Renaissance especially knew strange manners of poisoning, poisoning by a helmet or lighted torch, by a gilded pomander—"*

"Excuse me, but whose story is this?" Richard interjected as we came to a particularly gruesome reenactment of a witch strapped to a ladder, about to fall into a raging bonfire.

"Ah, we near the end of the exhibit. This diorama tells the story of the most recent witch-burning in Denmark," the Curator explained.

*Why hadn't he said* last?

"Anne Palles, executed in April, 1693," he continued. "Her case was simultaneous with those at Salem."

Looking at the lugubrious scene, Richard asked, "Was she burned alive?"

"No, I blush to say that we stopped short of reality in this particular scene. In the actual case, it was her headless corpse that was immolated. You see, Anne was seventy-three years old when she was condemned by the Supreme Court in Copenhagen to be burnt alive. Given her age, the sentence was commuted by King Christian the Fifth, and she was first beheaded."

"How... merciful," I ventured.

"Quite," the Curator said.

"If these women really were fooling around with poisonous plants, dancing around the cauldron saying 'Bubble, bubble, toil and trouble' and all that, then would you say that they were really *guilty* of being witches?" Richard asked.

"Ah, guilt. It's such a difficult matter," the fastidious man said, grimacing as he tilted his head to the side and waggled the index and middle fingers of his right hand. "Tell me, if the British had quelled your rebellion, no doubt George Washington and Benjamin Franklin and the others would have been hanged for treason, isn't that right?" the Curator asked Richard.

"I suppose so."

"And they would have been *guilty.*"

"W-well..."

"You see it's always the *winners* who determine who is guilty of what. And these poor women, I'm afraid, were not life's winners," the Curator concluded.

We arrived at the last panel, which summarized persecutions of more recent centuries, including modern "witch-hunts" like the McCarthy Trials, Stalin's purges, even the Holocaust. In the background were various newspaper articles. A photo caught my eye and my blood went cold.

"Richard, look!" I said, pointing.

"*For fanden,*" Richard swore. "That's Karl Damsgaard! What's it say?"

"It's old-fashioned language, but I can read it," I replied.

The article from *Berlingske Tidende* was dated July 27, 1897, ninety-nine years ago.

"The article is a report of a woman in Vendsyssel, near the town of Hjørring. She was chased by an angry crowd and lynched... the weather had been particularly hot... there'd been a drought that summer..."

"What in blazes has that got to do with Damsgaard?" Richard asked.

I struggled to find the connection. "I don't know," I said, shaking my head. "His photo is in the next column over. He seems to be commenting on some scandal or other."

"What is he saying?" Richard asked.

"Sin is only shameful in the first person, as in *my* sin, *our* sin. In the third-person, *their* sin, it is quite delightful, an opportunity for scandal-mongering and recriminations," I translated.

"Hm, what do you make of that?" Richard said, turning to the Curator. But he was nowhere to be found.

# 21. Richard

I knew going to see an exhibition about witches would break the mood between us, and sure enough, it did. Not only did we get a complete tour of "101 Decapitations" and an unexpected lecture on the Spanish Inquisition, but in the end we came face to face with our nemesis, Karl Damsgaard, whose photo showed up in an old newspaper article on the back wall of the exhibit. I wanted to ask the Curator about it, but he'd disappeared. Katrina couldn't get out of that place fast enough and waited in the car while I walked up to the ticket lady – the only one in sight with more than wax in her veins.

"Did you see where the Curator went off to?" I asked.

She gave me a shrug and a mealy smile.

Not one to be put off easily, I tried out my Danish, saying, *"Hvor er Herr Bangsgaard?"* pronouncing it first "bangs-god" and then "bongs-gore."

But the lady just nodded her head and said via a series of croaks and glottal stops, *"Museet er nu lukket, kom tilbage imorgen."* The Museum is now closed, come back tomorrow.

*Yeah right, I'd rather have root canal.*

When I got back to the car, Katrina was catatonic, staring out the window. I climbed into the driver's seat and started the engine. "That was whacked."

Katrina just stared straight ahead. "He's followed us here."

"The Curator? Did he come out to the parking lot?" I asked, looking around as if he might be hiding in the back seat.

"No, Karl Damsgaard."

"You mean the newspaper article?"

"Yes – didn't you see?" she asked, turning to me now. "It was the *same photograph* as the one in the dining room."

I pulled onto the two-laner and pointed the car northward, back toward our little sanctuary at Skagen. The sky had clouded up while we were in the museum; the late afternoon light was dull and I turned on the headlights.

"Old Damsgaard was a wealthy lawyer active in society at the time," I said. "The lynching happened just before the turn of the century, right? That was his heyday. No doubt his picture was in the Copenhagen papers all the time. It's just a coincidence."

"Remember *The Celestine Prophecy?*" she asked, reminding me of a book we'd both read last year. "There *are* no coincidences."

"You can't take that kind of thing literally, Skat. For me, 'no coincidences' means you've got to keep your eyes open. Even small things could lead to great opportunities – like that scientist who noticed little plants sticking to his trouser legs and invented Velcro."

"Like us seeing the poster about the exhibition outside an apothecary shop in a small out-of-the way town in Jutland. If we hadn't seen that placard, we would never have thought to visit the museum, so we wouldn't have seen Damsgaard's picture, and read his quotation," she said, her pace accelerating to a gallop. "Richard, don't you see? It's like he's speaking to us from beyond the grave!"

"Nah, that quote refers to some scandal or other that happened a hundred years ago. Probably one of his own, if what Søren was saying is true. What did he call him? A libertine. He was probably screwing half the duchesses in Denmark – pardon my French."

Katrina, ignoring my remark, plowed ahead with a hermeneutical analysis of the text. "Hm, let's see. What did he say, exactly? 'Sin is only shameful in the first person,' wasn't it something like that?"

"Yeah," I replied, recognizing that she wasn't dropping this. *"My sin is shameful, their sin is delightful, an opportunity for scandal-mongering and recriminations.* Something like that."

"What does it mean?"

"Well, scandal-mongering sounds like someone is on the lookout for scandal, probably his enemies, rivals," I said, playing along.

"And recriminations, that's like accusations, right?"

"Well, I take that to mean a counter-charge. So if you've been accused of something, and you hear about a flaw in your accuser's behavior, you can use 'their' sin to launch a counterattack. I guess that's why he calls it delightful."

"So, as Annika would say, Why has the Universe so organized itself to reveal this insight to us at precisely this moment?"

"I don't know," I said with a shrug. "It's just a little witticism – reminds me of Oscar Wilde or somebody like that. Why can't it just be a *bon mot* from a hundred years ago?"

"I don't believe in coincidences," she said, and then gasped and said, "Oh my God, what if he's talking about *us?*"

"What?"

*"Their sin.* What if 'they' are the two of us, the people living in the house he built?"

"Katrina, there's no sense in that – what sin have we committed?"

"I don't know – perhaps we've changed something, insulted him in some way."

"Well… did you ever come across anything when you were gardening, something like that? Did you disturb anything?" I asked, remembering movie-plots.

"No," she said.

We drove on in silence for a few minutes, the bleak landscape rushing by. I was glad we were getting closer to the Sea House.

Then Katrina said, "Richard."

"Yeah?"

"Remember that document that disappeared from the computer screen?"

"Are you still thinking about that? Documents get accidentally erased from computers all the time – as Eddé pointed out."

"Don't you think it was weird how it happened just when you said the word 'ghost' – when you said we had to *get rid* of the ghost?"

"A coincidence, just like Eddé says," I said, feeling quite proud of myself that I hadn't strayed from the Rationalist path.

"The letter that remained – it was a *D*, wasn't it? I don't know why I hadn't thought of it before – it was *D, like Damsgaard."*

I didn't like the feeling in my stomach. My saliva glands didn't seem to be working well, and I smacked my lips to water my mouth.

"You mean you think it was like Damsgaard's calling card?" I said.

"Of course. It all fits, doesn't it?" she replied, her eyes wide. "You insulted him, said we had to get rid of him. You declared war!"

The thought that she might be right flashed through my mind. A little flicker of panic. A sign flashed by. Thirteen kilometers to Jerup. That was the town where they burned the witch. Oh, this was all so damned creepy – witches, ghosts, waxworks – it was like a B-movie. It just couldn't be. But what if – what if Damsgaard *was* following us, haunting us?

"What does he want?" I said, my voice rising. "I mean what the hell does the man want with us?"

"I don't know!" Katrina said. She started crying, shaking. "I don't know."

She was melting down; I had to be the strong one. I had to think. But for some reason, it was hard to think. I felt like we were flying, flying down the road, over the road. *What to do to get grounded again? Grounded. Think, Richard. Take a deep breath.*

I said a tiny prayer, *Oh, please God, help me.*

And as if in response, it came to me: *Remember your basics: drink, eat, sleep.*

"Katrina, look, I'm sorry I yelled," I said gently. I touched her hand. "I'm sorry."

A sign with the black silhouette of a village announced that we were entering the jurisdiction of Jerup. I didn't really want to stop at a place known for persecuting witches, but it didn't seem like I had a choice. It started to rain, and I thought about the beginning of *Rocky Horror*.

"Here's a little town," I said. "Let's stop and get some water. And maybe some groceries. Pasta. Let's get some macaroni and chop'meat; I'll make a gravy and we can eat at home tonight, OK?"

"That sounds good," she said, with a little quiver in her voice.

I stopped the car and we got out. Katrina moved slowly, unsteadily, like an accident victim. I made sure we drank water right away, even before we paid for it. All that salted fish this morning didn't help. We were bone dry.

We bought some apples, and we found everything we needed for a nice Italian dinner, except the Parmigian. So we got some mini-rounds of Bel Paese, an Italian cream cheese, instead. We picked up a decent Chianti too, the kind in the old-fashioned wicker basket.

A gangly, acne-scarred kid rang up the groceries, one-at-a-time. It seemed like he was moving in slow motion. He must've heard us speaking English, because he asked in a thick accent, "Want to buy a lottery ticket, Mistah? Big lottery this time of year."

"No. No, thanks, we're in a hurry," I told him. I only had a five-hundred kroner note, and as the boy made change, I felt like I was hiking at high altitude, my synapses firing at half-speed. Counting—out—the—money, slo-ow. Getting—the—change. End—lessssss.

Finally, we climbed back into the car. We chugged the water and crunched the apples. As the sugar kicked in, we began to feel a little better. *And the water put out the fire.*

"You think maybe we were dehydrated?" I asked.

"Yes, and you're sunburnt from yesterday."

"You too."

"I was starving," she said, talking with her mouth full. "I didn't realize it – but we hadn't eaten since this morning."

As we approached Old Skagen, I gave her hand a squeeze and said, "I could really go for some spaghetti right now, how about you?"

"Sure," she said, and managed a weak smile.


Katrina scurried to and fro setting out tea lights as the sun sank low in the sky. I brought in the groceries and started puttering around the kitchen. The minced onion and garlic hit the hot olive oil, and a wonderful aroma began filling the atmosphere. We began to feel safe again, and our mood brightened.

Katrina sat on a bench by the rough-hewn wooden table reading the headlines in *Jyllands Posten,* the conservative rag. Like the British, the Danes had newspapers aligned with political ideologies; this was foreign to me, because American papers were strictly for entertainment value.

"What's happening in the world?" I asked.

"NASA says they've found primitive life forms on a rock from Mars…"

"…and they're more lively than Bob Dole," I said with a laugh.

"Hmph! Look at this, there's a new political party in Denmark!"

"Oh," I said, not looking up from the browning beef.

"It's called the Danish People's Party, Dansk Folkeparti."

"Folkeparti?" I said, as I added tomato paste and a jar of sauce. "Hmm. *Das Volk*— sounds like a bunch of Nazis to me."

"It is in fact the same name as the Nazi Party in Denmark during the war – but they deny any connection, of course."

"Gee, what a coincidence," I noted with irony. "So they're a bunch of skinheads or what?"

"No, no. Some very legitimate politicians are involved, and they're using the anti-immigration sentiment to win support. Says here they'll have seats in Parliament at the next election."

"It sounds like Le Pen in France – xenophobia," I said, adding black pepper, oregano, basil and a touch of cayenne.

"Fear of strangers never seems to go out of style," she said, no doubt thinking of Eddé's story from the other night.

I nodded and said, "Fear is one of the common factors in our lives. The word on Wall Street is that there are only two things that can move the Market – fear and greed."

"What's everyone so afraid of?"

"Being overrun, I guess – there's only what, five million Danes? The culture could get drowned in a sea of foreigners pretty easily."

"Or the culture could be *enriched* that easily…"

"True, I'd like to think so – I'm a foreigner too, remember."

"Hmph, the new party has gotten popular in a hurry," she said, continuing to read the article. "They have ten percent of the vote already."

The sauce started to bubble violently.

"That's a lot," I said as I turned down the heat, "for a country with about three dozen political parties."

"It is a lot. But just for the record, there are only eight parties in Parliament."

"Are you including the stand-up comedian who was elected last year after promising that he would eliminate *headwind* along Danish bicycle paths?"

Katrina laughed. It was so good to see her laugh.

"Okay, nine," she said. "But the Slesvig party was a joke. Nobody was more surprised than Jacob Haugaard was when he received over 20,000 votes and was thereby sentenced to four years hard labor in Parliament. He actually has to go to *work* now."

"Well, I guess I can't throw stones at countries that elect entertainers to high office, right?" I said with a smirk as I snapped a fistful of spaghetti in two and tossed them in the boiling saltwater.

"Why do you do that?" Katrina asked.

"Do what – elect Reagan?"

"No, break the spaghetti in two?"

"I don't know. My mother always did that. I guess to make them easier to eat?" I said with a shrug as I set the silverware and napkins out on the table

"Hm," Katrina said, and went back to the article. "Oh my God, listen to this:

*The Danish People's Party demands the Government support the National Church... opposes the European Union...*

*Denmark belongs to the Danes. We do not accept a transformation to a multiethnic society..."*

"Denmark for the Danes, huh? They didn't say anything about *lebensraum*, did they?" I asked, chuckling.

"No," Katrina said, not chuckling. "But they do call for a *Muslim-free* Denmark."

"Aw, Jeez. Listen, don't take this too seriously, Katrina," I said, pouring two glasses of Chianti. We were both still thirsty and didn't stand on ceremony. The wine tasted good, warming on the way down. "It'll come and go. Just a few manipulative bastards taking advantage of the anxiety people are feeling."

"I just can't believe serious people are walking about with 'Denmark for the Danes' on their lips. We were supposed to be above all that," she said, shaking her head.

"It's easy to be liberal about things like interracial marriage when it's a handful of grizzled American jazz musicians and their slinky blond wives."

"What about the Jews? Denmark was the only nation in Europe not to give up our Jews to the Nazis," she said with pride.

"Well, that *was* something," I said, running cold water over a few spaghetti and testing them. *Al dente.* Just right. "That's Eddé's story, right? His family would have been saved if they had been Danish Jews. But that was a long time ago."

"We hid them and saved them. It was supposed to *mean* something, Richard," Katrina said, her voice rising. "It was supposed to mean that inside all the cold, boring Danes, there was a heart, a sympathetic heart. Inside these identical villages where everyone goes about their everyday and nothing much ever happens, there were good people, people who defied the Nazis, defied evil. It meant that everyday people could be heroes, not just one extraordinary person like Schindler or Wallenberg but a whole nation. A nation of Wallenbergs."

I set the bowl of pasta on the table, poured the tomato sauce over it, set out the cheese, and sat down, ready to eat a nice meal.

"I don't know, Katrina. The people I've met are very nice and all – but they don't like foreigners much. Including me for that matter. I guess they're just scared – scared that the Copenhagen skyline will someday be dominated by minarets, scared that the church bells will be drowned out by the Muslim call-to-prayer."

"Richard, you're describing total paranoia. Danes have always been progressive, liberal. Danes are sophisticated and international – we look outward, not inward."

"Well, then, let's drink a toast to Denmark, to the way it used to be!" I said, pouring more wine.

"God preserve Denmark," Katrina said, and we "skoaled," clinking glasses and swallowing the hearty wine.

We ate and drank like lost hikers emerging from the wilderness. The Chianti, murky and robust, complemented the starchy, springy durum wheat of the pasta perfectly. The Bel Paese was rich and creamy and melted into the sauce, making swirls of white and pink. The food comforted us, and the wine made us drowsy. Soon overcome, we took shelter under the duvet. We didn't pause to do the dishes.

Or even remove them from the table.

# 22. Katrina

The clouds moved in during the night. I woke in the morning neither tired nor refreshed. I sat up, alone in the big bed and gazed west. Mist lay over the water like a shroud. The ominous blue-grey storm clouds gathering out over the North Sea inspired neither dread nor excitement.

I felt nothing.

Just a vague sense of drifting. Torpor. Weatherless. I would have been happy to stay sitting up in bed, leaning against the oversized feather-pillows, watching as the billows of fog rolled in – but Richard called from downstairs, "Katrina, you want some coffee?"

It took me several seconds to process this complex question.

"Okay," I replied finally. "I'll come down."

Usually I bound out of bed, but this day found me deliberate. I had taken another sleeping pill the night before. I fell asleep right away, but woke after an hour or so. I couldn't get to sleep, I kept thinking about the hellish exhibit, about Damsgaard's message. It was a trap. If I stopped taking the pills, I became sleep-deprived, which made me unable to think straight. But whenever I took the Ambien, I would feel lethargic, drugged the next morning – and I couldn't think straight. Strange that Edvard said it wouldn't make me drowsy. I'd just have to talk to Dr. Madsen about an alternative.

I eased into my slippers, padded to the bath, and went through the rituals of my toilette as if moving to the strains of a dirge. As if I were climbing at high-altitude, I felt stupid: simple tasks became challenging. Should I brush my teeth up-and-down or side-to-side? I had to focus intently on holding and inserting my pearl earrings. My fingers felt thick, like sausages.

Could it be that we had insulted Damsgaard? Going through a manifest, like at an auction, I listed various items of his: the grandfather clock, the piano, the sideboard, the telescope, the portrait. I had buried his photo in the closet, but that was pure – wait a minute. Pure. That was it; I remember thinking that, assuming he did have Nazi leanings – which seemed reasonable from the markings on the telescope – then from his perspective, it would have been a *sin* to bring a Jew into the house. Like Edvard – oh, God, that's when it had all started! The night of the Housewarming, the first time Edvard entered this domain. And the lights went out when he was speaking – what was he saying, something about international peace and understanding. Such talk would have made Damsgaard furious!

Usually, this thought would have made me panicky, but today, standing there brushing my teeth in front of the mirror, looking at my own haggard visage, a trickle of foam escaping the side of my mouth, I just made a funny face and spit.

I stumbled down the stairs and sat at the kitchen table.

"Richard," I said.

"Yes, Skat?" he replied, not looking up from the French press.

"Let's leave here today," I said.

Richard stopped what he as doing and looked across at me from under his brows. "Leave, why?"

"I want to leave."

"But it's only Friday – we have the rental till Sunday."

"Couldn't we just drive away from this place?"

"Yesterday still bothering you?" he asked, pouring out two cups of the thick coffee and sitting across from me.

"I've just had enough."

Looking out the kitchen window at the clouds, he said, "Well, it looks like it'll be a wet weekend anyway. Let's pack up, point the car south, and see where the day takes us."

"We can stop at the *Tilsandede Kirke* on the way – I've seen pictures, but I've never seen it in person."

"What is it exactly?" he said. "I mean how does an entire church get buried in the sand?"

"The dunes stop at nothing. The sand drifts over centuries until it covers everything in its path."

"Fascinating," he said, shaking his head. "Like Pompeii in slow motion."

We parked on the sand-strewn asphalt of a lonely lot surrounded by scrawny pines and walked up to a big sign that bore the story of the doomed kirk.

"What's it say?" Richard asked.

*"St. Laurence's, built in the late 1300s, was the largest medieval church—"*

"It must have been a Catholic Church then, right?" Richard asked.

"Yes, well, everything was Catholic in the 1300s, wasn't it?" I said, before continuing, *"...named for the patron saint of seafarers, St. Laurence's remained the center of religious life in Vendsyssel into the 1700s. By mid-century, the drifting sands began to threaten the church's continued existence..."*

"Where is the church, anyway – it's not completely buried is it? I mean it would be a waste of time to come out here to these pine barrens just to read this big sign..."

"No, it's not completely buried," I said patiently. "You can still see the bell-tower sticking out of the ground."

"You mean the sands covered the whole church up to the steeple? Wow, that's so *Planet of the Apes!*"

"It's just a hundred meters that way, through the trees. We'll see it soon," I said, pointing eastward. "Now do you want me to read the rest, or should we go have a look?"

"No, go ahead, it's just getting interesting. What did the parishioners do?"

*"Sands... threaten the church...* Ah, here it is: *so that the faithful had to dig their way in to reach the church door..."*

"They actually had to dig their way into church every Sunday? Talk about commitment!"

I furrowed my brows and glared at him.

*"By 1795,"* I continued, *"the situation had become so,* uhm, *cumbersome and unsafe that the church was closed by royal proclamation..."*

"Amazing, they dug their way in for forty-five years, two generations—"

"Will you let me finish?" I asked, and he put his hands over his mouth.

*"...and a new parish church built in the town of Skagen, some ten kilometers to the north. The altar was desanctified and the holy artifacts were removed and sold; under the surface of the earth, remnants can still be found, the old floor plus a baptismal font, which was not taken away and sold like the rest."*

"What made them leave the tower standing?"

"It's a marker for passing ships."

"Well, you said St. Laurence was the patron saint of seafarers, right?"

"Yes, that's right."

"So that's it?" Richard asked, screwing up his face and looking around, as if there might be a second enormous sign behind a tree or something.

"That's it," I replied.

"Well, let's see the thing," he said and we walked off in the direction of the ruin.

As we crested a knoll, the tower came into view. From this vantage point, we could see the soft hills as they made their way down to the shimmering waters of the Kattegat. Silhouetted against the blue of the eastern sea and sky with the brilliant yellow ball of the sun behind it, the spire loomed large. It must've been eight or nine storeys high, but appeared even taller, surrounded as it was by nothing higher than stunted pines, bramble bushes and purple heather.

"It's a shipwreck itself," Richard said.

"What?"

"You said it was a marker for passing ships, but the ship is a symbol for the church – our refuge in a sea of disbelief and worldliness – and this one is a wreck."

I saw what he meant: the steeple was like the mast of a sunken ship; the nave, lost beneath waves of sand, was just a hull that had been looted and left.

"Danish churches have anchors on their walls and model ships hanging from the ceilings. The 'nave' of a church in Danish is the *skib,* our word for ship. But the bell tower is too thick to be a mast," I said, looking at the polished white stone of the steeple, its red-tile roof, set ablaze by the morning sun. "To me it looks like a candle."

"A funeral candle," Richard said and gave me a look before entering the dank interior of what had been a church.

A middle-aged woman, her hair the color of liverpaste, sat in a green cardigan at a table in the vestibule, selling tickets, postcards, and Buried Church baubles and gewgaws. No crosses or religious articles were on offer, as it was not a Christian place. Whatever belief had once flourished here was dead centuries ago. A *kirkegaard* is a cemetery, but this was *the burial place of the Church itself. Kirkens kirkegaard.*

I noticed a demure button on the woman's cardigan. DF. She caught my eye and smiled. I compressed my lips and clunked down three gold coins for two tickets and we started up. Richard had to crouch down as we climbed the narrow medieval stairs of hewn rock. Once we were out of earshot, I said, "Did you see that woman's button?"

"What button?"

"DF – she's one of them," I whispered to Richard, then mumbled to myself, "It figures, way out here in the country…"

We encountered several landings where one could stop and rest or enjoy the view, but we kept going. At the top, Richard stopped and pulled me over to the sunny aperture on the east side of the tower.

"What were you trying to tell me on the stairs? What's DF?" he asked.

"Dansk Folkeparti. She's a member of the Party."

"I see," he said, looking out the window.

Patches of sand, meadow and moss were stitched together with pines to form a yellow-and-green quilt that lay in rumples across the tidewater, all the way down to the white fringe of the sea. As we gazed at the beautiful scene, it occurred to me that the colors in the foreground were deepening – shadows were creeping in – but it did not cross my mind that the weather was about to change.

"Richard, do you think it could be the same—" I said. Richard had gone over to the west side of the tower. When I turned to look at him I could tell something was wrong. His face was panicked, and the sky behind him was black.

"Katrina, we've got to get out of here!"

"Why? What's happened?"

"Look for yourself!"

An enormous mass of thunderheads had gathered; even though the eastern sky was clear and the sun shining, to the north and west of us, the skies were charcoal grey. The storm was closing in. As I watched, a crack of lightning rent the air and a peal of thunder rang out like a shot. My heart jumped.

The bell started bombilating. Not the measured ringing of the hour but an insistent clanging: an alarum. From inside the bell tower, the noise was painful. I put my hands over my ears.

"Let's run," I screamed inaudibly, and we trip-trapped down the stone steps as quickly as we could. Bounding through the foyer and out the front door, we were pelted with fat raindrops.

"That's some storm coming this way!" Richard shouted, trying to reach my ears over the incessant tintinnabulation.

We ran down the dirt path, which was quickly turning to mud now, and felt relief as the noise diminished from unbearable to merely deafening. The raindrops grew thicker and we soon found ourselves in a torrential downpour. The car was farther away than I'd remembered, and I flagged behind Richard, falling once in the sloppy path. He turned back to help me up and we continued running hand-in-hand the rest of the way to car. As we got to the parking lot, another bolt of lightning streaked across the sky, seeming to emerge from the very sand of the dunes, and a wild crash of Thor's hammer followed immediately. I gave out a yelp and threw myself into the passenger's seat.

The nerve-wracking clanging seemed more distant as we sat with the windows closed, listening to sound of our own heavy breathing and the pounding rain on the roof of the sedan. My dress was ruined; we were soaked to the skin, our clothes plastered to our bodies – it all would have been quite funny, I suppose, except that we were so anxious about the ominous murk that now stretched from west to east above us.

"The bell must be used to warn locals about impending storms. Should we try to drive back to the Sea House and wait it out?" Richard asked.

"The sky to the south looks more promising."

"You're right," he said as he floored the accelerator and we sped out of the parking lot, kicking up gravel as if we were being chased by demons.

We drove fast through the hideous Raabjerg Mile. I looked up at the series of immense, undulating dunes that rose from the Jysk plain like a great worm that had been turned to stone for its crimes. The rain became hail, and the hail ripped into the silicon flesh of the dune-dragon, and dinged on the hood of the Mercedes like so many ball bearings.

We sped over the flats of Jutland, bisecting towns like Jerup and Frederikshavn without stopping or even slowing down. After an hour of breakneck driving, we reached Aalborg, the city of aquavit; the storm finally let up and we stopped for lunch at a restaurant overlooking the city. As we ate and drank, we began to feel safe again. The panic subsided, though the ringing in my ears continued unabated. I shook my head with no effect.

"Something's not right about that story – it's been bothering me ever since you read me that sign," Richard said.

"What do you mean?"

"First of all, we're in the middle of nowhere. What was that big church doing out there anyway? Why didn't they build it in one of the towns?"

"I think there was a village there," I replied. "It got swallowed up by the sand too. The church was in the middle of the county. It was a compromise, equally convenient to the several towns that were up here at the time – Skagen, Frederikshavn, Hjørring, and so on."

"Hmm," he said, nodding his head. "Okay, let's go with that – it was a compromise – and then maybe the Skagen merchants get rich and decide they don't want to ride so far on Sunday morning. So they get this place condemned so they can build a nice *new* church in town – a modern, Protestant-style church, right?"

"What makes you say that?"

"The candlesticks," he said triumphantly.

"What candlesticks?"

"They sold the holy artifacts – the candlesticks, furniture, the monstrance, even the tabernacle. Everything. If they wanted to relocate the church, they would have moved everything to Skagen. Instead, they sold them because they didn't want to relocate the old Catholic-style church; they wanted their own little Church o' Denmark. So they buried the old one and sold everything, to get enough kroner together to buy all new, trim, modern furniture and altarpieces and baptismal fonts – and *candlesticks*. And whatever they couldn't pry off the walls, they left as grave-goods."

I couldn't figure out what Richard was driving at. I said nothing, just looked at him blankly, dumbly.

"Don't you think?" Richard asked, looking for agreement.

I didn't want him to think I was stupid, so I just nodded and said, "Yeah, I suppose so."

This seemed to satisfy young Sherlock, and I brought up the subject I was trying to raise in the belfry.

"Richard, do you remember the DF-button we talked about?"

"Sure."

"Do you think the return of – oh, it's silly," I said, swallowing a gulp of water.

"No, go ahead, tell me," he said. "It'll bug you later if you don't."

"You'll laugh."

"No, I won't."

"Do you think the return of a name like 'Dansk Folkeparti' signals a return of the old evil?"

His face became drawn. "The *old evil?*"

"Yes. Do you think that evil – like the evil of the Nazis – do you think it's destroyed by wars? Or does it just go underground and wait for the next opportunity?"

I expected him to crack up, but he didn't. When he finally spoke, his face was like stone. "You want my opinion?"

"Yes."

"Grass grows in the cell blocks and courtyards of Auschwitz, but the evil that created such a hell-on-earth never really disappears, no. It lies underneath the surface, and waits to emerge in a new place with a new name."

"That sounds awful."

"It is awful – you've read your European history," he said, putting up his palms. "These horrors return again and again. I don't know – my mother would say that our only chance is to climb aboard the ship of the church, which will sail us safely through a sea of troubles."

"But what if the Church is dead and buried?" I asked, and to this he made no answer.

From the roof of the multi-storey car park in Aalborg, we could see for many kilometers in all directions. To the south lay the peaceful fields of Jutland, enjoying the summer day, brimming with grain parched yellow in the light of August.

When we looked northward, we saw the furious, blue-grey thunderheads and the black heart of the tempest. The tapestry of nature's anger unfolded across the peninsula from coast to coast and as far as the eye could see. Long capes of rain swept darkly across the landscape; flashes of lightning illuminated the onyx plain; and distant thunder rumbled like a sleepless monster.

There was no turning back.

"Wow, we were lucky – looks like we just got out in time," Richard said, relieved.

"Yeah," I said nodding. "Or maybe we've only got one place left to go."

\* \* \*

"Hej, Annika, undskyld jeg kommer så sent – I hate to be late. I just don't know where my mind is these days," I said. "Say, is this place new? What a great name, Café Sneaky-pants!"

"Yes, it has quite a reputation," she said, getting up and giving me two kisses, the French way. "It was a gift for me to wait for you. I made good use of the time."

"Oh. Doing what?" I asked, as I sat down, still fluttering with my shopping bags and scarf and handbag.

"Observing my surroundings. Meditating."

The barmaid came by and we ordered two herbal teas. As she walked away, I said, "Listen, a lot has been happening – I went to the Buddhist Center. The Master was away, but I spoke with someone called Mette Falck."

"Oh, that's great," she said. "Mette is Associate Director, and has been apprenticed to the high Masters in Tibet. I just attended her talk on the evils of animal protein."

"Tomorrow she's coming to feng shui the house. It'll be our second session already; she's prepared a Ba-gua. Would you be willing to come along?" I asked.

Paging through her filofax, she agreed. When I told her that the original owner died falling down the cellar stairs, she said, "Hm, such a dramatic event may have seriously disrupted the energy field."

"You think this could be at the root of all the problems I've had? My insomnia, inability to focus, anxiety?" She toggled her head, noncommittal. I pressed my lips together and then told her about seeing the newspaper article about Damsgaard in the Bangsbo Museum.

"The picture in the newspaper article was the same as the one that was hanging in our dining room. His words appeared in print on the wall of the museum – *writing on the wall*, you know? It was a *message*. FROM HIM!"

The tea came. She frowned and stirred her peppermint infusion, raising up a storm of peppermint leaves, only to watch them settle again. She closed her eyes for a few moments, and then said, "There are no coincidences."

"That's just what I've been saying!"

"Katrina, you have every right – even an obligation – to reflect on this message, to interpret it as you would a dream."

I told her the message, and she said, "Reading this produced a strong reaction in you?"

"I almost *fainted.*"

"Then for you, it is meaningful. What does the word 'sin' mean to you?"

"Well, my first thought was that 'their sin is delightful' might be Damsgaard talking about us, about me and Richard."

"How so?"

"I found an eagle and swastika marked on the telescope in the front bedroom. I think he may have been a Nazi informant, watching the coast, from the front room, you see?"

She kept nodding and listening.

I continued, "So, when we brought Edvard, who's Jewish, into Sundhuset... Remember, all the trouble started at the Housewarming."

"When the wineglass exploded?"

"Yes: The lights went out while he was speaking—"

"And the wineglass cut his hand. There was blood everywhere," she said, nodding.

"So perhaps Damsgaard is telling us, from beyond the grave, that we've sinned."

She drank all this in with a shock of peppermint. I thought she was about to agree when she shook her head and said, "I don't understand. The quotation was 'Their sin is delightful.' Such a sin would not delight him."

"What do you mean?" I asked, caught short at the quick turnaround.

"Think more personally," she advised. "What does 'sin' mean to *you*? Is there something you feel guilty about?"

"Well, I have been feeling badly about how I've treated my mother and brother," I said. My lower lip started to tremble.

"Do you feel it was 'shameful' that you ran away?"

I looked down, embarrassed. "Yes. Yes, I suppose I do," I said. "And 're-criminations,' that means *counter-charges,* right? That may have to do with Claus too. We fell out amidst mutual accusations. And we *were* glad of it at the time. It was 'delightful' in a perverse way, because it allowed us to escape what was really bothering us: we were both in pieces over Fa's death. Over our guilt."

She seemed surprised. The word hung in the air for several seconds before she said, "Hmph. I am surprised to hear you say 'guilt.' After all, *you* didn't kill him."

"No. No, of course not. No one did. But..."

Now it was my turn to pause, sipping my chamomile infusion thoughtfully.

After a long while I said, "I don't know. I can't speak for Claus, but I felt very confused about the whole thing. I loved Fa', but I was so angry and resentful toward him. For never being there when it counted – for my birthday party when I was seven and my first ballet solo when I was twelve, and how many piano recitals and riding competitions and school trips. One time he showed up to a parent/teacher meeting and our teacher, Fru Sommer, was so flustered – Fa' could be intimidating – that she forgot herself and admitted that she didn't know I *had* a father."

"How was your brother's relationship with him?"

"One time when I was in first grade – Claus must have been in third – he drew a picture of our family in crayon. There we were: Mor, Claus, me, our cat Silke. But no Fa'. As if he didn't exist."

"What happened when your father saw it?"

"He never did. Mor took one look at it and completely lost control. She screamed at Claus – she didn't raise her voice very often, so I really remember it clearly. She said it would hurt Fa's feelings to be left out like that. '*He would die if he saw it,*' she said and ordered Claus to draw him in."

"Did he?"

"I never saw the drawing again. We never spoke of it."

She seemed to take this in. Then she screwed up her face and said, "I still don't understand why you use the word *guilt.*"

"I hated him sometimes. Then I would feel bad about how I, well, manipulated him. I used his feelings of guilt about being away to *get* things from him, material things. When he was gone, I became angry with him, blamed him for cheating me out of all those years. But then I felt guilty about being angry. And I felt guilty about accepting all the material things instead of insisting on what I really wanted, which was to *be* with him.

"Oh, why didn't I fight with him, why didn't I confront him and tell him I loved him and just wanted to spend time with him? That I didn't need the horses and boats and grand-fucking-pianos!"

Little rivulets of tears were flowing steadily down my cheeks now. Annika offered me a tissue, which I took and dabbed my eyes.

"Suddenly," I said through the tears, "without me ever *once* thinking about him dying – he was always healthy as a horse – suddenly, it was too late!"

I cried openly after that. I was beyond being embarrassed. Finally I collected myself and said, "Do you think I'm crazy?"

"Katrina, I really appreciate that you've shared all this with me. You are not crazy. What you are experiencing is the result of emotions that have been bottled up inside of you for years. Your normal feelings of grief – and anger and guilt and resentment – have escaped from their bottle, and like the genie in the story, when they emerge, they tower above us."

"Do you think it's good that I've let these monsters loose?"

"Yes, of course."

"Are these feelings are the true cause of everything that's been happening?" She took my hand. "We'll find out soon."


The next day we sat in the window seat like a pair of Siamese, waiting for Mette. Wearing an unbuttoned raincoat and loosely-wrapped scarf, she swooped down Rosenborgs Allé from the west, her outer garments flapping in the breeze. Skidding to a stop directly in front of Sundhuset, she stalked about in small circles, her head moving forth and back, forth and back. Her sharp, furtive eyes canvassed the property, and then she closed them. With her elbows at her sides and forearms outstretched, palms up, and first three fingers of each hand touching, she meditated for several minutes, giving no sign she was aware of our presence.

We stared at the display, not knowing whether we should join her.

*"Hvad gør hun for noget?"* I asked.

"I have no idea what's she's doing – meditating, I suppose," Annika said. "Based on her last visit, how would you describe her survey technique?"

"Very different. When my friend Hester assessed our apartment in New York, she noted carefully the locations of each table, chair, mirror, desk, and bed. So she could construct a proper Ba-gua afterwards. Mette took no notes. In each room it was the same: a quick series of rapid eye movements and then she would close her eyes."

"She's using the *inner* eye."

"Yes, I suppose so," I said, glancing out the window. Mette strutted up the walkway, stopped halfway and perched on the brick edging, facing east toward the water.

She stood there meditating.

"What sort of person is Mette?" I asked.

"She's what we call an *old soul,* the kind of person who can gaze into your eyes without blinking," Annika said. "At first I turned away, but then my eyes reverted. She regarded me so calmly, so peacefully that I wanted to return the gaze, to be worthy of being a mirror for such a person. It felt as if she was merely looking in the direction of my eyes, looking through me."

"You're sure you're not a little in love with her?"

"No, not the way you mean. Listen, I just love the way she has about her – she's never in a hurry. She always listens when you talk, she's comfortable with long silences. Time and space seem to flow over her effortlessly."

After what must've been about five minutes, she began walking the perimeter, grasping hold of certain trees and shrubs, circling the grounds once before coming to rest directly in front of the door of lacquered vermilion.

I opened the door. Dressed simply in flowing garments of deep blue, Mette looked ordinary enough; other than the crest of white hair, she would not stand out in a crowd.

We moved into the dining room, and Mette took charge, outlining the agenda for the session. She told us to take notes (we did), how much time we would spend together (two hours), and that her role was not to *fix* anything (the fixes were up to me).

Then she said an odd thing: "In the end, I sense that you may decide to leave this place."

"You mean move?" I asked, but she didn't respond. She did that annoying "allow the silence" thing, looking in my eyes as if trying to find a flaw in the retina.

"My goodness, is that the only way?" I asked. "We just got settled in. How could we explain it, justify it? And besides, wouldn't it be unfair to dump these problems on the new owners? Wouldn't that be – bad karma?"

Mette let the words hang in the air for a couple of seconds and then said, "No, not at all. There is nothing immoral about moving: the next family may be better attuned to the property. You would not suffer karmically."

Waving off further debate, she took out her homework. Extracting a scroll from a metal tube, she showed us the eternal form of the Ba-gua, an octagon superimposed on the floorplan.

Annika asked, "Are ghost-like phenomena the result of there being too little energy?"

"You've been studying, I see," Mette said with a smile. "A dwelling near a graveyard is the classic example of the sapping, sycophantic energy you are talking about. I have examined such places – they are dull, depressing, and the people living there are prone to clinical depression, constipation, and respiratory infections."

"That's just what I was thinking of," Annika said.

"Sundhuset is nothing like that," Mette declared. Annika's face fell. "This is Sound House. Strong, masculine *yang* energy blows in off the Sound. The front door is bright red. The open floorplan allows Qi to flow smartly through the living room, dining room, and kitchen, and right out the back door, like a wind-tunnel."

"Sometimes it does feel like that," I nodded.

"The stairs leading to the second floor are in the rear, protected from this torrent of energy," Mette explained. "This leaves them relatively protected. I suppose you feel less anxiety upstairs. Is that right, Katrina?"

"The feeling is worst on this floor, but I still have trouble sleeping up there," Katrina replied.

"Yes, I believe you do. Because the overall tuning is so high. But still it would be much worse if you tried to sleep on this level."

"You're certainly right," Katrina answered. "Even Richard doesn't even like to be down here alone late at night."

"I do not doubt it. If you are having trouble falling asleep, do not come down here to read or even to make tea. Once you are upstairs for the night, by all means, *stay there.*"

I nodded, and Annika asked, "How can we slow this energy down?"

"To lower the tuning of a room, one allows the energy to pool up, to form eddies – it must not blow through the rooms like a hurricane," Mette explained.

"So we have to chop up the house, put in walls?" I asked.

"That's the idea, but it needn't be so dramatic a solution. I would suggest we start with small moves: put a curtain between the living and dining rooms, for instance, or better yet, a Japanese screen. Also within the rooms, make sure you have centerpieces on the tables. Try to focus the energy on specific central objects – flowers, candlesticks, low tables, a bowl of fruit. These central objects should be simple, preferably made of wood, stone or natural fibers rather than metal or glass."

I nodded and took notes. Pointing to gaps in the diagram, Annika said, "The layout does not fit very well into the Ba-gua."

"Good, Annika. Can you show me where the gaps are?" Mette asked.

"Look here, for instance," she said, pointing to a spot on the east side. "There is an indentation in the floorplan where the Relationship Corner should be."

"Yes, that's a fact," Mette replied. "Katrina, if you don't mind, tell me about your relationship with Richard. How have you been getting along these past few months?"

"Fine. I mean, okay I guess," I said, looking down. "It was better in Skagen."

"Compare for me the time you have been here together with Richard with the time you spent together in New York. You were more intimate there, weren't you? Emotionally, sexually?"

"Yes."

"Katrina, you need to expand the energy footprint of the Relationship Corner."

"I placed a crystal there," I started to explain, "hung photographs of us—"

"Yes, I have seen this, and I must commend you on performing the gap analysis correctly; on the other hand, the cures will not sufficient to bridge the gap," Mette said.

"Why not?" I asked. "In New York, this is what all the feng shui practitioners do to energize a section of the Ba-gua."

"There are many paths, Katrina, but only one Way," Mette said with a flourish of her hand. "Hanging a four-ounce crystal can have no significant impact on the energy flow across the domain."

"Is that your interpretation?" I asked.

"No, it is a physical reality. You see, Nature is a living thing, an organism. Like all living things, Nature must breathe. Qi is the breath of Nature."

"So the flow of Qi is our connection to the breath of Life itself," Annika said.

"Yes, Annika. This is why the *flow* of Qi is so important. Too much or too little movement can disrupt Nature, disrupt Life itself. The results are discomfort, discord, illness, even death."

"I learned this also in New York: to seek a balance of warm and cool colors, place furniture harmoniously throughout the dwelling," I said, remembering why I got into feng shui to begin with. The harmony.

"Yes, you have learned well," Mette said. "And so you also appreciate that like matter or energy, if Qi does not move properly, it can get stuck, pile up, like oxygenless water in the depths of the sea."

Mette took a sip of the tea to allow this to settle in. "I feel a great deal of sadness and 'stuck' energy in the house. Are you surprised to hear this?"

"No, on the contrary, I'm amazed at how much you've understood in such a short time," I said. "I feel trapped, depressed."

"To change the flow of energy, you will need to make use of *kinetic* objects – things that vibrate, move, make noise – or *substantial* objects: furniture, walls, heavy structures; things that have mass – and therefore energy."

"Like Einstein's equation," Annika said, like the "teacher's pet" she used to be.

"Indeed," Mette said with a nod. "An example would be placing a large stone or crystal in that section of the garden. Or you could use color."

"Can we use red, I love—" Annika started to say.

"Excellent that you thought of red, and in many cases it would be the perfect color to employ. However, given that Sundhuset has so much strong *yang* energy, perhaps one should consider butter yellow or pumpkin—"

"What about wind-chimes?" I asked.

"Yes, I adore wind-chimes," Mette replied, taking a sip of green tea. "You also need to remove all mirrors except for those in the bathroom or inside closets."

"Why?" we both asked.

"Constantly at work, mirrors are unnatural and disturbing, often responsible for insomnia and anxiety. In a long-term study at a mental hospital, mirrors were the first objects attacked by the patients. None of them attacked pictures of natural settings."

Taking notes, I said, "Mirrors must go."

"Yes, and as we examine each section of the Ba-gua, let's keep in mind the five elements: fire, metal, wood, earth, water."

"Not air?" I said.

"Air is the medium," Mette explained patiently. "But it is not one of the five traditional Chinese elements which form a circle of creative destruction: water douses fire, fire melts metal, metal cuts wood, and so on."

"But feng shui means 'wind and water,' doesn't it? Surely air must have some role to play," I said.

"Feng shui refers to the healthy, renewing qualities of water," Mette said. "In arid steppes and deserts, tribes wander, restless nomads. Only at the water's edge do they find rest. So too is it in your home: the Qi that speeds through the air of your home can also be returned – *at the water's edge.*"

"So we need a water feature of some kind? Like a pond?" I asked.

"Or an aquarium?" Annika tried.

"Many design elements can provide the element of water – living plants for example. As we have seen, the main line of energy runs from the front door to the back door and out into your lovely garden which is full of green plants holding a tremendous amount of water. A secondary flow sinks down to the fuggy cellar."

"So you would add plants in the living room, right – to keep the Qi in there for a while?" I asked. "That's a great idea. I love plants. I can't think why I didn't add more of them myself."

"Yes, plants will also absorb pollutants in this urban atmosphere, and will produce oxygen. If you like fish, by all means add an aquarium as well," Mette said, with a nod to Annika. Removing a crimson folder from her bag, Mette said, "By now we have discussed most of the key elements of the plan, which is also described in writing in the report I will leave with you."

It felt like the session was ending, but we were only halfway through the two hours. "Are you going to survey the rooms again?" I asked.

"No, but," she said, lifting her head and inhaling, narrowing the eyes as if she were about to sneeze. "I would like to examine the cellar once more."

"I haven't been down there in weeks," I said.

"Is that so," Mette said and turned to Annika for explanation.

"Katrina fell down the cellar stairs a couple of months ago," Annika said.

Mette widened her lips into a smile. "I understand," she said knowingly. "We'll go slowly, Katrina – but we must face this. It's important."

I agreed and we got up from the table. Mette approached the small door under the stairs that led to the cellar and said, "I'll go first."

Mette went first, followed closely by Annika. I felt a bar of ice in my stomach. As we descended, when she reached the third or fourth step, Mette swayed visibly, and stopped.

"There's no need to push, Annika."

Annika made no reply, but gave me an innocent look. We continued down, and from the bottommost step, Mette spotted the trap.

"What's behind this wooden panel?" she asked.

"It's a crawl space," I said.

"Ah, another place for energy to dissipate. Unless you need to access this space regularly, I would advise you to seal it off," Mette said.

"But I thought there was too much energy," I said. "Isn't it good to have *yin* areas like this?"

"No. One must *never* energize a subterranean chamber. The consequences can be grave. You see, the moist, cold cellar draws Qi down from the living areas with great force – sucking the life out of the house. You might want to consider installing a wood stove or dehumidifier in the basement to heat and dry this area, reducing the flow."

"Maybe a box fan—" I started to say, remembering Niels Dahl.

"Oh, and one more thing," Mette said.

"Yes?"

Mette paused, and then pronounced, "You'll need a dowser."

# 23. Ingrid

Dowser. I had never heard the word before.

"*En hvad for noget?*" I asked my daughter as we sat in the solarium overlooking the Sound.

"You know, one of those men who walks through fields with a Y-shaped stick and finds water," Katrina explained. "Didn't you ever see one growing up in Jutland?"

"Oh, I've heard of that – one sees them in Westerns every once in a while – but no, I never saw one in Jelling. I don't suppose there's much call for their services in Denmark: one can dig pretty much anywhere and find water, Skat.*"

"But it won't always be *auspicious* water," my daughter told me, which was the first clue that something had gone awry.

"What's the difference?"

"Mette says that there are many paths but only one Way."

"Hmn, the woman talks like a fortune cookie," I said and took a long drag on my cigarette.

I narrowed my eyes and took a hard look at my grown-up daughter. Katrina seemed thin. *Was she was living on coffee?* And as we sat there, she kept fidgeting – she played with her hair, she scratched her teeth. This was not at all like her. *Was she on drugs?* Ever since she'd come home, I'd had the feeling that something was wrong. Yes, the years and miles had come between us, but there was something else. Something was not quite right inside her.

Now she'd dumped a full load of hocus pocus on me. Someone had pushed her down the cellar stairs; she's been hearing footsteps, smelling smoke. Now she'd gotten some Buddhist woman to come in and rearrange the furniture. She was really in the deep end of the pool. I didn't know where to begin.

"Let me get this straight," I said. "This woman—"

"Mette."

"Yes, indeed, Mette, whom you met in the corridor of the Buddhist Center, came in and analyzed the 'energy flow.' She told you that to 'cure' the house, you need to 'install' some plants and a Japanese screen, remove all the mirrors—"

"Except in the bathrooms and closets."

"Right," I said, nodding. "And hang bamboo wind chimes to energize your Relationship Zone."

"The Relationship Corner of the Ba-gua."

"Yes," I said, smiling and nodding the way one does to a toddler or incompetent. "Then she informed you that the cellar is damp, which I'm sure it is, and advised you to find a man with a forked stick to see if he could locate the source of the underground flow."

"Yes, that's right," she said. "What do you think? Does it sound crazy?"

"Oh, Katrina I had no idea you were so... superstitious," I said, looking away.

"Mor, I don't know what's going on, but there's something deeply wrong in the house." The look on her face was like when she was a little girl and she fell down and skinned her knees. Or when Per failed to materialize at one of her recitals.

"Skat, let's not get hysterical," I said. "What's happened? Has that husband of yours—"

"Richard's not the problem. He's been great."

"Well, what does he think of all this? Does he know about the man with the forked stick?"

"The dowser," she corrected, pulling away. "No, I haven't told Richard about that yet. He's in Paris till Friday."

"Your man seems like a practical cat – I don't think he'll go in for that sort of thing."

"Richard was very supportive of feng shui when we were in New York. You know it's a very respectable practice in America now – the Clintons had the White House feng shui'd, for goodness' sake."

"Yes, I've no doubt," I said. "And the Reagans consulted an astrologer on a daily basis."

"I was thinking of having my chart done," she said, looking at her hands.

I didn't say anything, just poured myself some more Earl Grey, and fortified myself before continuing. Katrina's eyes filled.

Putting my hand on her forearm, I said, "Skat, is there something *else* going on?"

"What do you mean?"

"I don't know, you and Richard haven't had any children yet. I thought perhaps—"

"There's nothing wrong with me!"

"I didn't say there was," I replied, trying to calm her down, but it didn't work.

"You always make things out to be my fault."

"I never said anything was your fault."

"Yes, you did. You wish I was more like Claus – my dutiful brother, who has never left your side, his productive wife pumping out blond babies on a regular schedule. Well, I'm sorry to disappoint you, but *I'm not Claus*, okay?"

I confess this made me angry, but Katrina wasn't quite herself, so I replied in an even tone, "Katrina, I care equally for *both* my children."

"Go on, admit it," she said. "You *always* wished I was more like Claus. And you wish I'd never left home to become a dancer. You would've had me marry some bloodless banker from Bispebjerg, then stay home and have babies like you did!"

This stung. But I bit my upper lip and managed to say, "I never regretted staying home with you. You and your brother were my life. After you and Per left—"

"Per and I *left* you? Fa' *died*, Mor! He's dead. He didn't leave you for another woman. And I left because I just couldn't bear it any longer, couldn't bear the insinuations and sniping, the favoritism. And all the *not-saying*."

"Katrina," I said, livid. "You've never talked this way. What have I done to deserve this kind of treatment? I thought you left to find opportunity in America, where they specialize in that sort of thing. And what do you mean, favoritism? I *never* favored either of my children. I treated you as equally as I could."

"It was always easier for Claus," she shot back. "He used to say he was a member of the 'original family.'"

"Oh, that's just something older children say."

"No," she said. "In a way he was right. The three of you were birds of a feather with your crossword puzzles and chess games and bridge. I would want to play tag or dance or explore. There was no room for me in the birdhouse."

"I'm sorry you had such a miserable childhood," I said quietly.

"Me too!" she said, as her sobs grew louder.

"A lot of children would have been grateful to have all the advantages you did. You say there was no room for you, but you had your own room – and your father got you a horse, a piano. You were his princess; he pampered you, spoiled you really. That's it. You're so spoiled you don't know how lucky you are."

"I didn't ask to be anyone's princess. I didn't want all those things," she said. "All I wanted was for him to come home, and by the time he got around to it, he was dead."

I thought about Per, and how the four of us used to be together. Oh, it wasn't so bad, I suppose, especially in the early years, before the drinking got the better of him, made him paranoid by the end. We had some good holidays. After a period of decompression – it would take two or three days for Per's work-fever to subside, for the angst and stress of his job to dissolve sufficiently for him to really be with us at all. But then it would be pleasant to be together, in the garden or on the water.

"Your father was a man of his generation, Katrina," I said with a sigh. "It wasn't always easy for me, raising the two of you by myself. But men of that era weren't comfortable with tots. Your father never changed a diaper, never made your lunch; he never took you to school or met with your teachers. That was my job. And to tell you the truth, I loved every minute of it," I added, my voice catching.

A tear poked out from the corner of my right eye, and I quickly wiped it away.

Katrina saw it and softened. "You did it well, Mor." And then she hugged me. Not the brittle, polite bend-at-the-waist, peck-on-the-cheek embrace of adulthood, but a child's firm clutch. My girl was trembling by now, and started to sob.

"*Saa, saa.* There, there," I said softly, patting her back.

"I love you, Mor," she murmured into my shoulder.

Katrina had been a happy child, brimming with curiosity, enthusiasm, *livs-glaede.* But she had never functioned as well in the family group as Claus did. Perhaps she resented being the youngest, lowest-ranked, or perhaps she was just more artistic, temperamental.

"I love you, Skat," I said.

After the longest time, we finally pulled away from the embrace – we hadn't hugged like that since she was a little child – and her eyebrows flew up.

"Mor, you're crying!" she exclaimed.

"I guess I am," I said, widening my lips to form a sad smile. My chin trembled slightly.

"Mor, I've never seen you cry," she said. "Not even at the funeral."

"Oh, of course I did. You just didn't see it."

"I was so angry, angry because he always promised to spend more time with us. And then it was clear it would never happen. I felt so cheated."

"You were cheated. When was that man... Skat, you were already nineteen years old and Claus was already at University – when was he going to wake up and recognize that he had a family?"

"He didn't know how to be a family member."

"Oh, he was a terrific family member – to his clients, to his colleagues at work. His partners *adored* him! Held dinners in his honor, gave him pens and plaques and a gold watch, but—"

Katrina held a hand up to her cheek and drew breath.

"What's wrong, Skat?" I asked.

She looked down, then said, "Nothing."

"It wasn't nothing. Tell me, did I say something wrong?"

"The gold watch, the one you gave me when I first returned to Denmark. The thing's cursed, I wish I'd never set eyes on it. And to think I ruined my relationship with Claus over it."

"With Claus? Oh, yes, now I remember," I said. "You both wanted it."

"It was so stupid," she said.

"Oh, Skat, people often fight about little things, stupid things. The biggest fight Per and I ever had was over a toaster."

"A toaster?"

"Yes, I wanted a two-slice toaster and he wanted the big four-slicer. He wanted the speed and efficiency of making four slices of toast at the same time, and I wanted more counter space." I paused as a thought dawned on me, then continued. "And I suppose, subconsciously, I didn't want him to eat breakfast so fast and run away so soon. And perhaps I didn't like him controlling things in my kitchen when he controlled so much in my life already. Anyway, whatever the reasons, we argued bitterly and it was a long time before things between us were all right again."

"I don't remember ever having a four-slice toaster at home," Katrina said.

I smiled and said, "No, we never did."

"So you won – good for you, Mor!"

I considered this, then said, "No, I lost. We both lost, walked away bruised. And while I did get to keep the two-slicer, I had to endure Per's glances every morning for a long time afterwards."

"The fight over the pocket watch seems so silly now."

"You weren't fighting over a pocket watch. You were fighting over an heirloom, a piece of your father, whom you had just lost, suddenly and without recompense."

"But it was just a gift-watch, the kind they probably give every partner after a certain number of years."

At this, I stopped and looked out at the waves, took a drag on my cigarette. She noticed.

"Mor?" she said. "It was just a standard gift watch, wasn't it?"

"No, as a matter of fact, it wasn't."

I remembered the Tribute Dinner like it was yesterday. The luxurious banquet was held at the D'Angleterre. Per was young then, and still more in love with me than the curves of a wine bottle. Trim and tall, he led me around the dance floor as the swing band kept up a raucous tempo.

"It was in the early sixties," I recalled. "There was a Gala for the Fiftieth Anniversary of the founding. It was quite a do! All the partners and their wives were there, plus the associates, office staff, and a few friends like Niels Vier Dahl. One of the original founders had died."

It was neither Justesen nor Svindborg but a third man, one who had to leave in some disgrace a few years after founding the Firm. I tried to recall his name, but couldn't, and it occurred to me that I may never have known.

"In his will," I continued, "he declared that certain personal possessions were to be bestowed upon the surviving partners, based on seniority. The eldest partners received the most luxurious items – diamond cufflinks, an extraordinary ruby ring set with amber and cobalt, an original oil painting by Eckersberg."

"And Fa' got the watch?"

"Yes, that's right – he had just been accepted into the partnership. He was very proud."

"So it's a valuable antique – is that why Claus wanted it?" my daughter asked, a bit cruel, but not entirely without warrant. My son can be quite pecuniary at times.

"No, I don't think so," I said. "Claus wanted it because it was his father's – and perhaps also because he knew *you* wanted it."

"Fa' did want me to have it, you know. He told me so."

"Yes, and he probably told Claus the same thing at some point: it was a *man's* watch, after all. And a lawyer's timepiece. I believe it chimes on the quarter-hour—"

"A chiming pocket watch, I've never heard of such a thing."

"Yes, it reminds the barrister in question to bill for the interval, you see."

"Do you still think Claus wants to have it? It sounds perfect for him," she said with a smirk.

I wasn't at all sure he would want it any more. He's so proud. He certainly wouldn't take it if he saw it as something his sister gave him out of pity.

When I hesitated, she said, "Can you help me and Claus make up? You promised you would."

"I don't know, I wouldn't want to get in-between—"

"You're *already* in-between, you're our mother," she interjected. "Oh please, Mor? Invite the two of us out for a sailing trip, the weather's still fine!" she said, crouching next to me, wrapping her hand around mine.

"Sailing?" I asked, incredulous. "Oh, it's too late in the season for that. Anyway, I haven't taken the boat out in years."

"But you still have it? It's at the marina still?"

"*Chancen*? Of course."

"So have old Herr Nansen get it ready and we'll take it out this weekend. Oh please let's do it – it's the only way Claus will see me. I invited him and his wife to dinner, they didn't even come."

"I know. But my boat is docked, and that's where it's staying. We'll just have to find another way—"

"Just think about it, Mor, please?"

I was reluctant, but she was right about one thing: the weather was fine for late August. I looked out over Øresund and the sun on the water, dappled and sparkling, tempted me. To venture out on the waves with my two children, my two grown-up children, was alluring.

"All right, I'll think about it," I said.

"You promise?"

"Yes, I promise. To think about it."

# 24. Edvard

The pavement was cracked, a jagged scar running diagonally across the heaved surface. I nearly tripped as I came up the walk. What could have caused it? The doldrums of summer were done drumming, but it was hardly time for frost damage. Hearing voices, I walked round to the back where the party was already assembled on the terrace in the garden.

Richard had called from Paris yesterday. From his tone of voice, I got the sense he wanted to talk with me about something privately. He asked me to come by for cocktails and a light supper on Saturday afternoon, it would be just the three of us, plus their neighbors, the Reverend Pearson and his wife. Richard was down there five days a week now, which I didn't like. Not good for Katrina to be alone all the time.

Katrina looked tired, but otherwise well as she introduced me to the Reverend George Pearson, a white-haired gentleman with a wry smile, watery blue eyes and flaring cheeks of burgundy.

Extending my hand to the old fellow, I said, "Please call me Edvard."

"It's a pleasure to meet you, Edvard," he said. "Katrina has told us so much about you. Please call me George."

"You say 'us,' but I don't see your wife. Will she join us?"

"Ah, well, I rather doubt it. I'm afraid she's a bit jet-lagged. You see we just returned from Canada yesterday."

"You were touring?" I asked.

"No, we were there visiting our youngest son, Alfred and his family. Unfortunately, none of our four children live in Denmark – we have three in England, and Alfred in Toronto."

"That's a great town, Toronto," Richard broke in. "Very international. Great Asian food."

"Indeed. What I love about Asian cuisine—" said the Reverend, who seemed about to launch into a story when Katrina interrupted.

"The punch is ready," she announced. "Come, let me give you a glass of Pimm's-and-lemonade."

"What's that?" I asked Richard.

"Pimm's is gin-based liqueur, bitter with quinine – so if any malarial mosquitoes show up, we'll be ready for them. Then to make the punch we add Sprite, pieces of citrus fruit and cucumber."

"It's long been a staple at English garden-parties," noted the Rector.

"Then maybe you'll know, George," Richard said, "Why do they call it 'Pimm's and lemonade' when there's no *lemonade* in it."

"Nonsense, my dear boy, our lemonade is just what *you* call Sprite," George said as he tasted the sticky, brownish elixir. "My goodness, it's delicious, Katrina. Reminds me of my days with the boat club at St. John's."

"Did you study theology at Cambridge?"

"As an undergraduate? No, I was a geography man," he said, pronouncing it *jography*. "Later on I went back up for my D.D."

I gave him a quizzical look.

"Doctor of Divinity," he explained.

"So when were you called to be the Anglican apostle to the Danes?" Richard asked.

"Oh goodness, that was many years later. After the Second German War, I returned to Kent – I'm a Kentish man, you see – and took up residence in a parish not far from my native Rochester."

"Did you raise your family in England then?" Katrina asked.

"Yes. I was Rector of St. Botulph's starting in the late fifties and held my position there for twenty years. We moved into the vicarage at St. Alban's, the sole Anglican Church in Denmark, in seventy-eight, and stayed there ten years. Then when I retired, we settled into Number Twenty, but we do spend a good bit of time traveling, what with all the visits to the grandchildren."

"Richard, shouldn't you start up the grill?" Katrina said in a stage whisper.

"Oh, yeah. This may be our last chance to barbeque this year," he responded.

"Richard, let me help you," I offered. "Nothing better than roasting meat over an open fire. Brings out the caveman in all of us."

"Sure, Eddé," Richard replied. "Let's go and get the charcoal briquettes and starter fluid out of the garage."

We set off across the grass, and Richard said, "Thanks for coming, Eddé. And on such short notice."

"Happy to be here. What was it you wanted to talk to me about?"

"It's Katrina. She's deteriorating," he said as we reached the garage.

"In what way?"

"In every way: she can't concentrate, can't sleep, has no appetite, no *libido*," he said in a hushed tone.

"Has she seen a doctor, Richard?"

He lifted the bag of charcoal and a maverick briquette rolled onto the floor. Picking it up, he flipped it in the air a few times nervously as he answered, "Yeah, this week, but the test results aren't back yet. What do you think it could be?"

"There are several different things that could be going on: depression, hypothyroidism, bipolarity…"

"Do any of those things affect teeth?" he asked.

"Teeth? What do you mean?"

"Her teeth have yellowed. The dentist can't explain it. And her skin isn't what it used to be either. Haven't you noticed?"

"I see that she's tired. Her skin might be a bit sallow. Lack of sleep can take its toll on the body. But the teeth," I said, turning it over in my mind. I'd never heard of that symptom except in smokers. "It implies a change of chemistry in the mouth. That might be hormonal too – I would have to consult an endocrinologist."

Handing me the starter fluid, Richard set off toward the barbeque pit, which was in the back of the lot near the garage. As he worked to prepare the pit, he said, "There's something else: she's suffering from *lost time*."

"Lost time?"

"Yeah, I'll call home. No answer. Then when I reach her later, she can't tell me where she's been. It's like she's having blackouts or something."

My mind flashed immediately to Søren, of the night on the beach, of the unexpected hostility toward Richard.

*Was Katrina covering up an affair?*

"I'm really worried," he said. "All she wants to do is play that damned piece on the piano—"

"*Le Gibet*. I looked it up. It's an obsessive work. Did you realize that the B-flat octave sounds 141 times in a five-minute performance?"

"She *is* obsessed. The latest thing is she's gotten involved with this feng shui lady—"

"Feng shui? You mean the Chinese interior decorating?"

"Well, this has gone *way* beyond where to put the sofa. This woman claims that the ghostly phenomena are somehow related to water movement underground. She wants Katrina to bring in a *diviner*."

"You mean a charlatan with a forked stick who tells you where to dig your well?"

"Yeah, the Buddhist lady took her down the cellar – Katrina admitted that she's been afraid to go down there ever since the accident. She's even been taking the laundry down to the coin-op on the boulevard."

"Afraid to go down to the cellar? That's not good," I said, thinking of stress reactions after a tragedy – people who drive miles out of their way to avoid the spot of a previous traffic accident.

"After they came back up from the basement, she gave Katrina a lecture on something called *ley lines*. She described them as alignments, natural conductors of energy in—"

"In the earth's crust," said a distinctly British voice from behind me. It was George. "Pardon me for bursting in like that. I didn't mean to eavesdrop, but Katrina sent me out to see whether you chaps would care for appetizers."

We were both startled, but before either of us was able to say anything, the old codger had turned on his heels and marched straight back to the veranda.

Richard and I exchanged shrugs and ambled back to the deck, where Katrina had set out a tray of smoked halibut, smoked salmon, and *gravad lax*, salmon soaked in a pepper-dill marinade. As I was just helping myself to some of the buttery white halibut, Katrina brought out the herring salads: curried, ginger, beet-apple, and Øresund salad, which is made with a tomato-based sauce fortified with egg-yolks.

"Katrina," I said, "You've outdone yourself again. All these *sildesalater*, you'd think it was Christmas."

"Oh, these are so easy to whip up," Katrina said, coloring and waving her hand at me.

"Do you care for these strong-tasting seafoods, George?" I asked.

"I enjoy the smoked varieties, but the sour marinades have never been for me. Puts me off my wine, you know."

"Ah, some of them are less cranky than others. This Øresund Salad, for example, tastes more of tomato than vinegar," I said.

"All right, I'll give it a go, since Katrina's gone to the trouble," George said, smiling at our hostess, and he helped himself to the pulpy dish of herring and crushed tomatoes.

Once the four of us had sat down to our starters and were sipping the bottled beer that accompanied the strong fish so well, Richard got up the nerve to ask, "George, it sounds like you've got some familiarity with ley lines?"

"Oh, yes, it's hardly possible to live in Cambridge for any length of time without hearing about ley lines. Most people have walked the Cambridge Ley that runs from Wandlebury down to Swavesy," George replied.

"Ley lines? Richard, you told George about ley lines?" Katrina asked.

"I hope it's all right," replied Richard before George could admit to overhearing.

"Of course. I just thought you didn't take them seriously," Katrina said.

"I don't know much about them," Richard said, carefully treading a line.

"Tell us, what are ley lines, George?" I asked.

"Well, the gentleman who invented them, Mr. Alfred Watkins, lectured at Cambridge before the War. I was a member of the Straight Track Club as an undergraduate. Many of the geographers were—"

"How can he have *invented* ley lines?" Katrina asked. "I thought they were ancient, thousands of years old."

"Watkins believed that. A tradesman himself, constantly traveling back and forth, surveying the English countryside, Watkins came to believe that the great standing stones like Stonehenge, burial mounds from the Bronze Age, pre-Reformation churches and other ancient landmarks were arranged in dead straight lines. There was nothing secret about it – his ideas were published in his book, *Old Straight Track* already in the 1920s."

"Did he think these leys were Lines of Power in Mother Earth?" Katrina asked.

"Good heavens, no," George said. "Alfred was a level-headed tradesman and amateur archaeologist. His theory was that ancient people built things along straight tracks as a kind of proto-motorway system. It wasn't possible to construct real roads until the Romans came. So the ancient Britons made do with markers, each one within line-of-sight of the next. Ingenious really."

"So his thinking contributed to the archaeological understanding of Ancient Britain?" I asked.

"No, it wasn't accepted," he replied. "The Club continued to chart alignments for years after his death, but the historical interpretation fell on deaf ears. There was a strong tendency to denigrate 'primitives' in the 1930s, and then the War came and leys were largely forgotten."

"How did ley lines get associated with lines of energy in the earth's crust?" Katrina asked.

"I don't know, but I suppose it must've happened in the sixties, like so many other things. The environmental movement got going and people began to see Mother Earth as something, well, something almost sacred."

"Doesn't that go against the Church?" Richard asked. "It's pagan to see the Earth as Gaia, some kind of Goddess—"

"Now wait just a moment, I didn't say anything about the Goddess," George snapped back. "The Bible does speak of stewardship, but—"

"Yes, yes," I said, impatient with the Biblical digression. "But are these lines real? Is there any evidence?"

"I don't think we know," George admitted. "Almost every month one reads of some church putting in heating and finding a pagan site buried beneath its sanctuary. There are teams out there now walking the countryside looking for alignments: collinear placements of rock, crossroads, burial mounds. Looking for a *pattern* that lies hidden in the white noise of our lives."

Patterns hidden in white noise reminded me of SETI, of the science fiction of Carl Sagan. Searching for truth, for meaning, for the Holy Grail. But there's no easy way out: meaning has to be scratched out from the thin soil of our everyday lives, not discovered by finding where X marks the spot on a yellowed treasure map.

"George, are there ley lines all over the world, or just in England?" Katrina asked. "I mean, if they're just in England—"

"People have found straight tracks just about everywhere they've looked," George explained. "The Bolivian Altiplano, California and New Mexico, Malta, Chile. And of course there are the famous Nazca lines in Peru. I read recently that one group has even found ley lines connecting Viking sites in Scandinavia."

"Are there really Viking sites that fall in a straight line?" I asked.

"Yes, so it seems. The article said that the main artery through Denmark goes from the old abbey at Løgum Kloster in Jutland through the altarpiece at the Cathedral of Saint Knud in Odense, to the last resting place of Danish Kings in Roskilde. I suppose there is some poetic justice in that the ley line should come to rest in the royal crypt."

"What does it mean for a ley line to come to rest?" Richard asked.

"No one knows exactly, but the theory goes that the line simply turns ninety degrees and burrows straight into the earth," George replied.

"Don't say anything important," Richard said, "I've got to put on the steaks, I'll just be a minute."

When Richard had left the table, I took another bottle of Carlsberg.

George turned to Katrina. "May I ask why the discussion of ley lines? It's hardly typical cocktail party banter. Do you have an interest in archaeology?"

"I had the house feng shui'd this week—it seems like there is a flow of water or some kind of energy running underneath," she replied.

I thought about the crack in the pavement, shook it off. Just a coincidence, certainly.

"I don't know much about feng shui," George admitted, "but I will say that it seems sensible to me that one's home should function something like a living thing, like the 'exoskeleton' of the family that dwells within it."

Katrina beamed. "I'm so happy to hear you say that. I think the same thing, George. Beautiful homes reflect beauty—"

"And a family's decline, be it financial or moral, is reflected in the decay of its physical surroundings," he said.

"Yet surely the house is just composed of bricks, mortar, pipes, and so on," I said. "What else is there? What else could there be?"

"That same reductionist argument has been made for thousands of years to 'prove' that a human being is nothing more than one's constituent parts: carbon, oxygen, nitrogen and the rest. Yet even if I had the constituent parts in the correct amounts, sitting in canisters here on the floor, still I would be a long way off from having a human being. It's the precise alignment of the ingredients, the recipe, the 'Form,' if you will – that makes us recognizably different from the pile of chemicals."

"Did I miss anything?" Richard asked, hurrying back to table.

I smirked and said, "Only the history of Western philosophy."

"What do you mean?" asked Richard.

"George was explaining how the house, like a person, is more than the sum of its parts; I was taking the opposite view. On both counts."

"Well then it will be quite a comedown for me to ask the question that's been on my mind," Richard explained.

"Not at all, Richard, ask away," I said, thinking he was trying to be humble about a philosophical query.

"How do you like your steaks?"

We all laughed, and the tension was broken.

"Rare," said Katrina.

"Medium," replied the Reverend.

"Well-done," I said.

"OK, but you may have to wait a little longer for yours," Richard warned as he walked back to the grill, which was smoking and flaming.

I couldn't resist bringing George back to the point of the argument. "Even if I grant your point that a human being is more than a pile of chemicals – for example, a human has moral value far beyond his constituent elements – still, the essence of the difference is no more than complexity. The result of chains of atoms and molecules, put together according to the great recipe that is DNA."

"Complexity, Edvard," George said, wagging his index finger at me. "You've said a mouthful in that one word. How did all that complexity get there? I for one can't believe for a second that it's happened by chance, by coincidence. No, there is a divine plan to that. Do you realize that if the hydrogen atom weighed a tiny bit more or a tiny bit less than it actually does – one-tenth of a percent either way – then life in the Universe would be impossible? Many of the world's leading scientists admit privately that they believe in a Supreme Being: it's all too blasted complicated to have arisen by itself."

Richard arrived back on the scene. "Here's the beef!"

Katrina scurried to bring out the potatoes and salad, and soon we were digging into the hearty meal.

"Ah, this is a real American barbeque, Richard," I said.

"Yeah, we like eating outside when we can," he said. "Say, I've got more beer in the cooler. Who wants?"

The motion passed by acclamation and Richard placed four more green bottles on the festive table.

I didn't want to continue the futile argument on the existence of God, so we ate in silence for a few minutes, then made small talk about the high quality of the steak and the pleasantness of the weather and company.

As we were finishing up the main course, I said, "Tell me, George, how have you managed to stay current in geographical topics for so many years?"

"I'm a member of the Royal Society of Geographers, of course, and have read the *Journal of Historical*—" he started to answer when Richard cut him off.

"Say George, do you think the Society has a website – I mean, could we go online to learn more about the Danish leys?"

"Oh, yes. The RSG database is accessible from anywhere in the world," George replied.

"What does it contain, George?" Katrina asked.

"An enormous store of information, I daresay it's one of the largest in the world. There are thousands of photographs and maps – millions, I suppose. It's just a tiny topic area for them, but they've kept track of ley lines since Watkins' days. The City of Seattle just commissioned a study of their lines," he explained.

"Could we look up Svanemølle?" asked Katrina.

"We could try. But as I'm sure you know, this whole area is an upstart relatively speaking. The large letters on medieval maps are reserved for Aalborg, Aarhus, Ribe, Odense, and Roskilde. Not Copenhagen."

"And those places are linked by a system of alignments?" I asked.

"Many of them appear to be, yes" he responded, opening his eyes wide and nodding his head.

"But wouldn't any set of points, no matter how random, fall into some kind of alignment?" I asked.

"Of course any two points define a line," he said. "But there used to be an informal rule that *four* points in a row are required to establish a ley. In the case of the Cambridge Ley, which I've walked myself, there are ten distinct points, all in a precise line. It's very impressive when you actually walk it. It goes smack dab through the chancel of the Church of the Holy Sepulchre in the center of Cambridge."

"How do you know it's not just a matter of Chance that some sites line up and others don't? It doesn't sound very scientific," I objected.

"Ah, but the Scientific Method is of no use in this case because there can be no control group. I believe one must test this type of knowledge by what we call 'discernment.'"

"Discernment?" I asked.

"Yes, as St. Paul tells us in his letter to the Galatians, 'If you are led by the Spirit, you are not under the Law.'"

I was baffled.

"So how do you 'discern' the truth – through prayer?" Richard asked.

"Yes, prayer is part of it – you see, one must determine whether the spirits that are influencing the mind are of heavenly origin. If so, then what they lead to is inspired by the Holy Spirit and all will be well."

"And if not?" Richard asked.

"Well, then things will not go so well. Right decisions are taken thoughtfully, with basis in reason. Foul choices are most often emotional, conflicted, made in haste."

"Couldn't this lead to serious errors? I mean, how do you know if your 'discernment' is correct?" I asked, worrying now that this old churchman's superstitious claptrap might mislead Katrina, who was vulnerable.

"The history and tradition of the Church serves as a useful check on one's – imagination," he stated carefully.

"But you offer no proof," I pointed out.

"For those who believe, no proof is necessary. For those who will not believe, no proof is possible," he quoted.

"So you actually believe in these so-called Lines of Power?" I asked.

We all looked at him and awaited his reply. He hesitated and said, "Let's just say I wouldn't rule it out."

I shook my head in disbelief and was about to object when Richard interjected, "In the online database you mentioned, are there actual maps?"

"Yes, the database contains everything one needs to find leys in the field: coordinates, landmarks, field notes, and detailed maps," George said.

"Well I for one would like to take a look at those maps. Can you help me download them?" Richard asked.

"Take me to your keyboard," George said with a glint in his eye.

I helped Katrina clear the table. It was beginning to get dark, so we turned on the outdoor lighting. Katrina put water on for coffee and set out a home-made chocolate cake. We had just sat back down again when Richard and George came back out carrying a large printout. Putting the cake to one side, Richard laid out the map on the table in the glare of the outdoor spotlights.

"You see, here is site of the original altar stone of the abbey at Løgum," George said, pointing at a spot near the west coast of Denmark.

"That's right by the town of Løgumkloster – not far from where I grew up in Southern Jutland," I noted.

"The abbey was founded by the white monks, the Cistercians, in 1173. According to the database, when they arrived in the area, the spot was *already* called 'place of the gods' in the local language," George explained. "The priests simply translated this *Locus Dei*. The Modern Danish *Løgum* comes from the Latin, *locus*.

"This fixes the Western terminus of the ley, which is one of the longest ever recorded by the Society. The alignment traverses nearly the entire country, binding together Jutland with the two major islands, Funen and Zealand. There are no fewer than 18 landmarks of various kinds: crossroads, Bronze-Age burial mounds, Viking-era standing runestones, and finally major cultural sites like the Roskilde Cathedral."

"Look at all these points," Katrina said, tracing them with her finger.

"There must be hundreds or even thousands of candidate sites..." I began to object, but the mood of the room was having none of it.

"I know some of these sites from *folkeskole* – the Starup runestone is here, and the Gørlev stones! They're famous," Katrina marveled.

"Yes, it says here that they are a prime source for our understanding of the *futhark* alphabet," George reported.

"The runic alphabet was the sacred, secret code of the Vikings, the knowledge Odin gave his eye to obtain," Katrina said solemnly.

Richard said to me on the side, "These are some of the most important holy sites in the country, Eddé. We should at least give it our consideration."

I replied, "Well, I hope you don't mind if I pour myself some coffee first before such a long journey."

Katrina, recovering her hostess sensibilities, said, "Oh, yes, of course. Please help yourself to some cake and coffee."

Richard said, "Saint Knud is the patron saint of Denmark. The ley line goes right through his cathedral."

"Yes, it appears that the High Altar of the Odense Cathedral is the central point, the pivot around which everything else turns, so to speak," George said. "Like the node at Løgum Kloster, the sanctuary was also connected with a major abbey, this one run by the Church's men in black, the Benedictines."

"Hmm... That's odd. That church is not particularly old by Danish standards," Katrina questioned, and I breathed a sigh of relief – *she's thinking for herself, not eating everything raw.*

"Yes, but the history of that location goes back much further," George explained. "In 1086, King Knud was murdered on the altar of a wooden church in Odense. After Knud's death, pilgrims came to the location from all over Europe. The miracles they reported led to his quick canonization – he is one of very few kings ever to have been canonized.

"No one knows how far back that wooden church goes – it may have been a pagan site," he said.

I noticed he wasn't reading any of this, so I asked, "Is all this on your printout?"

"No. No it's not. You see, the name of the church where Saint Knud sought refuge just happened to be *St. Alban's*, which just happens to be the same name as my church here in town – so you can well imagine I heard the story more than once when I was Rector."

"Saint Knud must have been legendary," Katrina said, looking up from the map.

"Oh, yes," George confirmed. "Odense Cathedral was built in the 1200s and dedicated to him, centered on the spot where he was martyred. Though largely forgotten today, Knud was a folk hero in Denmark in the Middle Ages, similar to Saint George, the patron saint of England."

"You mean the one who killed the dragon?" Richard asked.

"Yes, that's the one," George answered as he riffled through the text printout. "The *Sanct Albani* site held religious significance for the pagans. The Danish team believes Knud was murdered for religious reasons, in kind of a rear-guard action against the blossoming of Christianity in Denmark. They theorize that pagans chased the saint-king, his kinsmen and housecarls into the Christian church and slaughtered them on the altar purposely, in an effort to show that the Norse gods were more powerful than Jesus."

"I see," said Richard, nodding his head. "That's why they chose *Odense* as the site of the execution of the Christian King."

"Odin," I said, catching his meaning.

"Yes, the one-eyed chief-god of the Vikings who was supplanted by the Man on the Cross," George said. "What better place to murder the saint-king than in Odin's own sacred place?"

"But the whole thing backfired," Richard said. "The murderers inadvertently made a hero out of Knud, Christianity flowered more than ever, the cult of Odin faded, and the revolt went down in history as a tax rebellion."

I was growing tired of the history lesson. "So how do you determine that these places are truly aligned? Do you have standards for distinguishing whether two sites are on a line, or 'nearly' on a line?"

"The old rule," George replied, "was the thickness of a pencil-line on a standard topographical map. Modern methods have come in now. A ley line is reckoned to be five-and-a-half feet across, and GPS coordinates are used so the curvature of the earth can be taken into account. Still, it's all pretty obvious just by looking at a good topo-map."

I shook my head. All we had just reviewed was a series of speculative tales and some pinpoints lined up on a map, but the three of them were as excited as school children. I thought they were going to start sharpening dowsing sticks any minute. It was all so uncritical, primitive – I felt like I was watching a National Geographic special on folk beliefs of Papua New Guinea.

"Still, I don't suppose any of this has any relation to Svanemølle, though, does it?" Katrina asked.

"No, Skat," Richard said. "We looked, there's nothing at all in this part of the country."

"Of course one never knows what will be found in the future, but at least at present, nothing has been surveyed in our neighborhood," George agreed.

We all stared at the map. I looked to find points that were not *quite* in line with the others. Richard and George were dividing the points into four or five categories, ranked from most to least important.

"Wait a minute!" Katrina said.

"What is it, Skat?" Richard asked.

"Well, it's possible isn't it?" she asked George.

Her eyes were wide, expression elated.

"What's possible, my dear girl?" George asked, a bit alarmed at her change in mood from glum to ecstatic.

She grabbed the cake-knife, covered in chocolate as it was, and she laid it down right on the map, and looked at us each in turn, as if to see our reaction. She was positively beaming at first, but then as the three of us men looked stupidly at one another, not knowing what to make of her outburst, her expression started to melt. Her eyes sank.

"Don't you see it?" she asked. "What if the ley line doesn't end in Roskilde's crypt of kings? What if it keeps *going?*"

Ah, she was using the knife as a ruler. I followed it with my eye and almost jumped, for right there on the official Royal Society map of the Kingdom of Denmark, the sharp point of the cake-knife rested on the word

*Svanemølle.*

# 25. Søren

I was trimming my hedges on an idle Tuesday when Katrina emerged from the red door and said, "*Sikke en fin hæk!* Your *leguster* are looking sharp, Søren."

I smiled at the compliment and said, "Thank you."

Ceasing my clipping, I walked the few paces out to our common driveway. Once out of the shadows of my front lawn, I squinted in the bright afternoon sunlight.

"It's been so long since we've talked," I said. It had been two weeks since our last session and I'd missed her.

"You know we were away, in Skagen, Richard and I," she said haltingly.

"Ah, how lovely. How was the weather up there – sunny as usual?"

"Idyllic."

"Too bad the summer has been so overcast here on Sjælland."

"Yes, it has been dreary, but it's nice today," she said, toeing the gravel and twisting her wedding ring.

It seemed as if she wanted to tell me something, so I tried to help her along. "I hope you haven't had any more of those dreams."

"Oh, no," she said, looking up into my eyes. "No, not since our session."

"Good to hear it," I said.

"The hypnosis has worked perfectly," she said, biting her lip.

"Katrina, forgive me for saying so, but you seem nervous. Has anything *happened?*"

She looked away and exhaled before turning back to me to say, "Oh, Søren, I don't know where to begin."

My facial expression changed from curiosity to concern. "You haven't fallen again, have you?"

"No, but some things happened, while we were in Skagen." Taking a step closer, she said in a low voice, as if someone could hear, "We went to this horrid

exhibition on witches – then when we got back, a feng shui lady came and…
well, it's too much to go into standing here."

"Oh, dear," I said. "Well, it's so warm today – *you, like me,* must be thirsty –
shall we have some coffee? Come into my garden, won't you? Let me go and put
the water on, then I'll meet you on the veranda."

She agreed. I went inside, washed up a bit and put on a clean, white shirt
with a Nehru collar. In a few minutes' time, we were standing together on my
back porch, where I gave her an overview of the walled garden. The plot was
extensive, over two thousand square meters, and included flower beds, two herb
gardens, a small pond stocked with carp, two dozen trees, numerous bushes, and
in the center of it all, a statue in the Greek style. Grape vines, ivy and creepers
crisscrossed the yard, grabbing anything they could, throttling living things if
I let them.

"It's beautiful, Søren. I had no idea," Katrina said.

"Thank you," I replied with a gallant tip of the head.

I had put in a lot of work on the garden these past several months, and by
now I could be quite proud of it. Typical for August, almost everything was in
full bloom. The stems were doubled over with the weight of the blossoms, and
the air was heavy with the perfume of flowers in the heat of the afternoon. Katrina inhaled the intoxicating vapors that rose from the flowering plants. Her
blue eyes drank in the reds, yellows and deep green of the foliage; assessed the
height and thickness of the mature trees; and traced the coiled tendrils of the
clematis – also known as devil's hair – that crept over the stones and benches and
wound themselves round the marble statue.

"Who is it?" she asked, pointing to my alter ego, the consummate gardener,
Vertumnus.

"The shape-shifting god of the seasons."

"He's gorgeous."

I beamed and said, "Hah, better be careful of that one. He can be very
tricky."

When she just laughed, I lifted my hand toward the garden and said, "Shall
I show you?"

"Of course," she said, and we walked down the steps into the lush boscage.

As a lifelong lover of herbs and flowering plants, I was very much on my
"home turf" so to speak, and spoke easily about a wide variety of alluring plants:

foxglove, gelsemium, monk's hood, laburnum, lily-of-the-valley. She had no idea what she was dealing with, but I could see she was impressed. Upon spying the lemon-yellow flowers of aconite, she did a double-take, inhaled, and said, "Oh, my. I just got a powerful feeling of déjà vu."

"Do you get that often?"

"No, but then the whole garden seems familiar somehow, as if I've been here before."

"Perhaps you have," I said with a grin, and we continued over the footbridge in silence.

Once on the other side of the bridge, in the back-garden, Katrina relaxed. Her shoulders dropped into place; the tense muscles of her face let go, making her appear younger. As if tipsy from the heady perfume of the flora, she giggled when she spoke and took on a playful air, quite unusual for her, giving me a glimpse of the girl inside her. It was ecstasy to be alone in the garden with my Eve; it was all I could do to control myself. But I'd vowed I would be careful this time. The spider does not pounce.

"Søren," she said, stopping and turning to me in the most private part of the garden.

How I loved to hear her speak my name! The other times, she'd been silent, entranced. I'd been able to steal a kiss or a touch, but had received only the shadow of real satisfaction, for I knew it was not her will but mine that had been done. I was but a usurper in the temple of her body.

"Yes, Katrina," I said, taking her hand. It was as warm and moist as the plants around us.

To my delight, she did not remove my hand, but asked, "How have you managed to create such a wonderful garden in this awful climate?"

"This is a fantastic environment for green plants to grow up in – what they need most is moisture, which our little kingdom provides in abundance. Beyond that, I give them protection from the wind," I said, indicating the high walls of fitted stone, "plus a measured amount of sunlight and great deal of care and attention."

Her attention had fixed on a gymnosperm just off the path to the left. She reached out and plucked a light-green, fan-shaped leaf and examined it, running her fingers along the veins. Caressing the delicate triangle, she held it tenderly against her cheek and asked, "What kind of tree is this?"

"Ah, this is an East Asian temple-tree, a gingko," I said.

The leaf's shape resembled that most intimate angle where the protective down of a virgin grows. This form inspired the gingko's alias, the *maidenhair* tree. Yet I could not share this with her. So I folded the leaf, which snapped, bleeding a green stickiness onto the shafts of my fingers. I scented redolent chlorophyll, the stuff that life is made of, then held the broken body of the leaf to my lady's upper lip, allowing her to breathe in its lime-green secrets.

"In New York, we sold an extract of this plant as a natural supplement, gingko biloba," she said. "For sharpening the mind."

"Yes," I said, inclining my head. "Once again I am impressed with your knowledge of botany. The gingko, like everything else that grows on my property, has a purpose: the trees give shade; one patch of herbs is edible, the other medicinal; even the grasping vines produce fruit for birds. You will find nothing ugly or useless. I remove all the weeds, root and branch, for only beauty may grow here."

We walked deeper into the grounds hand-in-hand, dappled sunlight playing hide-and-seek with her noble features. When we reached the far corner, a shadowy spot where sun-shy denizens congregate, she crouched down to examine a spotted, golden-yellow flower of five petals.

"What's this one?" she asked.

I hesitated a moment, and then said under my breath, "St. John's Wort," reddening as I recalled the clumsy kiss at Midsummer.

"Oh," she said and looked away.

Whatever charmed moment we might have had was over. Katrina's head and shoulders drooped; my northern flower wilted at the very mention of Sankt-Hans, that insufferable day of African heat and flaring tempers.

I tried vainly to smooth over the awkwardness, babbling the first thing that came into my head. "Yes, the flower grows wild here in Denmark, but it can also be cultivated. And an extract of the herb can also help in—"

"Depression, yes. Yes, I know," she said, five drops that made a mockery of my torrent of words.

*Satans også,* I had spoiled the mood. Again. I could only watch, helpless, as my lady withdrew into a dark place deep inside herself. I soldiered on, trying to bring her out of it, showering her with words, words, words: *yes, how popular these alternative medicines are becoming; you must have used these in New York; oh, see here saw palmetto... and there's milk thistle... ginseng... Echinacea...* But it was no use. Glassy-eyed, her soul was crouched by the shore of a distant sea. By the time we got back to the terrace, silence reigned complete.

I stomped back inside in a murderous mood. In the kitchen, I brewed coffee and brooded about weeds and husbands.

*It would all be so much easier if she weren't married,* I thought to myself, setting off a familiar internal debate.

"Yes, but you're a great believer in marriage – Mother always said..."

*But he's a foreigner, he has no right, no standing...*

"Yes, but she's a grown-up; she's married him and what the Lord has joined together..."

*Nonsense, he's the one that barged in here, invaded my kingdom; he's neither useful nor pretty; weeds should be pulled up root and—*

"What? You would destroy him?"

*Gardens must be pruned, herbicide applied. Oh, it would be easily done. There's a recipe for eliminating such rapacious vines, such "southern creeper."*

"Oh, but you can't use it on a human being, you simply *can't.*"

*Why not, if anyone is beyond Good and Evil...*

"What would Mother say?"

*Oh. You mean the Rule.*

"Yes, Mother's Rule."

*Man skal aldrig bruge en Opskrift...*

"That's right. Never use a recipe unless you are sure you can reverse it."

I slammed a cabinet door, shut the lid on the coffee pot and stormed back outside. One day I would stop *dithering* and show the world the Man of Action that I am...

Katrina was staring blankly at Vertumnus encircled in woodbine. I poured libations: two steaming cups of strong, black coffee softened with chicory and sweetened with honey. Then I said, "So, tell me about your trip."

The caffeine jolted her out of her malaise, and she started to speak, though slowly, haltingly at first: she seemed to be off-balance, out-of-equilibrium. Yet rattled as she was, she managed to tell a fairly long story about the trip to Skagen. She had taken in the *Hekse i Vendsyssel* exhibition, of which I'd already heard good reports. I asked for her reaction to seeing Damsgaard on the wall of the exhibit. When she proposed there was "no such thing as a coincidence," I took the opportunity to bring up Carl Jung's concept of *synchronicity*.

"Synchronous events, separated by vast expanses of time or space, go far beyond all normal notions of coincidence," I explained. "Jung himself kept careful records of such exceptional pairings over many years."

"Why? What did he hope to gain?"

"Everything, what it means to be human," I said, with a touch of drama. "You see, he believed that synchronicity enables us to tap into the deep structure of meaning that lies at the foundation of our experience as a species, the *collective unconscious.*"

Katrina was rapt, nodding slowly. The she said, "I'm becoming more and more aware of these uncanny alignments..."

But as if her internal compass was broken, she kept veering off onto tangents: feng shui, ley lines, dowsers, and I-don't-know-what. I brought her back to the Jungian archetype of the Ghostly Father by saying, "The one who built the house is the one responsible."

"What do you mean?"

"I mean that Damsgaard created and seems to be steering everything – and he's trying to get a *message* through to you."

"You may be right, Søren..." she said, and then paused, looked up, a sign she was thinking visually. "What if we tried to talk back to him?"

"How do you mean?"

"I don't know, how does one do such things? Find a medium, hold a séance, use a Ouija board."

I blanched and swallowed hard, and said, "That can be quite... unsettling."

"Why? Have you had an experience communicating with the Other Side?"

"I don't speak of it," I said, looking away. Then I turned back to her and said, "But yes, many years ago, when I was just a boy. You see when Mother passed over, I was alone. No one to watch over me. I thought they were going to send me away. Then my Uncle Peder... well, we tried to make contact with her."

"How did you do it?"

"We went to a shop in Østerbro," I said, lifting my head and closing my eyes, as one does when one is trying to remember something from the distant past. "Into a back room, lit by a single tall candle. The three of us sat on stools around a small table. The medium was a scrawny, dark woman with leathery skin."

*The old woman on the bus.*

As I set the scene for her, I held out my right palm, and as I'd hoped, she put her hand in mine.

"Did you play spirit-in-a-glass?" she asked, using the Scandinavian term for Ouija.

"Not a glass, but there was a kind of planchette, heart-shaped, with a sharp needle below, and there was a board, but I didn't recognize the writing. It certainly wasn't Danish, perhaps Cyrillic."

"Or *futhark?*" she asked, inexplicably.

"What?"

"Rune-writing."

"No, the letters were curved," I said, not wanting to get distracted by the origin of the writing. "The clairvoyant started emitting a hum; the drone reverberated in the small stone chamber. Then Uncle Peder asked questions…"

I stopped, and put my head in my hands.

"What?" she asked, "What sort of questions?"

"Ach, damnable questions. Questions about Mother, about what she was doing… I don't remember. It was so long ago. Oh, I have a headache," I said, putting my fingertips over my eyes.

"Søren, don't, it's all right, we'll stop" she said, leaning forward.

With a wave of the hand and a dramatic exhalation, I continued, "At some point I must have blacked out. I remember waking up back at home, and my uncle was standing over me, assuring me that I would never have to go through that again."

She held my hands tightly and said, "Oh, you poor, poor dear!"

"No, don't say that." I adored basking in her attention, but I would not have her pity. "No, it was all worth it," I said and pressed my lips tight.

"Worth it?" she asked. "It sounds horrible, how could—"

"Before I blacked out, I got to ask one question myself." I looked away, then turned back to her and looked into her deep blue eyes, peered as deep into her soul as I could in this world.

Then I breathed in and said, "I asked Mother if she loved me. Mother had never used that word with me, not ever. She said she was happy with me sometimes, but she never said *love.*"

"Women of her generation," she said, shaking her head.

I nodded and said, "The planchette whirred forth and back, then stopped abruptly. The medium told us the spirit had spelled out *I love you and will be with you always.*"

Katrina said nothing, but I saw a tear stream down her cheek.

"I have felt Mother's presence in my life ever since that day. She inspires my gardening, you know."

"Is the medium still alive?" she asked. "Do you think we could ask her to help us with the Ghost?"

"I don't know, but the shop is still there on Østerbrogade; I pass by it every once in a while. The sign says,

*"The Psychic of Østerbro."*

# 26. Richard

Fat Street, Istedgade, is a seedy stretch of massage parlors and porno shops near the main railway station. Shop windows are filled with whips and chains, French ticklers and dildos, right down to the sidewalk. So the few children who roam these streets grow up fast. I heard one toddler say, "Look at the big thumb, Daddy."

As I was on my way down to catch a taxi in the plaza, I heard a girlish voice say what sounded like *"Lust-forn-pee?"*

Before me stood a doe-eyed teenaged girl, dirty-blond, not more than five-foot tall and ninety pounds sopping wet. A pixie in child-sized blue jeans. Flat-chested, wearing a khaki army jacket and carrying a day-pack, she looked about as sexy as Bambi. I thought she was on a school trip, figured she was asking for directions.

*"Lyst for en pige?"* she repeated, slower this time.

"Excuse me?" I asked, not sure I'd caught the slippery Danish.

"Would you like a girl?" she asked and flashed a McDonald's smile.

Finally it registered: Bambi was a professional.

"A-uh, no. Uh, no thank you," I said. I pasted a fake grin across my face and took a couple of stumbling steps backward before regaining my composure. I had to stop coming to this neighborhood.

I hailed a taxi and the driver helped me put the bags in the trunk. It was Thursday. I'd come home from Paris a day early to surprise Katrina, bearing duty-free gifts, bottles of Pomerol and Chanel No. 5. Katrina and I hadn't made love since Skagen – that's three weeks ago now – and I was hoping that somehow she'd get her spark back. I was hopeful, but not optimistic.

As I sat in the back of the taxi, I realized that I had lied to the streetwalker. The truth was, I *would* have liked a girl, just not a little one. Jeez, she didn't look old enough to take to the prom, even.

The cab left me standing in a Rosenborgs Allé that was deserted at the dinner hour. The house was looking peaked. The paint on the façade was cracked and peeling like an old lady's makeup at a summer wedding. The lawn needed clipping, a couple of dozen mushrooms had sprouted under the trees, which had grown over the summer. The ash tree had really taken over, reaching out onto the roof and grabbing at the red tiles. I'd have to get up there and trim it back one of these weekends.

I pulled my bag up the front steps and rang the bell. No answer. Rifling through my PC case, I found my key and opened the door. It was like the first time I walked into the place with Dahl, months ago – stale odor, trace of cigarette smoke, moldy smell. I had to step over a pile of mail. The living room was a mess. Dirty dishes stood out on the dining room table. I called for Katrina, no answer.

I put the shiny, airport-wrapped gifts on the dining room table, set down the laptop, and *thunked* my rollaway up the stairs. On the way up, I opened the window on the landing so the house could breathe a little. When I got to the top of the stairs, I noticed a dark rectangle on the goldenrod wallpaper where the mirror had been, and heard some movement in the bedroom.

"Katrina," I called out.

"Yeeaaah? Richard, is that you?" a croaky voice replied.

I stood in the doorway and said, "Hi, Skat. I thought I'd surprise you."

Katrina was sitting up in bed, wearing one of my gray college sweatshirts. Dark patches in the orbital areas under her eyes gave the impression of a fistfight, but I determined from the box of tissues on the nightstand that she'd been crying. When she looked up and saw me, her mouth twitched slightly in an effort at a smile.

"I'm glad you're here," she said.

I went and sat by her legs on the bed. I took her hand and said, "Me too. What's the matter, Sweetheart?"

She just looked down. Her lower lip started to tremble and then the corners of her mouth dropped down into a frown, and she started to cry.

"What's wrong?" I said and put my arms around her. She hugged me back, hard. "It's okay, Skat, just let it out," I said as she put her head on my shoulder and her body shook with sobs.

After a minute or so, I felt a sticky wetness on my neck, pulled back and said, reaching for the Kleenex, "Here, have a tissue."

She blew her nose a couple of times. I looked at her face and noticed that it was thinner. It made her look a little like her mother.

"Have you been eating?" I asked.

"I haven't had much of an appetite."

"Did something happen?"

"No, I just haven't been able to sleep at night."

"You having those dreams again?"

"No, I don't dream at all any more. I just keep rolling around in bed. I fall asleep, finally, at about four o'clock, but then I wake up again at seven or eight. So by late afternoon, I need a nap."

"But if you sleep at this time of day, then you won't be able to sleep tonight."

"I used to fight the urge to nap, but now I just take all the sleep I can get. It's still not enough, I can tell you."

"Did you get to see the doctor?"

"Oh he's such an idiot. These Danish doctors are all the same – *get some rest, exercise more, eat your rye bread,*" she said in a flat nasal mumble.

It was a pretty good imitation and I laughed.

"It was pathetic," she concluded.

"What's wrong with these doctors?" I asked rhetorically. "Well, did he agree to do the blood test at least?"

She nodded and said, "Yes, but I haven't gotten the results yet."

"There was some mail downstairs by the front door, maybe it's in there?"

"They were supposed to call."

"Eddé had an idea that it might be something to do with your hormones, right? What was it, your pineal gland or pituitary or something?"

"It was the thyroid, and I don't think it's that. Thyroid patients get fat – I've been losing weight."

"Well, I'm not a doctor. We just have to find the right man..." I started to say when I noticed she was just staring blankly out the window. There was something she wasn't telling me.

I took her chin between my thumb and forefinger and turned her face towards me. "Is there something else?" I asked.

"I don't know," she said and looked away again. "I spoke to Mor. Claus agreed to take the two of us boating on Saturday."

"This Saturday – that's great news!"

"Yeeaahh..." she said, as the sobbing returned. She started shaking.

I held her and said, *"Naa, naa,* is that what's got you all upset, Skat? You don't want to go?"

She shook her head and said, "Saturday is the thirty-first. *August 31ˢᵗ.* My blood just went cold. Of all the days in the year..."

I didn't remember what had happened on that date – it wasn't our anniversary or anybody's birthday that I could think of. I didn't say anything.

"It was the day Fa' died," she said, giving me a look. "It's the eighth anniversary of his death and we're going sailing."

"Ohhh," I said, nodding.

"I can't believe it. I feel like we're trampling on his grave."

I really wanted to help her get past this – she needed to reconcile with her brother. I had a feeling that this whole haunting thing would just dissolve somehow if she could make peace with her family, with her father's death. My instinct was to say something like "It's just a coincidence," but with her new-found faith in *The Celestine Prophecy* – there *were* no coincidences – I knew that wasn't going to work. So I went the opposite way, the way the wind was blowing you could say.

"Trampling on his grave? Gee, I don't think so," I said. "It's really very poetic if you think about it."

"Poetic?"

"Yeah, your father passed away eight years ago; his passing really tore your family apart. Now the family is coming back together, healing the old wounds, on the anniversary of his death. It's kind of nice if you think about it."

She took this in for a moment and retreated a bit, saying, "Richard, I've not been sleeping – the house is a pigsty, I'm a wreck, in case you didn't notice. I am just not up to this."

So far so good. Next I took the tack of arguing against going, so she would defend the idea:

"You can always back out, I suppose. Maybe go sailing another time."

"How can I back out?" she asked, lifting her arms. "It was my idea. And it's September next week. This will probably be the last chance we'll get to go out on the water before the cold weather sets in."

Okay, we'd established importance and urgency. Now I just had to steer the ship into port.

"Then you'll just do something else together. Go for a walk in the forest and take in the autumn colors. Maybe apple-picking..."

"No," she said right away. "Being out on the water makes perfect sense. It was what we did together when Claus and I were children, the whole family. It's what we have to do together. It's what I have to do."

Almost home! Now all I had to do was to tie down any stray lines of argument by being supportive.

"Well, it sounds like you've made your decision, then. I'm sure it will go fine. I believe in you," I said and kissed her.

Katrina still looked glum, so I said, "Come on, give me a smile."

She gave me a plastic smile, which disturbed me for some reason I couldn't put my finger on, reminded me of someone. I changed the subject before she could have any second thoughts.

"Listen, I brought you a present. From Pa-ree," I said, sing-songing. "What do you say you go wash your face and put something on, and I'll make us a nice dinner? I got a lovely bottle of Pomerol at Charles de Gaulle."

"Okay," she said, brightening a little. I got up and went toward the door. "And Richard," she added. "I'm glad you're home."

"I'm glad to be home."

I opened up all the windows. Mild, fragrant air wafted in, blowing away the pent-up staleness. I picked up the mail from doormat and set it down on the kitchen table. There wasn't much in the refrigerator, no meat really. We had eggs, and I found some ham in the crisper, so I could make omelets. No mushrooms in here – they were all out on the lawn – but I found half a yellow onion that was sprouting green, a couple of old garlic cloves shriveled in their skins, and grabbed a sweaty white cheese that felt like a cold, saggy breast in my hand.

I set a wooden cutting board on the table and lined up the ingredients. This reminded me of George's canisters of the chemicals that make up a human being. So I imagined myself the Dr. Frankenstein of eggs, constructing a "monster" onion-ham-and-cheese omelet, *cue the evil laughter.*

But as I put the soggy Havarti down on the table next to the mail, I spied the embossed return address: *Rigshospital Diagnostisk Center.* It was the test results, and from *The Kingdom* itself – Lars Von Trier's mini-series about ghostly goings-on in Rigshospital was one of the few decent things on Danish TV. I ripped open the envelope without thinking. This was doubly stupid: I would get in trouble for opening her mail, and probably wouldn't be able to understand the Danish contents anyway.

Finding a page entitled *Resultater,* I scanned the columns of numbers without understanding their meaning: *134... 3,45... 19,1... 6.000... 47,3...* Then I noticed that ranges of values labeled as *Normale* were given in the rightmost column. I checked every one: a few close calls, but all the numbers were within range. I put the letter back in the envelope carefully, stuck the envelope back in the pile, and breathed out through pursed lips. Good, she was not sick. But then again, it would almost have been better if something had been out-of-line. At least then we would've known what was wrong. Now we were back to Square One.

As I chopped the onions and garlic and warmed up a circle of extra virgin oil in the omelet pan, I reflected on our situation. My mother wanted me to sprinkle holy water, get a priest to come and bless the house. Like when I was a kid and Father McNamara would come from the rectory, smelling of Old Spice and sacramental wine, and bless our new car. Pennies in the backseat – put them in the ashtray, they're for good luck – new-car smell; St. Christopher, not yet "laid-off," on the dashboard. The brogued *Faather congratulatin' oss heaaartily* on the new Pontiac or Buick; then he'd sanctimoniously deliver us from Evil with a flick of the wrist. I was an altar boy, so I got to hold the little bronze bucket.

I placed the onion and garlic in the hot olive oil and the room was instantly filled with the smell of my mother's kitchen.

Of course nowadays I was something of a lapsed Catholic. Funny how the word "lapsed" is always followed by the word "Catholic." You don't get many lapsed Lutherans – what's there to lapse? They don't have to go to church every week, or confession or do much of anything. Of course, to be a Protestant in good standing, you've got to be part of a congregation – which involves a substantial donation – but once you're a member, you're in. Like carrying the *Christian Express* card, don't leave home without it.

On the other hand Catholics, at least according to the Rulebook, have to go to Mass every week. You're either Cal Ripken who never missed a game, or you're sent down to the minors – and it's a long way down.

In fact, I prided myself on being something of a lapsed Catholic. Not that I didn't have a certain respect for the immensity and completeness of the Thomist world-view of the High Middle Ages. And I was very fond of the softer side of Catholicism – forgiveness, loving-kindness, *agape*, the value of good works – but

I considered myself beyond all the incense and mirrors, the shiny trinkets and gewgaws. And I hadn't been to church in years.

"What's that girl doing up there?" I wondered out loud, and called out, "Katriiinaah!"

"I'll be down in a mi-nute," she called back, with more verve than I expected.

This gave me time to get the omelets ready. I removed the clarified onions and garlic from the pan, diced a couple of pieces of ham, beat four eggs and poured the mixture into the hot pan, where it started to sizzle immediately. I added back the onions and garlic and sprinkled the ham on top.

I didn't go to church because, well, I just didn't see the whole thing as relevant any more. There was still a residual "Mass appeal" – even after a thousand Sundays, the ancient Order of the Mass still retained a vestige of drama and an elegant beauty. But it was remote, fragile as the pale nobles in Flemish paintings or the fanciful beasts of medieval tapestries. As a man of the world, I had taken on the worldly view that religion was somehow "good for children." Like Santa Claus.

I grated the cheese and the white flakes fell into the bowl like Christmas in Vail.

You got the sense that the ritual had become dependent on us, instead of the other way round. Like in *Peter Pan:* if we stopped clapping, the lights of the fairy world would grow dark. Of course, Catholics didn't clap in church, it wouldn't be respectful. And I was never tempted in a Protestant direction. If I couldn't believe in a vision of Christ's teachings that was logical and consistent, a seamless garment woven over a hundred generations by the One True Church, how could I possibly accept an ersatz patchwork?

No, when I lapsed, it was for Nothing: I didn't join the ACLU atheists who spend Christmas Eve vandalizing crèche scenes, nor did I dance round the Solstice Shrub with the pagans. No, I didn't renounce my faith, I just didn't practice it too hard. I'd become what Jesus called the worst of all: I was lukewarm.

And I was quite content in my tepidness, really, but then like lightning ripping through pure blue skies, I was confronted by the Magick of the past. *The tramping on the stairs was like the beating of a tribal drum in the darkness.*

That reminded me of Steinbeck, the book where he travels across the country with his poodle-dog. Something about the darkness, looking out into the darkness...

I lowered the flame under the eggs, walked out to the bookcase in the living room, and found *Travels with Charley*. I sat down with Steinbeck, a true friend after all these years, at the kitchen table. The book fell open almost of itself to a dog-eared page with an underlined passage:

*"Oh, we can populate the darkness with horrors, even when we think ourselves informed and sure, believing in nothing we cannot measure or weigh... I thought how terrible the nights must have been in a time when men knew the things were there and were deadly.*

*"But no, that's wrong. If I knew they were there, I would have weapons against them, charms, prayers, some kind of alliance with forces equally strong on my side. Knowing they were not there made me defenseless against them and perhaps more afraid."*

That was it. That's why I've felt so antsy — I feel defenseless against the *Whatever-It-Is*.

The eggs had grown complacent, still gelatinous in their pan — I'd turned down the burner too far and the flame had gone out. Jeez, that's dangerous, I could smell the gas. I turned the knob until I heard clicking and the blue fire burned again.

Maybe this was why the old Protties panicked, why the witch-hunters in Denmark and Salem flew into a fury. They felt defenseless. They had no more beads, no incense, no holy water; no saints, no guardian angels. The reliquaries and candlesticks and monstrances had been melted down. The niches were empty. It was nothing less than unilateral cosmic disarmament — which would have been fine if they had quit believing in Satan, but *No-hoh*, quite the opposite. Think of Milton, Goethe, *The Devil and Daniel Webster*. No, the Protties did not "diss" Old Scratch — they recognized him as "Prince of the World." For them, the Invisible World was just as real as the Visible. So when the bearded elders encountered real, personal evil, they panicked like flocks before the Wolf.

I dumped in the cheese, which melted into a white gooey mass, pinched in sea salt, cranked in three rounds of black peppercorns.

The persecutions started with the "usual suspects," the old, the smelly, the homeless; Hose Mette squinting as she darned socks by the fire. But eventually, the accusations reached so far up the social ladder that it was clear to all and sundry that there was no way this upstanding Personage, so obviously one of the Elect, could *possibly* be a witch. And then came the wringing of hands. Thus it was that we learned that the three daughters of Belief — Magick, Religion and Science — could *not* share the earth.

The succeeding centuries have sorted out a victor: Science. The 18th Century suffocated poor, mad Magick in her sleep; the 19th, vampire-like, drained the blood of dainty Religion. God was dead and the Church buried. Nowadays, when the subject of God comes up, educated adults just blush and change the subject.

This is Eddé's Way. Yet when confronted with palpable, unexplainable observations – the man in the window, footfalls on the stairs – all Eddé can do is plead ignorance. He can't accept what his senses tell him, but he can't quite explain it away either.

The omelet was almost ready. I sprinkled in minute amounts of Provençal spices – basil, rosemary, thyme, fennel – you need just the tiniest bit, added late in the cooking process. Makes all the difference in the world.

Katrina and her friend Annika have turned to the East searching for a new spirituality. Laudable, but it reminds me too much of the seventies: pooka beads, mood rings, pet rocks. It looks okay, but don't scratch the surface or you'll see the "Made in Taiwan" sticker. *Eastern Mysticism for Dummies* doesn't work for me, because it just puts new names on the same old debates: placing a crystal and saying some lines of Sanskrit may be fascinating for somebody raised without ritual, but for me, it's just another motif. In our home, we had holy water from Lourdes, statues of St. Francis, and said our incantations in Latin. Sanskrit, Latin: same difference. Katrina would never accept the Catholic version because she sees it as going backwards, but put some Chinese characters on the same aphorism, and suddenly it's *au courant*. It's on the cover of a little square book on sale at the cash registers at Barnes & Noble.

I folded the omelet in two and smiled as I saw the brownish bottom.

How did the Clintons get away with this feng shui nonsense? Imagine the commotion if Jackie Kennedy had set up statues of saints in niches along the corridors of power. A hundred ACLU lawyers would have screamed, "Separation of Church and State." The truth is, feng shui is religion too, but because it enters your home under the cloak of "interior decorating" it's *chic*, like sushi or something.

I flipped the omelet over, pressed it lightly with the spatula, and slid it onto the plate. As she walked into the kitchen Katrina said, "Ah, that smells delicious, Richard."

"Well, I didn't see any meat, so I just thought we could have some omelets."

"Pomerol with eggs?"

"Well, I added Provençal spices, so it goes, *nestpah?*"

She laughed. Oh, it was so great to hear that little giggle. Her hair was wet. "Did you shower?" I asked, like an idiot. *What, was it raining upstairs?*

"Yes, it was great," she replied. "But we can save the Pomerol for steak-night. Let's open some Beaujolais or something." She held an envelope. "What's this, Richard?"

I forced my lips into a smile.

# 27. Katrina

I wished to God I were physically ill, that my pituitary had ceased to function, that at least one goddamned score was off. But they were all within range, and if I wasn't physically ill...

The days and nights were like the ups and downs of *Slangen,* the giant serpentine rollercoaster at Tivoli. During the day I might get excited by something, like when I found the ley line on the map. That was *my* idea! No one had thought of it. I've always been the one to see the lines that go outside the box – my schoolteachers didn't always like that so much – but who's to say the line doesn't go all the way to Sweden?

The medieval Danish Kingdom encompassed Southern Sweden. That's why Copenhagen is the capital: at the time, it was safely in the middle of the realm. But then armies swarmed down from Stockholm to conquer Skåne, to rape the women and Swedishize the population. This left Copenhagen on the edge.

Like me.

As evening came, it was as if a pall would begin to drop. *I hate to see that evening sun go down.* As the shadows lengthened, my mood would darken. Down I would go, down until there was nothing but blackness. One would think that as I grew somber, I would become somnolent and slumber. But such was the devilishness of my condition that only wide-eyed dozing was permitted. The best I could hope for most nights was to sit in a chair and stare with a jaundiced eye at the Victorian wallpaper for a couple of hours. At least it was kind of like being asleep.

The weekly routine included very few hours of real in-bed sleeping. On the nights when Richard was at home, Friday through Sunday, he would retire at eleven, and I would crawl into bed next to his bear-like body. We would read or talk. Sometimes I would have trouble concentrating on my book and he would read to me, his earthy voice imitating the smooth heroes and the gravelly villains.

But eventually he would want to sleep, which I couldn't, or he would want to make love, which I – couldn't. I would just get so distracted, so detached from it all. I would think about how his breath smelled, not that he had halitosis, I would just fixate on how it smelled. Or I would worry about my own breath, or armpits. Or whether the sheets needed washing. A million things. Sometimes I thought of Søren. His kiss was harder, leaner than Richard's. Forbidden. *My sin is shameful.* I blushed with shame in the darkness there, felt certain that Richard would notice, but I don't think he did.

Then there were the nights, Monday to Thursday, when Richard was away. I wish I could say I never thought about calling Søren, just to be with someone. I know he wanted that. I wish I could say I refrained from calling him because I was a good wife, because I was stronger than Annika with her nineteen-year-old barman. The truth was I didn't call him because I knew he would expect me to have sex with him. If not the first night, then surely the second or the third. And I had no interest in sex whatsoever. I found it vaguely distasteful, a chore like polishing brass or taking out the garbage.

On these nights, sitting alone, I would feel like a juke box with the plug pulled. No energy to do anything. I was sure there was something wrong with me. God knows I felt sick, tired all the time, I had headaches, stomach pains. I wasn't eating right, I knew that. But my blood work had come back clean.

At dinner, I flew into a rage, not only because Richard had read my mail, but because I wished I *had* been ill. I couldn't stand how he looked at me: not resentful, not angry. It was pity. He thought I was ill, mentally, and he felt sorry for me. Perhaps he was right: I was depressed. Sad, lethargic for no reason, that's depression, right?

I needed to get away from this place, away from... him. So, later that evening, I called Mor. The boat trip was in two days. I didn't want to risk a sleepless Friday, so I asked if I could stay at Mor's, sleep in my old room that night. It would be fun, like a sleepover. Given the early start we planned for Saturday, she agreed right away, seemed glad for the visit.

I was whistling a song I heard on the radio, a new one by Joan Osborne, as I packed an overnight bag on Friday afternoon. It was great to kiss Richard at the door and stroll down the walk to the waiting taxi. For once *I* was leaving *him* in this creaky old place.

As Sundhuset receded behind me in the rear window, I was happy to leave it behind, happy to have someone else spend the night alone there. Perhaps Richard would encounter some of the same things I had. That would wipe the smirk off his face. But then again, he wasn't smirking so much as feeling sorry for me. And the pity would be replaced with fear, which wasn't what I wanted. *What would he do? What if he needed my help?* Nonsense. My husband was a big boy, could take care of himself – or else order in from the Chinese Palace.

A few minutes later, I was standing atop the steps in front of my childhood home at the end of Strandparkvej. The brass "widow" nameplate was gone, replaced by a demure sign saying Nielsen. I smiled and rang the bell.

Mor opened the door and her face lit up. She was baking rolls for supper and the atmosphere was filled with the warmth of the oven and the aroma of bread rising.

"*Det dufter dejligt,*" I said. "What's for dinner? I'm starved."

"It'll be chicken, but I've not started it yet," Mor said.

"Can I go to my room right away?"

"Of course, I've made it up for you."

I took the stairs two at a time and swept into my room in a tizzy. As I cranked the casement windows open, the smell of Mor's roses rushed in to greet me. Pingvin, my plush penguin, held out his arms and I clasped him firmly as we waltzed around the room in rapture. I didn't know what to do first, so I did everything: opened old jewelry boxes, dusted off porcelain ballerinas, and extracted old albums of photographs and *glansbilleder*, collectible paper-dolls and sentimental scenes that I collected as a girl. The acrid odor of mothballs stung my sinus membranes as I dug through layers of clothing in my closet – *gymnasium*, upper school, lower school, pre-school – delving ever more deeply into the past, like an archaeologist unearthing artifacts from a Bronze Age burial mound.

Speaking of which, George told me that the ley-lines people are having a field day, quite literally, with my Swedish hypothesis. One faction is adamant that the "Main Line" ends at the royal crypt in Roskilde Cathedral, but a maverick group is intrigued and next weekend, an expedition is setting out for a remote Skånsk lake called Ringsjön, which is aligned with the Danish Main Line; in the center of the lake is a tongue of land where a Benedictine monastery called Bosjökloster was founded in 1080. Satellite photos of the site show several hillocks that appear to be prehistoric barrows.

"Oh, this is *hideous*," I said out loud as I examined the disco-era costume I wore to my first dance, a flowing gown of baby blue polyester with the front cut away to reveal a little triangle of flesh between breast and navel. Ugh, Barry Gibb's own mother couldn't love that dress.

I was thirteen year old. I padded my training bra with tissues and wore three-inch heels with platform soles in an effort to feel more grown-up. But no matter how well I did in school or ballet or piano, it was never enough. Perhaps I was never meant to grow up here: like some kind of rare transatlantic caterpillar, perhaps it was only by going to New York that I could metamorphose into an adult. If so, I had only one task left: to show my family, or what's left of it, the butterfly I had become.

"Katrina?" I heard from downstairs.

"Yes, Mor?" I replied.

"Would you like to eat now?"

"I'm coming!"

The roast chicken with brown sauce, boiled potatoes, and cabbage was comforting. I ate like I hadn't seen food in weeks.

"Can I ask for some more *boller*?" I said with my mouth full.

"Of course you can," Mor said as she passed the rolls. "Katrina, I haven't seen you eat like this since you were twelve years old."

"I know, isn't it great?" I replied, mixing my potatoes with a smear of Danish butter and pouring brown sauce over the whole thing, making a caramel-colored mash.

"You have been looking thin lately."

"I haven't had an appetite, to tell you the truth," I said, gulping down water. Looking at my empty glass and then across to Mor, I asked, "Do you have any milk? Whole milk?"

"Katrina, I haven't bought whole milk since you kids left home. I have *let-mælk*."

"Two-percent? That'll be fine."

We ate and talked contentedly for a long time. Finally, the wishbone was snapped and the skeleton picked clean and the carcass lay cadaverous before us — as if we had conducted an avian autopsy. I looked at Mor from under my eyebrows and smiled.

Drawing in her cheeks, she asked, "Would you like any more?"

This reminded me of Winnie-the-Pooh, and I replied, "*Is* there any more, Rabbit?"

Her eyes lit up and she shook her head. "No, Pooh, there isn't."

"Then I must be going now," I said in my best sticky-Pooh-voice, wiping my mouth as I got up from the table.

We laughed as we roused ourselves, said *Tak for maden,* and brought the dishes into the kitchen. I insisted on helping her put things into the dishwasher and we worked together to scrub the pots and tidy up the kitchen and dining room.

Just as we were finishing up, she said, "Shall we take our coffee in the winter parlor? Perhaps watch television."

"Oh, I don't think I should have coffee in the evening. It might keep me up, and I want to be fresh for tomorrow. How about hot cocoa? And can we play cards instead of watching TV? There's never anything good on anyway."

She agreed and I warmed the milk as she went to get the cards. I brought the cocoa into the winter parlor, where we set up the card table. Since we didn't have enough players for bridge or whist, we played Rummy 500, which was easy enough to follow, even for me. Nonetheless, Mor, who was used to keeping track of bridge hands, built up a lead most of the game. It was only by sheerest luck that, just as things seemed hopeless, I rose phoenix-like from the ashes to win in a dramatic style, earning two hundred points in the final hand.

"Ah! You got me," Mor said, smiling.

"Oh, this has been the nicest evening I've spent in a long time, Mor."

"Same for me, Skat," she replied with a twinkle in her eye. "Same for me."

Mor followed me upstairs to make sure I had everything I needed for the morning – towel, washcloth, shampoo, soap. Standing next to the ABBA poster that still hung on the bedroom door, I kissed her briefly, on the lips like when I was a child. She smiled and padded downstairs to secure the doors for the night. I went to the bathroom and brushed my teeth, reflecting on what it meant to be home, to be here, to be Mor's child and yet not be a child any more.

I was all grown up now, but just for tonight, I suppose it was all right for me to feel like someone's little girl again.

The cotton felt soft against my skin. I hardly ever slept in pyjamas any more, but dug these out of my dresser for the occasion. I opened the curtains a hand's width so it wouldn't be too dark in the room. I doused the light and crept in under the fluffy, fragrant duvet. I couldn't believe I was back here, in the very room where Mor used to read to me, play patty-cake, and sing the Danish version of itsy-bitsy spider, "Lille Peder Edderkop." I heard the Danish Radio coming from Mor's room and fell asleep before I could even think about nodding off. I dreamed like an angel, of Fa' and boats and swimming, and finding crabs on a beach of wave-worn pebbles and shattered shells.

I woke to the high notes of coffee brewing downstairs and a strident symphony of light invading the room. As I squinted at my childhood things gathered around me, I was momentarily lost. *Where was I? Oh, yes, I'm home after all these years, we're going sailing this morning.*

I no longer dreaded the boat-trip, but was actually looking forward to being with Mor and Claus, out on the aquamarine again after all these years. After breakfast, we walked the block to the yacht club in the brisk morning air.

Mor had no trouble striding over to the quayside, and I said, "You seem spry this morning, Mor!"

"I was going to say the same to you," she replied with a smirk.

"Tell me, do you always sleep with the radio on?"

Keeping her eyes forward, she said, "Yes, ever since your father died. Keeps me company, you know. Did you bring the watch?"

I handed the box to her. "Does Claus—"

"Let's talk about this later," she said as she walked away. "I need to nip into the marine shop for a few minutes."

I remained on the quay. *Chancen* had been brought right up to dockside, center-stage. Tomorrow would be September; I'm sure it's the latest Nansen has ever made a Danish vessel ready for her maiden voyage of the season. She looked gorgeous, her lacquered teak skin glinting in the morning sun. At twenty-eight feet, she was large and sturdy enough to sail confidently just about anywhere, yet she was rigged so that just one or two experienced sailors could guide her easily through the oft-tricky waters of Øresund, Kattegat and the salty Baltic. Still, she was a lot smaller than I remembered.

*"Dét må vaere min lillesøster,"* I heard from behind me.

I recognized my brother's voice immediately. Then I turned and saw him; at six-foot-two he was hard to miss, in a short-sleeved white sailing shirt, his dark, wavy hair wet. Pale and beaky, he looked the same as I remembered, though a bit thinner in the face and thicker around the middle. Not terrible, though – *for thirtysomething*, I thought with a smirk.

"Hi, Claus," I said with a shy smile as I walked over to him. At first I stuck my hand out, as if to shake his, and then we both realized that this was a *de rigueur* hug situation. We embraced, awkwardly but not without feeling, and after a few pleasantries, Claus said, looking directly into my eyes, "I'm sorry we couldn't come to your dinner party in July…"

"Oh, please don't mention it," I said, too quickly.

"No, it was stupid. Agnete and I did have another engagement that evening, but we really should have canceled the other thing."

"I thought you couldn't find a baby-sitter," I said, raising my eyebrows.

"Well, that's also true. The other event included children, you see; if you had invited them too, perhaps…"

"Was that the problem, that I didn't invite the kids? But you could have brought them, Claus."

"Well, like I said, it was a – stupid misunderstanding. Mother said it was a lovely dinner; I'm sure we would have enjoyed it."

"Speaking of Mor, here she comes now."

The oversized Nansen, laughing and joking, lumbered along behind the dainty matron as she walked out of the marine outfitters. When they reached us dockside, we made our greetings all around. Topping two meters, he towered over all of us, his wiry ginger hair coiled like copper-wool on top of his head.

"So who's going to captain this here fine craft today?" he asked in a hearty voice.

"I believe I've been selected," Claus responded, ever the able-bodied-seaman.

"That's fine. Now I'll need to show you a few things before you get underway. You'll need a gentle hand, y'see, as she's not been out much lately," he explained, and led Claus to the engines, leaving us girls behind in his ample wake.

"Oh, we didn't pack any food," I said.

"Oh, Hans took care of all that – we have boxed lunches for three, including sandwiches and fruit, and there's even wine onboard," Mor replied.

"You've thought of everything," I said, and then did a double-take. "Hans?"

"Yes, Hans. Herr Nansen."

"Why Mor, I do believe you're blushing."

"Nonsense," she said, turning away. "It's just the sun on my face. Good thing we have plenty of sun-cream. Let's get aboard."

It was a perfect day for sailing – not too cold, good wind, and nary a cloud in the sky – just a few puffy cotton balls strewn here and there across an azure tablecloth. The sunlight coming across the bow at an oblique angle glinted off the lacquered wood. I donned my Givenchy sunglasses, tied my Hermès scarf about my head and felt like Audrey Hepburn.

We made ready to launch, and Nansen waved from the dock as Claus revved the Volvo Penta inboard engine and we growled out of the Hellerup harbor for pleasure-boats. As the water turned from murky green to deep blue, Captain Claus cut the engine and made ready to switch to the sails. The west-wind blew in at a goodly ten knots. Very much in his element, Claus snapped orders and instructions without batting an eyelash – *Make fast that line! Trim the sail!* Flowing over me, the nautical words – *luffing – jibe – tack – coming about!* – brought back memories of childhood Saturdays on the Sound.

As the coastline receded behind us, I crawled toward the bow and lay on my stomach on the foredeck, flat enough so that I would not be molested by the swinging booms and sailwork. My hands gripped the steel gunwale just behind the bowsprit, my legs spread athwartships for balance. This was my all-time favorite position as a child. My body rose and fell with the motion of the boat. I was one with it. Another girl would have been scared or seasick – I was in ecstasy.

The waves banged hard against the hull; the spray soaked my skin again and again, until I was so numb that I didn't even notice it any more, and my fingers grew so icy and stiff that I couldn't have uncurled them if I'd wanted to.

As exhilarating as it was, the rocking motion of the boat was comforting, too, and would have lulled me to sleep if not for the unconscious but ever-present awareness of the precariousness of my position. It was impossible to look back, dangerous to lift my head and turn round to Claus and Mor. So I stared out over the uncountable whitecaps to an unreachable horizon.

After the longest time, Claus needed my help with navigation and called me up to the bridge. Standing next to the Captain as he steered, I tried to figure out the new GPS unit; Mor lounged astern, taking in the rays.

"Do you get out on the water much, Claus?"

"No, not in years. Agnete and I both work outside the home, and we have two little ones, so there's really not a lot of time."

"Are you working weekends too?"

"Sometimes. But even when I'm home on the weekend, the prospect of a major logistical challenge like taking the family sailing is just not that appealing. And Agnete is not much of a sailor anyway – unless the ship should be the QE2," he added with a chuckle. "How about you, did you sail much in New York?"

"No," I said shaking my head. "We lived in Manhattan, and even though it is an island, I never think of it that way. New York, for me, is a party-town, a town of arts and theatres and the ballet. Not boats."

"You got to dance in New York, right? That must have been incredible."

"Yes, it was. It took almost two years for me to get a permanent spot at the Joffrey Ballet, but it was a dream come true."

"You're not dancing any more?"

"Well, no, not professionally. I had my run, Claus. My body rebels when I push it like that now."

"You make it sound as if you're too old," Claus said.

"Every discipline has its age range. I'm turning twenty-eight soon. That's pretty old for a dancer," I said.

"Not in Denmark."

"True, the dancers last longer here – they're protected by the Union and the social fabric. Dancers here can go on maternity leave for a year and then come back. In the States, it's different. If you get pregnant, you're finished. You just don't meet many older dancers over there."

"Survival of the fittest, eh?"

"Something like that," I said, biting my lips.

"So what will you do now that you're home?" he asked.

"I've been working on a business plan to open a natural foods store, health food," I told him brightly.

"In Copenhagen?"

"Yes, I suppose so. I'm not exactly sure where. The concept is to feature lots of fresh fruits and vegetables, focusing on ecological produce. No pesticides, no poisons. Also organic grains by the kilo, fresh fish on ice and butcher-quality meat. And a deli counter where you can get sandwiches made to order, and salads

– not the pureed kind in an industrial plastic container, but freshly made salads with artichokes and Spanish olives and bulgur wheat."

"Stop please, you're making me hungry," Claus said, laughing. "Seriously, it sounds fantastic."

"But that's not all – we'll also have a whole health angle: natural vitamins and supplements," I said, starting to gush. "Alternative remedies like Echinacea, gingko biloba, ginseng. There's a huge boom in these products in the US, and the margins are astounding – a lot higher than traditional grocery items."

"Hmn, I didn't know you had such an interest in *margins*," Claus said, furrowing his eyebrows and lowering the corners of his mouth.

"Well, I don't," I replied, looking away. "But my husband coached me that if I'm ever going to get financing I have to talk about more than just philosophy and health benefits of organics."

"Your husband has a good point. If there's one thing I've learned, it's that just as water flows downhill, money will flow toward more money."

It was nice to talk with Claus again, but painful too. It was so obvious that we had become strangers. We were in the middle of the Sound now and the breeze was strong in our ears; Claus came about so as to tack against the wind as we wended our way northward.

I had to raise my voice a little to be heard as I said, "How did we grow so far apart, Claus?"

He gave me a look and then turned to stare straight out over the bow. "Katrina, you moved five thousand kilometers away. Then you barely contacted me or your mother for eight years. That'll do it."

He went back to steering, his jaw set tight against his upper teeth.

"Listen," I said. "I know we quarreled, but really it all seems so silly now."

He made no reply.

"You can *have* the watch," I offered.

"Watch? What watch?"

"Fa's gold pocket watch, the one you wanted. It chimes on the quarter hour."

"You think I'm still sore over that?" he asked, looking at me. Then he turned face forward and said, "I haven't thought about that watch in eight years."

"You haven't? Then what's bothering you?"

His features contracted into a tight ball as if he had extreme stomach pain, and his face went fiery. His voice became liquid sarcasm. "You think you can just go away, leave your mother and me right after the funeral *for fanden,* cut off all communication, pay no attention to us for eight years – and then waltz right back into our lives? Eight years, Katrina!"

"You're angry because we've been out of touch? But it takes two – I mean, it's not like you were making any effort to communicate with me, either."

"I wrote to you, once," he said, backing off. "When you didn't respond to that letter—"

"What letter?"

"About Mor, her condition."

"What condition, when was this?"

"Just after New Year's, the year you left. It would've been '89."

I frowned and said, "I don't remember any—"

"I sent it to the address we had for you. It was about Mor's... you know."

I stared blankly at him. His expression slowly changed from irritation to disbelief.

"Don't tell me that you don't know."

"Know what?"

"Hasn't Mother told you herself?" he asked, bending close to me so he could lower his voice.

"Told me what?"

I was getting a sick feeling in my stomach.

"Listen, Katrina," he said, snatching a glance over his shoulder to see if Mor was still sleeping, "after you left, things took a turn for the worse with Mother. She was grieving, we knew, but this went beyond the normal. She stopped going out, didn't see anyone but me. For months. She lost weight, started talking about how it would be better if she were dead."

"Oh my God," I said.

"At a certain point, I think it was in January, we had to make a decision. That was when I wrote you, telling you that the psychiatrist, Schroeder, wanted to get her admitted—"

"Admitted?"

"She needed help, medications. Had to be watched around the clock, Agnete and I just couldn't—"

"Admitted – you mean to a hospital? A *mental* hospital? For how long? Why didn't you tell me? Why didn't she tell me?"

"As I said, I did write to you – it seems you never got the letter…"

I had just moved into the apartment in Alphabet City. Mor wouldn't have had that address yet. She probably gave him the temporary address I had before that and the letter never reached me.

"She was in for three weeks, most of the time on suicide watch," he continued.

"Oh, I'm so sorry," I said hoarsely, starting to tear up. I took off the silk scarf and dabbed my eyes with it. Claus stopped me.

"Here, don't ruin it, take mine," he said, handing me a clean white handkerchief with a curlicued blue *C* embroidered in the corner.

I took it and threw my arms around him. "Oh, it must've been awful, Claus. I'm so sorry."

"It's okay," he said, patting me. "She's fine now. And she's so glad to have you home again."

I sat and tried to calm down; Claus went back to steering. I saw that Mor's jaw had dropped; still asleep.

"It must have been hard on you," I said.

"I went to see her every day," he said. "Agnete too."

"That's right, you were with Agnete already at that time."

"We weren't married yet, but she came with me every day. She was a great help to me, to us both."

That stung. But I couldn't really say anything: she was there *and I wasn't*. I felt just awful. I had no idea. After a pause, I managed to say, "I'm glad you had someone there with you."

"Anyway, you should know that Mother's really thrilled that you've come back to stay now, and she's been in a terrific mood lately – you saw her this morning. I think she was flirting with Old Nansen."

"Yes, it was amazing," I said, smiling through tear-filled eyes.

After this, the conversation and my eyes ran dry. We each waded into deep pools of our own thoughts. I wondered why he'd never contacted me again, never told me about Mor's depression. Never one for conflict, Claus was a chronic avoider, trying to solve every problem by working harder.

Soon Mor was awake again and calling us back for lunch. Claus dropped anchor and joined us as Mor doled out the provisions.

"Wud'ja get?" I asked Claus as I opened my lunchbox.

"Liver-paste and cucumber on black bread," he replied. "Yuck."

"I love *leverpostej*. I'll trade you for my Canadian bacon and cheese?"

"*Hamburgerryg* was always my favorite, but you can keep the cheese."

We realized Mor was listening when she said, "Goodness, you two! Sounds like you're back in *folkeskole*."

Still, we traded. The rough-cut ground pig's liver – this was not the fine spread the French call pâté – filled my mouth with the piquancy of organ meat, combining smartly with the crisp cucumber and the stiff, grainy rye bread. Food always tastes better out of doors. To combat dehydration, a real risk at sea, we drank quantities of *hyldeblomstsaft*, a traditional Danish summer soft-drink distilled from elder flowers.

"This ade really hits the spot," my brother said.

"And it's good for you," I added. "Elderberry fruit infusions can reduce pain and swelling. Many women also use it to help with inflammation from UTI – urinary tract infections."

"Urinary tract infections? Are you opening a food store or an apothecary?" Claus asked.

"I guess it's a bit of both," I replied.

"Well, be careful or you'll run afoul of Danish regulations. Retailers can carry televisions, toothpaste and top-hats, but in general they're not allowed to offer medicines or anything that claims to be a medicament."

"I never thought of that," I admitted.

"You may want to add a section on such regulations in your business plan," Claus said.

"Thanks," I said, and smiled, glad to have a big brother around.

Turning to Mor, he said, "*Tak for maden*. I've got to go back to the helm. Should I turn her around?"

"Where are we? Someplace north, I think," I said.

"Yes, we're just a little past Rungsted. There's Rungstedlund," he said, pointing.

Karen Blixen's old mansion overlooking the Sound was stately and elegant. Made famous in the US by the film version of her novel, *Out of Africa,* Blixen was a national heroine in her home country. Her portrait appeared on the Danish equivalent of the dollar bill.

"What's up ahead?" I asked.

"If we keep sailing, we can make Elsinore in an hour or two," he responded, using the Danish word, Helsingør.

"No, that would be too long a day for me," Mor said. "But wait just a minute, don't turn yet. This is as good a spot as any."

I asked, "As good as spot for what, Mor?"

Reaching into her purse, she said, "You'll see soon enough."

"What's in the box, Mother?" Claus asked. Evidently, whatever she was planning to do, she had not discussed it with him. That made me feel better.

"We're going to bury your father today, Claus, once and for all," she said.

"But he's already buried," Claus objected. "It's not as if we can cast his ashes upon the water."

"Yes, I realize that," Mor answered with dignity. "We will bury him symbolically. And perhaps then the three of us can become a family again."

As Richard had told me in Skagen, *You can't get your egg back, but you need to clean up the mess and move on.*

"This is the pocket watch that meant so much to the two of you after the funeral," she said, opening the box and holding up the gold timepiece. "Your father was very fond of it, took to wearing it every day. He even used the chiming feature to time his meetings. But I always hated this watch, a symbol of his devotion to my rival."

"Rival?" I asked.

"His career," she replied. "Per wasn't much for other women, or even other *people* for that matter. He was a great, impressive man, but very much concerned with building up an image for himself to gaze at in the mirror. Like Narcissus, bending over the water," she said, starting to tear up a bit now.

As if the melting mood were contagious, I felt a tear run down my cheek and Claus started rubbing his eyes.

"Well, Per finally fell into that water and drowned there," she said, her head bobbing up and down slightly. "Drowned in his work, his drink, his self-admiration. And today this watch will follow him into the depths."

"No, Mor," I said. "Surely it's valuable, and Claus could use it."

"I don't want it," Claus said, shaking his head.

"You can time your meetings with it," I offered sensibly.

"I won't have it," he repeated.

"That's all right, *Knecht*," Mor said, using Fa's old nickname for Claus. "You don't have to. But before I send this 'golden idol' to its watery grave, I think each of us should try to remember something about Per Nielsen, something positive, so we can grieve him with clear conscience. And move on."

We stood there for some minutes, lost in our thoughts. No large ships disturbed us, no powerboats whizzed by. We had seen some sailboats earlier, a regatta, but at the moment we were nearly alone on the Sound, bobbing up and down in the shadow of Rungstedlund. The only distraction was a persistent seagull that had been following us for a while, hoping to catch a snack, no doubt.

Finally, Claus said, "Okay, well, I guess I'll start. As I said at the funeral nearly eight years ago now, my father was a great man – a hard-working man, a family man. He wasn't perfect, but then none of us are, are we?"

I felt he looked at me when he said this last line, but perhaps that's just my own paranoia speaking.

"Dad and I did a lot of things together – he taught me to ride a bike, play chess, and bait a fishhook," Claus continued. "I remember very clearly the time he took me fly fishing up in Norway – standing in frigid water for eight hours a day, catching very little. But this taught me endurance, and I learned more about him on that trip than…"

Claus narrowed his eyes and grimaced as the words stuck in his throat. He wiped away his tears with his forearm – I still had his handkerchief – and I reached out my hand to touch his. He removed his hand from mine, not roughly, but as if to shake off any constraints. He was not done yet.

"You know, it's no secret that Dad was gone a lot, but we have to remember why – he was supporting the family. He never spent much on himself, he only wanted to give us the things he never had. He grew up poor, maybe poorer than we ever knew—"

"My in-laws never had much," Mor confirmed. "They lived in a working class neighborhood, Per's father worked at the beer factory. I was considered quite a catch at the time."

"Anyway, I drew a picture of the family when I was a kid, I couldn't have been more than eight or nine years old at the time," Claus recalled.

"I remember, and you left out Fa'," I said.

"I had you draw him in, didn't I?" Mor asked.

"Yes," Claus responded, "and I did. When I showed it to him that evening, he noticed that the drawing of him was different and separate from the rest of the family. He asked why, and I told him that I drew him gigantic and in the distance, like a mountain, which was how I saw him.

"At first I thought he was going to yell at me or even spank me. But instead he grabbed me and hugged me. He held me close so I wouldn't see the tears, but I knew he was crying. It's the only time I can remember seeing him cry. He blew his nose, pretended to have a cold, and sent me to bed. We never spoke of it again. But after he died, when I went to his office to get his personal items, I opened the sliding wooden shelf in his desk, a shelf he probably used every day. There was a current calendar, and next to it was my picture. On it he had written, as if to remind himself of his little boy waiting for him back home, *Husk Mig,* Remember Me."

And at this Claus broke down, and I went over and hugged him. He hugged back.

It was my turn. "I'm sure you noticed what day it was today – I guess you planned this, Mor..."

"You mean the anniversary," Mor said. "Yes, of course I noticed, but no, I didn't really plan it. It just sort of happened."

"Well, eight years ago, I wasn't ready – I guess no daughter is ever ready to lose her father, but at nineteen, I figured that Fa' had given me a lot of I-owe-you's over the years. I expected, finally, that I would be able to start collecting. Fa' was always better with adults than children, and now that I was going to university, becoming an adult, I thought he would start to take me seriously. So when he died so suddenly, I felt like he'd run out on a debt. It's like when an aged criminal gets caught years after the crime, but then dies before sentencing. It's like he got away with something. Dammit..." I realized that there was too much anger and not enough love in this, so I tried to switch gears.

"Anyway, I was devastated and I fled. Fled as far as I could think to go, and I'm sorry I left you at that time. I really wasn't thinking about your feelings, your needs, your grief, as I was entirely wrapped up in my own." I felt tears on my cheeks, but wiped them away and continued. "I hope you can forgive me – I hope you both can."

"There's nothing to forgive," Mor said. "You were nineteen, you acted how most girls that age would have." And she reached out and held my hand. After some seconds, she said, "Do you have a memory of your father than you'd like to share?"

One popped into my head, and I smiled and said, "Yes, I used to feel... *left out* a lot, but there was one time of the day when I had Fa' all to myself: early morning, especially on Saturdays. I'd wake up early, it must've been six o'clock. I would catch him with his razor, his face full of foam, or as he was slapping his face with after-shave lotion. Then we'd sit together at the breakfast table. He would make Irish oatmeal, the steel-cut kind that takes half an hour to prepare, and while the oats cooked, he'd read me the papers. Fa' loved the newspapers. When I was little, he'd read the comic strips to me; as I got older, he'd explain the headlines and the financial pages. The brown sugar would melt into the porridge; we'd add dried apricots or figs, or stewed prunes – for the taste, mind you," I said and got a laugh out of both of them, as we all knew that Fa' was perennially constipated.

Finally it was Mor's turn, and she cleared her throat as the boat bobbed up and down in the Sound.

"Well, being out here, I suppose I should say something about the water," Mor started. "Per *loved* to sail, you know."

"I don't remember him coming with us very often," Claus recalled.

"Och, it was Per who bought *Chancen*. You wouldn't remember, but when your father was a younger man, he was a great sailor. One time just the two of us went out in a 22-footer that we hired bareboat in Skagen. We'd spent all day cutting in and out of the shallow waters around Læsø and were on our way back. The sun was low in the western sky and twilight was just coming on. It was that time of day when you take out the merlot, relax and smoke a cigarette – we both smoked in those days, this is long before you children were even thought of.

"Well, there we were sipping our wine when all of a sudden AOOOOOOH! And then again, AOOOOOOH! We were directly in the path of the *Oslo Ferry*. Ten stories high and closing in on us, fast from the port side. Your father moved like lightning to tack and come about – not overdoing it, we couldn't risk a stall – just turning the vessel starboard, a little more, a little more. The current helped, thank God. Still, there was a point when we spoke about abandoning ship. At the last possible moment, we found ourselves heading south-southeast, out of the Leviathan's path. The wake of that monster was almost enough to tip us, but we held on, and it makes for a good sea-story now. But don't let anyone ever tell you Per André Nielsen wasn't a great sailor. For that he was."

It occurred to me that Mor and Fa' had held on to their marriage in the same desperate way – with alcoholism playing the role of the Oslo Ferry. In the end, it was Fa' – perhaps looking at his own reflection – who fell overboard.

Mor's expression then changed, and she drew in her cheeks slightly and her eyes got a glassy look as she stared at the gold watch in its case.

"You know, it's important to let someone go. I've never told anyone, but in the months following the funeral, I sometimes felt a... *presence* beside me. After I got into bed at night, I would even hear the bedsprings squeak a few minutes later, as if someone were crawling into bed with me.

"I had to tell Per – or whatever it was, perhaps just my own imagination – that he wasn't wanted in that bed anymore. Never came back after that, but God help me, I do miss him."

As if on cue, the pocket watch began chiming. Mor grabbed it and hurled it as far as she could toward the setting sun. As the hand-sized golden orb sank beneath the waves, I looked about, but no natural wonders were seen. No lightning rent the pure blue. The Danish colors flying over Rungstedlund did not miss a flap.

I pressed my fingers into Mor's hand. Claus gave her a big hug. After a few minutes, I said, "I suppose we should come about or we'll not make it back before nightfall."

"Of course you're right," Claus said, and he began the process of turning the craft.

Approaching the endless city of Copenhagen from the north, even from twenty kilometers out, we could see the sprawling conurbation, backlit and glowing yellow and amber in the final afternoon light of August. As Claus piloted us homeward, I sat astern with Mor, away from the worst of the wind.

"This is a little drier and warmer than where you were this morning, no?" Mor asked.

"Yes, it certainly is."

"Did you get a chance to visit with Claus while I slept?" I nodded. "I imagine you had a lot to catch up on. After all, you've never even met the children."

I doubt she would have noticed through the windburn, but blood rushed to my cheeks: I hadn't even *asked* Claus about his children. What were they, a boy and a girl? I wasn't sure.

"I'm really looking forward to meeting them. How old are they now?" I asked, fishing for the information.

"Marius is six and Cornelia is two."

"Hah, just like Claus and me."

"Same order, just a little further apart in age."

"Is Marius in first grade?"

"No, next year. He's in kindergarten-class now."

"Mor—"

"Yes, Skat?"

"Claus told me about how things were for you right after I left for New York," I said.

"He did, did he?" she replied, her head toggling gently.

"About the hospital. Everything."

"Well, I don't mind you knowing. It's good that you know."

"I never got his letter," I said.

"I never knew he'd written you. I should've told you myself, but then, what could you have done?"

"Was it a terrible time?"

"Yes, it was," she said, looking away.

"Did they put you on medicines?"

"Yes, thank God they did. I wouldn't be here otherwise. I'd be dead."

"Do you still take... I mean..."

"Goodness, no," she pshawed with a wave of the hand. "The whole wretched business blotted out two years of my life. *Two years.* But then, somehow, the fog lifted. I moved on with my life. I see friends and play bridge. I go shopping, attend the opera. Of course something has been missing. But in the past week, being with you, and today being together as a family, well, I think I've found it."

I clasped her hand, and felt for the first time that I'd really come home.

As we drew closer to the city, we gazed at the spires and steeples aflame in the afternoon sun, welcoming us. The greens of the countrified suburbs gave way to the quaint city skyline: low, terracotta roofs with occasional towers in the distance, more like medieval Tuscany than a modern metropolis.

"The wind has shifted," Claus barked from the bridge. "It's been blowing mostly westerly or southwesterly all day. Now it's whipped around and it's coming from the east. Can't you tell?"

I licked my right forefinger like they do in the movies and put it up.

"Ay, Captain," I said. "What's it mean?"

"Well, the tide's coming out this time of day, and we want to make for Hellerup, which is basically southwest of us."

"So the wind is at our backs – that's a good thing, right?"

"Yes, in a way. But if we come straight in, the tide'll be pushing out, directly at us. The wind won't be strong enough to overcome the tide, and we'll be tacking endlessly."

"So what do we do?" I asked.

"Well, luckily we've noticed the situation early enough. Since the tide and wind are contrary and of roughly equal strength, we can ride *between* the wind and tide. That is to say, cut a line South-Southwest all the way into shore."

"You mean ride between the wind and tide, all the way to the water's edge?" I asked.

As Mette had told me, *The energy of life, forced for a time to wander the dry earth, may yet return home again.*

"Yes, that's right," my brother said, "the water's edge."

*The water's edge.*

"Two grey old women, witchlike, with hanging breasts and dugs of finger-length, were busy there, between flaming braziers, most horribly. They were dismembering a child."

- Thomas Mann

*The Magic Mountain* ("Snow")

Trans. H.T. Lowe-Porter

# FALL
# 28. Richard

As I stood with Katrina on the front stoop on a summery Saturday afternoon, the wheels of a taxi screeched.

"Have fun galavanting out there on the Sound," I said, squinting as the late-afternoon sunlight glinted gold on her hair and sunglasses. "You sure you don't want me to drive you up there?"

"No," she said, facing me with a grin. "This is my turn to get in the cab and your turn to watch it drive away."

We embraced briefly, and she added, "And besides, you have chores to do!" Then she chuckled as she tripped, almost skipping, down the front walk, whistling a bouncy pop tune from the radio.

I smirked at the thought of my "honeydew" list – mow the lawn, trim the hedges, buy groceries. But mostly I felt relieved to see Katrina in such high spirits after the depression of the past few days. I was also apprehensive about spending the night alone. It was the stuff of B-movies, *Creature Features* on the snowy Zenith in my bedroom when I was a kid. Can you survive a night in the *House on Rosenborgs Allé?* Boris Karloff, Christopher Lee, Vincent Price. But for me it was not an old man's millions that I stood to gain but... what? My peace of mind? My marriage? My wife's sanity?

As I walked back inside, I went upstairs to pack for Monday. I started laying out my clothes. The familiarity of the task, my weekly ritual, was comforting. I packed four pairs of dark socks, four sets of underwear, four white dress shirts, shorts, t-shirt, athletic socks, Nike running shoes and my toiletry kit. Then I clunked my stout rollaway down the stairs one at a time, and stood in the dining room, quixotically appraising my swarthy traveling companion of five years. Trimmed in gunmetal, his dark skin reinforced by unbreakable carbon-fiber, El Señor Tumi was as sturdy, though not nearly as clever, as Don Quixote's legendary traveling companion, Sancho Panza. I felt like Don Q these days, tilting at windmills, laughed at by the locals. The Danish team hadn't accepted my hard-charging style, and now with the merger, who knew what was going to happen? I could get cut from the team, stranded here. Well, no sense worrying about it.

I patted my dumb friend, and went off in search of a more intellectual companion in the long bookcase in the living room. I found two intriguing titles: *The Magus* by John Fowles and Paulo Coelho's *The Valkyries*. The hard-shelled Brit weighed heavy in my hands; by comparison, the Brazilian was a lightweight. Both titles were misleading. The magus in question was *not* an Oriental astrologer searching for the Christ child, but a devious Greek millionaire who ensnares our self-absorbed protagonist in a "deadly game of political and sexual betrayal." Meanwhile, the valkyries in question were evidently *not* Odin's handmaidens carrying off fallen warriors to Valhalla, but a female motorcycle gang who communed with their guardian angels in the "starkly beautiful and sometimes dangerous Mojave Desert." I couldn't decide which I needed more – a good game of sexual betrayal or women on Harleys talking to angels – so I left them there, strange bedfellows on the dining room table.

Walking past Señor Tumi without so much as a nod, I went into the kitchen to make an easy dinner of ham and eggs – my cooking had never advanced much past Dr. Seuss – with a slice of whole-wheat toast, and a glass of OJ. The air was still heavy from the heat of the late-summer afternoon, so I parked my carcass out on the back porch.

As I munched the toast, crumbs fell on the firm, reassuring typescript of the *International Herald Tribune*. Election news: "Clinton Emerges Strong from

Chicago Convention, Proclaims Bridge to the 21st Century." The smooth-talking model of a modern TV President, Clinton was expected to win handily against Dole, a man better-suited to the Golden Age of Radio. He would've given *Calvin Coolidge* a run for his money…

My eyelids drooped and the typeface began to blur. It was the familiar somatic imperative of the late-afternoon lull: *Need caffeine!* Dutifully, I got up, crossed to the back door with the intention of going inside to make myself a cup of Café Noir, my favorite brand. But when I put my hand on the doorknob and twisted, nothing happened. I tried the other way, rattled the handle. No result.

Somehow, the door had latched itself. I was locked out! My stomach contracted and I felt a little ripple of fear. *How'd that happen? Who locked me out?* I dreaded the thought of having to call Katrina. But I didn't panic. Reassuring myself that the front door was open, I walked calmly into the yard, past the garage and down the driveway. As I emerged from the cool shade that dwelt in the alley between the buildings, I was blinded by a shaft of sunlight. A tall figure appeared before me and I jumped.

It was just Søren, and I said with a chuckle. "Oh, hi! You scared me."

"Good day, my neighbor!" he replied smilingly. "Playing the bachelor this weekend?"

I looked at him with eyebrows drawn, as if to ask, "How did *you* know?"

"I saw Katrina drive away in a taxi earlier," he explained.

I breathed out and said, "Oh, yeah. She'll be back tomorrow."

"That's good. Say, what are you doing this evening?"

"I don't know, maybe calling a locksmith. I just had to walk around from the backyard. I was eating dinner out on the patio, and when I went back to make some coffee, I realized the door was locked."

"Well, there's nothing to worry about. I can let you back in – you gave me the key when you went to Skagen, remember?"

"Oh, that's right," I said. "Well, let's see if we can get in the front way."

Glad to have the company, I motioned with my head for him to follow me. The front door put up no resistance, and we passed through the rooms unmolested. When we got to the back door, to my amazement, the handle turned easily and the door swung open.

"I don't get it," I said. "This door was locked just a minute ago."

"It seems to be open now," Søren confirmed.

We got on either side of the door and tried to recreate the situation, but no dice. The door wasn't sticky. The bolt slid easily. The latch wouldn't just fall by itself, even after multiple slammings. It was like the heart palpitations I had that time in college that mysteriously disappeared as soon as I set foot in the cardiologist's office in Philadelphia.

"These little things happen all the time in older homes," Søren said generously. "Don't let it bother you at all. Why don't we just share a little bottle of wine together and forget the whole thing. I have a nice Italian I've been just dying to open up for the longest time, a Brunello. What do you say?"

"I say that sounds great," I said, smiling bravely. "I have some tapas I can put out."

"That would be fine. And if you're not busy, there's a superb British film on DR1 tonight."

"Really? What is it?"

"*Rosenkrantz and Guildenstern are Dead,* Tom Stoppard's spoof of the Bard's Danish play. I adore Shakespeare, don't you? It's meant to be hilarious."

I agreed and a few minutes later, I had expunged the evidence of my eggy repast and set out snacks in the living room. Søren popped back over with the dusty bottle, its label stained with mold from the cellar, and a dark blue case. As we sat down, I saw it was a sommelier kit. From the velvet-lined box, he withdrew two goblets of leaded cut crystal, ghostly white on the unpolished faces, clear on the rim where the glass tapered to an edge so thin you could cut flesh with it.

Filled with anticipation, we said little. Søren poured the subfusc, turbid super-Tuscan. Even in the halogen bulb, I could see nothing through the murky elixir – it's called "brownie" for a reason. I swirled the glass, giving oxygen to the rusty liquid that had been suffocated for so many years. A whiff of vegetative rot reminded me of the dark earth it came from. I raised the sharp bell to my lips and as the complex acid tones filled my mouth, I felt a heady, medicinal rush like when you lick vanilla extract from the spoon. The finish was bitter.

Two men drinking alone are not given to oohing and aahing, but we both murmured appreciation of the moody wine. After that, we said nothing. The almost-ritual silence was interrupted only by the ticking of the clock and the occasional sound of our teeth crunching into cracked wheat toast with garlicky tapenade.

I tuned in the Danish national television station, and the incomprehensible drone of the Danish news came on. The first story was something about the Greeks not wanting Danes to use the word "feta" on their cheese – there you go, the EU in action. Then Bill Clinton's grinning face filled the screen, his speech from the Democratic National Convention. Wow, he was on a roll. Just as I was starting to enjoy the clip, the phone rang. I excused myself and picked it up in the "office," an alcove between the stairs and the kitchen. When I put the receiver to my ear, all I heard was a click and then the cold moan of a dial tone. I set the phone back in its cradle and saw the red light on the answering machine blinking. I pressed *Play* and heard the voice of the machine.

| | |
|---|---|
| **Machine voice** | "You have – two – new messages. First message." *Beeep.* |
| **Mom's voice** | "Hi Richard, It's your mother. Give me a buzz. I was just wondering what's going on over there. Did you see the President's speech Thursday night? Oh, he was wonderful..." *Beeep.* |
| **Machine** | "Second – message." *Beeep.* *Hissing.* |
| **Hoarse male voice** | "I've got you, now." *Hissing resumes for several seconds. Beeep.* |
| **Machine** | "No more messages." |

I couldn't believe what I was hearing. I replayed the message three times, but still didn't recognize the caller's voice. No one I knew. My finger reached for *Erase*, but held back. Maybe I should keep the recording as evidence.

*Evidence of what? That I really heard it?*

I only half-believed there could be such a thing as a ghost. After all, I was a modern, educated man. I had letters after my name! But I was weakening, slipping into the comfortable agnosticism of "keeping an open mind." A dangerous thing. As Pop used to say, "When a man opens his mind, he makes himself vulnerable. Like a woman when she opens her *legs*."

It's not that my father was closed-minded, but he always expected you to have a "point of view." At the moment, my point of view was that locking me out like that was exactly the kind of childish prank that poltergeists supposedly play on people. Maybe this was just a prank call, somebody having a good laugh at my expense.

Locking me out felt symbolic, though, like somebody wanted to get rid of me. Damsgaard was a womanizer; my wife is an extraordinarily beautiful woman. If he was really haunting the place, I could see how the old dog would like having Katrina around, be in love with her even. But then why would he push her down the stairs? Maybe he didn't mean to hurt her, just tried to embrace her, but startled her instead, and she fell. Then he locks me out and sends a threatening message when I'm alone in the house for the first time. *That means he knows I'm here alone...*

But what was I saying? I was thinking crazy thoughts. And who ever heard of a ghost who leaves telephone messages? That's ridiculous!

Still, I couldn't help speculating... What was a telephone call but an electric current? The electrical had been haywire since we moved in – bulbs blowing all over the place, the fuse blowing at the Housewarming, clocks running backwards – what if the dead could speak to the living using a series of electrical impulses?

"Richard!" said a voice.

I jumped six inches. Then I looked up and saw Søren.

"Oh, it's just you. You startled me," I said, laughing at my own case of nerves.

"I'm sorry to disturb you, but it's starting in a couple of minutes," he said.

"What?"

"The film."

"Oh, right, *Rosenstern and Gildersleeve.* I'll be right there." I paused. *Should I confide in him?*

"Uh, Søren, would you listen to this message for me?"

"Of course. What is it?"

"Prank call, I guess. It's hard to make out. Here, listen,"

We listened to the tape together. I was half-relieved to hear the menacing voice, that I hadn't imagined it.

"What do you think of that?" I asked.

Søren knitted his brows. "How long has that message been on the machine?"

I played back the envelope information. The call was from Friday.

"You haven't checked the messages since then?" he asked, surprised.

"No."

"Perhaps Katrina has already checked them?"

"No."

"How can you be sure? Perhaps you should ask her—"

"Nah, the machine said I had two new messages. This was one of them. And besides, if she'd heard that message, I'm sure she would have told me."

"So she hasn't heard it," he said. After a pause, he asked, "Are you going to tell her about it?"

After a moment's thought, I replied, "No, at least not right away. She has a big day tomorrow. I don't want to worry her."

"Ah, yes. Of course," he replied. He seemed to reflect for a moment, and then said, "Still she should know, don't you think?"

"Yeah, sure, eventually. But I don't want to call her tonight." He nodded. I couldn't figure out why he was so focused on whether Katrina had heard it. The room fell silent. Finally, I repeated, "So what do you think?"

"About what?"

"About the message – must be a prank, right?"

"I— I don't know."

"What makes you hesitate? It sounds like somebody on a hissy cell phone graveling their voice to make it sound scary, right?"

"Well, that could be, but—"

"But what?"

He just looked away, toward the dining room.

"You think it's Damsgaard, don't you?" I asked.

"I didn't say that. It's just – why would someone call you with such a message?"

"I don't know. As a prank, I guess."

Looking straight at me, he said, "Richard, the message is in *English*." The meaning of this did not register at first. "Are we to believe this is an *international* prankster?"

Then it hit me. Any local Bart Simpson would've spoken Danish. Søren shook his head slowly and I asked the question that we both had on our minds: "Did Damsgaard speak English?"

"Yes. Quite well in fact."

"So you think there's a real possibility that it's a call from Damsgaard." It felt surreal to say this. I expected him to dismiss the idea out of hand, but he didn't.

"Well, I don't know," he began. "I've never heard of a phone call from beyond the grave. But then again, haunted places report more auditory phenomena than any other – banging, footsteps, voices…"

I had heard enough. "Let's go watch the movie. I've got to get my mind off of this shit," I said, slipping into a New York patois that seemed to unsettle my guest. "Uh, pardon my French."

"Sure," he said. "Let's see that film."

As we sat down side by side on the green couch, the opening scene was just getting underway. Two guys on horseback, one of them flipping a coin as they rode along. Søren gave me some background. It seems that Rosenkrantz (the name means *garland of roses* in Danish) – and Guildenstern (*golden star*) are minor characters in *Hamlet.* They're some kind of royal heralds or something, who appear briefly and then are summarily reported dead. Talk about "shooting the messenger." In this version, we see the action from their point of view. The main characters, like Hamlet, the Queen, Claudius and the rest just walk on and off.

*I guess in real life, we all think we're the main character, right?*

The coin kept coming up heads. Every time. Heads and heads, and heads again. Dozens of times until you just couldn't believe it was coincidence any more. I tried to follow the action, which – like life, I guess – was at turns philosophical and meaningless, Shakespearean and slapstick. But my thoughts kept wandering back to the ghost.

If it was just one thing – the wineglass shattering for instance – you could write it off as a freak occurrence. The factory produced a glass with a hidden flaw that exploded when hit with a certain vibration. If it was two things – like the business plan disappearing just when I said the word "ghost" – then you could say it was some kind of coincidence. But there's been so many incidents…

*What happens to us after we die?*

Despite years of Catholic schooling, I did not have a strong point of view on precisely what happens after we shuffle off the old mortal coil.

Eddé says that consciousness is just the byproduct of electrical impulses in the brain: turn off that electric current, the "person" disappears. There's just a flat line. Forever.

My mother believes our souls are immortal. After death we appear before a judicial Jesus who separates the sheep from the goats, wheat from chaff – the latter in each case thrown into a lake of everlasting fire. Gnashing of teeth and all that.

Katrina is charmed by the idea of a Self beyond self that develops over multiple lives. Eventually, after entering more young bodies than Mick Jagger, the soul returns to the Great All like a water droplet returning to the ocean.

Søren – believes in spooks.

"Do you really believe in spooks?" I asked.

"What?" he said, stopping mid-laugh as he looked up from Gary Oldman's pratfalls.

"Do you believe in ghosts? I mean, isn't that unscientific?"

Without missing a beat, he said, "It's unscientific *not* to believe in ghosts."

"How do you mean?"

"Science is based on observation, evidence, universality. If you examine any culture, during any time period, you will find reports of spirits, ghosts, hauntings. One person can be wrong, even a whole society can be wrong, but all societies cannot be wrong."

Thinking of Eddé, I countered, "But some people would say that belief in ghosts is just primitive."

"Yet even so-called modern societies – if there are any that deserve the name – have their mediums, their Ouija boards, their séances. Why?"

"I don't know. Maybe because some people, the weak-minded, want something to believe in. It's too terrifying to look Death straight in the face."

"The 'weak-minded,'" he said with a roll of his eyes. "You're just disregarding the evidence that doesn't fit your theory. A clear violation of the scientific method."

"So you really think that a rational person has to believe in ghosts?"

"You must, at the very least, keep an open mind. And trust your data-gathering devices, your full five."

"Full five?"

"Your senses."

I took another sip of the cloudy wine. I realized the drink (and maybe the conversation) was going to my head. I put down the glass, sat on the edge of my seat and said, "Well, just for the sake of argument, let's say that there is such a thing as a ghost."

"As the ancient Greek said, 'Thou art but a little soul wandering about bearing a corpse.'"

"Okay, a little soul wandering around, *stuck* in this world when it should be in the next. Tell me, why can't it move on?"

"It's difficult to say exactly why spirits should get stuck. Juvenile souls may need help finding the way to the next world. Sometimes in the case of sudden deaths, a man may not even realize he's dead – a soldier killed in war comes home quite annoyed to find a stranger in his bed."

"So you're saying Damsgaard might not know he's dead?"

He shook his head. "He was an old, sick man by the end. His death was hardly unexpected."

"Okay then I give up – why can't he move on?"

"I don't know," he said, looking down. Then he fixed his eyes on mine and said, "But here's an idea for you: Karl Damsgaard was a man of the world, a man of *this* world. He loved to smoke and drink and make love to women. Perhaps he just couldn't let all that go." As if to emphasize the point, he took up a cracker piled high with cheese and gave it a loud crunch. I nodded and was about to agree with him when his face clouded over and he shook his head. "No, no, that won't work at all."

"Why not? It makes perfect sense," I declared. "Damsgaard doesn't want to lounge around in paradise playing a harp all day. Like the sign in the Irish pub says, 'I may be going to Hell, but at least all my friends will be there!'"

"Yes, but spirits don't have bodies, so they can't enjoy alcohol or nicotine…" Søren's voice trailed off and he was silent for a moment. Then his eyes opened wide and he said, "Wait. What if a ghost could get a kind of satisfaction from being close to the pleasures of this life?"

"What do you mean?"

"I recall a case in England where the ghost of a chemically-dependent woman haunted her lover, also a drug-abuser, to continue the 'high' after death."

"You mean an addict who couldn't get the monkey off her back even after she died?"

"Precisely," he said, punctuating his remark with his index finger. "In this case, I think *smoke* may be the telltale. Katrina tells me you keep smelling cigarettes?"

"Yeah, that's right."

"Well, perhaps Katrina herself is smoking secretly, and Damsgaard is participating in the nicotine buzz."

"Katrina, smoking? Aw, I can't believe that: she's a health-nut."

"Yes, I was surprised too, but the evidence is there, and she was a smoker before, no?"

"Yeah, she smoked years ago. What evidence?"

"I've smelled tobacco on her clothing, found *Prince* cigarette-ends in the driveway – that's not my brand. Most tellingly, there are her teeth."

"Her teeth?"

"Surely you've noticed the yellow stains?"

This stung me. I *had* noticed something different about her teeth, but somehow I had never thought of this rather obvious explanation: Katrina was smoking.

"You think it's from tobacco?" I asked.

"What else? And it would explain why you keep smelling smoke, wouldn't it? It's the simplest explanation – and that's most often the correct one, yes?" he pointed out, invoking Occam's Razor.

I mulled over this up-till-now unthinkable possibility. It seemed more logical than imagining Damsgaard strolling through the halls toking on a spectral stogie.

"I'm sorry to be the one to tell you," he said, decanting the last of the Brunello, careful not to let the dregs descend into our glasses.

Damsgaard had said, *Their sin is delightful.* Could it be that he somehow delights in our vices, our sins? I was dumbstruck. I stared at the screen. The movie was by this point in its last throes. Off-stage, the mad Ophelia was dead in her grave, soon joined by Claudius and the Queen. On-stage, Rosencrantz and Guildenstern were dead, but still continued their wordplay and tomfoolery, not knowing when to make their exit.

When the red velvet curtain on the small screen finally fell, Søren rose. "Well thank you for a most diverting evening. We must do this Boys' Night at the Biograph again soon."

"Sure," I said, as we walked toward the door. "Thanks for the company. I'm sorry to lay all my troubles at your feet."

"Not at all. I think it's very interesting. Mysterious. Makes one think about the stranger things that lie between Heaven and Earth."

"Good night, sweet Prince," I said, picking up on the reference.

"And may flights of angels sing thee to thy rest," he said as he descended the trio of stone steps.

I closed the door, collected up the remains of the nibbles. On edge, I wasn't sleepy; maybe I could make some tea. I shut off the lights in the living room and walked toward the kitchen. As I passed the crooked door to the basement, a burst of cold air rushed by me. I got gooseflesh and shivered. The hair on my forearms was standing at attention, as if I'd walked through an electric field or something. Out of the corner of my eye, I caught a glimpse of something, like a shadow running along the wall. I turned, but I didn't see anything out of place. The only sound was the ticking of the clock.

*Like a pulse, the house's pulse.*

Trying to shake it off, I said out loud, "Richard, get ahold of yourself."

I sought the shelter of the clean, well-lighted kitchen to make myself a cup of tea. Just as the electric kettle started to chug, the grandfather clock pounded out the hour, reminding me it was TEN PM, like the public-service announcements on Channel Five when I was a kid.

*Do you know where your children are?*

This reminded me of my mother – she had left a message on the machine. I owed her a call. What otherwise might have been a barren chore blossomed into a delight. With anticipation approaching glee, I took the cordless phone off the wall and dialed the familiar number.

"Hello?"

"MOM!" I almost shouted into the receiver.

"Richard! How *are* you? I was just thinking about you."

"That's nice. I'm just returning your call," I said, trying to sound cool.

"Yes, I left a message."

"I know. You asked if I saw Clinton's speech. In fact, I didn't – it was on at four in the morning over here. But I did see some clips on the Danish news. He was pretty good, huh?"

"Oh, he was inspiring. 'I believe in religious liberty. I believe in freedom of speech. I believe in working hard and playing by the rules.' What a thrilling convention – I wish I could have been there!"

"You probably saw it better on TV."

"But I missed all the excitement and energy of being in that room!"

"I suppose so," I said, thinking that having so much 'energy' in a room was not always such a good thing.

"How's Katrina?"

"She went to her mother's. I'm on my own tonight."

Pause on the line.

"Did you two have a fight?" she asked.

"No, nothing like that. She's going sailing tomorrow with her mother and her brother Claus, and they wanted to get an early start, so she stayed over."

"But her mother doesn't live very far away. Why does she have to stay over there? Are you sure she's not mad at you?"

"I think she just wanted to spend the night at her Mom's, sleep in her own room. She's been – a little down lately."

"Well, we all get the blues sometime. Are you okay by yourself? Did you make yourself something to eat?"

"Yeah, Ma, I'm fine," I said, pausing before adding, "I'm a little nervous, I guess."

"Nervous? Nervous about what?"

"I don't know," I admitted. "It's just. Well. I feel like I'm not welcome…"

"In Denmark, you mean?"

"Well, that too, I guess," I said with a self-conscious laugh. Then I told her about getting locked out and the threatening message.

"Wha-at?" she said.

"I know, it's weird."

"Oh, my, that's terrible, Richard. Tell me, do you have any enemies?"

"Enemies? You mean like at work?"

"Wherever. Did you cross anybody?"

"No, not that I can think of. I haven't been here long enough to really have enemies."

"Think. You said people found you 'rough,' right?"

"Yeah, but nobody from Fielding & Co. would ever play a trick like this – Fielding men pride themselves on their maturity and self-restraint."

"Say, wait a minute, didn't you say there was a big merger going on?"

"Yeah – what do you mean, that someone from AmeriBancorp is out to get me?"

"You never know – remember when you were in Saint Sebastian's School, and we got a call from that shrimpy kid with the wax in his ears, what was his name?"

I rolled my eyes and took a deep breath. "Stephen O'Reilly."

"That's the one. You could've grown potatoes in his ears. Well anyway, I remember one day you were home from school for lunch, and the phone rang, I'll never forget. You answered and that boy threatened you, didn't he?"

"Yeah, Ma, but…"

"What did he say?"

"It's not the same, Ma."

*"What'd he say?"*

"I don't remember. Something like 'I'm gonna get you,' something like that."

"There, you see, almost the same words."

"Yeah, but this was on the message machine. And it didn't sound—" I was about to say "normal," but what came out was, "human."

Silence on the line. Then she managed, "Not human? What do you mean, it was like a machine-voice, like a robot?"

"No, not like that either."

Silence.

"Richard, are you still there?"

"Yeah."

"What was it like?"

"I don't know. It was scary. I mean, a ghost can't leave a voice mail. That's crazy, isn't it?"

"Yes, that's crazy. Listen Richard, you get a priest in to bless the house."

"There aren't a lot of Catholic priests over here, Ma."

"So get a Lutheran priest."

"I don't think they do that."

"Well, what about that nice Anglican priest you have living next door, maybe he can help you."

"George?"

"Yeah, he's a doll. I love the way he talks. It's just like *Masterpiece Theatre*."

"I don't know if he's helping the situation. If anything, it's the opposite. Now he's got Katrina believing in ley lines."

"What's that?"

"You don't want to know."

"Why not?"

"They're some kind of energy fields in the ground. Evidently, they're a big thing over in England, and now George has got Katrina thinking that we have some kind of a geo-electrical superhighway running through here."

"Oh, my."

I paused and tried a new tack. "Ma, do you believe in guardian angels?"

"Yes, of course I do."

"Do you have one?"

"I guess so. I suppose everybody does."

"Have you never *talked* with your Guardian Angel?"

"No, why?"

"I don't know. I guess I just feel a little vulnerable."

"You want to ask your Guardian Angel for help?"

"Yeah. I think I will. It'll make me feel less – alone."

"Prayer really helps, Richard. Use the beads I gave you, they're from the Vatican. You still have them, right?"

"Yeah, Ma."

"And see if you can find yourself a Catholic Church over there, and go tell the priest what's going on. Or get some holy water and say a blessing yourself. You can get the holy water at the rectory, they won't even charge you for it, just bring a container."

"Okay, Ma. Thanks, it's good to have someone to talk to."

"It's my pleasure. And don't worry so much."

"Okay, I won't. Goodnight."

"Goodnight, Sweetheart."

I put the phone back on the wall-cradle, comforted. John Steinbeck sat alone with his dog Charley on the edge of unfathomable darkness, with no allies against the Night. But I didn't have to be alone, I could get somebody on *my* side, contact my Guardian Angel. Like the Valkyries.

My tea had gone cold, and I put the kettle on a second time. As I started to pour the water, I realized that there was a voice, barely perceptible, coming from the next room. Maybe the TV was still on.

But the living room was empty and the screen dark. Listening intently, I heard a man's voice, audible but not quite discernable. I wasn't even sure what language it was at first, though I guessed it was Danish from the smear of deep tones, like verbal peanut butter. There was a crackly quality to it, like an old-time radio broadcast, as if it came out of the Gothic-arched speakers of a wireless set in a bygone era, but instead of shooting out into space like it was supposed to, it had gotten stuck within the walls.

I stood in the dimly-lit dining room and strained my senses to make out where it was coming from. The voice seemed to emerge from the walls themselves. As the speaker rabbited on, he became agitated and the sound grew in intensity – I could almost make out the words. It didn't sound Danish anymore. I heard the spitting dentals and knew it was German; I picked out a handful of words that I recognized – *Deutschland* and *nacht* and *krieg* and *kampf.*

My eye caught a glimpse of light seeping out from under the door to the cellar. I didn't remember leaving that light on. I crept over to the door and stood there, listening. *Could there be somebody down there?* I put my ear to the door until the pine creaked. A breathy static scratched at my ears, rising and falling, as if the house itself was breathing.

I built up my courage and cracked open the door. A rivulet of light from the cold stairwell flooded the carpet. I eased the door open farther and peered down the narrow stairway. Recalling Katrina's fall, I braced myself and stood back from the brink.

No one was down there, I could see that, but still I called down, "Hello, anybody there?"

No answer. But the Voice seemed to fade a bit, as if placated by the acknowledgement. I reached out my hand to shut the light, which went off with a snap and a sizzle as of a bulb bursting. I jumped and shut the thin door of ancient pine, and stood with my back to it. I squinted into the darkened rooms, lit only by the faint gaslight glowing in the picture window. The shadows seemed to flicker and dance around the room. I rubbed my eyes, but the weird ballet continued.

The jabbering faded, turned into music, and slowly grew in intensity. It was the haunting melody that Katrina has been playing every day. The chords chimed like a church bell. I stood stiff against to the door and held my ears. Was this a funeral dirge for Damsgaard? I'm sure I must have imagined it, but my back muscles seemed to register a slight pushing, as if the door itself were bowing outward. I put my weight against the door and it creaked. The noise in my ears was deafening – surely the neighbors must hear it now! – yet no help was on the way.

No one was coming.

When I couldn't stand it any more, I threw myself across the room toward the nearest light fixture, the piano lamp. When the light came on, the sounds died away and all was quiet once more. *Oh my God, I'm hearing things now. The first clear sign of insanity.* But wait, didn't Søren say that auditory phenomena were the most common in hauntings?

I pressed a key at random, one of the black ones. The tone was the same one that had been repeated over and over in the hellish music. I snatched back my hand as if the keyboard had teeth, and backed away from the instrument.

There was nothing to do but lock up for the night and go to bed. Plucking up my courage, I strode through the rooms, flipping lights on and off and securing the front and rear gates with steel deadbolts. When all else was dark, I snuffed out the last light and, despite myself, took the stairs two at a time, like when I was little boy in Forest Hills, fleeing up the stairs to the safety of my bedroom.

To fulfill the promise to my mother, I did a meditation exercise called "Ideal House" that I'd learned during my years in the Jesuit school. Still in my clothes, my legs crossed with some difficulty in a half-lotus position, I closed my eyes and put my hands on my knees. My thumbs made contact with my fore- and middle-fingers. My muscles were tight as guy-wires, my head throbbing so I could count my pulse at the temple. I breathed, focused on each body-part in turn, loosening, relaxing, slowing my inhalations and my heartbeat until the headache left me and my muscles softened to wet fettuccine.

I imagined myself in my favorite room, a wood-trimmed study lined with built-in bookshelves worthy of Oliver Twist's benefactor or the Reform Club of Phileas Fogg. Cluttered and dusty, the library had been set up fifteen-twenty years ago, and hadn't been tended to; I considered tidying up, but couldn't seem to find the dust-cloth. Accepting the disorder in my mind, I nestled into the burgundy wingback armchair facing the elevator that enabled visitors to come and go. In my schooldays, it had brought me important advisors like Vergil, Dante, Gil Hodges. But I must've fallen asleep because I was no longer in control. I wanted my Guardian Angel to appear, but when the light on top of the elevator finally came on and the door opened, what emerged was no angel.

A tiny man dressed in tails and silk top hat appeared, like Toulouse-Lautrec on his way to the Opera Populaire. It was the curator from the Bangsbo Museum.

He seemed pissed off. Thinking he'd felt snubbed because we left without saying goodbye, I explained that we had looked for him at the end of the tour that day, but he'd disappeared. But the Midget made no reply, just nodded, appraising me silently. When I asked him about Karl Damsgaard, what he made of the coincidence of the quotation, he began to laugh. A horrible, derisive laugh.

Frightened, I tried to wake myself – I knew it was a dream by this point – but then he was on me, knocking me backwards and kneeling on my chest. *I've got you now.* He had me pinned. His asymmetrical face was in mine, his hot breath on my skin, stinking, as if he'd eaten garbage. Pressing his hand onto my jaw, he forced my head to the side. I felt a burning sensation, as if he was pouring a scalding liquid – poison, it occurred to me at the time – into my ear canal.

*Oww!* I jerked awake and felt real pain. My head was crammed onto the nightstand, the wooden corner jutting into the portal of my right ear. The light was on. I sat up and fell back against the pillows of my bed, holding the side of my head. My fingers were orange-red, drenched in a sticky substance – my own sweat tinged with wax and blood. I was soaked, my shirt glued to the skin of my arms and torso. Taking off the shirt, I pressed it to my aching ear.

I had the feeling I was being watched, and looked up. The scene was well-lit, even superrealistic. Every detail in focus. By this point, I was *not* asleep. The LED readout of the clock was 02:00, exactly. Across from the bed, the wardrobe stood open, and I saw something in the looking glass on the door – one of the few mirrors that'd survived the feng shui purge. Something that should not be there.

It was not a menacing face, not the fierce Midget. It wasn't scary at all, at least not at first. It was just a pointy hat, in the shape of a mitre, jet black with a dull silver stripe down the middle. Something a warlike bishop might have worn during the Crusades. The outline was very sharp, like a poster would be.

As I sat up to take a better look, it fell. It did not disappear or fade away, it slipped away *slowly* down and to the right. Had there been a poster like that hanging on the wall behind me? My head whipped around. No poster on the wall, not on the floor. I got out of bed, scrutinized every inch, but there was nothing.

I was mystified. But then, wait a minute, a *black hat*, that rang a bell. Katrina had just been telling me about a Tibetan holy man that could see remotely into the homes and lives of others. He wore a black hat. The feng shui lady had asked him to help us. Is that how he does it? Was he peeping in our bedroom mirror?

*Ewwh,* I shuddered.

I got up and went to the bathroom, splashed cold water on my face. The evening was chilly, and I went around and shut all the upstairs windows. I brushed my tongue and teeth to remove the Velcro that had accumulated since dinner, slurped some water from the tap, then felt my stomach roil. I belched and felt a dollop of vomit burn on the back of my tongue. I rinsed my mouth again from the tap and chewed a couple of lemon antacid tablets for the agita. Then I went back to my room, making sure that all the doors on the hallway were sensibly shut.

Stripping down to my jockeys, I put on a dry undershirt. I checked again behind the bed for the poster of the black hat, but found just a couple of dust bunnies. I snapped off the light and the room was enveloped in darkness. As my eyes adjusted, I saw the moonlight cut through the ash and oaks, impaling a dappled pattern on the wall. I was tired, but too freaked out to sleep. My thoughts whirled. This isn't happening. Voices, threats, visions.

*It can't be real.*

I said a prayer, one from my boyhood, and as long as the glow of the sacred words lingered upon my lips, I felt warm and protected. But as soon as they had flown up to heaven, the room grew cold again; the darkness closed in around me. My rational mind knew that darkness was nothing more than the absence of light, that it would flee at the flick of a switch. But at that moment, darkness felt like a material thing, a sticky, suffocating substance. The shadows surrounded me, crowded and jostled me with a blackness that was not cool like onyx stone, but soft and smothering like crushed velvet, enfolding me, enrobing my body in its inky wrap. My pulse quickened in my ears, my breathing shallowed. I gulped at the air like a codfish on a pike, but couldn't get enough, as if my windpipe was being held closed.

Breathing hard, I whipped on the light again. The room took on a morose appearance as I sat there panting. The carved chair back frowned, the armoire loomed, the jacket slung casually on the pegboard took on the shape of a hanged man.

The room was close. I'd sweated through my shirt again. What was wrong with me, did I have a fever? I placed my hand on my forehead, which was warm and sweaty. I opened the window wide and let the damp night air roll in until I shivered. I closed my eyes and prayed again, manically repeating the same prayer over and over, as I changed shirts again. The soft dry cotton felt good next to my overheated skin. I ratcheted the window down to the first notch, left the curtains wide open. I crawled back in under the covers, exhausted, and slowly, my breathing became easier again. The wind in the trees made a doleful sound, but at least the stifling, crypt-like atmosphere was gone. It was 3 AM.

I was about to turn off the light when I realized the doors to the wardrobe had swung open again. *Was that a twinkle in its glassy eye?* I dragged myself out of bed, shut the door of the disobedient chifforobe, and placed a chair solidly in front of it to prevent any further shenanigans. I had to get some sleep.

Resolving to sleep late in the morning, I lay back down and switched off the light. The feeling in the room was much better with the window open. Turning onto my side, I gave myself strict orders to fall asleep, and drifted off into an uneasy sleep. But it was not to last. The bed was shaking. It was a gentle rocking, but unmistakable. This had happened before, always with Katrina lying next to me. At first it would seem like the rocking was a result of me jumping awake. But it would continue for forty seconds to a minute or so. Sometimes I would hear a train whistle in the distance, affording me the illusion that the incident was the result of remote locomotion. But no palliative whistle blew. The red diode read 04:00. Four o'clock in the morning, the hour when human capabilities reach their daily nadir.

Just then, I heard tramping on the stair. The footfalls were so clear that I felt sure somebody was out there purposely trying to make racket. I shot out of bed – bravely, I remember thinking – and went to the head of the stairs. The mumbling was audible again, coming from downstairs. The smell of tobacco smoke was heavy in the hallway; I turned on the hall light, and I saw smoke drifting about.

"Is there anybody there?" I asked, almost inadvertently.

My fear had by this point turned to indignation and anger. I strode up and down yelling into the rooms and down the stairs like a crazy person.

"Get out of here!" I yelled. "You don't belong here – this is my home – leave me alone!"

Sure enough, just a few seconds later, all was silent once more. I said a prayer of thanks to my Guardian Angel, and a sense of contentment came over me. Evidently, there was a battle of wills between the current and original owners of the real estate, and I was acquitting myself well. I smiled as sleep came over me for what felt like the umpteenth time.

*Tap, tap.*

I felt two pokes, insistent on my shoulder. Distinct, as if somebody was trying to get my attention. I lifted my head and looked around, bewildered. The room was bright now, filled with silvery moonlight – or more likely the graying of dawn, it must've been five o'clock. I started to fall back asleep again, convinced that the taps had just been part of a dream. But in the moments before losing consciousness, I heard a gentle *plop,* and then another, as if a couple of magazines had fallen over in the room. That was the last thing I could remember.

I woke to the peals of church bells on Sunday morning and squinted around the room, embarrassed by the evidence of my vigil: the wardrobe barricaded by a chair; the window open to the first notch, curtains flying open, allowing in the peeping of the songbirds; the hall light still on, its glow faint in the light of day. Joyous as Scrooge on Christmas morning, I grinned from ear to ear, jumped out of bed and stopped just short of doing a victory dance. Was I mocking the superstition of the wee hours now that I was standing in the enlightenment of the bright morning? Or was I celebrating the victory of Light over the forces of Darkness?

*Maybe a bit of both.*

For the first time in my life, I knelt by the side of my bed and said matins. As long as the tintinnabulation continued, I prayed and thanked my Guardian Angel for protecting me. I stumbled to the bathroom. Bloodshot eyes looked back at me from the mirror; I looked as rough as I felt. Evidently hung over, I put my mouth under the faucet and drank loudly. The fuzz on my tongue and bad taste in my mouth reminded me of last night's brutish Brunello. I brushed my teeth, opened all the doors and windows and took a long run, making a complete circuit of the bastions of Kastellet. When I got back, I took a steaming shower, dressed and made a bacon-and-eggs breakfast. The late night cat-and-mouse games were forgotten as I sat and read the papers, hovering over them with my coffee. I ginned up the Mercedes and went to pick up my shirts; I did some food shopping. At about one o'clock, I mowed the lawn, pulled weeds – I got rid of those mushrooms too – and removed some dead branches from the shrubbery. I was just looking up at the high branches on the ash tree when I saw it was almost four o'clock. Katrina could be home any minute, so I went inside and washed up.

As I came down the stairs, I was planning to sit down with a book, probably Coelho. Overnight, I had developed a keen interest in guardian angels. But when I walked into the dining room, the books were not on the table where I'd put them. Thinking they'd fallen, I looked on the floor by the table, but out of the corner of my eye, I saw the two of them, huddled together on the wood floor.

In a universe ruled by gravity and entropy, it was hardly a surprise that a couple of books should fall off a table. But these two were lying clear across the room; and as I approached them, it was clear that they were not lying randomly. On the contrary, it was an *impossible* position. They were vertical and at right angles to each other, "making a box" with the corner of the room. *The Valkyries* was even pages up – imagine that, a flimsy paperback just standing there like that. The tapping on my shoulder at 5 AM and the plopping sounds of magazines falling in the room came back to me, and I realized – there *were* no magazines in our bedroom.

I felt the blood drain from my head, and just before I hit the floor Katrina's cheerful voice rang out behind me.

"Richard, I'm home! Where are you?"

# 29. Søren

The time I spent with my neighbor on Saturday evening had gone exceedingly well. Of course I was disappointed that Katrina was away, but it had given me the opportunity to open up the Italian, and I really enjoyed that. I slept late into the afternoon on Sunday, rousing myself only when I heard Katrina come home in a taxi.

I had frozen some fish stew – Mother's recipe – some days ago. I put it on the stove to warm as I went to bathe and make myself presentable. At about five o'clock, I strolled across the driveway and rang the bell. Katrina opened the door looking radiant but preoccupied.

"Oh, Søren – it's you."

"I can see I'm disturbing you. I'm sorry. It's just that, well, I've made a mistake. I misjudged and now I have an enormous tureen full of bouillabaisse – I couldn't possibly finish it myself. Would you like some?"

"Who is it, Katrina?" said a voice.

"It's Søren. He says he's made too much soup tonight."

"Well, ask him in!"

"Oh, of course, please come in, Søren."

I stepped gingerly into the foyer. My neighbor was reclining on the sofa, a package of frozen peas on his forehead. He looked awful – bags under his eyes, lump on the head, bandage on his ear.

I said, "What happened to you?"

"Oh, nothing, I hit my head," he said.

"It was just when I got home, just an hour ago," Katrina explained.

"Yeah, I went for a long run. I guess I overdid it..." Richard added with a sheepish grin.

"Oh, I'm so sorry," I said, "and after we had such a pleasant evening together last night."

"Yeah, thanks for coming over," he said, and then to Katrina, "Søren and I watched a movie on TV last night, Sweetheart."

It always annoyed me to hear him call her by pet names, but of course I didn't say anything. Katrina seemed surprised that I was chumming with her husband.

I didn't want too much examination of my motives, so I said, "Well, I don't want to disturb your rest, but I thought I would bring over some of the bouillabaisse, seeing as I've no chance to finish it myself, and it's never the same next day."

"Well bring it over – we've got some stories to tell!" Richard said.

"Oh, I really hadn't meant to invite myself..."

"Nonsense – after all you're bringing the dinner! And very nice of you it is, too," he said.

So it was settled. I was coming to dinner.

I went to fetch the tureen of piquant fish stew, and brought it to the back door. While it had not been my intention to eat with them – Mother's bouillabaisse always gave me a headache the next day – I decided to make the best of it. I would investigate how yesterday had gone, and look for an opening to steer them toward the Psychic.

*"Var det fornøjeligt på vandet i går?"* I asked, alone in the kitchen with Katrina. "Was Poseidon in a good humor?"

"Yes, it was a fantastic day. It was great to get together again with my mother and brother. I hadn't seen Claus in ages."

"He is doing well, your brother?"

"Oh, yes, really well," she said with some hesitancy in her voice.

"You two were... estranged?"

Katrina reddened to the roots and said, "It's complicated."

Then she told me about an antique pocket watch that she and her brother had quarreled over.

"This pocket watch, it was among the items left by one of the founders of the firm?" I asked.

"Yes," she said.

"And who was this founder?"

"That's just it. No one seems to know – evidently he bowed out early on, due to some scandal or other."

"Scandal?" I asked, intrigued.

"Yes."

"Tell me, was there an inscription on the watch, something to link it to the original owner?" I asked.

"Why do you ask?"

"Well, the pattern fits, doesn't it?" I asked.

"What pattern?"

"You come to live in the home of a prominent Copenhagen lawyer who lived at the turn of the century..."

"Ohh, Søren," she said, realizing. "You mean the mystery founder could have been Damsgaard?"

"Even the newspaper clipping you saw—"

"Referred to scandal, yes. Oh my God, Søren!" she said, putting her hand to her mouth.

"Now let's not jump to conclusions," I said, putting on an air of coolness. "We just need to examine the watch, open up the case—"

"Never," she said, the corners of her mouth drooping.

"Why not?"

"Because it's at the bottom of Øresund."

Just then the Italian came in, asking for his supper, and the topic of conversation shifted. We brought out the simple Provençal meal: bouillabaisse with fresh baguette, along with some tapenade left over from last night, and a bottle of Chateau Morgon.

"I had quite an adventure myself yesterday," Richard said as we sat together in the dining room.

"An adventure?" I asked.

"Well," he said, "you know about the strange things that have been happening, and I played you that phone message last night."

"Yes, quite mysterious," I said, nodding. "I've never heard anything like it," I said.

"I thought it was horrible," Katrina said.

"Yes, well it wasn't funny," I concurred.

*Perhaps it wasn't meant to be.*

"So do you think it was a prank?" she asked.

I thought about this for a moment. If I said "Yes," then I couldn't say how it was in English. But if I said "No," then I couldn't explain how a ghost left a telephone message.

So I said, "I suppose I don't know what to think about it."

"Well, I know what it is," Katrina said.

"What?" I asked.

"Another message from, you know, *him*," she said.

"You mean this isn't the first time?" I said.

"Well," she said, "it's the first phone call—"

"I just don't see how a dead person can talk," the Italian interrupted, "much less leave a voice mail."

"You said it yourself," Katrina said. "A phone call is just a series of electric impulses."

"Have there been other electrical phenomena?" I asked.

"The lights went out at the Housewarming," Katrina said. "Remember, Søren? And the clock in the kitchen can't seem to keep good time. In fact, the only clock that seems to work is the grandfather clock," Katrina added.

*Grandfather, indeed.*

"And that's not electric," Richard said.

"And it was *his,*" she said, her eyes wide.

I tried to lighten the mood a bit. "Well, what if there is a ghost? Many buildings in Europe are haunted. It's an antique continent. Most people seem to live with them quite contentedly. It might even be fun to have a ghost!"

"This isn't like that, Søren," the Italian said.

"How so?" I asked.

"Because most of the ghosts you hear about in English castles and so forth just walk back and forth, rattle their chains, maybe moan a little. This is more like a *poltergeist* – and it's up to no good, I tell you. It's... malevolent," he said.

"Oh, is it as bad as all that?" I asked, pursing my lips like Derek Jacoby.

"Yes, it is. Last night, I really came to understand what Katrina has been going through here all by herself when I'm away," he said.

"What happened?" I asked.

"Well, first the lights in the basement came on by themselves. And then, I know this sounds crazy, but I heard things – voices and music – coming out of the walls, like. And there was definitely smoke — it was so thick I could see it in the hall light upstairs."

"Yes, well we talked about the smoking yesterday," I said, raising my eyebrows in reference to the idea that the closet smoker might be sitting among us.

"Yeah, but I was completely alone, Søren."

"Hmm, that is unexpected. Very strange. It does really seem as if you have an unruly spirit in the house," I concluded.

When they nodded, I saw this as a good opportunity to say, "Will you try to contact the spirit?"

"Yes, that's what I want to do," Katrina said. "Like we talked about the other day, Søren."

*She did remember! How much more did she recall?*

"So you want to bring in a psychic," I said.

"Well, I was thinking about using a Ouija board," Richard said, pronouncing it *wee-jee.*

"Spirit in the glass," Katrina reiterated.

"We used to play that game as kids," Richard explained. "My cousins and I would ask questions of any spirits that might be nearby. There were *always* spirits around. Nobody ever admitted to pushing the needle."

"But Richard, we talked about that — it's too dangerous!" Katrina said.

"But isn't communication always the first step?" he asked.

I weighed in. "No, I agree with Katrina. Listen, you don't do your own electrical wiring, do you?"

"Wiring?" Katrina snickered. "Richard doesn't even do his own shirts!"

"You mean we need a professional?" Richard asked.

"Yes, a Guide through the process," I said, thinking they would need Vergil himself.

"It's true, Richard. I wouldn't even know what to ask," Katrina said. "You know, I tried to evict the spirit myself once through visualization."

"You did?" Richard asked, sitting up straighter.

"It didn't work, though," she said with a shrug.

"What happened?" I asked.

"I imagined myself grabbing hold of Damsgaard's ghost and escorting it out the front door. It fought me all the way. I finally wrestled it outside and closed the door behind it. I heard it wailing."

"It sounds too rough," Richard said. "They say you're supposed to lead the soul to the Light, not dump it on the stoop like the kitchen trash bag."

"He wasn't gentle with me when he pushed me down the stairs, was he?" she asked. "Anyhow, the spirit just came back in through the vent in the basement."

"Spirits are said to seek refuge in dark, damp, dirty places like garages and cellars during the daylight hours, so they can emerge refreshed again after sundown," I said.

"Katrina, do you think we could lead the spirit to the Light?" Richard asked.

"Frankly, no," she said, shaking her head. "He doesn't want to go. But even if it is possible, I wouldn't know how to do it myself. We would need a professional."

"Quite right," I concurred, and sat back in my chair.

"Katrina has found a psychic, but we don't even know if she'll work with us," Richard said. "She's called them several times and left messages; they don't even call back."

*Don't they?*

"Maybe we should go down there together," Katrina said.

"Yes, by all means, go together. It's the best way," I said. "It's the only way. And if you need my help, just ask."

"Thanks, Søren," Richard said. "We just may have to call on you before this is over."

"I hope you do, Richard," I said, smiling. "I hope you do."

# 30. Richard

Saturday morning dawned cold and bright, and though it was only the middle of September, the trees were beginning to blush along the boulevard as Katrina and I rattled along in the Number 18 bus on the way into town. Getting off at the Triangle in Østerbro, we started walking uptown. But we got distracted by a lurid poster for an upcoming Styx concert – ironically entitled "Show Me the Way" – and we made a wrong turn.

*Halfway down Vortlivsvej, we found ourselves*
*In a shady part of town, the right road lost.*

It's hard to say how we found the place at all – we were so confused and the entrance so well-hidden. The door to Østerbrogade 47B was invisible to those on the surface, buried at the bottom of seven stone steps and protected by a black gate of wrought iron.

The featureless redbrick building was wedged between an abandoned butcher shop and Hope Mediterranean Travel Agency. The sign above the mahogany door said *The Psychic of Østerbro,* providing ample warning to all those who enter here that behind the dark wood lay journeys to a realm far beyond Tuscany.

I rang the bell with trepidation. The thin, leather-skinned lady who opened the door was foreign – hard to say where from, Eastern Europe? Southern Europe? – but she spoke her heavily-accented English fluently. Her dark eyes and raven hair contrasted sharply with her chalky countenance. She eyed us warily through the twisted bars of the grating.

"Hello," Katrina said. "I'm Katrina Nielsen and this is my husband Richard. I believe we spoke on the telephone?"

"You'll have to excuse me," said the older woman, squinting slightly. "I speak to so many people. What about?"

Katrina and I looked at each other. Then Katrina ventured, "We've had some – ghostly – phenomena in our home."

"Oh," she said, brightening, "we're good at that. We've been very successful with ghosts."

And without a further word of welcome or explanation, the gate swung open, and we crept into the damp shade of the subterranean premises.

I had never been in such a place. I didn't know what to expect; if I had any preconceptions, they were rank stereotypes – a crystal ball on a round table draped in spangled velvet, a kerchiefed Gypsy with hoop earrings of false gold, Professor Marvel's trailer.

We found ourselves in what looked like an overstocked Catholic gift shop. Hundreds of figurines of saints and martyrs perched in every corner of the room – I recognized St. Stephen carrying three stones, St. Sebastian pierced by arrows, St. Bartholomew carrying his skin. A sea of painted ceramic fonts offered holy water; and regiments of unlit votive candles kept their dark vigil. Illumination, dim and flaring as it was, came from fluorescent tubes hung from the ceiling, along which I could just make out a faint cloud of smoke, apparently from burning incense. The alluring, sweet-woody aroma wafted in from the back room along with the haunting strains of the *Canto Gregoriano* of the monks of Silos, a surprise hit on the pop charts a year or two ago.

Discordantly, New Age trinkets twinkled. Transparent orbs of cut crystal swung from the beams, reflecting the inconsistent effulgence of the lamplight. The shelves groaned with geodes, glistening in the artificial light like bizarre Asiatic fruit, sliced open to reveal obscene yellow and purplish innards.

While the old lady was polite, there was nothing welcoming in her disposition. She did not introduce herself, and as there were no chairs, Katrina and I stood there awkwardly as the small woman leaned against a counter. Her demeanor was one of well-worn toleration, like a super who's come take a look at a drippy faucet or spray for roaches.

"Tell me," the small woman said with a sigh, taking out a tiny pad and eraserless pencil. When she exhaled, I got a strong whiff of garlic.

"It started almost from when we first moved in," Katrina explained.

"When was that?" she asked.

"In April," Katrina replied.

"What day?" she asked

"What does it matter the day?" I asked.

"Do you remember what day it was, my child?" she asked Katrina.

"It was a Saturday... Saturday the 13th, I believe."

The birdlike lady made tiny scratchings in her journal – it was in no language I'd ever seen.

"And then?" she said, staring fixedly at Katrina.

We described the goings-on in the house in great detail, and at the end the crone nodded but remained silent.

"So do you think we really have a ghost?" Katrina asked.

"Oh, you definitely have a ghost," she said as calmly and confidently as a roofer announcing you have water damage.

"How do you know?" I asked.

"There are four classic symptoms of a haunting," she said coolly, as if she had explained this many times before. "Running on the floors, voices, apparitions, and pulling on clothing. Unprompted, you have described all four. So either you have been reading accounts of true hauntings and are here to trick me, or you have yourselves a ghost."

"I assure you, we're in earnest, Mrs. – oh, I don't know your name," Katrina said.

"Belasquita. Please just call me Belasquita."

*Spanish?*

"All right, Belasquita," I said, "you said you have a great track record getting rid of ghosts. What do you do?"

For the first time, she really looked at me. Her eyes, the color of burnt umber, were watery, the skin around them lined, sunken. Touching my forearm, she said, "You decide what *you believe in. Me,* I trust in my religion. The Church *you know you can trust – me,* I put my faith in the Good Father. Of course, we don't know how much longer we will have him..."

"A priest? What kind of priest?" I asked.

"Cath-o-lic," she said, pronouncing it with three syllables.

"What parish?" I asked.

"The Good Father is not with the parish, but a member of the... a monastic order. He is of the *Tradition*," she said *sotto voce.*

*What Tradition?*

"I was raised Catholic myself," I said, to let her know I would understand if she said Jesuits, Franciscans or Benedictines.

"Ah," she said, brightening and coming out from behind the counter, "*You, like me,* are Cath-o-lic?"

"Yes," I said.

Belasquita beamed, revealing crooked teeth. I didn't know why, but I believed in her, trusted her. For some unknown reason, despite her garlic breath and leathery, reptilian face, I liked her.

"Do you think you can help us?" Katrina asked again.

"Oh, yes. I will contact the Good Father, and we will pray on this matter. Please write down your name and telephone number for me," she said, handing Katrina her pad of inscrutable scribbles. (Whatever it was, it was not Spanish.) Katrina inscribed her name in the book. We said our goodbyes, and emerged squinting into the cold sunlight.

A week later I answered the phone on a Friday evening and heard Belasquita's voice say, "I have good news. My colleague, Rowena, will be able to visit your home already this Thursday."

"Gee, I won't be home on Thursday, can we do it Friday?"

"We would prefer to start the process Thursday night, as the planet Mars is leaving Cancer on that day, and we feel this will make for an auspicious beginning."

"But I'm still in France that night. We have a review of progress on Friday morning. Right after that, I can come straight home and we can get to work."

Silence on the line. Finally after several long seconds, I heard a sigh so deep I could almost smell the garlic. Then she said, "All right, if you insist, I will see if Rowena can accept such terms."

A few days later, Katrina spoke with Rowena and agreed on Friday. The week in Paris was marked by long days with the team – the merger with AmeriBancorp was not going well, and everyone was tense – and longer evenings talking with my wife on the telephone. Katrina reported incidents and I rationalized them – another prank call; the garage light and electrical appliances kept turning themselves on and off.

At one point, she said, "I saw a shadow run by me."

"Is there a particular place where this happens? Maybe it's a passing car."

"No, it's not one place – but it does seem to happen more on the side toward Søren's."

"The east side? You think there's something coming from that direction?"

"That's what Mette said. The negative energy is coming from that direction, from the Sound."

I had spent most of the week preparing for the client meeting on Friday. It was finally on the plane ride that afternoon that I was able to focus on the homefront. I decided to do whatever was necessary, spend all weekend if that was what it took. The house was ripping apart our marriage, our life together.

That evening, we ate an early supper and sat over coffee in anticipation of Rowena's arrival. We did not speak. The clock seemed to tick more slowly than usual as we waited. 5:45 PM – *ding-dong* said St. Michael's languid chimes. 5:52...5:57. I sat on the edge of my chair. Six o'clock arrived and Grandfather chimed so lethargically that I wondered why he bothered to toll at all. Still no sign of her. 6:02. Oh, this was endless.

"Didn't she say she'd be here at six o'clock?" I asked.

"Yes. I'm sure she'll be here," Katrina responded. Sitting down at the piano, she started to play scales to pass the time, but I asked her to stop.

At 6:12, a shapely woman in a long black dress strode up the front walk. The doorbell rang and Rowena swept into the front room and into our lives. At no more than thirty, she was younger than I expected.

*Belasquita's daughter?*

"Hi, you must be Rowena. I'm Katrina, we spoke on the phone," my wife said, extending her hand.

"I'm Richard Marchese," I said, noticing the heavy scent of perfume drifting in with her.

Rowena gazed distinctly into our eyes before saying with a slight accent and a bit of drama, like a doctor visiting a sick child in a remote village, "I'm so glad I could come."

The compressed heels of her black, lace-up boots clunked on the oaken floorboards as she strode to the dining room where we all sat down.

Rowena had an air of authority and immediacy, like she could only stay a few minutes, so you'd better pay attention. Buxom and clad in a dark, diaphanous outfit that was low-cut, her long nails covered in glossy red polish, Rowena exuded feminine power. A real *femme fatale*. I had to consciously raise my eyes up to face level, away from her fragrant breasts.

"Would you like some tea or coffee?" Katrina offered.

"No, no thank you," she said.

I noticed that she was breathing a bit heavily. A large woman, I wondered if she was winded from the walk.

"Can you feel something already?" Katrina asked.

"I felt it already outside – as I was coming up the walk – it knows I am here. It wants me to leave."

"It knows you're here?" Katrina said.

"Yes, it tried to stop me from coming in. But don't worry, she said, raising her right palm in assurance, I have encountered such resistance many times before," she explained, and exhaled.

"Maybe we can start by telling you about what's been going on here?" I proposed.

"I have read your transcripts," she replied, as if we had sent her our scholastic records. "I will of course want you to narrate the entire story, but before you say another word, I must establish some basic protections for us."

"Protections?" I asked.

"Yes. This work can be very dangerous; to be honest, especially for me. You may have noticed that when I came in, I placed a medallion by the front door."

I hadn't, but looked up and saw that there was indeed a yellowish medal hanging from the hinges.

"That is Saint Michael the Archangel. He will be our special protector throughout this process. As I said, the entity does not want me here, so I must use the cleansing rituals to create a space in which we can work safely. The smell of sage will not bother you?" she asked Katrina.

"Sage? No, not at all," replied Katrina.

Rowena reached into the black leathern bag she had brought with her. Reminded me of when I was a kid, the bag that Doctor Milano used to carry when he made housecalls. My sphincter muscles contracted involuntarily. But what Rowena took out of her bag was not a thick rectal thermometer, but wands of sage, which she lit up with a butane lighter. The rich smell of sage filled the room, and I was reminded of the endless dry, brown drear of Nevada tumbleweed country.

Rowena then proceeded to walk around the ground-floor rooms, waving the smoking sage, and went as far as the landing of the stairs. She wanded the seams but did not open the five-sided basement door.

Next she brought out holy water from a flask marked "Lourdes."

"Is that from the holy shrine at Lourdes?" I asked.

"Miraculous healing waters," she replied, nodding.

Again she walked all around the first level sprinkling the holy water, and halfway up the stairs, but not elsewhere.

"Why don't you have to go farther than the landing or down to the basement?" I asked.

"I am creating what we call a 'fane-space,' a zone of safety in which we can work and talk freely," she explained as she continued flitting around. "Nothing can interrupt us as we do our work this evening, as long as we remain in this area. Later we will address the various chambers and any outbuildings on the property, but first we must set up our war-room, so to speak. For, make no mistake, this is a battle of sorts."

"A battle?" Katrina asked.

"You want your home back. You have, how you say, 'squatters,' who are residing here. They do not wish to leave, and can be expected to put up something of a fight. But don't worry, you are the landlord now, and shall prevail in the end. The true Master of the House always does."

When she was done sprinkling and wafting, Rowena sat down, visibly relieved. Reaching into her bag, she extracted a large votive candle with a picture of a warrior angel on it.

"This is a seven-day votive candle, made of special holy wax that is only available at the abbey of Mont-Saint-Michel in France," she explained. "The angelic light will shine throughout our journey together. We will move it about as needed, but you must not extinguish it for any reason. Do you understand?"

I said, "We'll keep it burning, day and night."

Her mouth widened into a smile, and she gazed into our eyes for a moment. Then, taking out the little pad and pencil, she said, "So, tell me."

As we told her the story Rowena scribbled the same unknown language in the same cramped hand as the crooked-toothed woman in the shop.

When I told her about the suspicious telephone calls, she asked, "Can I listen to the recordings?"

"No, I erased them," I answered.

"I see," she said. "What precisely did he say?"

"I've got you now," I reiterated.

"In Danish?" she asked.

"No, it was in English," I told her.

"In English? Interesting. With an accent, yes?" she asked.

"Hard to tell from how raspy the voice was, but maybe a British accent," I said.

"Not a Danish accent? This Damsgaard, he was Danish, no?" she asked, looking at Katrina.

"Yes, he was," she said. Then she cocked her head and added, "Wait. I don't know why I didn't think of this before. All Danes were taught to speak with an upper-class British accent in those days – like the little man in the Bangsbo Museum."

I nodded and turned back to the soothsayer. "So you really think that a ghost can leave a voice mail?"

"Absolutely," Rowena said. "This spirit is trying desperately to communicate with you. The incident at the Museum was no coincidence. I cannot tell you yet what he is trying to say, but it appears to be a warning of some kind. Of course I can't tell for sure, now that you've erased the messages."

I felt reproved, like I had destroyed evidence at a crime scene.

"I just didn't want those recordings hanging around," I said sheepishly.

"Yes, of course I understand," she said, nodding and scribbling.

I went back to telling the story of my vigil. I gave a detailed account, not knowing what might be important. Rowena took copious notes, and seemed satisfied with the retelling. When I had finished, she announced, "Now we are ready to see the rest of the property. Let's start outside, shall we?"

Night had fallen and we stumbled along behind a single flashlight as we paraded out to the garage. I opened the side door.

As we walked in, Rowena's knees nearly buckled as she said, "*Ahgh!*"

"What's wrong?" I asked.

"The feeling is very strong here. *Ich!*" she said, as if the musty smell of the garage disgusted her. I smelled nothing out of the ordinary – exhaust fumes and motor oil, gasoline and turpentine. At first I was alarmed to see her reaction, but then I felt a sense of relief: we were finally getting to the bottom of this thing!

Rowena doused everything with holy water: the car, woodpile, tools, workbench.

"Do you think an 'entity' would be in a garage?" I asked.

"Spirits avoid bright light," Rowena explained. "They prefer shaded, dirty, moist spaces to inhabit during the day; they walk abroad in the night. In the dark..." Then she shrank back in horror and said, "Oh my God."

"What?" I asked.

Her hand trembling, she pointed at the license plate. I stared down at the black numbering: MRC666. The Number of the Beast – I had never thought about this before.

"You think it means something?" I asked.

I looked at Rowena who returned my glare, then at Katrina who raised her eyebrows.

"It's just a license plate. I'm sure the numbers are assigned randomly," I said.

"Get it changed, as soon as you can. We have to close as many portals as we can, Richard."

"Okay," I said, glancing back at Katrina, who had grown very quiet.

As we walked back inside, she asked, "Rowena, that number, 666... it's in the house too, isn't it?"

"What do you mean?" Rowena asked.

"We're #18. That number contains three sixes."

Rowena said, "Three is the holiest number, referring to the Holy Trinity, the Holy Family. I've never been called to a #3 or 30. It's usually something with a six, like #16 or #616.

"But the number 18 is the perfectly *ambiguous* number. It's composed entirely of threes, but unfortunately, there are *six* of them. So this number has within it the potential for perfect good or..."

"Perfect evil," Katrina said, finishing the thought.

We followed Rowena back inside and through the various rooms as she cleansed them with burning sage and blessed them with holy water.

Finally, we stood before the crooked door leading to the cellar. I got a knot in my stomach, like waiting in line for the confessional when I was seven.

*What horrors lay behind that door?*

"Richard, do you have a Bible?" Rowena asked.

"Yes, upstairs," I replied, and went to get it from the bookcase in the hallway.

A few minutes later, I returned and Rowena explained the role each of us would have to perform as we explored the cellar. I was to read from Psalms, Katrina was to hold the votive candle, and Rowena would sprinkle the *aqua sancta* from the sacred spring at Lourdes.

Rowena nodded, and I began walking down the basement steps, reading out loud in my best voice, "A reading from the Book of Psalms, Chapter 23.

*"The Lord is my shepherd; I shall not want. He maketh me to lie down in green pastures: he leadeth me beside the still waters. He restoreth my soul."*

At this point I stepped onto the basement slab. As we were all arriving in the small room, Rowena exclaimed, *"Agh! Ew!* The sulphurous fumes are unbearable! You can smell it, can't you?"

Katrina was coughing violently. I recalled the stink of sulphur from the showing with Dahl. It was close in the damp cellar-room. Beads of perspiration glistened on the plaster walls.

I tried to focus on the text and continued, droning now, *"He leadeth me in the paths of righteousness for his name's sake."*

Rowena blessed the laundry room and the storage area, and then stood facing the trapdoor that led to the crawl space. She pointed dramatically, and asked, "What's in *there?*"

"Just a crawl space. I've never been in there," Katrina replied.

"Open the door, please," Rowena said to me, "and then step back."

I had never been in the dirt-floored chamber at the root of the house – I never had any reason to go creeping around down there – but I had of course opened the door and looked in during the inspection when I bought the place. To enter the crawl space, you needed a chair or small step ladder, as the trap was chest-high. About four feet high, six feet deep and twenty feet long, running as it did along the east side of the building all the way to the front, the space was shaped like a shoebox – or a coffin.

*"Yea, though I walk through the valley of death, I fear no evil,"* I continued.

I prayed silently, *Deliver me O Lord from this valley of death, this pit into which I have fallen.* I felt lost, desolate. A tear almost escaped my right eye, and I choked it back, my voice catching.

I lifted the iron latch and swung the door open, never stopping my reading. A blast of bad air rushed out of the tenebrous vault. The psychic reacted physically, gasping and holding a handkerchief to her mouth so as not to breathe in the foul, moldy air emerging from the hole.

I raised my voice now, as if I had to shout the Lord's word to be heard above the draft. *"For thou art with me; thy rod and thy staff they comfort me. Thou preparest a table before me in the presence of mine enemies."*

Rowena stood on the chair and put her head in the crawl space and, reaching in, blessed it inwardly. Then she stepped down, stood back and doused the portal with the holy water.

Finally, she said, as if finishing a surgical procedure, "Now we shall close."

I shut the door promptly, but she had more in mind. Holding out her left hand, she produced an oversized ring set with an aquamarine stone. Rowena then opened the ring – it was a signet ring – and asked Katrina to allow several drops of molten candle wax to fall upon the exposed metal surface.

Meanwhile, I kept reading, *"Thou anointest my head with oil; my cup runneth over. Surely goodness and mercy shall follow me all the days of my life: and I will dwell in the house of the Lord for ever."*

Rowena then took the ring of hot wax and set a seal on the edge of the trap-door. After repeating this three times, she smiled and breathed out, and nodded for me to lead us back upstairs.

I held up the Bible before us, and led the way singing the first hymn that popped into my head, which turned out to be, "O God Our Help in Ages Past." When I sang the words, "Our shelter from the stormy blast," I thought of the blast of air coming from the crawl space; and at the end of the hymn, my voice caught and a tear came to my eye at "and our eternal home."

By this point, we were standing in the dining room once more, and Rowena was congratulating us. The mood was celebratory – as if we had just won a big football game or something.

"Oh, you did a superb job, Richard. And you too, Katrina, thank you. That was wonderful. Just wonderful," she said, sitting down. "I will have that cup of tea now, Katrina," she said, and Katrina went into the kitchen.

I was trembling slightly. Rowena reached out and took my hand and looked into my eyes.

"That was a very intense experience for you, wasn't it Richard?" she asked.

"Yes. Yes, it was," I said.

"You have a special role to play in our ritual, Richard. As the man of the house, you are the priest. It is *your* home that is being occupied. Only you can drive out these usurpers. Do you understand, Richard?"

"You mean there's more than one?"

"I have encountered three so far."

"Oh my God," I said.

Katrina walked back in and saw my face. "What happened?"

"Rowena thinks we have multiple spirits dwelling here."

"You mean it's not just Damsgaard?" Katrina asked.

"No, I'm afraid not," Rowena said. "But you mustn't be afraid. I have extended our safety zone to include the entire domain, with the exception of the crawl space. It is there the spirits will congregate until we can return to finish what we have started. We've done all we can tonight."

"You mean there's more we have to do?" I asked.

"Yes, of course. But don't be afraid, I will be with you until it is finished," she said.

Then she added, "Tomorrow night we shall enter the crawl space together."

"No way," I said, almost involuntarily.

"Yes, but don't worry, having seen you in action tonight, I feel certain you will be able to handle it. And you too, Katrina, I can feel you are ready for this," she said, squeezing her hand.

Katrina poured out the chamomile tea, and I stared at my cup for a moment before asking, "Why don't we just move?"

"It will follow you." Rowena fired back.

"But if we go far away," I tried, "back to New York—"

"It doesn't matter how far you go. There are no distances in the astral plane," she said matter-of-factly. "This entity has gotten hold of you now, and will not let go until it works its will, or is defeated."

"It can follow us?" I asked, dumbfounded.

"It already has, once – to Skagen," Katrina pointed out.

"And fleeing from it will only give it more power over you. No," Rowena said, shaking her head, "you must stay here."

I was suddenly depressed. I could only manage, "So what do we do?"

"I will be with you as long as it takes. As Katrina and I agreed on the phone, there is just a single amount that you must pay. This covers my time and the supplies." She turned and asked Katrina, "Is the check prepared?"

"Yes," Katrina said, and whispered the amount to me – a significant sum, but not exorbitant if we could put this whole business behind us.

"Is this just for tonight," I said like a shrewd negotiator, "or does it cover everything?"

"When I leave, you'll be totally cleaned out," she said.

"All right then." I nodded to Katrina, who handed over the check.

"Thank you," Rowena said. "Now I will give you some instructions for tonight. First you will each take a bath in rose petals."

"Rose petals?" I asked.

"I have brought with me two dozen roses," she said, pulling flowers out of her seemingly bottomless bag. "Each of you will take a dozen into the bath with you. As the tub fills with hot water, unfurl the rosebuds and allow the petals to fall gently into the bath water. Then you must bathe in the healing rosewater. This will restore your spirits in preparation for the work we have to do tomorrow."

"Next, I would like you to play sacred music all night long on the stereo, to sanctify the atmosphere. I have brought a cassette of Gregorian chant – I hope that is acceptable to you?"

"Yes, of course," Katrina said.

"Finally, I would like to see the photographs of your family that we discussed, Katrina." Katrina went off to get them.

While she was out of the room, Rowena turned to me and said, "This has nothing to do with you, Richard. The haunting is directed toward Katrina. I believe we are dealing with a deeply malevolent, male force. This force wants nothing but to molest, possess, devour; even I have been attacked lustfully this evening."

I looked away, thinking about my own wandering eyes.

Katrina's hand was quivering slightly as she held out several photographs. "Here they are," she said. "Perhaps I should tell you—"

Rowena put up a hand to stop her, and touching each of the photos in turn, she separated them into two piles.

"I have a gift for picking up faint vibrations from photographs," she said. "There are twelve photos here, yes? I have sorted them into two piles, six on the left and six on the right. The six on the left... are dead, or will be soon."

I looked at the photos and then at Katrina – several were relatives I had never met. "Is that true, Katrina?" I asked.

"Oh my God, yes, it is true – how did you know?"

"Just something that comes to me through my fingers," Rowena said with a shrug. "Obviously the living persons play no role in this, so we will put them aside. Now of these others..." she said, flipping them over, swirling them around, and finally placing them in a cross-like pattern.

Rowena then closed her eyes and placed her hands over the photos, not touching them, but twitching her fingertips just above the surfaces. She appeared to be meditating. After a minute or so, she picked up the one at the top and asked, "Who is this man? He is a father... maybe your father..."

"Yes, that's my father, Per André Nielsen."

"I get strong feelings from the picture of your father – you were very close to him, weren't you?" Katrina nodded. Rowena got a far-off look in her eye and gazing toward the top of the wall, she said dreamily, "Your father loves you, Katrina. Your father is worried for you. He is watching over you..."

Katrina was silent, but I saw the tears welling up in her eyes, and then she sniffled and I got out my handkerchief and handed it to her. She dabbed her eyes.

Then Rowena placed Per back at the head of the cross and took up the photo in the center. Quickly she dropped it again, as if it were ablaze.

"Ay! Who is that man! Another father, I think, but not yours!"

"That's my *morfar*, he died before I was born."

Rowena looked as if she had just seen the Devil himself. I looked at the deckle-edged, black-and-white shot of a man on a farm in Denmark, probably was the 1930s. The man looked weathered, a bit cold maybe, but did not strike me as particularly evil-looking.

"Do you know how this man died?" she said ominously.

"I don't, really. He was old I guess. I would have to ask my mother."

"The fact that this photo landed in the middle of the spread means that he is in control of the astral plane within this domain. I am getting extremely negative energy radiating from the photo of your mother's father. You must find out more about him."

"Did you also want to see Damsgaard's photo?" Katrina asked.

"Yes, let me see him, too," Rowena responded.

Katrina produced the daguerreotype, wrapped in brown kraft paper like butcher's meat. Unwinding the parcel, Katrina turned the framed picture to face the psychic.

"Ah, a handsome devil, isn't he?" Rowena said.

"Do you feel anything? Is he here among us?" Katrina asked.

Rowena closed her eyes and said, trancelike, "Yes, Karl is here. I feel... I feel Karl wants to be close to you... that he is in love with you, yes, desperately in love... and what's that? *Lemur? L'Amour?* What's that, a name?"

After a pause, Katrina almost shouted, "*Lommeur*, pocket watch!"

"Is that right, Karl?" Rowena asked out loud and then, nodding, continued with the question, "Where is the pocket watch?"

"Lost," Katrina said.

"He says not to worry; he wants to *forswear* you – forswear?" Rowena continued.

"Maybe *forsvare* – protect," Katrina tried, translating from the Danish.

"Yes, protect – he wants to protect you from someone... protect you," Rowena said, slumping in her chair and slowly coming back to normal.

Katrina said, "The pocket watch – so it *is* his after all!"

"What pocket watch?" I asked.

"My father's, the one he got from his firm – it was an heirloom from one of the founders..."

"Yes," Rowena said. "Katrina, such an object can be very important. It links the past with the present – and the future. This pocket watch, how did your father obtain it?"

"One of the founders – the one who had to leave under cloud of scandal – left various items of value for his partners," she explained.

"Soon after the scandal?" Rowena asked.

"No, decades later," Katrina said.

"I knew it – and then when you moved back to Copenhagen, decades after that, you just *happened* to move into this domain – did you really think it was a coincidence?" Rowena asked, shaking her head.

"What else could it be?" Katrina replied, distressed.

"It wasn't like she inherited anything – we bought the property voluntarily," I pointed out.

"On the surface it may appear that way, but underneath, there is a connection. There has *always* been a connection, Katrina, between your family and Damsgaard – your father wore Damsgaard's watch, worked in his office, perhaps sat at his very desk…"

Katrina blanched. "So you mean that Damsgaard lured us here – but why?"

"I cannot be sure of his original motives, but by now he is definitely in love with you – and he is terribly jealous."

"Jealous of what?" I asked.

"Of *you*, Richard – of the love between the two of you." She opened her eyes wide and asked me, "The bond between the two of you, it is special, isn't it?"

"Yes, I suppose it is unusual – the way we met, what we had to overcome to be together."

"I feel Karl will not harm you. He is very sad. He wants to be with you, Katrina – and he wants to warn you."

"About what?" I asked.

She replied by asking Katrina, "May I borrow these photos? I want to share them with the Good Father, and pray over them."

"Yes, please take them, take all of them!" Katrina said.

"You may go wherever you like, except for the space behind the trap door," Rowena said. "Under no circumstance should you break the seals. We have created a kind of vortex there, a place for the spirits to congregate. It can be opened of course, and we will open it, but it must be done properly. I would like to come here again tomorrow night, at six PM. In the meantime, you can eat – but eat lightly."

I walked her to the front door, thanked her for coming and said, "We're in your hands, Rowena."

# 31. Katrina

By the time Rowena left at nine o'clock, I was exhausted. Richard and I sat in the living room talking for a while. We were both buzzing after the night's session.

"I need a drink," Richard said, as he got up to make a bourbon on the rocks, his new favorite. "You want one?"

I did, desperately, but declined. As he clinked ice into the glass, I said, "You know, Richard, while you were upstairs, I told Rowena that sometimes I feel like he's *inside* me."

"Really?" he said, coming back and sitting next to me on the couch.

"She said it's common, that spirits seek the same things that we all do – love, comfort, contentment but also…"

"Also what?"

"The darker desires – revenge, power, sex, alcohol…"

"Alcohol – that's what Søren said. That they can enter the body of someone who is drinking, and somehow feel the buzz. That's why so many pubs are haunted!"

"It seems that spirits can experience sensations, if they are strong enough. You know how in Sweden, they eat *surströmming* – a delicacy of half-rotted fish?"

"I had to attend that Fielding dinner a couple of months back in Stockholm! The stench is so overpowering that if a restaurant serves it at all, they have to serve it to everybody."

"Rowena says that in some places, it's tradition to put out one empty place setting at each table."

"I saw some empty chairs. You mean they were for the ghosts?"

"As a sign of respect," I said with a wry grin.

"Amazing," he said. "But ghosts can only enter into people in the movies. Like Whoopi Goldberg!"

We laughed, but I could not get the thought out of my mind that there was a man in me, *entering* me at will, for his own dark purposes.

Finally, I started to fall asleep in the chair, and Richard said, "Why don't you take a bath like Rowena said. I'm sure it'll make you feel better."

So I left him there reading the Bible. I took a dozen roses from the dining room table and brought them upstairs to the bathroom. I placed tea lights around the room and lit them, releasing a fine sandalwood aroma.

I doused the overhead lamp and sat on the edge of the porcelain tub to draw the water, hot as I could stand. Steam rose up and filled the room. My muscles ached and I longed for the warmth of the bath. I unwrapped the flowers and breathed in the familiar scent of roses. I relaxed.

Removing my clothes, I wrapped myself in a clean white towel of thick, uncut pile. The window was shut, so as the bathtub filled, a Turkish-bath feeling of dampness and sweat began to permeate the atmosphere. I poured the bottle of essential oils into the receptive waters, and lavender joined the chorus of delicious scents in the small space.

I turned off the tap and took up the first rose. Rowena had said to unfurl each floweret, petal by petal. I was supposed to pray – *but how?* The idea came to me that I should meditate on each of the people in my life as I deconstructed the rosebuds. The first person that came to me was Richard – we were going through so much together – and I prayed for him and I watched the petals fall into the oily water.

Then as the petals dropped from the second rose, I thought of Mor – I felt so sorry for her, and sorry that I had left her in her time of grief. *How could I have been so selfish? She could have died!* The third rose was for Claus, the good son who had stayed with his mother while I was so far away.

And then I thought of Mette and Annika and Christian. Halfway there. And it was easy to remember Edvard, Angelina, Søren, and George. But at ten I got a little stuck – I barely knew Una, and I didn't really like Agnete. But why limit it to living people? Fa' became number eleven.

But then suddenly I couldn't think of anyone else. I grew uneasy. I held the twelfth rose in my hand. I brought it to my nose, ran my lips over it.

The identity of the final rose was already known to me, I think, before I started, but I resisted. I struggled to think of someone else, anyone else. I did not want to acknowledge *him.* I sat there until I shivered, from a chill in the air I suppose, and gave in, allowing the petals of the final rose to waft into the water as I contemplated the portrait of Karl Damsgaard.

Had he called me, used the link of the pocket watch to summon me to Sundhuset? It was somehow perversely romantic to think of him calling to me – like Mister Rochester calling to Jane Eyre across the moors.

*But what does he want from me?* By all accounts he was a blackguard. I recalled his quote – *their sin is quite delightful.* What would a man of his era have meant by sin? Vices – smoking and drinking, opium perhaps. And most of all, sex. While outwardly virtuous, even prudish, Victorian men secretly brought the prostitution trade to heights never seen before or since. I imagined vile habits, what was the phrase? *Unnatural acts.* I wondered what he would have been like. I imagined him, tall and strong and lean – on top and in control.

Allowing the towel to fall to the floor, I submerged my naked form through the layer of petals and sank into the oily, warm, womb-like fluids below. I heard a slight fizzing as the molecules of essential oil combined with the roses and acid mantle of my exposed skin in the moist interior. The rose petals stuck flat to my breasts and belly like fig leaves in a bowdlerized Eden.

Dizzy, from the steam I suppose, I lay my head back against the cool porcelain and closed my eyes. I touched myself and relaxed into the floating feeling that the steam rising from the waters gave. I allowed my fantasy full sway. After a few minutes with my hands under the roses, I experienced a great release, and I heard myself say audibly, "Aahhhh!"

I felt reborn. I stared at the ceiling, yellowish and flickering in the candlelight, and I smirked. I was elated, but when I put my hands on my knees, something did not feel right. I opened my eyes, brought up my knees and stared at my legs. I say "my legs," but they weren't my legs, at least I didn't recognize them. I gasped but did not cry out.

The legs I saw were *man's* legs, tawny and muscular; tight bandy calves below thighs like tree trunks. And covered with a mat of ghastly, black man-hair, wiry, like the legs of a goat. When I lifted the feet out of the water, they were massive and bony, bunioned. Grotesque. The man-toes were all knobbly, the toenails horny and yellowed.

Closing my eyes in terror – *was I going mad?* – I put my head under the surface of the water, hoping that the hellish vision would be gone when I emerged again.

After I'd held my breath as long as I dared, I emerged, gulping air. I looked down with anticipation, but nothing had changed. I felt the coarse hair on the calves with my fingertips, pulled on the hair that grew from my big toe.

*Ouch!*

I was appalled, but still I did not call out. I couldn't let Richard see me like this!

Closing my eyes, I whispered, "Dear Jesus" – how many years it had been since I had uttered that name in prayer? – "Please take this hateful vision from me and restore me to myself."

I opened my eyes again, and my legs were smooth and womanly once more. I thanked God for expelling whatever it was that had invaded my body. Tears of gratitude made little rivulets along my cheeks as I let the water run out. I touched all the parts of my body that I could reach, as if to make sure they were all still female, and then wrapping myself in the big white towel, I sat on the side of the tub for a long time, just holding myself and crying softly.

Finally, I collected the hundreds of sodden rose petals in the little wastebasket. I opened the door and called Richard up for his bath. I embraced him in the doorway.

"How was your bath?" he asked.

I hugged him close and said behind his back so he couldn't see I'd been crying, "I feel like a new woman."

# 32. Angelina

I was up early this morning on a Saturday, reading in the *Lives of the Saints* about Good King Wenceslas (like in the Christmas carol). September 28<sup>th</sup> is his feast day. The saint was murdered by his own brother while he was praying before the tabernacle in 938. It must've been about 7:15 when the phone rang.

"Hello, Mom?"

"Hello, Richard – this is early for you to call!" I said.

"Gee, I'm sorry, were you sleeping?"

"No, I was up – I was just reading about Saint Wenceslas—"

"Listen, Ma, you got a few minutes? I really need to talk about something."

This was not like my son. Richard did not like to admit weakness, and since he was eight years old anyway, he's avoided running to Mommy for help. Of course I was happy he was turning to me, but the story he told was worrisome, and when he finished, I was speechless.

Silence on the line.

"So what do you think?" he asked.

"I really don't know, Richard. It's good that she's working with a priest. And you say she studied to be a nun?"

"She said she *was* a nun, but she had to leave the Order so she could use her God-given gift as a psychic and perform the extra-ordinary duties she's since taken up."

"O dear God," I uttered, without really meaning to; I was glad he couldn't see me cross myself – I didn't want to scare him.

I tried to be encouraging. "Well, she used holy water from Lourdes, and I'm glad she put St. Michael on the door. He's very powerful. You know, his feast day is tomorrow, they call it MICKel-mus."

"No kidding," Richard said.

"Yeah, if you go to Mass tomorrow, I'm sure they'll talk about it. And afterwards, it's traditional to eat gnocchi."

I looked down at his picture in the book of the saints; he looked extremely handsome, tall with blue eyes, his muscles bulging as he carried a heavy sword. The article said Michael is one of the most powerful beings in the Universe – he will lead the Lord's armies in the Last Battle, slay the Dragon and defeat the forces of darkness.

"My confirmation name is Michael," Richard said.

"You chose that name yourself when you were just twelve years old. You had your pick of thousands of saints. What made you pick one of the few that aren't human beings?"

"What do you mean, not human?" he asked.

"Saints are pretty much all fallible people who rise above their faults by the grace of God to become role models for everybody. Only a handful of angels – Michael, Gabriel, Raphael – are called *saint*."

"Gee, I never thought of it like that. Most saints' names seemed namby-pamby to me – Francis, Julian, *Blaise.* I liked the image of strength, a masculine warrior-saint who fights evil. And flies, almost like a superhero!"

"Why?" I asked. "Were you afraid of something?"

"Well, I was never afraid of anyone my own size – it was the bigger kids, the ones with the longer reach."

"So you wanted a saint who could fight the big guys for you?"

"I don't think it was conscious, but Michael, he was one tough guy."

"Well, maybe you need his protection right now."

"Do you think angels really exist?" he asked me, out of the blue.

"What do you mean? Of course they exist. Some people say that they meet angels, that when somebody does something to help them, it's really an angel in disguise. There's even a show on television – *Touched by an Angel,* it's called. Della Reese plays the head angel."

I watched that show every Sunday night.

"I've heard of it," he said.

"Every week, this lovely Irish girl, she's an angel too, gets an assignment, to help somebody in trouble."

"You know, I've been reading a story about angels – this guy goes into the desert and tries to *see* his Guardian Angel. It's kind of scary."

"Well, don't read it if it's scary. I don't know if we're supposed to go find the angels – they come to us when we need them, like in the show. Angels are God's messengers, you see… oh, my goodness."

I had just remembered something.

"What?" he asked.

"Remember when I came to visit you?"

"In July, yeah."

"Well, when I was in the cab on the way to the airport, we got stuck in traffic. We just sat there. I was so nervous, I thought I was going to miss my flight."

"Yeah."

"We must've been stopped there on Woodhaven Boulevard for 15 minutes, the wheels not even moving – it turns out a tractor-trailer was jackknifed – anyway, there we were, right in front of St. Michael's parish. You know that beautyfull statue of Michael the Archangel slaying the Dragon from Revelation, the one on Woodhaven Boulevard down by the mall?"

"Hunh," he said. "It's funny that you just happened to get stopped right there, but it's a coincidence. I mean, it's not unusual to hit traffic on the way to the airport, is it?"

"No, but you know where St. Michael's is – it's not even on the way to JFK," I explained. "The taxi driver took a wrong turn on Woodhaven or we wouldn't have passed by that church at all!"

"You were going north on Woodhaven."

"So maybe it's meant to be, Richard. Saint Michael's watching over us! I prayed to him to help you and Katrina. Then you find this woman, a Catholic Nun in a Lutheran country – I mean, what are the odds? And when does she arrive on the scene but the day before Michaelmas!"

"And she's coming back tonight to finish the job."

"Oh, is she? That's wonderful. Maybe it'll all be over tonight!"

Silence on the line.

"I'm really dreading it," he said.

"Why?"

No answer.

"Richard, are you there?"

"Yeah, Ma."

"I asked why are you dreading it?"

"She says we have to go down into the crawl space."

"Crawl space?"

"Yeah, in the basement."

"You have to go *into* the crawl space? Oh my God."

"She says that's the only way to get rid of the spirits."

"*Spirits* – you mean there's more than one?"

"She says there's at least three. She says when you have a ghost, you almost always have more than one – they seem to like to hang out together."

"Oh dear Lord," I said.

"Does this whole thing seem right to you, Mom?" he asked me.

I thought about this for a minute. After all, you can't be too careful.

Then I quoted, "By their fruits you will know them. This woman is making you pray and read the Bible; and she's working with a priest, right? I mean, they're the professionals, and they can call in specialized help when it's needed. Is the priest going to be with you tonight?"

"Yes, I think so."

"Well that's good," I said. "Ask him whatever questions you have. He'll explain what they're doing. I hate the thought of you down there under the house. It all sounds very dark. But it's always darkest before a dawn, right? I wish I could be there with you, but that's not possible. So I will do what I can from here: I'll say the Rosary for you. You have the Rosary beads I gave you?"

"Yeah, Ma."

"Then say the Rosary, Richard. Recite the Rosary day and night until you beat this thing. Nothing can defeat that prayer! You know there was a mission in Hiro-sheema where they said the Rosary every day. And you know when we dropped the A-Bomb, that flimsy wood-frame building was the only thing left standing. I tell you with that prayer, you're invincible."

"Hiroshima?" he replied, pronouncing it Heh-ROE-shimma. "Really? Is that true – you're sure it's not just Catholic propaganda?"

I was a bit offended, but not altogether surprised by this remark.

"Didn't you pay attention in Catholic school, Richard? It was a mission run by German Jesuits. Almost at Ground Zero. I saw the pictures on TV. It wasn't made of concrete either, it was a ticky-tacky wooden building, just like all the others over there. Everything else was completely flattened, everyone killed instantly. And not just killed, they were pulverized where they stood – you could see the human form burnt into the rubble, like a shadow on the wall."

"I've seen those pictures, Ma."

"It was a miracle."

"It's amazing they survived – but then again, I guess they just died from radiation sickness later…"

"No, that's the thing – the priests were able to work with the radiation victims for months and continued living there in that area for years, but they never got sick. I saw them interviewed on TV, it was many years afterwards – they lived to be old men."

"Wow. That's amazing," he responded. "Okay, I promise I'll say the Rosary. I'll even get Katrina to pray."

"Oh, would you? That would be wonderful," I said. "Do you think she will? I mean, she doesn't seem very religious."

"Yeah, maybe – we'll see. Anyway, thanks, Ma. I feel a lot better."

"And go out and get yourself some gnocchi for tomorrow, okay?" I said, trying to lighten things up a bit.

"Sure, Ma. Sure thing. Gnocchi, okay. I'll let you know what happens."

# 33. Richard

The moon was down. I sat by the front window, waiting for the familiar silver disk to show itself and for the psychic to arrive. I was nursing a glass of bourbon, not my usual drink, but somehow this American version of whiskey was more comforting to me at that moment than any European liquor could've been. I looked at my reflection in the glass and turned over in my mind what was being asked of me tonight.

The crawl space. Even the name was frightening – a place where a man cannot walk, but has to crawl along, like an insect or a snake, humbled. Going down there was like going into a cave, or underwater. I hated putting my head under the water.

My parents, never strong swimmers themselves, did all they could to make sure I learned to swim. God knows, with all the CYO day camps and lessons at the salt-water pool in Whitestone summer after summer, I should've learned. But all I could ever do was paddle with my nose sticking out of the water, like a dog. When I tried to do the "Australian crawl," I would take in sea water, and come up retching and spitting, nauseous from the fetid brine of the Long Island Sound.

And now here I was, up against a different Sound, being asked to dive under the earth. I had to overcome the house by going under it.

*The crawl space was like a test of manhood,*
*Like going under the chassis of a Chevrolet –*
*Or a woman! – for the first time.*
*I had to hold my breath and dive,*
*It's what a man had to do.*
*Going under, going down;*
*Overcoming fear and darkness, the sulphur,*
*The stench, consumption. Poh! Poh!*

I had a bad taste in my mouth. I swigged the last of the bourbon, and suddenly saw the moon, not shining silver, but round and orangey like a pumpkin floating above the tree.

But it wasn't the moon I had to conquer. *What was there to overcome but myself?* This wasn't TV. The angels were not going to show up at the door and ring the bell. A person had to get away from it all, away from all the props – the fancy job, the suit and tie, the money, the car – go into the desert, up a mountain, or into a cave, deep in the earth.

You had to strip everything away, make yourself completely vulnerable, if you wanted to see your Guardian Angel.

The shriek of a night-owl woke me from my musings. I heard the mellifluous sound of the monks of Silos pouring out of the stereo speakers, and then, the doorbell.

In a moment the pensive, laconic day of waiting transformed into a frenetic, talky evening. Rowena flowed into the living room, loosing the sluice gates and unleashing a waterfall of words into our quiet Saturday:

*Did you take the rose-petal bath?*

*Did you see anything?*

*Did you say your prayers?*

*Did you read the Bible?*

*Were you able to sleep?*

*What did you eat today?*

As we sat around the dining room table, I finally managed to get a word in edgewise. "What about the photos? Do you think Katrina's grandfather is involved?"

"I have prayed over the photo, and discussed it with the Good Father. I even tried to communicate with the entity, but it resists. I get a name – Rasmus or Erasmus. Does that make sense to you, Katrina?"

"Yes, that's right, his name was Rasmus," Katrina replied. "Rasmus Søgaard, I suppose. Søgaard was Mor's maiden name."

"This spirit is highly energetic – but also resentful, remorseful, wretched. Do you know how he died, Katrina? Was it a violent or unusual death?" Rowena asked.

Katrina looked down. We hadn't talked about this during the day.

"Yes," she said quietly.

"Katrina, you didn't tell me!" I blurted. "Did you talk to your mother today?"

"Yes," she said again.

After some stammers, she finally managed to look up at Rowena and say, "It was suicide."

"Oh Katrina. Oh, I'm so sorry," Rowena said.

"And you never knew?" I asked.

"No. It happened before I was born," Katrina explained. "I guess depression runs—"

"What?" I asked.

"Uh, I mean, I guess it was during the Depression. Life was hard."

"Yes, of course," Rowena said. "But you must understand that suicides are cursed for all time. This is God's will. The soul realizes its error immediately upon death. Some may try to escape or at least defer their terrible judgment by tarrying in our plane of existence. I am sorry to say that quite a few of the 'stuck' souls that I have encountered in my calling have been the result of suicide."

Hmm. Free will is essential to human nature. Such a thing would not change just because we die. So, a suicide could, I suppose, choose to become a kind of renegade, a fugitive from justice. If Hell is real, then it stands to reason that anything is better than that – tortures designed specifically for you...

*Cain, cold-blooded betrayer of his own flesh and blood, doomed for eternity to be immersed up to his neck in a lake of ice.*

"What happens to them," I asked, "these fugitives from God's Justice? Are there some kind of cosmic bounty hunters that come after them?"

Rowena hesitated, as if she wanted to tell me something but could not. Finally, she said, "Ultimately, no soul can avoid the justice of God. Staying in the physical plane requires energy – the spirits we encounter, especially the poltergeists, are generally the souls of the *recently* departed. You see, spirits fade, Richard. Eventually, all spirits limp to their eternal home."

"Rasmus has only been dead for forty years, so he could have plenty of juice left. So you think he's been haunting Katrina. But why? The man was dead before she was born, he never even met her."

"I can't be sure," she said. "We know spirits follow blood lines. Perhaps he lived in poverty, may be jealous of Katrina, may not think that she deserves to live in such luxury."

"So he wants to drive her to financial ruin?" I asked.

"I believe the entity desires the break-up of your marriage," she said.

"Our marriage?" I asked, incredulous.

"Yes. Without your money, Rasmus would be appeased that Katrina has only what she herself has earned."

I put two and two together: "And Damsgaard would be happy if I was out of the picture, because he wants Katrina to himself. So does this mean were talking about *cahoots* here?"

"Excuse me?" Rowena asked.

"The two of them are working together?" I asked, raising my voice.

"Uh, well, I'm not sure about that," she replied. "I don't know if spirits would be able to..." she paused as if thinking of the right word, "collaborate in that way. But it is true that both spirits would be pleased to see Katrina on her own. The only way to satisfy them would be if the two of you split up – then the energy would be released."

I looked at Katrina, who stared straight ahead, catatonic. I reached out and held her hand, and said, "Don't worry, Skat. We'll get through this. We won't let them split us up."

Rowena backed me up. "Katrina, don't be afraid. You are not guilty of anything, so there's nothing to be afraid of."

But Katrina did not respond, so I said to Rowena, "Maybe it would make us less, uh, apprehensive, if we knew what was coming. What are we going to do tonight?" I asked.

"I have spoken with the Good Father—" Rowena started.

"Will he be here tonight?" I asked.

"No," she said. "He doesn't usually come onsite in this kind of situation."

"Why not?" I asked.

Rowena tilted her head slightly, looked directly in my eyes with her features softened, and answered, "The same reason I had to leave the Convent. Active religious are not allowed to get too close to this kind of work. It can contaminate them spiritually, leaving them unable to administer the sacraments for a period of time. That's why after three years I had to choose between being a nun and using the psychic abilities that God gave me."

"Oh," I said, feeling a heaviness like a bar of lead in the pit of my stomach.

"But as I told you yesterday, Richard, *you* are the priest here."

I remembered that in early Christian communities, the husband acted as the priest at the weekly ritual, but this didn't make me feel any better. I didn't want to be the priest if it involved the casting out of spirits. And there was something else, but I couldn't quite put my finger on it, something nagging at me in the back of my Jesuit-trained mind.

"How will you get the ghosts to leave?" Katrina asked.

"The power to evict these entities resides in you," Rowena said. "You see, Danes, like all Indo-European peoples, live in what we call a 'Guest' culture. The mutual obligations of Host and Guest are what sets them apart from all the other peoples in the world. In these cultures – Greek, Roman, Celtic, Persian – *ghosts* are, in a formal sense, *guests*."

"How is he a guest?" I asked. "We didn't invite him!"

"Damsgaard was here before we arrived," Katrina pointed out.

"Nevertheless, he *is* your guest. Listen to the words themselves – ghost, guest," Rowena said. "As the Germans put it, *Der Geist ist ein Gäst* – and an unwanted guest can only be expelled by the Master of the House."

"You're saying that I can evict these spirits – but then why aren't they gone already?" I asked. "I've yelled at them to leave—"

"Richard, it's not that easy – the entities here are strong, and very much afraid of being homeless. We must function as a team, a 'Triad' technically, in tonight's ritual. Katrina, you are the offended Hostess who tells your guests politely that you find their behavior objectionable. They must understand that you know what they are after, and that they're not going to get it. Richard, as the Host, you will formally evict them. I will lead us through the ritual process, and..." She stopped mid-sentence.

"And?" I asked.

"And one more thing," she said, hesitantly. "I will also block the way to compromise. There may come a point where you will believe it is better to live with the spirits than go through with the ritual. You may think that you can change them or help them. The truth is that it's too late for these spirits, and I must block this dangerous path."

Then the room went silent, and Rowena asked us for wineglasses. Katrina got them from the kitchen, and Rowena brought forth from the bottomless pit of her black bag a flask of sweet rust-colored wine. The color and smell reminded me of the sacramental wine of my days as an altar boy at Mass at Saint Sebastian's.

I got out the Bible, and Rowena placed the Holy Water from Lourdes, several candles, incense, and wands of sage on the white linen tablecloth. The ritual was about to begin.

Then she handed an enormous purple crystal to my wife, and said, "Katrina, this crystal is for you. Taken from the Mojave Desert in Southern California..."

*Like Coelho's Valkyries on their Harleys.*

"...it is one of the largest Hauser geodes ever unearthed. Our practice is extremely fortunate to have access to it. When I leave tonight, this crystal will stay with you. It is precious, so keep it safe. Keep it near you all night. Will you do that, Katrina?"

Katrina nodded gravely.

"Good," Rowena said, smiling. Then she decanted three pools of the tawny liquid. I drank mine down, but as we hadn't eaten much all day, the wine went right to my head. As I looked at the familiar words in Psalm 23, the letters wouldn't stay still for me.

I concentrated, and managed to make out the entire psalm successfully as we processed down the stairs to the cellar. Once again, I held the Bible aloft as a shield against the darkness, followed by Katrina, an acolyte holding the votive candle which cast shadows ahead of our little contingent, and Rowena, bearing the smoking shafts of sage.

When we arrived at the bottom and the final words of the psalm – *I will dwell in the House of the Lord forever* – rang in our ears, Rowena asked if there was a chair we could use to enter the hole more easily. I volunteered to get one. She also asked if I could raise the volume so the chanting could be heard more easily.

I ran up the stairs, attended to the stereo, took a chair from the dining room table, and walked it gingerly down the tight stairwell.

When I arrived again in the close room, lit by the single flame of the blue votive, Rowena said, "You recall last night we sealed off the crawl space with holy wax, taken from the citadel of Mont-Saint-Michel. The house has been very quiet today, no?"

"Yeah, dead quiet," I replied with an unfortunate choice of words that the women gracefully overlooked.

"This is because the spirits have been contained inside the chamber, the blue wax of Saint Michael holding back the torrents of spiritual energy, even as the

Norman fortress of Mont-Saint-Michel holds back the waves of the North Atlantic," Rowena explained.

"When we open the door and go inside, what can we expect to happen?" I asked. "Will the spirits attack us somehow?"

"Physically, you may experience some mild effects such as nausea, dizziness or palpitations," she said. "This is normal. Don't be afraid: you are in no physical danger.

"On the psychic plane, we will meditate together. I will attempt to get you down to alpha level. It is difficult to predict what you will experience at such a deep level of consciousness. Some people see unexpected things – monsters, demons – but whatever you encounter, remember that our purpose here is holy, and we are protected by Michael and his army of angels."

I know she said this to make me feel better, but it had the opposite effect. I just wanted to make this all go away, to go home, to see my mother. But that wasn't possible. Here we were, we had come this far; there was no way out. I looked over at Katrina and saw she was white as... well, let's just say she was pale.

I was just steeling myself for the moment when Rowena would open the trapdoor when she turned to me and said, "Richard, are you ready?"

"Yeah, sure," I said a bit too hastily.

"You may open the portal any time now," she said.

"Me? Why does it have to be me? I don't even want to go in there—"

"As the priest in tonight's ritual, you must open the seals."

"Open the seals – how do I do that?" I asked.

"You will use the water from the sacred spring of Lourdes."

"I'm going to open a wax seal with water?"

Handing me the oddly furry sprinkler, she said, "Simply dip the *goupillon* – it's the tail of a fox – into the holy phial. Then douse the entrance with the blessed water three times, in the name of the Father, the Son, and the Holy Spirit. Do you understand, Richard?"

"You want me to bless the trapdoor with the sign of the cross," I confirmed.

"Say the holy words as you soak the seals three times. Then you will see the wax respond to water's touch," she explained.

I was completely out of my element by this point. I don't know if it was the wine or lack of eating, or what, but I felt like I was in a dream. I took the bronze bucket from her hand, and dunked the sprinkler carefully, making a circular movement to get the fur as wet as possible.

Gathering myself, I said in my best Master-of-the-House voice, "I bless thee in the name of the Father..." and flicked the tail toward the wax, moving my whole arm to drown the seam as much as possible. I needn't have bothered, as the wax reacted to the first drop, immediately fizzing up and emitting an odd, hissing sound.

I continued, saying, "...and of the Son," sprinkling a second time. The hissing became a high-pitched squeal, like the air being let out of a balloon whose end has been stretched taut. I could see the water eroding the wax, like decades of corrosion collapsed into seconds. Katrina breathed in audibly.

And finally I said, "...and of the Holy Spirit," dousing the seam of the door so thoroughly that bluish liquid dripped down visibly onto the white wall below the trap. The three, thrice-blessed waxen seals of deep phthalo blue not only opened but virtually disappeared, yielding to the healing water.

If I hadn't seen it with my own eyes, I wouldn't have believed it.

Rowena, businesslike, treated the magical opening of the seals with no fanfare. All in a night's work, I suppose.

She nodded to me, and I lifted the latch and swung open the door. I noticed the usual stale, damp odor, but nobody's head spun around or anything, so I looked to Rowena, as if to say, "Now what?"

"Very good, Richard. The vortex has now been opened. Guard your thoughts, now, both of you. If an entity attempts to communicate directly with you, especially if you hear something like – 'This is for your ears only' – alert me right away, reject the entity, and begin to recite the Our Father or the Hail Mary. You know these prayers, don't you?"

We nodded.

Rowena produced three small tapers and we lit them from the large votive candle in its stand. Rowena, remarkably spry for a woman of her size, was the first to clamber in. Then Katrina dove in with ease, taking her tiny flame into the the endless blackness of the hole.

Finally, I stepped up onto the dining room chair and peered into the void. My eyes could dimly see the two tiny candles twinkling like eyes in the darkness. The vault was not sealed; there was a draft and I held the vulnerable flame close to my breast so it would not be extinguished.

Cold air rushed by me. I shivered…

*…on the high-dive at the Whitestone Pool. An overweight ten-year-old, frozen ten feet up. I knew the others were waiting impatiently. The line was growing.*

*"His Mommy better get him down from there before he gets huht."*

*"Hey Lard-ass! Move it, we ain't got all day!"*

*"C'mon ya Fag-it, you can do it, ya just got to go down!"*

*…and my ears burned.*

*I plunged into that vault of air – Down, down I come; like the glistering Sunlight – but I fell flat on my oversized belly, and hit the surface hard.*

The candles went out.

I felt a smack, as if I'd shattered the glassy surface of a subterranean lake. Light-headed and sea-stomached, I flopped ungracefully onto the base court, the base court of dirt and stones. Dust flew up. I coughed and sputtered and sneezed.

Rowena said, "Bless you, Richard."

# 34. Katrina

Rowena and I were alone in the cellar. Richard was upstairs fetching a chair. The monotonous, medieval sound of chanting drifted down to us from above, and I heard a man's voice.

*Now you are like the soul in torment that distantly hears,*
*But derives no comfort from the music of the spheres.*
*For though beams of yellow Sun penetrate the night,*
*Even to distant Pluto, no warmth is in that light,*
*No more than a flickering votive candle may deliver.*
*Nay, here in the world of shadows, our souls unsooth'd, we shiver.*

Rowena, her eyes closed in meditation, made no reaction. When the voice stopped, I was too stunned to say anything, stunned and sad. I imagined myself on the desolate surface of Pluto, seeing familiar Sol, so tiny and unimaginably far away. How maddening it was to see the Sun and yet feel no warmth! Just endless night, endless cold.

*Like being buried up to the neck in ice.*

I considered whether I'd imagined the whole thing. But the voice spoke a kind of poem – it was none I'd ever heard, and I'm no poet.

I became frightened and whispered hoarsely, "Rowena!"

"What's wrong?"

"I heard a voice inside my head – is he *inside* me?"

"What did the voice say?"

"I don't know. It was a poem, something about souls in torment."

"Ah, it starts," she said gravely.

For the first time in my life, I didn't trust myself, my own judgment. I worried that a ghost might be able to penetrate not only brick walls, but the gates of my *mind* as well. Was that how I knew the piece by Ravel on the piano, was he playing through my fingers?

"What's happening?" I asked, frantic.

Rowena gazed into my eyes and said, "You are very sensitive, Katrina. You may have psychic abilities yourself, able to feel the vibrations of entities around you. When I am in touch with the spirit world, I feel lighter, resonate at a higher frequency, *fade* a bit."

"Lighter – that's just how I feel sometimes. Like I'm just floating around, my head in the clouds."

"Fight it, Katrina!" she urged me, grabbing hold of my wrists. "The feeling of fading is an increase in the frequency of your own vibration, as your aura moves toward ultraviolet. When I am communing with the spirits, I also reach such a frequency. Then after the session I go directly to a heavy meal – grilled sardines, black pudding, Guinness stout, even kebabs. Anything to slow me down, anchor me to the physical plane.

"Tonight after I leave, as you lie in bed, you may feel thinner, very thin. You may feel vibrations as the spirits come for you. But you have a body, you can resist them. You will fight them, Katrina, and you will win, even though it may take a lot out of you."

Mesmerized by her words, I nodded, and just then I heard Richard creaking and clunking down the stairs with the chair. Rowena asked him to bless the door. To my utter amazement, the blue seals dissolved like sugar candy at the touch of the holy water. Each of us lit a tiny white candle with a flimsy circular hilt to protect our hands. Then Rowena swung wide the portal and we clambered inside the opening. Richard hesitated for a moment at the threshold, then flopped in clumsily, dousing the candles.

We lit the candles again and sat cross-legged in a circle on the earthen floor. Good thing I was wearing jeans, as the surface was rough and cratered, composed as it was of dirt, rocks and the leftover plaster of the Belle Epoque. I removed a particularly vicious pebble that was biting into my Victoria's Secret.

We could just glimpse the flame of Saint Michael's candle through the hatch; otherwise the world around our little circle was entirely black, and the tiny tapers cast monstrous shadows on the walls of the chamber.

Rowena spooned out the incense and lit the coals of a small censor that she placed in the middle of the floor. The scented smoke rose up to fill the small chamber, enveloping us in intoxicating fumes.

Holding hands, we were three persons in one triune ring. In a flash of insight, I saw that we each had a divine role to play:

Rowena was Creator and Guide in our world of the ritual;

Richard played the Son's role of priest like at the Last Supper;

I was the Third Person, the vessel to be filled with the Holy Ghost that would drive away the unholy ones.

Rowena asked us to close our eyes, count our breaths. She must've talked to us, but I cannot remember what she said. Perhaps it was like one of those relaxation exercises where you sit on a beach and then walk into the ocean but have no trouble breathing underwater. After what seemed an eternity, she clapped her hands and we woke refreshed and receptive.

Somehow Rowena had managed to carry in the wine and the glasses. I was slightly mushy-headed already and not inclined to more drink, but she was insistent – and I was so desperate to get my mind back that I would have downed a shot of antifreeze if I thought it would help.

Richard took up his cup of wine and said, "Dear Lord, we give you thanks and praise. Please bless our actions this night, in the name of the Father and of the Son, and of the Holy Spirit."

Then we drank. I tried to just take a little sip, but Rowena admonished me saying, "We must all drink deep from the cup."

"Good," she said. "Now, Richard, why don't you ask Katrina how this all began?"

"Katrina, how did this all begin?" Richard parroted.

"I don't know where to start," I said.

"When did you first begin to suspect that you were, uh, not alone?" Richard asked.

"At the Housewarming," I said.

The conversation went on like this for some time – Richard asking questions about my experiences, me answering as best I could, and Rowena commenting, guiding.

After some time, Rowena turned the tables and asked Richard, "What was it like to be alone all night in Sundhuset?"

"I felt like I was in Katrina's shoes for once. Trapped. And ridiculed, like someone was having a good laugh at my expense. It really made me appreciate her point of view."

"And Katrina, what were you feeling as you drove to Hellerup that day?" she asked.

"I was worried about Richard."

"Worried about what?" she asked.

"I wasn't sure what it would do to him," I said. "Being alone in the house."

"What did it do to you, Richard?" Rowena asked.

"It freaked me out – those books moving…"

"So you realized that there was an external force at work, one that does not play by the rules?" she asked.

He nodded and said, "Only by rules of its own making."

"Up till then did you just think I was crazy?" I asked.

"No, I never thought you were crazy, Skat," he replied.

"What did you think then?" I asked.

"I just – I just didn't know what to think," he said.

Rowena then tried to bring us together saying, "The two of you have been granted a rare gift. You've been able to see the world from each other's perspective. Richard, you saw what it was like to be trapped in a house that you perceive as hostile. Katrina, you have seen what it's like to go away and worry about your partner who remains alone, at home and at risk."

We could see it was true, and embraced there in that dark place.

Rowena smiled then and said, "I think we have made great progress tonight. All that remains is for the Paraclete to come and dwell among us. Richard, please say after me, *Come Holy Spirit…*"

"Come Holy Spirit," repeated Richard.

Then Rowena intoned and Richard repeated, "Penetrate with your Light the deepest part of our souls."

Finally she said and we all repeated, "Amen."

When we got back upstairs and sat around the dining room table, I felt elated, giddy even. I just couldn't stop grinning.

"I feel *so* much better," I said.

"Yeah, thanks so much, Rowena. This was a great session," Richard said.

"I'm glad. You were wonderful, both of you," Rowena said.

"So is it over now?" Richard asked hopefully.

Rowena shook her head and said, "We have opened the portal but not yet vanquished the Foe. There is more work to do."

Then she proceeded to give us our instructions for the night. "Richard, before you sleep tonight, I would like you to read two passages from the Bible: the story of Abraham and the Book of Job. Will you do that, Richard?"

"Sure, I guess so," Richard replied.

"Good. Katrina, I would like you to take the crystal with you to your bedroom tonight. Keep it close by you."

"I will, of course," I said.

"Good," she said, smiling. "Tomorrow, you need to cleanse the body. Fast if you can. Drink plenty of water. You can eat if you must, but nothing heavy."

We agreed, and Rowena said, "Good. Then tomorrow evening, we will meet again, perhaps for the last time."

"Will Father be able to join us tomorrow?" Richard asked.

I was a little annoyed at the question. Obviously all that Catholic schooling made him dependent on authority figures.

Rowena grimaced.

"I will ask him," she said. "But as I said earlier, he normally does not come onsite."

"Please ask him," Richard said.

Rowena agreed, and took her leave of us, no doubt off to hunt down a kebab shop that was still skewering at 10 o'clock on a Saturday night.

Richard and I sat down to a cup of Russian Earl Grey.

"How do you feel?" Richard asked.

"Ecstatic," I replied.

"Me too. Like I'm flying. What an incredible experience. She is really amazing," Richard said.

"Did you see the seals dissolve like that?" I asked.

"Yeah, that was unbelievable," he said with his eyes wide. "And the ritual was not at all what I expected – I thought there would be some kind of trance or séance or something, like in the movies. Instead it was very devout – very Catholic."

"Well, she was a nun," I pointed out.

"Yeah. Did you catch the reference to Jesus in the Garden?"

"No, what do you mean?"

"You didn't want to drink from the cup. Just like Jesus who asked God to 'Take this cup away from me.' Rowena told you to drink deep, just like the Father told the Son. Maybe what we have to go through is painful – but unavoidable."

"Amazing, I missed that entirely. But I did notice that the three of us formed a trinity – she as the Creator of our ritual, you as the Priest, in imitation of Jesus, and me as the vessel for the Holy Spirit."

Richard's mouth hung open. "Wow. That's incredible. The connections are everywhere!"

As we crept up the stairs to bed, the haunting stepwise strains of the Benedictine monks of de Silos repeated and reverberated on the cold plaster walls and ceilings of the ancient house, and in the dining room, the flame of Saint Michael's candle stood watch.

We sat up in bed and Richard began the story of Abraham. The theme was trusting in God no matter what. I winced at the part where Abraham, at God's request, raises his knife to butcher his only son Isaac, only to be stopped at the last moment by the shout of the Angel of the Lord. *Was this Michael?* Then Abraham looks up to see a ram stuck in the thicket, conveniently provided by Jehovah to replace the human sacrifice. It was a good story but it went on and on, and before we had disposed of Abraham, I had fallen into a deep, dreamless sleep.

Next thing I knew, Richard was saying, "I had no idea how long the Book of Job was – forty-two chapters... Katrina, what do you say we take a shortcut? Oh, were you asleep?"

"Mm-hm," I said, rubbing my face.

"That's okay. I'll just read the first and last chapters, and then we can call it a night," and then he read aloud, "There was a man in the land of Uz, whose name was Job..."

I must have fallen asleep again, the crystal cradled in my arms, because the next thing I knew, I felt this incredible buzzing going through my body. Like an electric current. I sat bolt upright and looked at Richard who was sleeping peacefully. There was a hint of tobacco smoke in the air. I reached out my right foot to touch his left.

Richard woke with a start and asked, "What's that? Oh, Katrina it's you."

"Do you feel that?" I asked.

"What?"

"I'm buzzing. Do you feel it?"

"Oh, yeah, now that you mention it, I do feel something. Like a tingling in my legs," Richard said.

"Do you think it's one of the ghosts?" I asked.

"I don't know. Let's pray together," he said, looking into my eyes and reaching out for his Rosary beads.

"My Mother gave them to me when she was here. They were my father's. They got them at the Vatican when they went to Italy about 10 years ago. The nuns make them out of rose petals. See, they still smell of roses, even after all these years," he said, holding the beads up to my nose.

The scent of roses made me flinch.

Richard held my hand and led us in the Rosary. The buzzing came in waves. When it wasn't so intense, I could pray along with Richard. At other times, I was just too overwhelmed.

Strange visions came into my head, Copenhagen as it was a century ago. An Ibsen play at the Old Theatre. Saint Alban's Church as it was being built, stone by stone. A lady's boudoir. A young woman, shapely but overly rouged. My hand on her slip, caressing her inner thigh. Her skin so smooth. *Ahh.*

Then I heard a chime – the pocket watch! I was running out of time! I tried to call out, and then I heard Richard's voice, as through a fog from a great distance, saying, "Katrina!"

"Katrina, how are you feeling?" he asked.

"I'm so tired," I replied. "What time is it?"

"The clock just struck twelve. Are you still feeling the buzzing?"

"It comes and goes."

"I feel like there's someone in the room with us."

"Yes," I said. "Sometimes it's like he's inside my head."

"Who?"

"A man," I said.

"Damsgaard?" he asked

"Yes."

"Does he seem – malevolent?"

"No. Just like he wants to be with me. Inside me."

"Well, he's not allowed. You tell him to get out, y'hear?" Richard said, his voice panicky.

*Rowena told me to resist.*

*Karl Damsgaard, you must leave. You've no business being here. The house is ours now. You're dead, and must move on.*

I saw in my mind's eye a figure walking toward a shaft of light. In my imagination, the spirit was reluctant, but I told him there was no other way, that his time as a Guest was at an end. But then the figure turned towards me and a strange thing happened – instead of Damsgaard's goateed face, I saw my father. As he was when he was alive. In the spotlight, but where were we?

His offices. There was Dahl, and I recognized some of Fa's partners, men whom I hadn't seen since I was a girl – a fat, bald guy with a large, brown mole on his cheek; a gangly man with thick, greasy spectacles. We entered a conference room. *Wannsee,* I recalled the name. This was where Fa' died.

As we sat there, the furniture changed – this was a dream, must've been some kind a dream or vision – old paintings in gilt frames appeared on the walls, a spittoon, a wooden, roll-top desk. And at the desk sat Damsgaard, smoking a cigarette. Yet Fa' and a younger version of Niels Dahl were still sitting there at the modern table, talking as if nothing had been altered.

Damsgaard looked at me as if to say, *You see?* But I didn't understand.

Then he turned toward Fa' with a withering look of hatred, got up from the desk, and moved toward him – I called out, but could not be heard – and I watched as he placed his hands around Fa's neck. The coughing was mild at first, as if he were clearing his throat before speaking, then it grew more violent, a chesty smoker's hack. Finally, Fa' stood and turned, coming face-to-face with Damsgaard.

*I've got you now.*

Fa' brought his hands to his throat, but it was no use against spectral fingers. His face turned bluish and his features contorted into the death mask I'd seen before. He fell to the floor, and Dahl ran over to him, too late, as the scene grew dim.

The tingling sensation stopped. I placed the crystal on the nightstand and fell back against the pillows, exhausted. I felt tears on my face.

"It's gone now, isn't it?" Richard asked.

"Yes," I said. "Yes, it is."

"Good. Rest now."

"Richard?"

"Yeah?"

*How could I tell him what I'd seen?* Hesitating, I said, "Can you fetch me a drink of water?"

"Sure."

As he turned to go, I said, "I'll come with you!"

And we *both* went to get a drink.

We kept the lights on in the hall. The window was open; the night air rolled in. I slid back into sleep to the lulling sound of Richard's voice praying and softly singing Catholic songs from his boyhood. I did not dream.

After I had been asleep for some time, a shaft of moonlight penetrated the ash tree and shone directly into my eyes. Still half asleep, I felt a distinct puff of air in my ear, my left ear, and detected a soft mumbling. It was Richard, no doubt, talking in his sleep. The words made little sense to me, like the grumbling of old men.

It was as if Richard were arguing with himself in his dream. I caught snippets only: "you put me down there... *rumble-mumble*, ashamed of me... *rumble-mumble*, for years now, how dare you... *rumble-mumble*, since the war..."

Sleeping on my back, I rolled over onto my side, to turn away from the sound. My face plowed right into Richard's shoulder! He was sleeping on my right-hand side.

*Who had been whispering in my left ear?*

Startled, I shook my face awake. The clock was striking two. I felt thin, faded, as if Damsgaard was tapping all my energy. My legs started tingling again – and then waves of buzzing started traveling up and down my legs. I sat bolt upright in bed, looked toward the doorway, and my eye caught sight of something, something white and wispy.

The hall light was on, but the door was mostly closed, and the figure appeared in the shadow behind the door. It was a girl, a girl in white. Preternaturally tall, over two meters, but adolescent in appearance – small breasts were visible through her sheer white negligee. She seemed sad, gaunt, and very thin.

*Anorexic.*

All this I saw in the second it took me to call out, "Aeh!"

"Huh?" Richard said sleepily.

I turned to switch on the lamp on my side of the bed, and when I turned back toward the door, the spectre was gone. Richard sat up and said, "What happened? Did you have a bad dream?"

"No, it wasn't a dream," I replied.

"Do you feel anything?"

"There's a gentle buzzing in my legs."

"Again?"

"Yes – but."

"But what?"

"This time I saw something," I said, hating to admit it, hating to sound like a crazy person.

"You saw the Ghost? You saw Damsgaard?"

"No, this was a girl, I saw a girl."

"A girl?"

"In leotards, white leotards, like a dancer. But unnaturally thin, like she'd starved herself to death."

"Was she here in the room? Where?" he asked.

"Over there, toward the door," I said.

"Don't you think it was just something from your dream?"

I shook my head and put my hands on my mouth.

"Let's just say a prayer and go back to sleep, okay?" he suggested. "I think we're both getting sleep-deprived. You know, they say you should sleep eight hours a night. For every hour less than that, you lose one point of IQ. And it's cumulative."

"Then I'm all out of IQ points," I said.

Then we said a little prayer and he kissed me on the cheek before rolling over and going back to asleep.

I looked at the clock – 2:11 AM. I took the purplish crystal from the night-stand and placed it over my sternum, clutching it in both hands. I was so exhausted that, despite the eerie circumstances, my heavy eyelids closed and sleep washed over me once more.

At 4 o'clock, I woke a third time with a start, pulses coming up my left leg, stronger than before, radiating through my entire body and down my right leg. My foot was touching Richard's and after two or three waves, he moved and then woke up.

"It's coming again, isn't it?" he said.

"Yes, I feel it again."

"What is that?" he asked.

"I don't know. Buzzing like before."

"I feel it coming out of your body and right into mine."

I moved my foot away. Richard reached out for my hand and put his foot back on mine.

"I want to help you through this," he said.

"Okay," I said, starting to tear up.

He got his Rosary beads out again and started praying aloud. I prayed silently along with him. The waves grew more intense, like electric current flowing through my limbs, and I was no longer in the room.

The air was stuffy, the air of a bunker. Concrete walls were hung with paintings in ornate frames, traditional landscapes; some were amateurish, others master works. One stood out, the same work that hung in Damsgaard's office – an aging painter, in his dimly-lit bedroom surrounded by his life's work. Sitting up in bed, he beholds Death in the wardrobe mirror and screams. It was an art critic's nightmare: grotesque like Dürer or Bosch, but painted in the lush style of the Danish Golden Age.

Fluorescent tubes hummed in their hoods. I sat on a cot, an ash-blond toddler in my lap. Where were the others? Already taken, I knew. The boy was the last one. He clung to my breast. He could not live, and this made me sad beyond any sadness I'd ever known. They were coming for him, *he* was coming. I heard footsteps outside the metal door, or no, not footsteps but a clunking. *Scrape-clunk. Scrape-clunk.* And then I knew who it was. The door opened...

Richard was shaking me. "Is it Damsgaard again?"

"No," I said. "Darker, much darker."

I didn't dare tell him what I had seen.

I prayed for the images to be taken from me. I tried to call out to my Guardian Angel – if I had one. I tried, but it was as if the angel could not reach me, as if the ghosts had come between us. I buried my face in the space between Richard's throat and collarbone, and broke down. Richard held me and stroked my hair.

Then I noticed a feeling in my stomach, a burning, acid feeling. It crept up my esophagus. Vomit. I started retching. Suppressing the feeling as best I could, I ran into the bathroom, threw myself on my knees and emptied myself, again and again, a dozen times or more. It seemed like it would not end until crimson blood rained down upon white porcelain.

Richard buzzed about me uselessly. Finally, heaving dry, I collapsed with a whimper on the cold rectangles of the bathroom floor. He held me then, and brought me back to bed.

The mood in the room had cleared. Whatever it was that caused the buzzing and the visions was gone; the sun was just coming up, and I could hear the early birds chirping in the oaks as I lay back on the pillows, exhausted.

I fell back asleep to the call of a lark.

# 35. Richard

Just before midnight, we began our watch of contemplation and prayer, our dark night of the soul.

Katrina and I were sitting up in bed. I was reading out loud from the Bible, the assignment that Rowena had given us. But it was getting late and we were exhausted, so when I had finished with Abraham, I took a short-cut on the plagues of Job.

I read the beginning where Job's three friends show up to comfort him and then skipped to end where God speaks to Job from the whirlwind, asking him what right he has to question the unique credentials of the Creator:

*Can you lead about Leviathan with a hook,*
*Or curb his tongue with a bit?*
*Out of his mouth go forth firebrands;*
*Sparks of fire leap forth.*
*From his nostrils issues steam,*
*As from a seething pot or bowl.*
*His breath sets coals afire;*
*A flame pours from his mouth.*

Just as Job was admitting that he wasn't quite up to slaying fire-breathing dragons, Katrina let out a little nose-snore. She had long-since been asleep. Closing the book, I crossed myself and turned out the light.

The beads in my hands, redolent of roses, amazed me; it was as if the tiny spheres had been crafted days instead of years ago. Certain saints, whose bodies were said to be incorruptible, when exhumed, smelled of roses. I prayed silently.

Then I noticed that Katrina had become increasingly restless, shifting position and whimpering softly. Caressing her face, I felt her damp hair and forehead, hot as a stove. I uncovered her a bit – the duvet was thick – and she seemed to rest again.

Just as I was coming around to the end of the beads, Katrina sat up suddenly. I didn't like the wild look in her eyes. Her right foot touched my left and a wave of tingling shot up my leg, like touching a live wire.

"What's that?" I asked.

"Can you feel it too? Buzzing."

I felt somehow it was important to get her to pray, not just pray for her. I held her hand, and led her through the Rosary. She said the Hail Marys and Our Fathers in Danish, and didn't say anything during the other prayers. Her hand was very hot to the touch, and I kept my foot over hers as well. We seemed to make some kind of electric circuit, because that buzzing feeling continued, and grew stronger and stronger, in waves.

After we completed the five decades together, I asked, "How are you feeling?"

"I'm dead-tired," she said.

"Are you still feeling the buzzing?"

"It comes and goes."

"Do you feel like there's something in the room with us?"

"Yes. A man. I think it's Damsgaard," she said. "He wants to come inside me."

"He's not allowed," I said, raising my voice. "You tell him to clear out!"

The moon was full, but it must've gone behind a cloud, because at that moment the room became dark, and it was as if a black mist pervaded the air, as if a knot of darkness occluded my eyes. I couldn't see past the end of the bed. The blackness came from the left side, toward the door. I was afraid and prayed.

*Please, dear God send an angel to help us!*

Then I visualized – I will not say "saw," though the experience seemed real enough at the time – an angel. Not exactly in the room with us, but as if the scene I witnessed was taking place on a level higher than my line of sight, as if on a stage or raised platform. I could see that the personage approaching was brightly illuminated, as if in a spotlight.

Built like a wrestler, this was a muscular man of God. Like a swarthy Roman gladiator, this was nothing like the angels you see in pictures. He was bald, though he had plenty of stubble on his face and seemed otherwise hirsute.

The angel paid little attention to me, but instead addressed himself to the blackness, what Katrina perceived as the ghost of Karl Damsgaard. I continued to say Hail Marys and hold Katrina's hand as I watched, dumbfounded. The contest did not last long. The angel held no weapon, nor did he need one. Instead he opened his mouth in the direction of the nest of blackness. I heard an immense boom like thunder, though there was no rain or lightning that I saw. And immediately the air was clear.

*Such a boom could bring the walls down… ah, it must be Gabriel.*

Then he turned to me and though he did not speak, I somehow received the message that I was to continue what I was doing, and above all get Katrina to pray, to hope. Then he was gone the way he came.

The moonlight illumined our bed and furniture, and the room was normal once more. She was thirsty, and like Jack & Jill, we went to fetch some water. I didn't tell her what I had seen. I hoped of course that the visitations were over, but somehow I knew they were not. It was just after 12:30 when we got back to bed, and Katrina fell back to sleep immediately. I dozed off soon enough myself.

Waking to the sound of Katrina cries, I asked, "What's the matter?"

She had seen the figure of a tall, thin girl. I took Katrina's hand – it was now as clammy as it was feverish before. I told her we just needed some rest; it was 2 AM.

As we prayed together, I felt a damp coldness in the room, especially on the left hand side, which is strange since one would expect any night chill to come from the window-side of the room, and a damp whitish film seemed to be over my eyes, like cataracts. I rubbed my eyes, but the haze remained.

Katrina fell back to sleep, but I kept watch. I prayed silently that the angel would come once more, a healing angel. For a second time, I visualized a beautiful presence, male but slender, light and smooth-skinned, almost feminine. Nothing like the first warrior-angel.

The smiling angel carried with him green grapes in one hand and a sheaf of yellow wheat in the other. I could see white light all around him, and he moved in a circular motion about the room, as if feeding or nurturing the blanched void. As he did so, the film upon my eyes seemed to clear. He reached out his right hand and touched my face, and I was filled with calm and confidence. *Raphael.* Then once again an angel was gone as he had come, and all was as before.

At 4 o'clock, I woke to the sound of the grandfather clock downstairs tolling and the unsettling feeling of the bed shaking. Taking up the beads, I went back to work like a union man on nightshift returning from his break. Katrina was awake. I took her hand and kissed her. Buzzing shot up my leg, coming right out of her body and into mine. Like an electric current.

I started praying the Our Father out loud, raising my voice a bit, as if to force the spirits away with the sound of God's own words. The waves grew more intense, and Katrina seemed very unsettled, as if she was in physical pain.

"Is it Damsgaard again?" I asked.

"No," she said, swallowing, "It's darker, much darker."

Closing my eyes tightly, I prayed for a third angel. But none came. Instead, a blanket of night enveloped me. My throat started to swell. I couldn't breathe. Panicky, I gasped for air and opened my eyes.

To my horror, there was no change: it was just as black with my eyes open as with them closed. I was blind. Even the window seemed black as pitch, not a crack of light seemed to enter the room. All was darkness visible.

My heart beat furiously, fast and irregular. Was this a heart attack? Would I die this very night? I started to cry silently. I squeezed Katrina's hand, but we did not speak. We were together, yet completely alone.

I despaired, saw my life and my work as worthless. With disgust I recalled the vanity, wasted time, the lost opportunities for love. Of what worth was I? The days of my life flipped over like pages in a Rolodex – wine tastings, sumptuous galas, driving past shanties in the limo in Bombay, trips to the porn shop in Vesterbro.

Finding nothing of lasting worth, I broke down and cried. I reached back for the pure faith I had as a boy, felt in my stomach the leaden loss of my innocence. Softly, I whispered a sincere prayer, to be restored to the faith of my childhood. I saw my words fly up to heaven.

Then all at once, I saw him, piercing through the mist of darkness. This was one serious angel. All-business, not a trace of mirth in his chiseled features. Much larger than the previous figures, he was enormously tall with white wings behind and seemed to fill the entire room; he carried a shield in his right and a sword of pulsating celestial blue flame in his left hand.

This was Michael. Incalculably powerful, older than imagination, predating any story, any religion known to me.

Ignoring me completely, the angel addressed himself to a creature in the shadows that I had not seen until the angel's brilliance illuminated him. A creature of deep hatred and self-loathing, in human form: a man with squinting eyes and hawklike nose, and a sharp goatee. Of an evil house, and grown strong in his wickedness, he held a wooden cane with a silver top in the shape of a dog or maybe a wolf. The man beat his stick against the Angel's shield and a report rang out like thunder. Michael showed no reaction, but accepted the blow, and then lifted his sword until it was vertical in front of his eyes, illuminating both figures with its neon light. The creature was much afraid of this sword, and retreated.

Around the image of Michael, more and more light effused until the room was lit with millions of candlepower, overwhelming my retinas. I don't know how to describe it – like standing in a darkened squash court which is suddenly illuminated by the lights of Shea Stadium; millions of candlepower, so bright you can't make out the seams.

The aftereffect of the sustained flash on my sight was like the spot of blue-blackness you see after looking directly at the sun, but in this case, the afterimage was solid black in all directions.

Yet through the darkness emerged a vision, as if I could now see with a new kind of light.

*Jesus on the Cross, from the perspective of the women.*

I looked up at Him, dying. Writhing, stretching for another gasp of air. Blameless; beaten and bleeding – beyond all comprehension, beyond all measure. My own breath held.

*How dare I breathe when He cannot?*

And then I saw that He was dead, that God was dead and we had killed him. Swollen, bloody, obscene – I had to look away. Then it sank in that I had been let in on a secret, the secret the modern world has been keeping from itself for a hundred years.

"It's all true," I said out loud in a voice that ached. "It's all *true*! Yet *nobody* believes it. Not even the priests, not even the religious – that's why she cries. That's why the Mother cries for the world, because her Son died for us, and nobody even believes it. And it's all truuuue."

And I wept – for the Mother, for myself, for the world.

Just then Katrina woke and ran to the bathroom. She was violently ill. It was 4:30 by the time I got her back into bed; the sky was just starting to think about lightening. Magenta was replacing black as the heavenly base tone.

I lay back on the pillows and placed Katrina's head on my shoulder. As we lay there, exhausted from our night together, the window flew up – there's a chain mechanism on it, and I guess the ratchet gave way – and a sudden gale blew in, whistling and rattling the window shade, evacuating the noxious vapors of the night and filling the room with a heavenly aroma. It was as if the exasperated angels, after hours of contending with who-can-say-what, finally shook their wings to finish off their shadowy adversaries. Sweet dawn arrived, bearing with it an indescribable joy and relief.

I mouthed the words, "Thank you," then turned to Katrina and said, "What do you say we go to Mass this morning?"

# 36. Katrina

*What if God was one of us?*

I listened to Joan Osborne's lyrics at the breakfast table as I nibbled my toast and inhaled the bergamot of my Earl Grey.

"Is that the song you've been humming all week?" Richard asked.

"Yeah. It's all over the radio right now," I responded.

"It's pretty religious for a pop song," he commented as we heard:

*If God had a face, what would it look like?*

*And would you want to see?*

*If seeing meant that you would have to believe*

*In things like heaven and Jesus and the saints?*

"Wow. That hits the nail on the head, doesn't it?" he said.

"What?"

"People don't want to accept all the logical conclusions of their faith."

I said nothing, but grimaced and shook my head.

"If it's all true," he said, "that Jesus died on the cross for our sins – then you can't just stop there. You have to reform your life, follow the commandments, go to church every week. You have to believe in *everything*, you can't pick and choose."

This didn't strike me as logical at all.

"I think we have to decide for ourselves what's right and wrong," I said. "And going to church every week is a Catholic thing. Danes, even Christian ones, don't do that. It would be, I don't know, fanatical."

"So church is like a health club," he said with a smirk. "Look for convenient opening hours and easy parking. Show up when it suits you."

"Why are you so focused on church attendance?" I asked. "Some people go to church a couple of times a year – does it make them bad people?"

"See, that's where the song lyrics come in," he said, shaking his hands for emphasis. "Joan's not talking about going to church or doing good deeds."

Richard had this annoying habit of referring to famous people as if he knew them personally – Jagger was "Mick," Kennedy was "Jack." One time he even called the Queen "Maggie."

I let it go.

"She's talking about *seeing God's face*," he continued, his eyes wide. "That's a mystical thing. What do you think you'd do if you saw the face of God?"

I shook my head and said, "I have no idea – what does that even mean?"

"It would be completely overwhelming. Like Moses at the burning bush or Saul on the Road to Damascus. Nothing else would matter. That single moment of Light would overshadow every other moment of your life, and you would never be the same again."

I tried to understand where this religious zeal was coming from, but couldn't.

So I changed tack and said, "Religion for me is morality. People should be decent to each other…"

"Sure – but if you really encountered the Divine, like Thomas putting his hand in Jesus' side, you'd put Christ in the center of your life. Not a sideshow. You'd put down your fishing nets and follow Him."

"Richard, this is the 20th Century!" I protested. "People aren't going to throw off their clothes and go live among the birds like Saint Francis. We're modern people."

He said, "You're right," but then added, "Christ didn't call us to be *modern*."

I was about to argue the point with the Mystic who was masquerading as my husband at the breakfast table, when I noticed it was 7:30.

"Say, didn't you want to go to church today?" I asked. "I think your mother went to an eight o'clock service at Saint Ansgar's in the city when she was here."

"You want to come with me?" he asked.

"Okay," I said, a bit reluctantly. "We don't have much time though, I'd better get ready."

"What do you say we walk down there and catch a later Mass – it's a beautiful day. We can walk along the water."

I agreed, but insisted on wearing sneakers.

We walked along the Promenade by the harbor, looking out over the many quays, cranes and ferry-docks. Since it was Sunday, the machines were still and there was little traffic on the coast road.

"I didn't know you were so religious," I said as we walked along.

"I guess I didn't either," he said with a short laugh. Then added, "I was religious as a kid."

"Angelina likes to point out you were an altar boy."

"Yeah, I prayed every day, I wore medals of the saints. And of course we went to Mass every Sunday. Sometimes I ended up going three or four times a week if I was serving. I went to dozens of weddings and more than a hundred funerals before I hit puberty – that was my first lesson in making money. People who are happy pay you better – I could get a twenty at a wedding."

"You didn't get paid at funerals?" I asked.

"Maybe a couple of bucks, a five-spot if you were lucky."

"You did it for the money?"

"No, not just the money. It meant something, gave me something that everyday life never could. In my neighborhood, everything was a joke, nobody took anything seriously. But Mass was different, the 2,000-year-old tradition, the seriousness of it. And as an 8-year old, I knew secret things: words like alb and chasuble, chalice and paten. And where they kept the wine for communion."

"You haven't gone to church regularly in years."

"No, I haven't," he admitted. "I guess I just couldn't find the right community. But then, no, that's not it either. That's just an excuse. I think the real reason is deeper: I lost touch with the *meaning* of it all."

"The meaning of what?"

"Of religion. In college, I got all caught up in the social issues – birth control and abortion; the role of women in the church and problems with the hierarchy. That's all superficial stuff."

"Those are some important issues, Richard," I pointed out.

"Yeah, sure they are, but in arguing about the conclusions, I think I forgot the premise."

As we crossed the little bridge that goes over the moat to Kastellet, Richard said, "I saw angels fighting the spirits in our bedroom last night."

I was speechless. Angels! My experience of last night was so dark, ending only in pure exhaustion when I got several liters of pestilent vomit out of my system. Meanwhile, he was seeing angels – how could our experiences be so different?

"What was it like?" I sputtered.

"Each time a ghost would come," he said. "I think there were three in all, right?"

"Yes, I think there were three different ones."

"Yeah, well, each time, I would pray and an angel would come and drive it away."

"What was it like – did the angels have wings?"

"It was – like nothing else. I saw the ghosts as misty presences in the room with us – not really defined but clearly in one area of the room – and then, each time, an angel would come and drive out the spirit. And yeah, they did kind of have wings."

"Did they speak to you?"

"No. But I got a strong sense from one of them that I should continue praying – and get you to pray too."

I didn't know what to make of this. Somehow seeing angels sounded way more crazy than seeing ghosts, but then again a lot of people in the New Age community were starting to believe in angels – there were books and posters and calendars filled with angels these days.

But Richard wasn't finished. A few minutes later, we were going over the footbridge that led from the castle to Saint Alban's, and he said, "There's something else.

"As the last bit of darkness had receded, the room filled with tremendous light, a blinding white incandescence that overwhelmed me. Like a flash bulb that went off in my head and somehow stayed at its maximum intensity. My retinas were saturated with light, and then that Light became black. Like when you look at the Sun for a second and then look away, you see a spot of blackness – but this was everywhere."

"So you were blinded?" I asked.

"Completely, everything was black. And then through the blackness I saw..." He choked on the words.

"What did you see?" I asked, putting my hand on his forearm.

"Emerging through that sphere of blackness, I saw – I saw Jesus. Jesus, on the Cross."

"You saw *Jesus?*"

"It was like I was standing there with the women at the foot of the True Cross. The sky was cloudy and dark; it was raining, I felt the rain on my face. But it wasn't like in a movie – there were no thunderbolts, no cheesy music, no John Wayne – it was dirty and smelly and kind of grotesque. He was bloody and battered and already dead. I started sobbing. I felt like I'd been let in on a secret that the modern world has been keeping from itself, and I just kept saying the same words to myself over and over again, 'It's true, it's all true.'"

And then he started crying right there on the bridge, as if he were reliving his vision or dream or whatever it was.

Putting my arms around my big, blubbering boy, I kissed him and held him. This was a side of Richard I had never seen before – a softer side, more emotional, more in touch with the spiritual. I decided I liked it.

After a long time on the bridge, we continued down along the Esplanade to Bredgade and the Catholic church, Saint Ansgar's. We arrived at the church just before 9, and read the bulletin board in what my Art History class had taught me to call the "narthex."

*High Mass – 10 am, with Gregorian chant.*

"Hmph, Gregorian chant," I said with a grin, "Just what we need."

I had never been in the church before, and we walked around like tourists in Saint Peter's. The nave was a pleasant surprise. I had imagined a pre-Reformation church, a sombre Romanesque remnant of old Catholic Denmark. But of thousands of medieval churches in Denmark, not one was left to the Catholics, who were banned here for centuries.

St. Ansgar's was a 19th Century marvel of new-found religious toleration and assiduous Victorian workmanship: stained glass windows, hand-carved wooden pews, imported Italian marble. The apse was covered with an immense mosaic mural of Jesus, the apostles, and various saints. The side altars featured Romantic paintings: one of Mary holding Jesus, the other of Saint Joseph.

The Cathedral was more stony and formal than its piney Lutheran neighbors, but it still conformed to the general light, spare style of Danish design. I expected windows like Rouault – heavy black leaded eyebrows brooding over deep blue eyes and tawny faces. Instead, the many high stained glass windows were filled with airy, almost clear colors, allowing what arctic sunbeams there were to enter the nave largely unfiltered and unfettered.

Next we visited the adjoining Museum, passing by glass cases filled with various religious artifacts – an ivory crucifix from Emperor Ferdinand, a gem-encrusted silver chalice from the time of Saint Knud, and the golden bishop's crosier of Ansgar himself.

As we emerged from the Museum, Richard noticed a small box hanging on the wall with the sign *rosenkrans* on it.

"What's that, Skat?" he asked, pointing.

"Those are Rosary beads – I guess they're for sale," I responded.

"*Rosenkrans* means Rosary?"

"Yes – why is that so strange?"

"Hunh. You know the movie I saw with Søren the other night? It was about a guy named Rosenkrantz – I didn't know the name meant Rosary."

He bought a set and handed them to me. "I already have the beads my mother gave me," he said. "Here, why don't you take these – they're made of rosewood."

I said, "I don't know, Richard," but put them in my purse.

As we walked down the hallway, we noticed a table displaying several books with names like *Saint Michael, God's Warrior Angel* and *My Name is Michael*, evidently in honor of today's angelic feast day.

Richard picked up one of the books and started paging through it. After a minute or so, he said, "Would you mind if I took a look at the library for a while?"

"Not at all," I said. "I'll see if I can find the toilet."

It had been a long walk.

Richard popped into the Reading Room, and I walked farther down the stone corridor in search of the facilities. I passed by a doorway that was emitting warmth, the tinkling of glasses and a great buzz of conversation. The room was filled with people; it seemed like a reception of some kind.

I succeeded in my quest for the ladies' room, and was on my way back to the library when I was arrested by an incredible stained glass window. Beautifully backlit in the morning sunshine, the window shone gold and azure, illuminating two figures, one a young woman, the other an angel.

"The Annunciation," I heard from behind me.

"Excuse me?" I said, turning to see a tall, ruggedly-handsome man with slick, dark hair and twinkling eyes.

"Forgive me for intruding," he said in heavily Slavic-accented English. "I was just saying the name of the scene: the Annunciation is when the Archangel Gabriel gives Mary the news of her coming baby," and he smiled and tilted his head as if to say, *Of course, you already knew that.*

"Oh, no I didn't know the name in English," I said, smiling back. I didn't know the name in Danish either, but somehow I did not wish to admit that at the moment. "It's a very beautiful piece. But Mary seems so placid. Don't you think she would be afraid at the sudden appearance of a fully-grown angel?"

"No, somehow I don't think so. Although I have seen icons of this scene in Poland where Mary is obviously troubled."

"Are you Polish then?"

"Yes, Michal Glemp, at your service." He brought his heels together like a cavalryman and bowed slightly at the waist.

"Katrina Nielsen, pleased to meet you," I replied, offering my hand. The gentleman took it, and for a moment I thought he was going to kiss the hand, but he refrained, content to hold it at shoulder-level for several seconds while gazing into my eyes.

"Tell me... Katrina Nielsen," he said, releasing my hand and turning to the angel in the glass once more, "do you believe in angels?"

"I don't know. I've never seen one myself, and I've always been somewhat skeptical of those who say they have," I replied.

"I was too," he said, looking at me again with a slight grin.

"Then what happened?"

"You must understand I grew up in Gdansk in the industrial depths of Communist Poland. The State did everything it could to undermine religion, to make it seem old-fashioned, unscientific, not worthy of consideration. So I grew up an atheist – everyone I knew was atheist in the '70s. Only a few tattered elderly people clung to the old ways. Then when I was 17, I had an experience..."

Just then, a stocky man with reddish hair came up to Michal from behind and spoke some words in Polish into his ear.

*What a coincidence that I've met this man, just after Richard's experiences of last night. Or are there any coincidences?*

Without turning, Michal nodded, and said, *"Oah,* excuse me, please, I must speak with the Bishop before Mass begins."

"The Bishop?" I asked.

"Yes. Forgive me, it was very nice to meet you."

I remembered that the sign said *domkirke,* cathedral, so of course there would be a bishop, especially for High Mass.

"I'm sorry not to hear your story," I said.

"Oh, but you will, my dear. You will."

Then Michal turned on his heel and marched off toward the sacristy.

I glanced at my watch – 9:55, just five minutes before services were to begin – and walked hurriedly to the Reading Room where I found Richard in the stacks, immersed in a thick tome. I glimpsed some Latin – *Exorcismus Rituale Romanum.*

"What's *that?*" I asked.

"Oh, nothing. Just a book I picked up," he said, cramming it back in the crowded shelf.

We rushed over to the church, and settled into a pew toward the back of the church just as the first sounds of chanted "introit" were washing over the nave. Closing my eyes, I listened to the meandering Gregorian music, and felt myself going up and down long, gently sloping passageways. The effect was hypnotic, and Richard several times had to nudge me into standing or tug on me to sit down.

Before I knew it, the Bishop – the stocky reddish-haired man – was preaching from a lofty pulpit, dressed like something out of a Renaissance painting in his burgundy vestments and skullcap.

"As you all know," he said in Polish-accented English, "today is the Feast of Saint Michael and All Angels. And as many of you know, my family came to Denmark from the country of Poland, across the waters of the salty Baltic. After my installation as Bishop here in Copenhagen last year, I had the opportunity to return to the land of my genesis, where I had the honor of visiting the birthplace of Karol Wojtyla, the man we now call Pope John Paul II, and I concelebrated Mass in the Wawel Cathedral in Krakow where our Holy Father served for many years as Cardinal. At that Mass, one year ago today, I met a man whose faith impressed me greatly, and whose story I felt should be told. Michal Glemp..."

"Oh my God, Richard, that's the man I was talking to in the hallway!" I whispered.

"Shhh!" we heard from the elderly women sitting behind us.

"...instead of getting a lengthy homily from me, I would like you to listen to Michal's story, and then I will say just a few words afterwards. It's a story that won't soon be *glemt*," he concluded with a chuckle, making a rather lame pun on Glemp's name which sounds like "forgotten" in Danish.

Michal stood up and walked to the front of the center aisle. He held no microphone, yet we had no trouble hearing him, even in the back of the church. Completely relaxed, he began to tell his tale.

"Thank you. His Excellency mentioned the waters of the salty Baltic. It is to these waters and to the year 1973 that I would like to take you this morning. I was swimming at the beach in Brzezno, not far from my home in Gdansk, a blue-collar town of shipbuilding which became famous some years later as the birthplace of Solidarity.

"I was together with my best friend, Tomasz, but we had gotten separated at lunch, and I went swimming on my own. It was a sunny day, but also very windy, and although I was a strong swimmer, that day I swam out too far. I tried to fight the current, but the waves kept knocking me back out to sea. The more I struggled on my own, the farther I was getting from my goal.

"I looked around. No one was near me. No boats or swimmers, no floats. I was suddenly all alone. Yet on the beach, it was a crowded Saturday, and I could still see the reds and yellows of the umbrellas."

As he spoke, he stretched out his arm, as if he were seeing the umbrellas at that moment. I could almost see them myself.

"Surely I was not going to die within sight of the beach!" he said to the hushed congregation. All the children were quiet, not a cough or sneeze was heard. It felt as if all breathing stopped.

"But I was freezing and my legs were getting numb. I began to take in seawater; I choked; I couldn't breathe. My vision was fading, and I knew in my heart that I was about to drown. A wave took me under and I remember thinking that I was too young to die – I was only seventeen. I did not want to leave my family.

"I had never been religious. It was the Communist times, and like all my friends, I was an atheist. But I knew my name, Michal, was the name of an angel. So there in the water, I prayed, 'Please God send me Your angel. Please, dear God, save me. I don't want to die.'"

His features melted as he spoke these lines, and his eyes filled with large droplets that remained welled up.

"I will never forget the hand that reached into the water and grabbed my arm. With one forceful pull, I was up and out of the water. I had the sensation of being carried to shore, and set down on the coarse sand. I wiped the water from my eyes" – as he said this, he stopped and actually wiped the real tears from his eyes – "and I saw my friend Tomasz running up to me with fear in his face.

"He asked me if I was alright – he had seen me from a distance and came running. He told me I was too far out and asked me how I'd gotten back into shore. I told him a powerful lifeguard had carried me to shore. I looked around and said that I wanted to thank him.

"But Tomasz just shook his head and said, 'What lifeguard? I didn't see anyone.'

"It was then I remembered then that there *were* no lifeguards on the beach in Brzezno. I realized an Angel of God had saved my life.

"But why?" he asked, and took a dramatic pause.

A chair scraped and someone coughed. A baby started fussing and was whisked out of the nave by an embarrassed mother.

"Six years later, when I met the leaders of Solidarity for the first time, I encountered the *Why* in my life. It was God's will that I should play a very small role in bringing down the evil Communist system, to replace the cold State with the warmth of Jesus Christ. And thanks be to God, this struggle was successful.

"Praise be to God," he concluded and nodded to the congregation.

Several people said *Amen,* and then everyone clapped wildly. A few, including my suddenly emotional husband, were in tears. Then the Bishop got up again, pumped Michal's hand and climbed up the spiral staircase once more.

"As usual, Michal is far too modest. An early associate of Father Jerzy Popieluszko, who became a martyr to the cause, and later personal secretary to Lech Walesa himself, Michal Glemp was a pivotal figure in Solidarity, the movement that ultimately brought down the Curtain of Iron that had surrounded his suffering nation for two generations.

"Thank you, Michal, for an inspiring story. We all struggle at times in the stormy seas of life. It is worth remembering that left to our own power, we will drown, but that God's power can save us. Thank you for coming all this way to our little outpost at the north of Europe to remind us of this lesson."

Then he told a remarkable story of his own:

"As the last century neared its end, Pope Leo the Thirteenth, while in conference with his cardinals, fell to the floor. The cardinals immediately called for a doctor. No pulse was detected, and the Holy Father was feared dead.

"Just as suddenly, his Holiness awoke and said, 'What a horrible picture I was permitted to see!' In his vision, God gave Satan one century to do his worst work against the Church. The devil chose the 20th Century. So moved was the Holy Father that he composed the prayer to St. Michael the Archangel, which you'll find as an insert in your missalette today.

"Now that we approach the end of this century of trials, our Holy Father John Paul II has once again urged the faithful to offer this prayer. So please let's say together, *St. Michael the Archangel…*"

And the entire congregation joined him saying,

*Defend us in battle!*

*Be our protection against the wickedness and snares of the devil.*

*May God rebuke him, we humbly pray, and do thou,*

*O Prince of the heavenly host, by the power of God, thrust into Hell*

*Satan and all the other evil spirits who roam about the world seeking the ruin of souls.*

*Amen.*

The Bishop then returned to the altar and made ready for Communion. I hesitated about receiving – this wasn't my church after all – but Richard encouraged me, and I went up. It was pretty much the same as in the Danish Church. After all the fasting, I felt strengthened by the bread, wafer-thin as it was.

After Mass, we remained in the nave and Richard went over to the Mary side-altar to say a prayer. As we left the church, I looked down the corridor for Michal, but everyone had disappeared.

We started the long trek home. As we strolled along, Richard said, "I loved that. And I couldn't get over that Polish guy. What a great story!"

"I was trying to tell you, that was the gentleman I met in the hallway," I replied.

"When I was in the Reading Room, you mean?"

"Yes. I had no idea he was the guest speaker. The Bishop held a reception for him before the service."

"The Bishop's Polish, I guess?"

"A Polish-Dane. About 100 years ago, many Poles came to Denmark to help with farming sugar beets. Some stayed. I suppose the Bishop must be from one of those families."

"I see. You know what else I loved?" Richard asked.

"What?" I asked back.

"The bells at consecration. I used to get to ring the bells when the priest raised up the host. Somehow I felt like it all depended on me, the bread turning into the body of Christ depended on me ringing them in just the right way, at just the right time.

"I imagined all the Masses, all over the world on a Sunday morning, and bells going off all at the same time, making a joyful noise so loud that it could be heard in Heaven. And God would be pleased, because we remembered."

"Remembered what?"

"Jesus. *Do this in memory of me.*"

"Oh, right," I said.

We continued walking northward in the bright sunshine. There was a light breeze off the Sound, and seagulls darted to and fro, playing tag with small children who cast breadcrumbs upon the waters.

As we passed Kastellet, I pointed and said, "There's the Little Mermaid."

"And there's a café. What do you say we have a bite to eat? I'm starving," Richard said.

"Do you think we should? After all, we're supposed to be fasting."

"I didn't say you had to order the Lumberjack Special. But I've got to eat or I'm not going to make it till tonight."

"Okay. Just a little something."

We got a table by the dock, and I ordered sparkling water with lime, followed by *smørrebrød*, an open sandwich with shrimp and dill sauce. Richard ordered a large orange juice, ham and cheese omelet, toast, and a cappuccino.

"Isn't that a bit much?" I chided him.

"I'm hungry," he whined, and then said, "Okay, I'll skip dessert."

And we laughed. Richard never was one for fasting.

After the food arrived, I asked, "So what were you reading while I was mingling with Polish politicians?"

"I came across some unusual material."

"About exorcism?"

Richard put his fork down with a clatter and said, "How did you know?"

"I saw the cover – *exorcismus* isn't hard to figure out," I told him.

"Well, I wasn't looking for stuff on exorcism," he said, his voice lowered. "I was reading about angels. But then I came across the topic of fallen angels, and I found a reference to the Roman Rite. So I thought I should read about it."

"Surely you don't think I'm – possessed?" I asked, with an outward smirk but inward worry.

*Can ghosts possess people?*

"No, in fact you're definitely not possessed," Richard said.

"How can you tell?"

"Because you can pray, be blessed with Holy Water. You even received the Eucharist with no ill effect. In the accounts I read today, people who were possessed would scream at the touch of holy water. Receiving communion would be completely intolerable for a demon."

"What if it's not a demon?" I asked.

"What else would it be?"

"Well – theoretically – what if it were the spirit of Damsgaard?" I asked and the question hung in the air. I wasn't sure if he would laugh.

"I don't know," he said, taking the question seriously. "But ghosts seem to haunt places, they don't possess people."

"Didn't Rowena say that ghosts sometime get inside people?"

"She did say that, but listen, the exorcist in the book said that he had never encountered a case where the victim was completely innocent. All of them had fooled around with something – black magic, witchcraft, Satanism. Since we've never done anything like that, there should be no danger at all."

I didn't say anything, just pasted on a smile and nodded. But this remark worried me, and later on, in the afternoon, we were sitting in the front room – I was trying to do a crossword puzzle, and Richard was reading the Bible – and I said, "Richard?"

"Yes, Skat?"

"There's been something I've been meaning to tell you. About Damsgaard."

"What is it?"

"I was in the front bedroom one day, I think it was right after your mother left, and I was taking the sheets off the bed. I was folding the sheets when I was overcome with the loveliest aroma of wildflowers in the room. It was a hot afternoon and the window was open. I couldn't resist the temptation to lie down."

"Yeah," he said, with a leading tone in his voice.

"I lay down and removed my clothing. The sunlight felt so good on my skin."

"OK," he said, not seeming to understand where I was going with this.

"Well, you can imagine what I started to do… No one can see in that window…"

"Gee, Skat, this isn't confession – I mean, I guess everybody masturbates once in a while," he said, looking away. "Why are you telling me this?"

"Richard, I started to fantasize. I imagined *him,* coming to me…"

I was hoping he wouldn't make me say it. We made eye contact as the seconds ticked slowly.

"You fantasized about *Karl Damsgaard?*" he asked point blank, his eyebrows shooting upwards.

"Yes," I admitted, glad to have it off my chest.

"Oh my God," he said. The blood drained from his face, and he quoted, "Their sin is delightful."

"What?" I asked.

"Don't you get it? Damsgaard said 'Their sin is delightful' and everything is revolving around vices – smoking, drinking… the fancy meals, that could be gluttony… and sex."

"Sex isn't sinful."

"It is if you're not married!"

I blushed when I thought of my encounters with Søren – but surely they were innocent. *Or were they?* After all, I couldn't always remember everything – I suffered from blackouts, from 'lost time.' And the times I had been with Damsgaard – oh God, this isn't real, this can't be happening!

"I tried to stop, but I couldn't," I said. "Damsgaard just kept coming back to my mind. I kept on doing it and doing it, and finally I came, I came hard and then, I smelled it."

"Smelled what?"

"The odor of cigarette smoke in the room."

"Oh my God, I can't believe this – and you never told me?"

"Would you have wanted me to?"

"No, I guess not," he replied. "But it sure blows my belief in our 'complete innocence.' You invited trouble in, Katrina. You allowed him into the… the *temple* of your body itself."

Then he looked away and said, "You realize we'll have to tell Rowena. Maybe we'll be needing that exorcist after all."

# 37. Richard

A ravishing creature entered our home on Sunday evening. When I opened the door, I saw her as if for the first time, a *femme fatale* wrapped in a mantle of black velvet, her raven hair braided with dwarf diamonds twinkling like the night sky behind her. She was well-prepared for the occasion: made up, coiffed, and dressed to the teeth.

"Good evening, Rowena," I said, helping her off with her cloak. Her arms were festooned with billowed cloth like pirate sails; her curvaceous body covered by a tight-fitting "second skin" of emerald green, tufted in hexagons with tips of yellow ochre. Her long throat was accentuated by a golden breastplate studded with blood-red garnets.

*The psychic business must pay well,* I concluded from her regalia. But as she slinked into the room, I noticed how her necklace clanked like armor plating and thought, *Hmm, maybe it's just brass after all.*

"You look stunning, Rowena," Katrina observed.

"Thank you," she replied. "But I should have worn a warmer outfit – I'm freezing!"

"Gee, I didn't notice the cold," I said.

"I've always been very sensitive to temperature changes," Rowena admitted.

"Come in and we'll make some tea then," Katrina said.

As I followed the women to the kitchen, I couldn't help but notice the contrast between them – where Katrina was lithe and firm, Rowena was powerfully-built, ample and supple. Following her hind quarters, I marveled at the enormous tail that meandered back and forth as she sashayed on her high heels with serpentine smoothness.

I put the water on, set out some macaroons, and we sat down together at the kitchen table. Katrina told about last night's ghostly visits. I didn't tell Rowena about the angels; somehow I felt they were none of her business.

I poured out the chamomile. Rowena devoured the chewy cookies greedily and I had to get more. Bits of sticky insides clung to her teeth and she smacked her lips. Wrapping her fingers around the mug, her long red-enameled fingernails bit claw-like into her own flesh. She must've still been cold. I crossed to the counter and shut the window, and stood leaning against the counter with my own tea.

Katrina described the experience she'd had with Damsgaard in the front bedroom. It was embarrassing for both of us, but Rowena took it in as if she'd been expecting it the whole time. Once the story was told, including a vivid description of my wife's orgasm with her ghostly lover, Rowena's face stiffened as if she was preparing for battle, and she exhaled audibly. "So that's how it happened."

"That's how what happened?" I asked.

"Such a union contaminates the soul itself," she explained. "Katrina, the entity that came to you as Damsgaard has become *commingled* with your soul."

"You mean it *wasn't* Damsgaard?" Katrina asked.

"We don't know for sure," Rowena replied quietly, and she seemed to hesitate over what she had to say next. She bit her lower lip, leaving red marks on her upper teeth; she opened her mouth slightly and stuck her tongue between her front teeth and upper lip a couple of times, and rubbed it along her upper incisors, further smearing the redness.

Finally, she looked into Katrina's eyes and said, "I think we can agree on the origin of the..."

She seemed to want Katrina to say something, but nothing came.

"Of the *what?*" I asked.

"The voices?" Katrina said, nodding.

"You're hearing voices, Katrina?" I asked. She had never told me that.

She nodded.

"Opening yourself up to a spirit of unknown origin was most unwise," Rowena said. "Katrina, a dark spirit has *penetrated* you, penetrated your very mind. Now it appears this entity is dwelling much of the time inside of you, influencing you, telling you what to do."

"What will happen to me?" Katrina asked.

"If we do nothing, the entity will take over by degrees and finally seize complete control. At that point, there is nothing anyone can do. You will be lost to us."

"And the dreams," Katrina said. "The visions I see – the knives, the blood, the hangman's noose –"

"Will become reality for you and those around you – unless we stop it in time," Rowena said.

"You mean there's some kind of time limit?" I asked.

"Katrina, when is your next birthday?" Rowena asked her.

"December 30th," she said.

Rowena nodded.

"Ah, then we have time – till the end of the year," she said, and began rummaging in her alligator-skin bag.

I couldn't believe what I was hearing, the downward path this had taken. When Katrina first mentioned a psychic, I thought it might be interesting – like the Sanskrit incantations we intoned during the feng shui period. Maybe we'd play with a Ouija board, hold a séance like in the movies. But I was in the wrong theatre: instead of an Abbott-and-Costello comedy, I had stumbled into *The Exorcist*.

"What can we do?" I asked Rowena.

"The Good Father has advised me to take the safest possible course in this case," she replied.

"What do you mean?" I asked.

"Such a dark spirit must be trapped, contained so it cannot enter another person ever again," Rowena explained.

"What will *happen* to the spirit?" Katrina asked, with a bit too much sympathy for my taste.

"It will be isolated from Mankind until the end of the world," Rowena said, as nonchalantly as if she were talking about burying trash in a landfill.

"I see," Katrina said, and looked down.

"Richard," Rowena asked, "what is the holiest vessel ever constructed?"

"The holiest vessel – I don't know, Noah's Ark?"

"Well, it was built for a kind of ark..."

"You mean the Ark of the Covenant?" I asked.

"Precisely, and where did the Jews keep the Ark of the Covenant?"

"In the Holiest of Holies," I replied, pleased with myself.

"Yes, and before the Temple was built, they built for the Ark a golden tabernacle, yes?"

"Tabernacle – like where the host is kept at church?" I asked.

"This is what we need."

"You want to take a tabernacle from a Catholic Church and bring it here?" Katrina asked.

"Let me explain," Rowena said patiently. "This ritual must be done in a holy place, in a controlled setting. There is a refuge, in the mountains where I have connections; there is a room, specially-built for this kind of work, dangerous work that cannot be done here in the city."

I was stunned. Silent.

Finally, I asked, "What kind of place is this, a monastery?"

"It is a place of natural power," she explained. "A place where one finds crystals, amber, cobalt…"

"Is there a church there?" I asked, thinking it was where the priest was located.

"No," she said, her head down in her skin-bag again. "We could not risk defiling a sanctuary. Let me show you – here is a photograph of the setting." She handed me a brochure.

I took the glossy trifold showing picturesque German mountains just west of a town called Lutherstadt. The brochure was a little cheesy – smiling peasants in their native costumes – and unsettling, like we were looking at time-shares in *Transylvania*.

The absence of a priest was still bothering me, so I asked, "Will the Good Father be there to perform the ritual?"

"No, Richard," she said. "*You* are the priest, you will perform the necessary rites. I will be there, and there will be two helpers – burly men, I can tell you – with whom I work in such dangerous situations."

I bit my lip. I knew she did not welcome this line of questioning, but I couldn't help myself – I guess it was my tenacious Jesuit training. "Can't the Good Father come here tonight?"

"Definitely not – we can't risk that," she said.

"Well, can I talk with him on the telephone, then?"

At this, Rowena hesitated. "Well. Perhaps by telephone…"

"Could you at least ask him?"

"All right, let's get set up for tonight's session and then I'll call him." She spoke calmly, but there was fire in her eyes – she did not like being challenged.

"Katrina, do you have the crystal?" she said.

"Yes, it's on the dining room table," Katrina replied.

"Get the crystal and we shall gather in the front room. Richard, raise the volume of the music now," she ordered.

I raised the volume on the endless Gregorian chant – we had played it now for three days and nights, to the point where I barely noticed it anymore – and sat down with the women in the living room.

From the bottomless hoard in her bag, Rowena produced a wand of incense, which she lit and blew into a red glow. She put Katrina on the couch with the crystal perched on her solar plexus, and then began to pass the fragrant punk over her. Unknown words passed from her lips, growled and rumbled hotly under her breath. I recalled the strange language on the little pad in the shop. After a few minutes, Katrina became completely stiff and rigid, and Rowena handed the punk to me, motioning for me to step away from the couch.

Rowena stood close to me in the entry, in front of the grandfather clock, and said, "I am going to leave you alone now while I contact the Good Father. You will continue using the incense in the same way I did – just say the Hail Mary or Our Father while passing the incense all the way up and down the body, from head to toe. Can you do that, Richard?"

"Yes, of course."

Rowena took a step closer – she was uncomfortably close to me now, looking directly into my eyes. She grabbed hold of my wrist and twisted. I felt her nails in my flesh, but said nothing as she held my gaze. Her throat extended toward me; there couldn't have been more than six inches between our faces. I felt her hot breath.

"Katrina may get restless or unruly," she said. "I expect she will be sick to her stomach. If she needs to throw up, get a bucket for her, but she must keep the crystal by her heart and you must keep praying over her, all the time burning the incense. Can you do that, Richard?"

Rowena's snout was so close now that I winced at the acrid halitosis emanating from her mouth, so cavernous at this distance that I could see the meat stuck between her teeth. Yet somehow I managed to reply with heroic civility, "Yes, of course." And out the front door she flew.

As if in a trance, I dutifully wanded my wife's near-comatose body, up and down, and said a decade of Hail Marys. Katrina was quiet; my thoughts were unruly.

*Driving out unclean spirits – this was something Jesus did, and he granted the apostles this ability. It's Biblical. But the priest – why wouldn't the priest want to talk with us?*

From the volume I'd read in the church library, I knew that the Rite of Exorcism – for what was the driving out of an evil spirit but an exorcism? – had to be performed in a Roman Catholic Church. By a Roman Catholic priest.

I was filled with anxiety, perplexed in the extreme. I was *waaay* out on a limb here, and I needed help. But the environment of the past week created a mistrust of outsiders, of anyone who had not been through the rituals with us.

"Katrina?" I said.

"What?" she said from far away, as if she was drugged.

"I want to call someone in, someone to help us."

As I said the words out loud, they gave me confidence.

"Who can help us? Our friends wouldn't understand!" she said. "Oh my God, I think I'm going to be sick."

"Don't move! I'll get a bucket," I said, running into the kitchen.

Who could we turn to? Who could help us? Edvard would help us – but he was an atheist, he wouldn't understand this at all, and anyway he was off in Norway someplace, another plane... Søren would help us, and he was right next door – but he looked down on anything Catholic.

When I got back to the living room, I gave Katrina the bucket and she retched a few times, but little came up – she hadn't eaten much of anything the past few days. Just then I looked up through the stained glass window on the west side of the building and saw George's flags: the English standard, crimson cross on a white field, was flapping happily, just below its inverted Danish cousin.

"I want to call George," I said.

"But we barely know him, he'll think we're crazy! No, *please* don't call him."

"Listen, George is a man of God. He knows the New Testament, the driving out of unclean spirits. He'll know what to do," I said with a growing sense of confidence. "Just stay here, and keep the crystal on your chest, and keep saying your prayers – can you do that, Katrina?"

"Yes, of course," she replied.

I went to the phone and dialed the number.

"George, is that you?" I said, my voice cracking under the stress.

"Yes, Richard," he said.

"Thank God you're home – can you possibly come over here right away?"

"Of course. I hope nothing's happened."

"Me too," I said.

I saw him cross the front yard and found myself willing him to hobble faster. But he kept the same steady pace. He was in great shape for ninety – but he was still *ninety.* I opened the door before he even rang the bell. I shook his hand and said, "George, thanks for coming." It was how I greeted people at my father's funeral. "I'm sorry to bother you on a Sunday afternoon."

As he took off his jacket and cap, he said, "Nonsense, not a bother at all. I was just preparing for the Feast of Saint Jerome, it's this week, you know."

"Is that right?"

"Yes, I was reading his commentary on *Bel and the Dragon*," he said as he walked into the living room. "It's a deuterocanonical story in the *Book of Daniel.* You see, Jerome was the first to explain how to ascertain whether a given text should be accepted as *authentic—*"

I touched him on the arm. "You're a man of God, aren't you, George?"

He paused for a moment, as if confused by the question, then answered, "Why, yes – yes of course."

"Do you think it's possible for a person to be inhabited by unclean spirits, like it says in the New Testament?"

"No, as a matter of fact, I don't."

"Don't you believe in the Bible then?"

"Yes, of course, I do. But Richard, that model of the world doesn't work for us today." He stopped when he saw Katrina on the couch. "Say, what's this all about? What's the matter with Katrina? Is she ill?"

Just then, she leaned over, convulsed and spit into the blue bucket. I took up the punk and said, "Oh, I'm sorry, George. I'm supposed to keep this incense going until Rowena gets back."

"Why don't you leave that for a moment so we can chat?" he said and led me to the dining room. "How did all this start?"

I quickly told him about the footsteps on the stairs, the sounds, everything. Finally I asked him again about demonic possession – could the ghost really be a fallen angel?

He repeated the bit about the ancient view of spirits not working for modern people, and asked me a simple question. "Tell me, are you paying her anything?"

"Yeah," I said. "Do you think that's important?"

He nodded and said, "Well, where there's money's involved, one has to wonder."

This got me thinking. I was on the defensive now. "Rowena said she was working with a Catholic priest. But whenever I ask to see him, she says he can't come here or he'll be contaminated. The reason she's not here right now is she went to try to convince him to talk with me by telephone."

"Well, I'll be surprised if she can produce an authentic priest of any religion, but if she does, I'll be happy to speak with him on your behalf."

Just then, we heard Katrina retch again, and we went to check on her. She was embarrassed for him to see her like this, looking like an accident victim – emaciated, bluish patches under her eyes, her hair in disarray. Nothing like her usual self.

"What's this on your chest?" he asked.

"It's a crystal," I said.

"May I see it?" he asked, taking it in his hands. "It's heavy, must weigh five pounds or more. What's going on here, Katrina? Why the crystals and incense?"

"The psychic is helping us get rid of the ghosts – you know we've had ghosts in the house for months." She made it sound like it was something shameful, like cockroaches.

"You've talked about some odd happenings in your home, yes," he said. "But I don't think you have a ghost, and I certainly don't believe there is any kind of 'evil spirit' inside you." She looked away. "Tell me dear, how long have you been fasting?"

"Three days."

"No food at all for three days?" he asked, raising an eyebrow and looking at me.

"Well, I've had a little food, but... well, I've been throwing it up again," she said.

"Food and water," he said. "That's what you need. Have you been able to sleep?"

"No. I've slept only in snatches. The ghosts, you see..."

"All right, all right. That's quite enough for now."

We went to get her some water, and she took some crackers. "You can take this away, Richard," he said, handing me the bucket. "I don't think she'll be needing this any more – will you, Katrina?"

"No. I suppose not," she said.

George said later that all she needed was an authority figure to release her from the spell that made her sick to her stomach – she was under some kind of hypnosis.

"Let's all go sit by the dining room table and wait for this person to return, shall we?" he suggested, and asked me to turn off the stereo, which had been chanting in Latin for three days now. I looked at the objects on the table, and felt suddenly ashamed, like Adam and Eve when they realized how naked they were. There was a large votive candle, bags of incense, half-burned wands of sage, angel medallions, a vial of holy water. There were also some papers in a blue folder.

"Are those papers hers?" George asked.

I nodded and showed them to him. "This is a brochure for a place in Germany where she wanted to take us—"

"Lutherstadt," he said. "That's in the Hartz, isn't it? Lovely tourist area. Why the devil was she going to take you there?"

"She said we needed to go through a special ritual to remove the dark spirit, and we have to do it in a special, holy place," I said.

"In the Hartz Mountains?"

Katrina, who had been drowsing, almost asleep on her elbows, suddenly woke with a start saying, "Hartz Mountains – that sounds familiar... A peak..."

"There, there, dear – of course it's familiar. A common tourist destination," he said, patting her hand.

"Yeah, but not a Roman Catholic Church, which is what you need for an exorcism," I said.

"And you don't *need* an exorcism, Richard," George said. "Say, look at this!"

I took up the pages. "It looks like some kind of price list – tabernacles?"

"Yeah, she said we needed the holiest vessel on earth to contain the dark spirit."

"Yes, no doubt – and it seems as if tabernacles are expensive these days – look at these prices: $10,000 – $20,000 – $35,000. My goodness: gold, diamonds, jewel-encrusted…"

Then he gave me a look that said, *So that was the scam.* I closed my eyes. This wasn't happening. The bell rang and I opened my eyes. It was no dream. I went to open the door, and Rowena strode in, eyes on fire, a real dragon lady.

"Who is this?" she demanded.

"This is our next-door neighbor, George," I said. "George, this is Rowena."

"I've been learning about what you've been doing to these nice people," he said.

"I really don't think we should be bringing in outsiders at this point in the process," Rowena said.

"Rowena, listen, George is just here to help," I said.

She closed her eyes. "I feel Unbelief in the room!" she said. "I cannot continue in the face of skepticism."

"Of course you can't, you monstrous woman," George said. "That's exactly why I'm not leaving."

"I really think you should go," she said hotly, her eyes staring at George as if they meant to burn holes through him.

"Not until you explain yourself – what manner of lies and blasphemy have you been telling these people?" George asked.

"These people called me to help them with a problem in their home," she said. "I have been in touch with certain entities that are dwelling within the house…"

"So your only mission here is to help them?"

"Of course – I want them to find peace," she said.

"And what's all this about evil spirits and exorcism and tabernacles?"

"I am under the direction of a priest, a Catholic priest—" she started to say.

"Were you able to reach the Good Father?" I asked, still hoping.

"He cannot come," she said, turning to me. "It's too dangerous."

I couldn't look at her after that.

"I am a priest, a *real* priest," George said. "Who are you really working with? Give me his name!"

"You're a priest?" she asked, taking a step back.

"Yes, George is an Anglican priest," I said.

"Why don't you come clean," George said. "This priest's tale is just a smoke-screen. Admit it, there is no priest!"

"I cannot say the name of my Guide, but I assure you I have one, someone more powerful than you!" she spewed. "Richard needs to find the power within himself, the priest within him. He needs to stop relying on authority figures, old men in robes…"

"That's enough, Rowena," I said, still avoiding her eyes. "You kept telling me how I had to be the one to evict the evil spirit from the house – well, I'm finally doing it. It's time for you to leave, Rowena."

She turned on me, snarling like a sick dog. "Mark my words," she said. "You can evict me, but that which is lodged within your wife shall not leave as easily. The stories you two have told me – the bath, the books, the fall – this is not just footsteps!"

"You know what I think, you beastly woman?" George said, stepping be-tween us. "I think that there are no ghosts or demons here, but that *you* have conjured them! You should be ashamed of yourself!"

Receiving this like a blow, Rowena cried out. Her shoulders slumped, as if her fire were finally put out. Her head fell forward and she seemed to physically deflate, like a papier mache dragon in the dumpsters on Canal Street, the day after Chinese New Year's.

The room fell silent.

Then from nowhere, the con artist came to life, carrying out a salvage opera-tion. She snatched up the rare geode. "Well, I've never been one to stay where I'm not wanted. I'll just collect up my things and go."

"What are these things anyway?" George asked, in hot pursuit. "Religious medals, incense, votive candles, magic crystals – you've really put on a show here, haven't you?"

"The tools of my trade," she said, not looking up.

"These are the tools of a conjurer and a cozener – take your rubbish and be off before I ring the police!"

In a matter of seconds, she got her gear together and beat a retreat to the front door. Her parting shot was: "Richard, you have my number. Call me when you come to your senses!"

"*Honi soit qui mal y pense!*" George pronounced.

Unlike me, she must have understood the French, because her mouth opened wide. She yelped a little, and limped off.

"Back into the twilight world from whence you've come," he said.

"Gee, what did you say to her?"

"There's a long story behind it, but essentially it means *evil is as evil thinks*."

"Richard!"

Oh, my God, it was Katrina, we'd nearly forgotten her in all the struggle. "Are you all right, Skat?"

"Why don't you come over to our place," George said. "Una's made some lovely roast beef tonight, and I know there's extra."

But Katrina just said, "No, thank you, George. I'd just like to go home, please."

## *LE GIBET*

*What's that up there, still stirring on the gallows? – Faust*

Ah! Those sounds I hear, would it be the north wind that moans in the night, or the hanged man who breathes a sigh atop the gallowstree?

...Or would it be some spider that weaves from a half-measure of muslin a cravat for his strangled neck?

No: it's a bell slowly tolling from the walls of some distant city beneath the horizon; and a hanged man's corpse, swinging back and forth, reddened by rays of the setting sun.

- Aloysius Bertrand
*Gaspard de la Nuit*

# FIRST FROST
# 38. Edvard

Incommunicado for weeks at a time, more than a thousand kilometers north of the Arctic Circle, I carried a .308 caliber Winchester rifle throughout September, due to the risk of polar bears. The ice mountains of Spitzbergen, glittering incessantly in the midnight sun, were like something out of *The Snow Queen*, but the grisly task at hand was no fairy tale.

Vnukovo Airlines Flight 2801 was en route from Moscow to Svalbard Airport on the 29th of August, carrying 141 passengers and crew, mostly Russian coal-miners and their families. Despite initial news reports, the cause of the crash was not bad weather, inexperienced crew or equipment failure. The greying Siberian pilot had earned his wings over tundra; the morning skies were cold and clear, the machine a reliable workhorse. It was a series of tragic – if it weren't disrespectful, I would say tragicomical – misunderstandings, mistranslations and human error that put the plane on course to land at a phantom runway, some 3.7 kilometers off to the right.

Following a mistaken vector, the jet got caught up in turbulent airspace amidst the bowls of a windswept wall of frozen rock. At 10:22 local time, the Ground Proximity Warning System turned on with nine seconds to impact, too late for the sluggish Tupolev to climb out. Staring straight at annihilation, the captain screamed "Horizon!" and the aeroplane plowed into the forbidding face of Operafjell, one thousand meters above sea level and fourteen kilometers from the landing strip.

All souls were lost.

The next day, I got a call from an old friend in Oslo asking if I could lead the team that would counsel airport staff and rescue workers. The greatest disaster in the history of Norwegian aviation, personnel here had ever seen anything like it. Few have. There was an endless parade of mangled corpses, many of them women and children. Emergency workers, used to saving lives, felt helpless, useless as they trudged through the lifeless dunes of snow with neither urgency nor ceremony. It took over a week just to recover the bodies. Giant Russian military cargo planes, some of them still marked with the hammer and sickle, had to be flown in to repatriate the remains and remove pieces of the aircraft for analysis.

Mobile telephones don't work up here, but somehow Richard Marchese managed to find me at the Spitzbergen Hotel in Longyearbyen – I suppose there aren't many others to choose from. On the last day of September, just a few hours before I was planning to leave, I received a message at the front desk, handwritten by the clerk in pen and ink on a pink *While You Were Out* slip:

*Need your advice urgently.*
*Please call right away.*
*Richard.*

On the way back to my room, I considered postponing my response: after all, it was very expensive to call home from the high arctic. But this wasn't a social call – something had to be very wrong for Richard to leave a message like that. I dialed the scrawled Danish digits. It wasn't the home number. I reached an older woman whose voice I didn't recognize and was about to hang up when she agreed to put Richard on the line.

"Richard!" I said, my voice raised unnecessarily.

"Eddé? How is it up there?"

"I'm freezing my butt off – I wish I were in tropical Denmark!"

"Nah, you'd be surprised," he said, lowering his voice. "We've already had our first frost here."

"That's early," I remarked.

"Yeah, it is. Tell me, Eddé, how're you holding up? Must be tough."

"It's grim, Richard – but it's the kind of thing I've seen before," I said, trying to put a good face on it.

"Eddé, listen, I know you're busy, I hate to bother you up there, but something's happened, and we really need your advice. Your professional advice."

"I'm listening," I said as neutrally as I could.

The conversation that followed was long (and costly). Richard explained that they'd called in a psychic to help get rid of the "ghost." A fraud, of course, the woman had duped them out of some money – *Why do the authorities allow these criminals to operate?* – but what worried me were the cult-like tactics she had used. It was the kind of thing we used to call "brainwashing" – isolation, withholding of sleep and food, neuro-linguistic programming, post-hypnotic suggestion. Even sensory deprivation in a darkened crawl space.

"What a witch!" I said after I heard the full story.

"I could tell you more," he said, "but I think the most important thing is for you to talk to Katrina. Even though she is exhausted; she could barely sleep last night. She keeps thinking that Rowena can see where we are, can infiltrate her thoughts. She's a wreck. I don't know what to do."

"Hmm, it sounds like a post-traumatic stress reaction," I said. "Is she there now? Put her on."

"Hi, Edvard?" said a timid voice that I wouldn't have recognized.

"Katrina, how are you doing?"

"Not so good."

"Tell me all about it."

"Well, you heard about the psychic, right?"

"Yes. Richard tells me you may have been drugged, possibly amphetamines – you say you were awake for three or four days in a row?"

"Yes. And we both, uh, *saw* things."

"You saw a ghost?"

"Yes, and we both *felt* the ghosts in our bodies, it was like a buzzing, electrical feeling. And when I looked down at my legs in the bath, I saw hairy, muscular legs, like a man's."

"You were hallucinating, Katrina," I said, trying to reassure her. "That could be from some chemical agent that this woman gave you or it could be due to sleep deprivation and dehydration."

"The buzzing didn't stop, though," she said. "We felt it again last night. Every time I would drift off, it would start again and wake me. And when I close my eyes, I can see…"

"I didn't catch that, what can you see?"

"Her eyes, huge eyes so filled with hatred and anger – oh, Edvard, it's awful! It's like she's watching me. I hesitate even to tell you this on the phone. I have to watch what I say, what I'm thinking even. She was furious when she left, like a woman betrayed. Maybe she'll try to take revenge…"

"I understand. It's natural to be concerned." Katrina was not only frightened, she was paranoid. "Do you believe she knows where you are at this moment?"

She thought a moment and answered, "No. Sitting here in broad daylight talking with you, no, it seems silly. Of course she can't see me. But in the night, in the dark, I'll see her eyes glowing amber-brown, almost yellow eyes, like an animal. I'll believe she can see me, that she can read my thoughts and—"

"Hold on there, Katrina. Just take a minute. You may be experiencing something like post-traumatic stress disorder, PTSD. It's often associated with soldiers, but I see it quite often in relief workers and accident victims. Think of it as a psychological echo."

Silence on the line. I could hear soft sobbing in the background.

"Katrina?" I asked. "Are you there?"

"Yes."

"Are you okay?"

"Uh-huh."

"Listen, I recommend something called 'Luminal' for you. It will help you get some sleep, which is probably what you need most right now."

"Is it like Ambien? Because that doesn't work at all for me. It seems to have the opposite effect, it keeps me awake!"

"Really?"

"It worked at first, the very first bottle. But then after that, I got immune to it or something."

"That's very unusual. I've never heard of that before with Ambien. Anyway, Luminal is a barbiturate. Nothing at all like Ambien. I'll give you enough for a week or so, and then we'll reevaluate. How does that sound?"

"That sounds great, Edvard. Thank you so much."

"Have you been eating alright?"

There was a pause.

"I say, ARE YOU EATING WELL?"

"Yes. Yes I am. Mor has seen to that," she said chuckling.

It was good to hear her laugh, and it broke the tension a bit.

"It's great to hear you laugh. Listen, everything is going to be fine," I reassured her.

Then I decided to take a small risk and challenge her delusion: "Tell me, Katrina, do you still believe there has been a ghost?"

"I don't know what to call it, but yes, something was going on. Too many unexplainable things happened, Edvard."

"Remember you were in the hands of an untrustworthy person – there is nothing you've seen or heard the past few weeks that you can trust. Nothing!"

"We got those threatening phone calls…"

"They were placed by the psychic – of course they were!"

"But we hadn't even met her yet."

I didn't expect that. But I pressed on.

"Think, Katrina, was there any way this woman could have gotten your phone number?" I asked.

"Well, now that you mention it, I had left our number on their answering machine."

"There, you see? Instead of calling you back right away, she started manipulating you, softening you up."

"Oh my God, you're right!"

"Of course. Surely you didn't think a ghost was leaving you voice mails!"

"No… of course not. But what about you? You saw something yourself, in the window that night."

"Oh, yes, I've been meaning to tell you about that. I think I know how that happened," I said brightly.

"You do?"

"Yes, well, I can't be certain of course – we would have to test it – but, I think it was what they call a Window/Mirror Effect."

"A what?"

"What is a mirror? A surface that makes objects on this side of the glass appear as if they are on the opposite side. You look at yourself in the mirror and you appear to be standing on the other side."

"Yes, but a window is not a mirror – you see through a window to real things on the other side."

"Usually. But any piece of glass can *become* a mirror with the right lighting. Imagine a flat pane of glass. If you put a candle on the near side and a glass of water on the far side, and look in the glass, the candle will appear to be burning under water. The pane of glass functions like a mirror and what is really on this side appears to be on *that* side."

"So what happened that night?"

"I saw what appeared to be a man in your kitchen," I explained. "No one was there. But I believe there *was* someone there that night, not in the kitchen with you but out in the yard with me, that is to say, *behind* me."

"A man standing behind you? But he would have been in the dark."

"No, Richard had just bought that torchiere, remember? The man would have been standing in a pool of light."

"Then you would have seen him!"

"Not necessarily. I think he had been standing in the shadows, possibly watching you. He unwittingly moved under the garden spotlight, and then retreated back into the darkness after he realized I had spotted him in the glass."

"Incredible. Who would be hiding in our garden? And why?"

"*That*, I'm afraid, I can't tell you. But I can assure you that there's no such thing as a ghost. That's simply not possible. Strange things happen and one looks for a rational explanation."

After a moment of silence on the line, I said, "Now is there anything else you wanted to talk about?"

She paused, and then said, "No, not now. I just need to sleep. Thanks, Edvard."

"Okay, I'll call Dr. Schroeder and let him know about your situation. I won't tell him anything more than absolutely necessary. Then he'll make out the prescription and call it in to your pharmacy. It's awkward to do from here, and I think you should establish a relationship with someone there in Copenhagen anyway. Should I tell him to call it in to Boulevard Apotek?"

"No, we're up at my mother's. Tell him to use Hellerup Apotek."

We said our goodbyes, but as I put down the old-fashioned rotary dial phone, I felt a twinge of remorse. I hadn't been looking after this pair of starlings as closely as I should have been these last few months. I knew they were drifting off course – first talk of ghosts, then feng shui, then ley lines, such a lot of hocus-pocus!

But I never thought they would get caught up in a whirlwind like this. Katrina had really crashed, already feeling the classic signs of lasting trauma – flashbacks, paranoia, anxiety. Richard and Katrina would both need serious counseling, and quite likely medication for some time to come. PTSD symptoms usually fade away over time, but it can take many years, and the truth is, unscrupulous use of such powerful mind control techniques can leave permanent scars.

Later that day, as I walked up the stairs to the DC-9 that was waiting for me on the frozen tarmac, I got the distinct feeling that I was embarking on yet another mission.

# 39. Søren

Ice crackled on the pavement as I crunched along, knees bent, on Jagtvej at the northern edge of Assistens Kirkegaard, the final resting place of Søren Kierkegaard, H.C. Andersen, Niels Bohr and so many others. The trees were bare now, stripped of all defenses. It had turned cold suddenly as it sometimes does in October, and what leaves had clung to the branches were down now, lying in heaps on the frozen ground.

Spying a tasteless green sign, I slid up to the grimy entrance and pulled open the heavy door, but received neither warmth nor welcome from the unheated taproom, deserted as it was at eleven o'clock on a Tuesday morning. Mullioned windows set with green glass the color of beer bottles lent a greenish cast to the dimly-lit interior. The atmosphere was unpalatable, smelling strongly of cigarettes and spilled beer, faintly of vomit. The upper halves of the walls were stained brown from years of smoke. I took a seat at a table in the corner under the statue of a verdigris sprite that had clearly seen better days; a dilapidated Green Knight leered at me from across the room.

*Matter of life or death,* she said in her note. But why not meet in private, at her home or mine? Why in this seedy bar in Nørrebro? *La Fée Verte*, I'd never heard of it. It had been years since I stepped foot in a pub. Other than work and the occasional errand, I didn't get out much. I hadn't gone outside in two days, had called in sick. And it was true enough: I was sick unto death after the debacle on Sunday...

A disheveled publican entered, stamping out his cigarette as he came, and grumbling as if I had interrupted his morning coffee break. I didn't feel like a drink, but couldn't very well sit there empty-handed, so I said, "Grøn Tuborg."

Standing at the tap, he grunted and poured out three glasses of froth before the amber liquid ran clear. He served the beer without peanuts or small talk. I lapped at the foam listlessly.

Then a cold shaft of air hit me full in the face. I looked up and saw *her* standing in the doorway. Flamboyant as always, she wore a mink coat, ermine muff, hoop earrings and makeup thick as pancake batter.

*Simply can't help herself; well, she is foreign, isn't she?*

"Good day, Rowena," I said, standing for her though she was no lady.

"Is it? What's so good about it?"

"I was being polite."

"I hate this weather of yours, Søren," she said, as if I was to blame for the cold snap. Then she said to the barman, "Bring me a Deva 70. I need something to warm me up!"

"What is that?" I asked.

"Spanish absinthe," the waiter replied as he walked away.

"*Hah*, the man is an imbecile," she said under her breath as soon as the publican was out of earshot. "Deva is *Basque,* not Spanish."

*Was Rowena Basque? She'd mentioned Logroño once...*

"As I'm sure you'll agree, Sunday was totally unacceptable," she said, suddenly all-business.

"You make it sound like it was my fault," I protested. "I was ready, standing at the window. I knew something was wrong when you walked out the front door and went to your car – and then that ancient Englishman comes crusading across the lawn..."

"It's not anybody's fault," she said, putting up her hand. "Richard wanted to talk to the priest. He just wouldn't let that drop. So I went to make a phone call, but, well, there was nothing I could do. I'm sure you can understand that, can't you Søren?"

"Well, yes, I suppose..." I started to say when I got distracted by the entrance of several other patrons. A towering immigrant with a flattop haircut walked in along with a dwarfish, greasy-looking fellow with thick glasses. Behind them, a ruddy-faced couple, regulars almost certainly, stumbled in, eyeing us as if we had taken their usual spot.

The barman was suddenly very busy and the pub suddenly very public. I leaned over and said with a lowered voice, "Why did you want to meet here, in such a public place?"

"Neutral ground. I want to discuss terms with you."

"Terms? What terms? Given what happened, I can't see how you'd expect me to pay anything."

Rowena allowed my words to hang in the air for a moment, and just then the waiter arrived with a silver tray containing the accoutrements of the infamous Absinthe Ritual. An acid-green layer of wormwood diffusion lay in wait at the bottom of a tall glass; alongside stood a decanter of chilled water, a bowl of cubed sugar with tongs, and a filigreed silver spoon. Rowena put the grated spoon atop the glass, and placed the sugar cube on the grille. Icy water dribbled over the die-shaped lump of sugar. On contact – as if by magic or alchemy – the chartreuse liquid transmogrified into an opalescent louche. As iridescent as it was, it still looked disgusting, like dirty milk.

"You simply don't understand the situation you're in, Søren," she said smiling as she lapped her murky draught. "The way I see it, I'm out a lot of money."

"How much are you talking about?"

She handed me a business card. *Rowena Morgana, Psychic and Spiritualist,* it said. I look at her, nonplussed.

"Turn it over," she said with a roll of her eyes.

On the back side was written a very large number. I raised my eyebrows, and looked at her, more perplexed than ever.

"And that's dollars, Søren. Not kroner: *dollars!*"

"But this makes no sense. You would never have gotten so much money. I would have come in and saved the day just as the Englishman did – that was the plan, remember?"

"No, you see I never intended to call you in until *after* I had the bank giro safely in hand. Then you would have had your moment in the sun, but the money would have been mine."

"You don't think the Italian would have stopped payment on the cheque?"

"On a Sunday night? I don't think so. And I would have made a deposit the next morning in a little branch I know of that opens an hour early. The transfer is immediate, and can be in Switzerland in minutes."

I was flummoxed. I had no idea she planned to bilk them out of so much money.

"So Søren, here's what I'll do," she continued. "You put up *half* of what I was expecting – so you see I am being very reasonable about this – and we can both forget the whole messy business."

"That's not possible, I don't have that kind of money!"

*And if I did, I wouldn't give it to you, you lying witch.*

The nerve of this woman! She didn't have anything on me! – or so I thought.

"I expected you might react this way," she said, rummaging in her bag. "But you'll raise the money, and you'll do it by the end of the week, or I will put a copy of the materials in this envelope into the nearest post box." She handed me a large yellow envelope.

I started opening the package and was working the clasp, when I noticed a dwarfish man walking over to me. I realized I'd met him before – *what was his name? Grønnegaard or Grøgaard or something?* I could see the reflection of myself in his glasses as he approached the table with a crooked, toothy smile. Then to my utter surprise, he thrust a camera in my face and said in lofty British tones, "Say *cheese,* Søren!"

Two incredibly bright flashes flooded my retinas. I rubbed my eyes and blinked. When I came to my senses, I was sitting alone in the cold, empty taproom. I watched in horror as an overexposed photograph of Rowena and me materialized slowly on the abandoned tabletop.

# 40. Katrina

I lurched and wobbled as the Number 18 snaked its way down to Svanemølle on Tuesday afternoon. I had finally slept, the peaceful dreamlessness of Luminal, and it was noon before I ventured out of the safety of my childhood home. Instead of driving, my plan was to take the bus, do a little shopping, and then pick up my bicycle on Rosenborgs Allé and ride back up to Hellerup.

Once in town, I walked along the Boulevard and browsed at a book store – James Redfield had come out with a sequel to *The Celestine Prophecy* – but I didn't buy anything until I found the most adorable little azure scarf. I put it on immediately, as the day was chill and the ride back along the coast was sure to be brisk.

I felt fine shopping, but as I walked down Rosenborgs Allé toward the Sound, I began to feel unsure of myself.

*Would the psychic be waiting there for me?*

*Are her collaborators watching me?*

*Could she read my thoughts even now?*

*Ach, nonsense!* I told myself, thinking what my mother would say to all this. I stopped to take a deep breath and was overwhelmed by a sweet aroma. Looking about, I saw, prominent in several of the front gardens, seven-petaled white flowers with hearts of gold, unaffected by the frost. Asters were still in bloom, up and down the shady Allé, like weeds.

Feeling a bit better, I continued down the arcade, walked past the familiar red door and up the concrete driveway, making for the garage in back. I hadn't been back inside Sundhuset since that night.

Søren was standing by the twin garages.

"Hej, Søren!" I called out as I strode up the drive. *"Længe siden."*

"Hello, Katrina. I thought you were at your mother's."

"Did George tell you?"

"Yes. And he told me about Sunday. I'm so sorry. Is there anything I can do?"

"No, it's for the best, Søren. We've given up. We're moving to Hellerup, to be closer to my mother."

Søren blanched at the news and said, "I'll miss you." He scrutinized my face like a painter trying to fix each detail. He kissed me goodbye, and I gave him a hug. *This terrible time has bound us together.*

He was a bit choked up, so I said as I pulled away, "Søren, we're going to miss you too. But it's not as if we're going to be in another world. It's just a few kilometers – we'll still see each other from time to time, I'm sure." He seemed to appreciate that.

We said our goodbyes and I cycled up to Hellerup following the coast-road. Despite the gale that came in off the Sound, I enjoyed the ride; the sea air cleared my head. I felt alive, more like myself again. When I arrived at Mor's, I put my two-wheeler in the garden shed like when I was a child. Just as I closed the door, I noticed something white in the basket, an envelope. A note from Søren, handwritten in shaky ink.

*1 October.*

*Dearest Katrina,*

*These are the hardest words I have ever had to write. The past six months have been for me Paradise and Inferno mix'd, as my forbidden love for you has grown as desperate as it is hopeless. It is indeed Heaven on earth when you smile at me, when we have been alone together as on those delicious but unwise days in my garden; but I have also come to know Hell. Damned to tortured evenings alone, conscious of your presence just out of reach, knowing that I can never fairly taste more than your honest courtesy.*

*If I have wronged you, know that I never meant you harm. That I have been but over-wrought, perplex'd in the extreme. That I have loved you but too well.*

*Remember me, and know that I have suffered, suffered for your sake; and that I would have given all for you, that I have.*

*Yours, truly,*

*Søren*

I bit my lip and my hand trembled. Was it a love note, an apology, a suicide note – all three? I recalled how he was sobbing when we said goodbye, how he said *Farewell.*

"OH, SØREN!" I shouted.

It was three o'clock exactly. *Was there still time?*

I ran inside, frantic. Empty rooms – Mor was out playing whist, wouldn't be home for hours – *What should I do?*

Called Søren's number, no answer.

Richard's mobile – no answer – I waited for his fatuous recording to end, left a hurried message.

Then his office, listened once more to his stupidly cheerful greeting.

Hit zero, reached the front desk... *Oh, where was he?*

"*Reception, goddag,*" a voice sang out.

"I'm trying to reach Richard Marchese – it's an emergency."

"I'm sorry, he's not picking up. I'll connect you with his secretary."

Seconds ticked by.

"*Hej Katrina, Richard er næsten færdig. Det er kun Niels tilbage...*"

"Niels? Oh, of course, he's with Niels Dahl," I remembered. Then I stopped cold. *Det er kun Niels tilbage.* Only Niels remains.

A million images flashed before my eyes, my brain zigzagged, neural spinnerets weaving a spider's web of connections. The dream – the door – the Scraping Man. I'd always assumed that when I saw "NIELS" in the dream, it was a remnant of "NIELSEN." The Scraping Man wanted to remove my father's name, Nielsen.

But what if he really was telling me that *Niels* was the only one left? The only one who... *what?*

Knew something about Fa's death.

In my vision, Dahl was in the conference room when Fa' died. He was at the Gala, Mor said that. What was he doing there? He wasn't in the Firm, he was – *the Damsgaard Family lawyer.* What if he was the executor of the will, there to hand out the mementos? That means he would know who the Founder was, why he made such an odd bequest. It all made so much sense:

Dahl was the executor.

Oh my God, Richard was in his office right now!

Jette's voice in my ear said, "Katrina, are you still there?"

"Yes, I'll be in the house. Please have Richard meet me there."

Later, Mor asked why I didn't just call the police. I don't know, what would I have told them? All I could think about was Søren. I got back on my bike and rode as fast as I could.

It was just a few kilometers, I told myself.

And yet, a world away.

# 41. Søren

By noon I was sitting at my own kitchen table, opening the blackmailer's envelope with trembling fingers. Within, I found three malicious letters, relating the unlucky deeds of the past few months:

The first was a letter to Katrina, which referred to the newly-taken Polaroid. In it, Rowena claimed that I had been working with her the whole time, had been manipulating Katrina for months, so she would feel vulnerable and get into bed with me. The thought of her reading this made me sick;

The second, addressed to the Pharmacological Review Board, alleged numerous irregularities in my prescription records;

And the third was addressed to the Police, Division of Controlled Substances, alerting them to the growing of various dangerous and forbidden plants in my garden – belladonna, aconite, calamus, heliotrope, lobelia, silvervine and others – again with photos.

While not everything Rowena claimed was strictly true – she had extenuated – the contents of the envelope would ruin my life. Coming up with the money, however, was simply not possible. I had exhausted my own resources long ago.

No one to turn to now.

"Belasquita's Dragon," the Midget had called her, and her hunger knew no bounds. The harpy would pursue me for all eternity.

"Oh, I should never have made a deal with that ravenous woman!" I said out loud.

Anxious and desperate, I read the letters over and over. Finally, I began to sob. I considered medicating, but decided that for once I should face my troubles without anodyne, my nerves raw and exposed as they were. Slowly, a picture of what I had to do came into focus. Now was the time for *action*.

I built a roaring fire in the black porcelain stove and burned Rowena's letters and photograph. It felt strangely satisfying to watch her burn and melt, even if it was but in effigy. The Polaroid even emitted a little squeal as it burned up. *A nice touch.*

Of course I was witnessing my own destruction as well.

At my roll-top desk, I wrote a note to Katrina. I placed it in a white envelope and considered how to deliver it.

*Should I leave it in my pocket, next to my heart? No, someone else would find it first. In her mailbox? No, Richard might destroy it in a jealous rage.*

Ah, there was Katrina's cycle leaning up against the garage. I took action. Bidding goodbye to Mother's picture on the wall, I strode out the side door into the chilly air, crossed the driveway and had just inserted the envelope in the basket, under the cycle-lock, when I heard her voice say my name. At first I thought it was my imagination, but then I heard it again.

*"Hej Søren, længe siden."*

"Katrina!" I said, turning and nearly starting to cry again. *Could she tell I'd been weeping?* "I thought you were, ah, at your mother's or something."

"How did you know that?" she wanted to know. *How did I know that?*

"Uh, George. George told me. And uh, listen, I'm *really* sorry about what happened Sunday night," I said, truthfully.

Nodding, she said, "So he told you."

I smiled, my mouth quivering as it was, and bobbed my head up and down, dumbly.

"I'm so sorry, Katrina. If I had known..."

"No, Søren, it's alright. It's finished. We've given up. I don't know if there's something rotten in the house or the ground or what it is. But we've decided to sell."

"You're moving?"

"Yes, I know," she said putting up her hand. "We just moved in and fixed up the place – that's what everyone says. But we've made up our minds – we've already started looking for something up in Hellerup, closer to my mother."

"I see," I said biting my lip. "I'll miss you," I said sincerely, and peered into her cyan eyes, perhaps for the last time.

With the carelessness that comes from having nothing left to lose, I kissed her, as I did at Midsummer. Her cheek was softer than a hibiscus flower, and to my amazement, she did not pull away. Her mouth was wet on mine. I drank in the taste of her like a man climbing the scaffold who suddenly scents daffodils.

Embracing her, I buried my nose in her honey hair, and kissed her neck, sobbing openly.

Pulling away, she reached out her hand to my cheek. I grabbed it, held it there, and said, "*Farvel.*"

"Farewell, Søren. Listen, I'm going to miss you, too. But it's not as if I'm going to another world. It's just a few kilometers!" And she made dimples on her cheeks. "You'll check in on me from time to time, won't you?" she said, not knowing what she was asking.

"Of course. Of course I will."

I watched as she mounted her bicycle and rode toward the Sound, growing ever-smaller as she approached the circle of blue at the end of the street. Then she vanished. She never glanced in the basket, nor did she look back to wave. My wristwatch read 2:42. I determined, Man of Action that I was, to be done with the matter by three. There must be no time for regrets. This gave me 18 minutes.

I walked into the garden one last time. Rummaging around in the storage shed, I found a sturdy rope, one I'd used to sustain saplings. With this coil, I could still cheat Rowena. The fury of the old cozener would be frightening, but there was nothing she could do. She would have nothing to gain and everything to lose from posting the letters after I was gone. It was a Pyrrhic victory, but the only way to be rid of her once and for all.

After six minutes had ticked away, I let myself into Sundhuset. I still had the key. There were still candles everywhere – some lit, others extinguished – like at a funeral. I blushed at my part in the whole business, but I was so desperate, I would have made a deal with the Prince of the World himself. In a way, I had. But now I could atone for my errors by sacrificing everything for the one I loved, just like Mother did for me. *Mother.* Yes, I would see Mother again.

Twelve minutes after my last hope for tenderness in this life abandoned me, I chose the spot for my martyrdom, for my mortality and immortality – an exposed beam, an eastern arm akimbo, so to speak, easily visible from the street. All who pass shall see me and know fear – and my Love, know what Hell I traversed for her sake. I began to twist the rope into a simple knot. As it evolved into a heinous noose, I thought of the *Spejders* of my childhood, the Scouts. I was a good *spejder*, everyone said so. Mother said so too. Strange to think the knot-tying badge from so long ago would come in handy now.

Perhaps this was the only real choice a human ever has – to take one's own life. Everything else is conditioned, manipulated, rigged... Rigged, indeed – what if I got caught in the rigging, caught in the web of my own making? What if I should jump out and regret? There was no ten-day grace period after all. But then I saw Rowena's eyes turn from malice to hope. No, I could not turn back now. The point of no return.

Fifteen minutes after her blue form disappeared below the horizon, I tested the strength of the rope. *It's not as thick as a cable, and its weave is worn, but 'twill serve. Twill serve.* I laughed a hollow laugh at my own inadvertent pun. *Ask for me tomorrow and you shall find me a grave man.* Kneeling at the windowsill, perched before my self-made doom, the cold air rushed against my face. There was nothing to protect me from the winds that would blow now. For once, I was working without a net.

Seventeen minutes after I saw my angel for the last time, I heard music. Or rather, I imagined I could hear the piano playing downstairs, the haunting piece that had sounded incessantly these past several months. As if its phantom still echoed in these halls out of all reason. I had heard this music before, years ago when I was little. I hadn't remembered till now – it was before Mother died, before the Accident even. We were here visiting Uncle Peder, all three of us. We were sitting on the veranda when that music started coming from the house. Uncle Peder grew angry and stormed inside. We heard men shouting. Mother took us back to our garden to look at the poppies in bloom – it must have been August – when Uncle Peder came out again, I remember thinking that his face was as red as the flowers.

No one mentioned the incident again.

Exactly 18 minutes After Katrina, the grandfather clock chimed the hour of three – or was it not a church bell? Yes, a church bell in the city began tolling. A church bell slowly tolling from the walls of a distant city beneath the horizon...

Brushing back a single tear from my right cheek, I threw wide the window and stood on the sill. It was a long fall, no doubt this would be my end. A thrill rippled through my veins as it became clear to me that I should finally become the Man of Action I had always dreamed of being.

I slipped the noose over my head and put the rope in its place along my collarbone, the knot by my left ear. I felt the rough ends of the hemp against my skin – and heard a slow banging sound, like a pile-driver.

How annoying – it must be the construction in the next street. And yet it sounded nearby, ominous. What was that infernal hammering?

I looked up and down the street, but saw no jackhammer, no sign of workmen. Yet the hammering continued, steady and unabated.

BONG... BONG... BONG... BONG...

*Was it my heart, pounding in my ears?*

No, it was my watch, an Omega that Uncle Peder had given me long ago. My left wrist pressed against my ear as it held the noose close to its tender quarry. With each beat, the pulse seemed to grow slower, and... slower.

They say that each man's heart is designed to contract a specific number of times in his lifetime. No amount of exercise or struggle can alter this fixed number. The only hope is to lower the pulse rate; the only freedom, to select which one will be the final beat.

As I stepped past the ledge, I heard my name. It was Katrina's voice! Had she come back for me? I looked back toward the open window. In my haste and distraction, I kicked over a candle that had been sitting on the sill. I heard a man's scream.

Dazzled by the sunlight as I emerged from the shadow of the eaves, my eyes became slits and I grimaced. Felt a slight falling sensation in my stomach. I expected a jolt, but the rope must have come loose from the rafter, because I felt myself falling and falling.

I could still hear the echo of Katrina calling my name. Or was it an angel?

Then the voice was drowned in bells, chimes and carillon calls that rebounded and resounded in my head. Grandfather clock called and called the hour – it was three – marking the moment of my choice.

*What moments chose me?*

The instant Katrina said my name in springtime; the kiss at the bonfire at Midsummer; the summer night I contracted with the harpy...

Then the church bells faded. Down, down I fell. The brightness of the day turned black, as if I had fallen into a well. I found myself in Uncle Peder's basement, in the crawlspace there, where I was sometimes punished as a boy. There was a mound near the front of the vault that I was always afraid of. Yet I found myself crawling toward the soft, black earth...

Then I cried out for Mother, and could hear her voice, calling me.

What of my own father, whom I called Uncle?

What of the grandfather I never knew?

*I've got you, now*, said a man's voice.

*Grandfather.*

*Was it my grandfather playing the Ravel on the piano?*

I was gripped by the thought that the Player had been played.

The bells stopped.

*Oh, God, it can't be! Am I Time's fool?*

Then there was a tremendous crack, as of a great oak suddenly sundered by lightning. And my body, its neck broken, swung gently from side to side beneath the rafters of the house.

# 42. Richard

I didn't expect to see the inside of this office again for a while. I sat in the waiting room, looking at the wall of properties (mostly apartments) available at the Østerbro office of Löhff & Dahl. Before long, the slick old-timer walked in smartly and sing-songed, "Hello, Richard!"

"Hi Niels," I responded, nodding and shaking his hand.

"Please come into the conference room," Niels said, and added, in a conspiratorial tone, "I must say I'm surprised to see you back in the housing market so soon again."

"Yes, it's quite a surprise to everyone concerned."

"I hope it wasn't the house that was lacking something?"

"Oh, no," I said after a moment's hesitation. "I can't really say that."

"Trouble with the neighbors then? You're not moving back to the States already, are you?"

"No," I said shaking my head. "We're not moving back to New York, at least not yet. We'd like to find something up in Hellerup, closer to Katrina's mother. Say, why'd you ask about the neighbors?"

"You'll love Hellerup..." he started in before I cut him short.

"Is there something you know about the neighbors, Niels?"

"Well, you know I've been working in the north end of Copenhagen for a long time. I just celebrated forty years in the business..." he said with a self-conscious laugh.

"You must have seen a lot."

Dahl was hesitating, obviously he wanted to say something but was unsure how to say it. Finally he said, "How have you gotten along with the Jensen boy?" as if the forty-year-old pharmacist was our paperboy.

"Søren? Fine. He's helped us out a lot, we've had him over to dinner. In fact he and I watched a movie together not long ago, one night when Katrina was at her mother's."

"Good, I'm glad to hear that you've become such good friends. Really glad. I knew his mother, you know. She was a fine woman, a fine woman. But it was a sad story – you never can tell how it'll affect a child like that."

"What story?"

"Well, just between you, me and the lamp post... Gerda came from a fine family, you know, an old Copenhagen family. But she had troubles, always troubles. Health problems of her own – she was a nervous woman – and then her older boy, Holger, he was always sick. She was taking him to the doctor all the time; the boy was what we used to call 'accident-prone,' falling down stairs, that kind of thing. He must have had four or five concussions by the time he went to school. And then she had Søren out of wedlock. Holger was three or four years older. And Gerda, a single mother! This must have been the late fifties, early sixties: an unmarried woman just didn't go and have a child like that in those days."

"She wasn't married to Søren's father?"

"I believe she had been married to Holger's father, a shipping man who had died at sea before I met her, went down with the *Princess Victoria*, I believe. Left her some money, they say. I can't tell you who Søren's father was, but I'm certain she wasn't married when he was born. I sold her Rosenborgs Allé 16 when Søren was an infant, and it hasn't changed hands since."

He shook his head, but I couldn't tell if it was because of the sad story or all the commissions he'd missed.

"So what happened to Holger?" I asked.

Dahl's face grew very serious. "Well, one day Holger was playing in the backyard and accidentally swallowed something – once I heard it was cleaning powder, but someone else said it was poisonous berries. Anyway, his mother rushed him to the hospital, but it was too late. Holger died, just nine years old."

"Oh, that's tragic."

"Yes, but the story doesn't end there. You see, the doctors reported it to the police. Social services came to believe that Gerda was *intentionally* harming the children."

"The children, you mean Søren too?"

"Yes. After Holger's death, the state threatened to take Søren away from Gerda. She fought them, God knows, she fought them 'with beak and claws' as we say. But finally the judge's order came, and Søren was to be shipped off to a children's institution. It was all just too much for the old girl. She put her head in the oven, and turned on the gas. The boy found her like that."

"Oh my God, what a horrible thing to happen to a little boy! So did he end up in an orphanage then?"

"No, he never did. Peder Damsgaard, the neighbor, stepped forward and said he'd look after the boy if the court were to award him custody. A trust fund was set up, a nanny was hired, and so on."

I wondered why a neighbor would come forward like that – usually orphans go to the next-of-kin. Putting two and two together, I asked, "Do you think Peder Damsgaard was Søren's real father then? I mean why would he step forward like that?"

He took a breath. "Some people said that at the time. I suppose it's possible that Gerda moved in next door to Peder after having the baby, just to be near him. But whether biological or not, I can tell you that he was a father-figure – losing him last year must have been hard on the lad."

Since Niels was being so incredibly open with me, I felt I had to tell him a little of our story. "Gee, you've shared a lot with me, Niels, so I feel it's only fair that I tell you the real reason why we're selling again after only six months."

"Yes, by all means, why?"

"Well, to tell you the truth, a lot of strange things have happened. Unexplainable things."

"What do you mean?" He narrowed his eyes.

"Well, for example, Katrina fell down the cellar steps, but said that she was pushed. Then Søren told us that Karl Damsgaard fell down those same steps to his death."

"*Karl* Damsgaard?"

"Yeah, you know, Peder's father."

"Oh, I never met him, he was dead long before I started in the business."

"I thought you were the family lawyer."

"I was Peder's lawyer, yes," he said, examining his fingernails. "The only thing I can tell you about Peder's father is that he was a newspaper man."

"A reporter?"

"Editor, I think. Like Peder."

"That's funny. Didn't they have an awful lot of money for a family of newspapermen?"

"Peder was editor at a right-wing journal. I'm not sure where the money came from, but they always had it. His father was editor at *Berlingske* for years before the war, must've been an influential man."

Hm, *Berlingske,* that rang a bell. That was the paper we saw in the Bangsbo Museum, the one with the quote from Damsgaard. Funny, Søren never mentioned that the old man was the editor.

"Did you ever meet him?" I asked.

"No, not as such," he said, looking out the window. I waited, and sure enough, he turned back to me and said, "Well, I really shouldn't go into it, client privilege, you understand, but well, it did affect your family, your father-in-law certainly. And anyway, everyone involved is long since dead and buried..." His voice trailed off.

"Please tell me, Niels. Who am I going to tell?"

"The year was 1961. I'd only known Peder for a couple of years. He was a fine man, a cultured man – I don't want you to think ill of him, though he could be a bit stiff and old-fashioned about things. One day he told me he wanted me to handle his father's will. I read the testament, which was unusual in many ways, and found inside the envelope the key to a safety-deposit box. In Berlin. That's how I remember the date. You see the East Germans had just closed the border and started to build the Wall. The city was very tense. It seemed like every day someone would make a run for it, jumping out of windows or climbing over the fences. Some, smart or lucky it's hard to say, would make it; others would stop, palsy with bullets for a few moments and crumple to the ground."

"I've seen pictures," I said.

"I found the address on the outskirts of West Berlin, in a pretty area not far from the lake, Wannsee. The bank building was a converted mansion, the vault in the cellar. I expected to insert the key into a small coffer, certainly nothing bigger than a strongbox or filing cabinet. Instead, I found the key unlocked an entire room full of valuables. No one realized what was in there. Paintings, jewelry, ingots. Now this wasn't my field at all. I'm a real estate man. This was complicated – estate taxes, rules of inheritance, international tax treaties. But it was my duty to execute the will, and that's just what I did."

"So what happened? Did Peder inherit everything?"

"Everything was liquidated, and Peder received the proceeds after tax *except* for certain named items, seventeen in all. Each of these were to be given to the partners in Justesen & Svindborg, in order of seniority. The will had a clause that stated these items should be given to the partners upon the fiftieth, the golden anniversary of the firm's founding. You see, every item was made of gold – the watches, rings, and so on."

"But not the paintings."

"Ah, well, there was gold in the frames – and one of the paintings was from the Golden Age." He smirked.

"So that's how Katrina's father got the pocket watch." He nodded. "But wasn't all this stuff suspect, I mean, wasn't it stolen?"

"Why should it be stolen?" he asked, silver eyebrows furrowed.

"Well, I don't know, but didn't the Nazis loot, steal stuff like that? I mean the vault was in Berlin and all…"

"That's pure speculation. Damsgaard was a wealthy man, a man of property. The items were in Germany, it's true, but so was he often enough. He was criticized for having been so pro-German in the thirties. But people forget what it was like before the war. At the opening ceremonies for the Olympic Games in Berlin in 1936, the athletes marched in with a Nazi salute.

"*Sieg heil!*" he said, and made the stiff-armed motion with his right arm. His eyes widened and his hand remained in the air a bit too long for my taste.

I squirmed and said, "You mean the *German* athletes, don't you Niels?"

He lowered his arm and his tone of voice, and chuckled, "Not only them. Many others did too: the Italians, why even the *French* athletes…"

My cell phone rang. Jette. Something about an emergency – Katrina would be in the house, I had to meet her there right away. So I finished up quickly with Niels – he agreed to help us get rid of the property on Rosenborgs Allé and help us find something in Hellerup, closer to Katrina's mother – and jumped in the car.

As I drove up the boulevard, I started to get worried. Sirens whined and klaxons blared. The street was choked with emergency vehicles, and more were still arriving – police, ambulance, hook and ladder.

*My God, what was going on?*

*Could this have anything to do with Katrina's message?*

I parked two blocks away and ran the rest of the way. Rosenborgs Allé was transformed. Usually quiet as the grave, the street was noisy and crowded with people. I didn't know we even had so many neighbors. The acrid smoke assaulted my nose and eyes even before I saw the black billows.

The house was on fire!

I couldn't believe it. I bulled my way through the tumult and found the man with the biggest helmet. He seemed to be in charge.

"Excuse me!" I shouted.

No response – the chief was talking with another fireman. I grasped his elbow and said, "Excuse me, but that's MY HOUSE!"

"Oh, I'm sorry," he replied as he turned to me. "Do you know if there's anyone inside?"

"I don't know. I don't think so," I said.

*Katrina's message: she would be in the house.*

*I froze.*

*Oh my God, was she trapped in there?*

The second storey was completely engulfed in flame, and there was smoke visible in the front room downstairs as well. The firemen were having trouble with the hydrant because of the frost, but finally got the hose turned on and started dousing the second floor with a jet of water. But the pressure was low. For such a huge conflagration, it was a paltry stream, like trying to piss out a forest fire. They would *never* get the blaze under control at this rate.

What if Katrina was in the back bedroom, trapped?

Should I go around back and take a look?

Wait, she would have her phone with her – I grabbed my cell phone and called Katrina's number.

*Thank God for modern technology!*

One ring...

Two...

*Oh God, Katrina, please answer the phone...*

Three rings.

"Hallo?" a voice said faintly.

"KATRINA!" I nearly screamed into the phone.

"Yes – Richard?"

"Katrina, where are you?"

I heard only coughing.

*Oh my God, she's trapped in the house!*

"Katrina, are you all right? Where are you right now?"

"Richard, it's you – I tried to call. WHERE *are* YOU?"

"I'm here on Rosenborgs Allé, where are you?"

"You're here? But I'm here. I don't see you!"

"I'm across the street, on the..." I started to say, but then put the phone back in my pocket. Katrina was fifteen feet away from me, just behind a hulking Danish fireman. I ran over to her and hugged her until I thought she would break, and then held her in my arms, not wanting to let her go. She was crying, I was crying, from fear, joy and relief.

"Oh, it's horrible!" she said.

"How did it happen? Were you inside when the fire started?"

"No—" she started to say, but then pulled back and looked at me. "You don't know, then."

"Know what? The goddamned house is on fire, what else is there to know!"

"Richard, there's something you should see," she said. We walked toward the heat of the flames, weaving through the crowd of rescue workers and curious neighbors, none of whom seemed familiar – who *were* all these people? As we came around the long fire truck and I stepped onto the lip of the driveway, I saw it. Hanging from a beam over the alley. I couldn't see it before because of the eaves. Just hanging there, swaying slightly as the waves of heat emanated from the burning building.

I knew it was a dead body right away. But I couldn't see who it was or think of a reason why it would be there, hanging from the rafters like that. Grainy, black-and-white images of lynchings came to my mind – a corpse dangling obscenely from a tree, torch-flames all around, a noisy mob. The neck was broken, head cocked to one side. I strained to see who it was through the clouds of smoke. Waves of heat poured off the structure; the firemen yelled at us to move off the walkway. The face was distended and tinged reddish-orange by the light of the fire and the evening sun behind it.

Then all at once I realized.

"IT'S SØREN!" I screamed. "Oh my God! What's happened?"

I grabbed Katrina, pulled her to my chest, and turned away from the horror.

"For Christ's sake, why don't they cut him down?"

"It's not safe, Richard. They wanted to, but it's too close to the flames," Katrina said.

The fire hose, under high pressure now, focused its spray on the front bedroom, causing a draft that sent flames leaping out the side window, setting fire to the beam, the rope, the body. Katrina screamed and buried her face in my chest. I held her and turned my face away as Søren's clothing ignited and I caught the unmistakable scent of burning flesh. Then without looking back, I walked Katrina away from the house and its self-immolation.

# 43. Edvard

The house – what was left of it – stood silent against the cool blue of the autumn sky. The roof was gone, the second storey had collapsed, and the personal possessions were ruined, charred beyond all recognition. The façade was still standing, but black tongues of smoke damage licked upwards from the doorway and window seat in what had been the front parlor. The empty outlines of what had once been dormer windows stared blankly like eyes that had been put out. A copper tube lay half-molten along one sill, like frozen tears.

It didn't take an expert in forensics to see that the blaze started upstairs, near the front of the dwelling – in the "frontal lobe," so to speak. Here much of the structure was simply gone, and what remained was charcoal.

"It's a total loss," Richard said through tight lips as we stood on the curb.

"The insurance will cover everything, I suppose?"

"I don't know, but it's not the money I'm thinking of. It's the life we were trying to build here." He wagged his head back and forth. "There's nothing left."

A breeze blew in off the Sound. The smell of sour ash and smoke made me wince. I turned toward Søren's place next door, shut up as it was, so snugly safe. The firemen had focused much of their effort in protecting the nearby dwellings, having admitted defeat at Number 18.

I thought of the irony of how the one who started all the trouble was himself protected from its consequences, when as if to upbraid me for my thought, I caught sight of the charred beam jutting out from the right hand side of the façade, a gibbet coal-black against the sky, and I regretted my thought. Søren had paid for his misdeeds, and paid dearly.

Richard pushed past the yellow cordons that the authorities had set up around the property and we walked the grounds. We poked at the rubble, Richard with his shovel and me with my hoe. Just under the surface, it was still smoldering. Smoke and ash would fly up at the touch of our tools, the last gasps of the inferno.

What were we looking for? It's hard to say. Perhaps we hoped to discover what we could about the origin of the fire, or pluck from the ashes some prized memento that had somehow survived the blaze. Richard picked over the remains like a detective, holding up this and that in his gloved hands, asking questions. Perhaps young Sherlock hoped to find a magical clue that would solve the mystery of what happened here. But at my age, I was under no such illusions.

Even after all these years, people still ask me why I never went back to Germany, never visited the camps where my family met their fate. But there wasn't anyone to visit and nothing to be gained by sifting through the remains. In fiction, one finds the conveniently-dropped meerschaum pipe or Trichinopoly cigar; in real life there are no answers hiding in the ashes – only bones and shoes.

The rear was the least damaged, and ironically, the wooden deck and garden furniture were largely intact. So we sat there out of the wind and drank coffee from a thermos I had brought with me.

"Nothing like this has ever happened to me, Eddé."

"You lost your father."

"Well, yeah, but Pop was sick, lung cancer, you know. By the end, it was a blessing that he got the chance to rest after all he'd been through. This is so unfair – the house is a total loss, and poor Søren's dead – and Katrina, will she ever be the same? Oh my God, we should never have come here..."

"Now wait, Richard, don't say that. I for one have been very happy to get to know you and Katrina..."

Stopping me, he said, "Oh, sure, Eddé – I feel the same way. You were just a figure to me, a legend – somebody my father knew a long time ago. Now I know you as a real person. And I'm grateful for what you've done for me and Katrina, I really am."

"Aw, I haven't done much," I said, truthfully.

"Oh, but you have! There were several times when I thought about what you told me – 'Strange things happen and you look for rational explanations.' You kept me from going off the deep end, I don't mind saying. But – I don't know, I feel like now we're starting all over again. And I feel so alone – my family is so far away – Katrina's a wreck, I have to be there for her, but who's there for me?"

"Don't you have any friends at work, any colleagues?"

"No, not really," he replied, looking down.

"Richard, tell me, you were raised in a close-knit, working-class family with a strong sense of religion, weren't you?"

"Yeah, you know I was."

"You have no close friends at work, is that right?"

"No, I tend to keep my professional relationships at the office – who wants to bring work home?"

"And would you say your colleagues do the same?"

"Well," he hesitated and looked away. "No. They're always going out for a drink after work and stuff like that. But I want to go home after work."

"Like your father did?"

"Yeah," he said with a tip of his head.

Richard's sense of loneliness and alienation stemmed from being a fish out of water, a working-class kid in a white-collar world. So I asked, "Richard, did you ever consider that you may be caught between two worlds?"

"How do you mean?"

"You left the world of the working class a long time ago – but some of the behavior patterns are still imprinted on you."

"You mean like keeping work and home life separate?"

"Yes – like a typical working class man, you don't make real friends at work, yet like a typical member of the professional class, you've moved away from family and neighborhood. This leaves you isolated – and vulnerable."

Richard took a moment to drink this in with his coffee, and then said, "I never thought of it that way – I never really have fit in at work. I mean, I've been very successful and all, but not by being any good at office politics. I've always made up for it by being better at the work."

"You had the tools your parents could give you – but as charming as Vinnie could be, he was never one to 'suffer fools.'"

"Nah, Pop would always speak his mind no matter what. I guess you can 'take the boy out of Queens' – maybe the answer is to just go back to New York, huh?"

"I'm not sure one can ever really go home again," I said, thinking of the cold reception Katrina got on coming back to Denmark.

"Why not? Now that this merger's gone through, I've got better opportunities in New York than here. My old mentor is running the place now, he called me last week, offering me a corner office. And you know my Mom's not getting any younger. It would be nice to be closer to her – and maybe it's time to start a family. That would get Katrina's mind off all this – darkness."

I let that hang in the air a second as I took a drag on my cigarette, and then asked, "Richard, do you really think Katrina is *ready* to move back to New York?"

"What *is* she ready for? She's a basket case, Eddé! A change of scenery might really do her good." He was trying to convince himself.

"Richard, Katrina's had a great shock, she's just getting reacquainted with her family, and starting therapy with Dr. Schroeder."

"But look at this mess!" He said, pointing at the hulk. "I don't even know where to begin picking up the pieces. It all seems so meaningless."

"Meaningless?" I asked, surprised at his choice of words.

"Yeah. What's the point of living if we never get anywhere – I mean, we worked so hard to get here, to get the house and everything. And now it's all gone," he said, as the words caught in his throat.

Psychiatrists know to listen for certain words. "Meaningless" is one of them. Existential depression, the deep-seated feeling that one's life is meaningless, is a common result of tragedy and isolation. I tried to get Richard to see the good things in his life and establish more of a task-orientation.

"But your life's not all gone, Richard. You're young and healthy. You can re-build. And you're *not* alone – you and Katrina are so lucky to have each other!"

"I know – I know how lucky I am to have her. But she's in a bad way, Eddé, and I don't know if I can help her anymore. I'm way out on a limb here – where do I go from here? How do I fit in? I feel like the extra puzzle piece that doesn't fit in anywhere. I'm such an outsider – I don't even speak the goddamned language!"

"It's hard," I said, putting my hand on his arm, but he pulled away. "Richard," I said, pursuing his eyes with mine, "you can build bridges to other people, you can learn the language. You can *choose* your attitude to any situation – this is the great lesson that the 20th Century has taught us."

Richard just looked away again. I decided to share a bit more of my personal history as a way of wrenching him out of his self-pity.

"Richard, when I was a teenager, I went through a moping period," I said. "I was self-absorbed, melancholic. I dressed in black and ignored my schoolwork.

I read everything I could about the camps, about how people suffered there. I imagined what my family went through and spent my days crying for them and for my own loss."

"That doesn't sound like you at all, Eddé."

"I wasn't always like I am now."

"How did you get through it?"

"By reading the accounts of survivors, of people who, despite the sadistic SS men and capos, managed to walk out of that living hell. Some could even manage to be thankful for the good things. I'll never forget the account of one survivor who made a point of the fact that, despite not being able to clean their teeth for months or even years, the prisoners' gums were healthier than ever!"

"That's incredible – I don't know how they managed to survive at all, let alone see a positive side of the experience!"

"Richard, those who survived talk about how they focused their whole being on getting through one day at a time – to live till sundown. Then, when even that became too difficult, *part* of a day. Imagine that, getting through the morning by being completely focused on not dying before noon. Which capo could be bribed? How could you manage to get a scoop of the thicker soup at the bottom of the pot? Making it through morning inspection by scraping your face with a piece of glass, or smearing blood on the cheeks in a cheap imitation of health.

"Humans, no matter *how* traumatized, can live. Must live. I realized just how lucky I was to be the one Hans Müller knocked down that day. I owed it to him, and to the memory of my family, to look forward, not backwards. And that's how I found my own calling in traumatic psychiatry."

"And you're a wonderful counselor, really you are. But the thing is see, you didn't do anything *wrong*. I feel like such an idiot – falling for a psychic! I failed to protect my family, that's the first rule of being a husband, right? I blew it. I got to marry the most wonderful woman – I still don't know why she would ever want to be with me – and I blew it."

"Listen, Richard, it's okay to feel bad – that's the basis for self-improvement, self-overcoming. But you're not the first person to be taken in by a swindler and you won't be the last. The key is to *learn* from your experience. 'That which does not kill me makes me stronger.'"

"What's to learn?" he said, shaking his head. "That I shouldn't trust anybody?"

I reflected on what made Richard lose his way, get blown so far off course.

"For one thing, don't give in to irrationality so easily," I told him. "I saw a ghostly man in the window one night in July, but I *knew* there must be some kind of rational explanation – and sure enough, there was. The window was functioning as a mirror, and the man I saw was standing behind me."

"Søren?"

"Of course, he was *stalking* Katrina, and in his twisted mind, my presence there that night was a threat. He probably saw me through the window, consoling her, helping her after her fall, sleeping over..."

"Katrina told me that he tried to kiss her on the beach at Midsummer – he must've been green with jealousy. And I can imagine that Søren was responsible for some of the things we experienced – the smoke, the phone message – but I can't pin everything on poor Søren. There must have been something else going on. I mean, the books moved and I heard voices and Katrina fell down the steps..."

"No one was in the house," I said in my most confident voice. "The combined effect of several coincidences is to give the illusion of a pattern or magic, but it's just a series of misunderstandings... Listen, you know I don't like to talk about my work – it's unpleasant and very confidential – but I read the final accident report from the Vnukovo Airlines crash just this week. There were many errors that led to the crash, Richard. In fact, a total of *18.*"

"How can that be?"

"The Russian crew did not speak English well, procedures were lacking or not followed, there were a host of reasons, but my point is that it took many separate things to go wrong for the tragedy to occur. Now you might say it would be impossible for so many things to go wrong – an impossible set of coincidences, but it did happen: I watched them carry away the dead bodies, 141 of them."

Richard became pensive and we sat there in silence for a time. The wind in the trees made a mournful whistling sound.

Then finally he said, "The night Søren came over, we watched a movie together. There was this guy flipping a coin over and over again, and every time it comes up heads until you're absolutely sure the coin must be fixed. But then, after something like a hundred heads in a row, the coin comes up tails. Turns out it was a series of coincidences the whole time."

"Yes, that's it, that's what I'm trying to tell you. It's much more believable that you experienced a series of coincidences or misunderstandings than to say that the Laws of Physics have been repealed and dead people are rearranging your books!"

"I suppose you're right, Eddé, but I'll never quite understand it."

"Perhaps someday you will. Until then, the most important thing is to take care of Katrina. Give yourself time to recover from the shock and pick up the pieces of your lives. To do that, you'll need to minimize change for the time being. The last thing you need is to move thousands of miles away, back to the hustle and bustle of New York."

"You're right, Eddé," he said, brightening. "Let's see what we can salvage from the garage. At least that's still intact."

The garage at the rear of the property was unharmed by the fire. Richard selected a few tools and put them in a wheel barrow. The door to Søren's garden stood ajar, and I walked up to it casually and pushed.

I was amazed. It was a cold October day, yet beyond the gate was an intense jungle of flowering plants and vines and overhanging trees. In the center of the garden, a headless classical statue reigned over the chaos, tendrils crisscrossing its torso.

"This is incredible, Richard," I called. "You've got to see this!"

He came to the gate. "What a mess!"

"It seems like it was a lovely garden at one time – but it certainly is over-grown now."

"Poor Søren – he was as messed up as his yard – but from what Niels Dahl was telling me, it seems like it was his childhood that did it."

"What did Dahl tell you?" I asked as I stepped tentatively into the ruined but still-aromatic garden.

"Well, evidently Søren's older brother died under mysterious circumstances. Social services accused his mother of poisoning him. They were going to take Søren away from her, but before they could do it, she committed suicide."

*Just like her son.*

"Evidently, Søren was the one who found the body," he continued. "It must have been gruesome. Have you ever heard of a case like that?"

"The facts are consistent with MSP, Munchausen Syndrome by Proxy."

"Oh, I have heard of that. That's where the mother hurts her kids to get attention."

"Yes, often the mother plays the hero or the long-suffering martyr, even though all the while she's the one who's been causing the medical problems to begin with. Poison is a common modus operandi for these women."

"You wouldn't think such evil was possible."

"For a long time, few gave credence to the anecdotal evidence of maternal abuse. But in the 1980s, well-documented cases started coming out, and since then we've had to reckon with the fact that some mothers do this to their children."

"What's the impact on a surviving child like Søren?"

"There is very little information on the long-term effects of MSP, though I will say that I noticed a strong tendency in Søren to seek attention, to play the expert or hero."

"Yeah, he was always making himself the center of attention, always pronouncing on something. I know this sounds paranoid, but you know that Søren was a pharmacist; he filled prescriptions for us. And he was always bringing over gourmet food – strong cheeses and wine, *bouillabaisse*. You think he was trying to poison us?"

I considered this while puffing out my lips and tick-tocking my head back and forth. I recalled Søren's xenophobic comments that night during our "chess game."

*Was he really capable of murder?*

Finally, I said, "If the man was trying to kill you using arsenic or something like that, you'd be very sick, probably dead by now. But perhaps he was manipulating you. For example, I remember Katrina saying to me that the Ambien affected her in reverse after a while."

"Yeah, the Ambiens kept her up."

"I don't believe that's medically possible. So it is conceivable that Søren was putting a stimulant like caffeine in the sleeping pills."

Just at that moment, my ankle touched the prickly fruit of a plant that looked familiar.

"Hello, what's this? Datura!" I said, pointing to the trumpet-shaped flowers.

"Is it poisonous?" he asked.

"It contains alkaloids, which can be used as poison, and in smaller amounts, as a hallucinogen. Some people use it, uh, recreationally."

I lifted up a willow branch that was shading this part of the garden, and what lay underneath looked like a page out of a natural-pharmacology journal.

"Good Lord," I said.

"Wow, would you look at that – look how many are still flowering!" Richard said. "You'd think they'd be frost-bitten by now."

"They must've been protected in this shady corner. I wonder if Søren was using these plants medicinally. Many of these plants are pharmacological – foxglove, the natural source of the heart medication *digitalis;* that dark flower is deadly nightshade; the pretty one is St. John's wort which is widely used for depression, and the yellow flower there is henbane, which also has psychotropic properties."

"Yellow – that reminds me. How do teeth get stained?"

I suppose we'll never know whether Katrina's teeth were stained by henbane, smoking in secret or the citrus Earl Grey she drank every day. But I wrote down the incidents that occurred over the six months that Richard and Katrina lived on Rosenborgs Allé.

Curiously enough, there were 18 of them. I haven't explained them all yet, but I haven't given up, either.

1. Footsteps on stairs
2. Wineglass exploding
3. Ghostly man seen in window
4. Katrina's fall down cellar steps
5. Smoke
6. Document disappearing from computer
7. Angelina's dream of Damsgaard
8. Katrina's proficiency in Ravel's *Le Gibet*
9. Bed shaking
10. Damsgaard quotation at Bangsbo Museum
11. Alignment of Danish monuments ("ley line")

12. Threatening voice messages
13. Door locking self
14. Unexplained voices/music
15. Black hat in mirror
16. Relocation of two books
17. Hairy legs in bath of rose petals
18. Feeling of "buzzing" in limbs

# 44. Richard

As I walked away from the smoldering ruins, my hands were shaking, my heart pounding. I found it hard to breathe. *What was I afraid of?* Our ordeal was over – Søren was dead, the house was razed. About the only thing we didn't do was sow the ground with salt. But this was not fear. Fear has an object, like an invading army or a monster under the bed; it spurs a man to activity: run away, fight back, look under the bed. Anxiety, without cause, freezes you, stops you in your tracks. Like when you stand on the double yellow line, smack in the middle of Wood- haven Boulevard, traffic whirring by in both directions: you can't go forward, there's no way back, and you're terrified standing where you are.

So I decided to leave the tools in the wheel barrow and take a walk down by the water to clear my head, the same route I used to run. The air was crisp and I started to feel better as I strode briskly by the working docks, their cranes continually in motion, like an ant colony. I watched as heavily-built guys worked with their industrial-strength equipment in the harbor; Edvard said I was caught between two worlds. Part of me loved the money and status of the Mercedes- filled world of finance, but another, primary part of myself was envious of these guys working in the open air, the honesty of it.

Edvard told me that straddling the two worlds had made me isolated and vulnerable – and I guess that's right since I fell for a psychic. I felt so ashamed, but I did survive to tell the tale.

Thank God that George was there! Think of it. We were saved by a ninety- year old – and an *Anglican.*

*Help is often right next door, but you have to ask for it.*

Kastellet was a five-pointed fortress overlooking the Sound; the walls were topped with sandstone that glinted gold in the afternoon sunlight. It was an enormous golden star, *Guildenstern.* On my way up to walk the ramparts, I missed the first bridge, so I had to climb a ladder that had been left there, by some workmen I suppose. It was a hard climb – I was out of shape! Stopping to catch my breath, I admired some beautiful wildflowers that were growing out of a crack in the wall.

*Now who put these here?*

When I reached the top, I looked out over a vast vault of air – the view extended all the way across the Sound to the Swedish side. It was breathtaking. I surveyed the harbor, the ships, the docks, and the islands beyond. A group of sleek, three-bladed windmills were wading in the shallows there, standing guard over the city. I counted 18 of them.

*In a way, all of us are like those windmills – our arms, our actions, revolve around our own center; and as close as we sometimes get to each other, our blades never quite touch. But our movement is not random, not coincidental. The truth is that all of us are stirred by the same unseen breeze.*

I patrolled the perimeter, deep in thought. I felt guilty. All these months, Katrina was getting more and more detached from reality, falling deeper and deeper under the spell of the house, playing that damned tone poem on the spinet again and again. Meanwhile where was I? Out galavanting all over Europe, instead of taking care of her.

I thought I could trust Søren to take care of her while I was gone. But my so-called friend, who ate at my table countless times, was possibly trying to poison us. Such the gourmet with all his tapenade, goat's cheese, and Fumé Blanc – but what better way to hide the taste of a foreign substance?

At the first bastion, overlooking the north harbor, someone had carved the word *Fellowship* in stone next to the antique cannon. I continued my tour, reconsidering Søren's guilt.

"Nah, it sounds too paranoid!" I said out loud.

After all, Søren was a victim in all this. He couldn't have been responsible for the the books moving, the banging on the stairs, Katrina's fall. Anyway, why would he want to play tricks on us? It just didn't make sense.

I reached the second bastion, *Generosity*. I continued walking, going east now.

What if it wasn't Damsgaard who was after Katrina, but Søren himself. Maybe he wanted her to feel insecure so he could take advantage of her. What was he doing in all those hypnosis sessions? My ears burned.

At the third point of the star, the word *Purity* was engraved.

*Must be a list of virtues.*

I had to shade my eyes as I walked southeast toward the fourth point.

*So what do I get, the horns?* It was like an Italian comedy: the fatuous husband plays host to the lecherous neighbor. I was "host" to Søren, to Rowena, to Damsgaard – only instead of "guests," I had *parasites.*

The fourth was the bastion of *Courtesy.*

As I walked toward the last point in the star, I could see the sea again, and I said piously, "Please God, let me be enlightened so I can see the truth – but not my will but Thy will be done."

The fifth bastion read *Piety.*

Reaching the point, I got an unmistakable whiff of a pinewood fire, of fish being smoked by the harborside – like Fisherman's Wharf in San Francisco. I realized how hungry I was, and made straight for the smoke.

A lanky Danish fisherman with a light moustache and distant gray eyes had moored his boat and set up a small grill, not far from the Little Mermaid. But I had to get down off the ramparts and by the time I reached him, the smell had turned from delicious to disgusting. I walked up to the fisherman and said, making a face, "What are you roasting there, rotten fish?"

"This? This is the guts."

"What are you cooking that up for?"

"Nobody was coming today, so as you can see I'm packing up early. I'm cooking up the insides of this catfish for my dog." He motioned with his head to a tired-looking golden retriever in the back of the boat.

Judging from the heaps of stinking flesh on the grill, the whiskered fish must have been enormous – the organ meat spat and stank as it cooked. I turned away and walked across the plaza.

A hot-dog cart stood just in front of the war memorial. I was still hungry, so I ordered a hot dog and a regular coffee from a foreign-looking guy with delicate features and long eyelashes. His skin was the same color as the milky coffee. I took him for Middle Eastern or Greek maybe.

"Where are you from?" I asked.

"Me? I'm Italian," he said. His nametag said *Raffaello.*

Smiling, I said, "Me too," but before he could start speaking Italian, which I don't, I added, "Four generations back."

Handing me a blue paper cup with a Greek motif, he said, "Ah, I see. So what, you Danish now?"

"No, American – my wife's Danish." I sipped the coffee from the cardboard cup. The hot liquid felt good going down. It was very sweet, the way I like it.

"Is no' easy to becoma Danish. But I lika Dannamark – whaddabout you, you like it eeah?"

I hesitated. It had been a tough year. I answered, "I guess so."

"You shouldn' guess. You should know," he said as he put the frankfurter in its bun and without asking, slathered it in brown mustard and cooked onions – just how I like it. "Wherever you are, you should like. You know why? 'Cause every day is a gift."

I was about to agree with him in the good-natured way you agree with philosophers who sell hot dogs or drive cabs in their spare time – when I noticed a statue above his right shoulder, on top of the war memorial. I must have run past it a hundred times, but it's tucked behind a clump of trees and mounted high atop a column. I'd never looked up before.

So instead I said, "What's that?"

"I say every day is a gift," he said, a little louder.

"No, I mean what's *that,*" I said, pointing.

"Oh, you mean *who's* that!"

"What?"

"It's a *who*, not a *what*."

"It's a *who*?"

"Yeah, that's right, she sure is."

He gazed up at the statue, nodding.

We had stumbled into an Abbott-and-Costello routine, but sensing my confusion, Raffaello broke the pattern. "No, you no understand – an angel, she's a person, see? So you gotta ask *who* it is, no' what it is. People t'ing an angel is some kinda mysterious being with wings, but i's no' right. Angels, dey'r just like us."

"So this is an angel?" I asked, walking over to the column and staring up at the figure.

But the sun was behind it, and it was hard to see clearly. I desperately wanted to see what the angel looked like. Maybe it was *my* angel...

"Yeah, shu'," he said. "Angel o' Victory, i's a girl, y'know? Every time I come down eeah, I see my angel. She's a very beautiful, no?"

I squinted up at the angel, clothed in sunlight as she was. I started to feel strange, dizzy; the world started to shimmer, what they call "tunnel vision." I put my palms over my eyes, but could still see exploding starbursts of light. Like in third grade, when Nick Azarias was kicking up his heels as he ran up the stairs; I got too close, and got a uniform-shoe heel in my right eye.

I staggered back a couple of steps and collapsed onto a park bench, or I would've fallen to the ground. My left hand released the cup and it fell to the pavement, spilling over the pentagonal cement paving stones of the walkway. Putting my hands over my face, I doubled over. It must've been a migraine or something. I couldn't stand the light and felt sick, overwhelmed, just wanting to block out all light, all sound, all sense.

The last thing I remember was hearing a voice yelling, *"Hjælp! Hjælp! Tobee-as!"*

When I opened my eyes again, after what seemed like a long time, I was lying down on the bench looking up at the street vendor who was holding my head in his hands.

"What happened?" I asked in a weak voice that was hardly my own.

"Ah, you' life, she's a miracle! I thought you were gone for shu'!" he said with a wide grin.

I realized I must have blacked out, and asked, "How long was I out?"

"I dunno, maybe five-ten minutes. Tobias, he's the fish-man, he go get 'elp, but he no come back yet."

"I *was* gone. I mean I was someplace else. I remember looking up at the gray stone of the statue and then suddenly finding myself among such stones, on a rocky height, above a plain stretching out in all directions. The air was dry and thin. The wind blew shrill. I was so thirsty. I gulped in each breath. The terrain was rugged, unforgiving, and I cried out."

"You were struggling for breat', I thought maybe you were 'aving an 'eart attack..."

I continued recounting my dream, if that's what it was. "Then I was tumbling, jogging and stumbling down a stony path. The sun warmed my face. At a rushing stream, I plunged my head into the cool water."

"I 'addapour water on you' face – see you' still wet."

"The water revived me. As I walked along the river bank, my feet sank into its muddy wetness. I descended from mossy stones to reedy estuaries, and finally walked the plain among herds of cattle and wild ponies. I drank from a clear pool."

"You calm' down at one point. I give you some water to drink."

"Then the river grew wider, more tropical, and a huge crocodile—it must've been twelve feet long—came from out of the water and attacked this cow. The jaws yawned and bit off one of the hind legs first, drenching the green monster in blood and gore."

"Shh… It's over. Don't upset you'self now," he said, smoothing my hair like my mother used to when I came home with a skinned knee.

But I went on, more excitedly now, "As I descended farther, I entered a third realm, hotter still – I was sweating! And it smelled awful, like rotted things – the fumes burned my nose, it was so bad."

"'At was how I woke you up – I put some o' the fish under you' nose. Boy that got you' attention!" he said with a grin – his teeth were perfect, small and pearly white. Then he got serious again and said, "You musta had some kin' of a seizure – or 'eh, you no eat you hot dog?"

He went and got me a nice beef hot dog. I sat up and, despite my nausea I was able to eat easily – and greedily.

What did the vision mean? Maybe these past few months I had entered a whole nother realm – in reality or my own brain. A kind of Third Realm – not the desiccated heights of Eddé's skepticism, but not the rich plain of my childhood beliefs either. A world where a dark spirit can fall in love with a beautiful woman. Where illusion mixes with reality and you must wrestle with your deepest fears. And you can only save yourself by seeking help in the least likely place.

As I chewed on this, Raffaello came over.

"Listen, Richard," – *when had I told him my name?* – "I'm gonna leave you alone for a little while, but I won't be far away," he said with a wink.

"Okay," I said, thinking he would be back in a minute.

I finished the frank and went to tell him not to bother with the paramedics. But he had vanished. The hot-dog wagon, which had been just around the bend, was gone. There was no boat, no brazier. It was getting dark. I figured they had gone home for the day. I looked down at the wrapper in my hand.

*Hebrew National.*


I lost the Amphora cup, but still have the hot-dog wrapper in a frame over my desk, like it was Veronica's Veil or something. I went back to that spot a few times, but never saw Raffaello or Tobias again. My mother tells me I met an angel, maybe two – it turns out that October 2^nd is the Feast of Guardian Angels. Honest Injun, I had no idea that there even was such a thing. Edvard insists I just suffered a mild post-traumatic stress attack and was saved by a kind-hearted Italian street vendor.

Either way, I guess I was kind of lucky. And I remembered what Edvard had told me: that we could rebuild, that the most important thing now was to take care of Katrina so we can both move on with our lives.

That evening after my seizure, I was left alone on the park bench as it was getting dark. There were no cabs to be had, so I had to walk down Borgergade toward the D'Angleterre, where there was a taxi stand. All the cars had their lights on now, and I hugged myself in my herringbone coat to keep warm. As I passed Studieskole, a Danish language school, on the left hand side of a tree-lined block, I walked in, on an impulse.

"*Jeg ville lære mig dansk,*" I said, explaining in halting tones that I wanted to learn the language.

A pretty, dark-haired lady with a sharp nose and librarian glasses smiled and said she would have to give me a placement test. Within minutes, I was trying to imitate the *thirteen* vowel sounds of the Danish language. This experience proved beyond doubt that Danes are physically distinct from the rest of the human race, possibly the forerunners of a new multi-vocalic species, *Homo hyperglottis*.

I was assigned to Level One only because there was no Level Zero. The teacher scrawled the school's address on the chalkboard and asked me to pronounce the street name.

"Bor-ger-gad-uh," I said.

"Nej, det er *Bo-ga,*" she explained (*o* like *slow* and *a* like *had*).

"Bo-ga."

*It was going to be a long winter.*

And I smiled.

# 45. Ingrid

Claus and I were setting out the plates and silverware for the *julefrokost*. I was holding a traditional Christmas Luncheon the first Sunday in the month of December. My son had picked up the food at the caterers, his wife Agnete was in the other room with the children, and the other guests had not yet arrived.

"*Så hvad skete der virkelig?*" he asked. "What really happened?"

"You know what happened. The house burned down, and Katrina and Richard moved in right down the street here in Hellerup."

"No, I mean before that. What happened that night, the night they came up here."

"Yes, well, it was a Sunday, about ten o'clock in the evening. I was just having a cup of tea in the kitchen, in my bedroom slippers. I jumped halfway out of my skin when I heard the phone ring. It was Katrina, and she said that she just couldn't possibly sleep another night in the house."

"Why not?"

"She was afraid – but I'm coming to that. The next thing I knew, Katrina, her husband, and an English priest by the name of Pearson were sitting around my kitchen table at eleven o'clock on a Sunday night."

"That would be a first; what did they say to you?"

"That was the problem, they all started talking at once. It took me quite some time and several sandwiches to get them to calm down and tell me the story."

"Sandwiches at that hour?"

"Well, that was the first thing I learned: they were famished. Katrina had called in a *psychic*," I said, raising my voice and my eyebrows, "to help her communicate with the so-called ghost..."

"She *what?*"

"She called in a psychic. The Psychic of Østerbro, she calls herself. They had been up all night reciting prayers and incantations – fasting for days at a time, so by the time they got here, they were starving to death."

"I'm really very surprised," Claus said, shaking his head. "I never knew my sister was so superstitious."

"It was all part of an elaborate scheme in which she was going to trap the 'evil spirit' in a golden tabernacle."

"Let me guess – which she would have them purchase for a large sum of money."

"Yes, that's it."

"So your sharp banker son-in-law was taken in by a common *svindler.*"

"A swindler, yes, that's exactly what she was," said a man's voice from behind me. Evidently Agnete had let them in while we were talking, and Richard and Katrina were standing right behind us. We said our hellos with a touch of embarrassment, and then my son-in-law continued saying, "I feel so stupid now. Just like all the crime victims you see on TV."

"Oh, you mustn't blame yourself," Claus said. "That woman took advantage of you."

"That's right," I concurred. "She isolated you from you friends and family, deprived you of food and sleep… and then she was playing tricks on you – like those phone calls."

"What phone calls?" Claus asked.

"We got these weird messages on the answering machine saying *I've got you now,*" Richard explained. "We hadn't even met the psychic yet, but Katrina had left our phone number on their answering machine, and I guess they left those messages as a way of softening us up."

"The psychic was *gaslighting* you," I said. But Richard just furrowed his brows and Katrina puffed out her lips. Evidently they didn't get the reference.

"*Gaslight* – the film with Ingrid Bergman. Honestly, young people today," I said. "The Frenchman, Charles Boyer, plays the villainous husband who is driving his young bride mad, so he can steal her inheritance. Boyer keeps telling her that she's ill, isolates her – won't let her see anyone – and then starts playing tricks on her – moving pictures about, hiding things, walking on the upper floors at night."

"Gee, I should have paid more attention in film class," Richard said.

Katrina couldn't accept the idea. "Mor, I know the psychic was a fraud. But there were a lot of strange things that happened earlier. That's why we called her in to begin with!"

"What sort of things?" Claus asked.

"It started with banging on the stairs. Then there would often be the smell of smoke. I fell down the cellar steps – just like the original owner. And at night, the bed would shake, wouldn't it Richard?"

When he didn't answer, she repeated, "Wouldn't it?"

"I don't know – maybe we just whipped ourselves into a frenzy, just like Eddé says," Richard said, looking down.

There was an awkward moment. I was happy when Claus took her hand and said, "We believe you, Katrina. I'm just glad it's over."

"We are too," Richard said.

"I'm curious, though," Claus asked. "How did you break the spell? What saved you?"

"Well, all along the Psychic told us she was working with a priest," Richard said. "A Catholic priest. First he was going to come to the house, then he couldn't come in person but he would talk with us by telephone; finally, of course it turned out that there was no priest."

"I was so far gone, I didn't care about the priest. I would have done anything, given her anything," Katrina said, shaking her head.

Richard continued. "The psychic left us alone for a few minutes, I guess to go see if she could get someone to play the part of the priest. That was her one mistake, leaving us alone. She lost control of us momentarily. I was standing there in the living room, waving a stick of incense over my wife..."

"I was completely out of it," Katrina said. "Catatonic on the couch, clutching a big purple crystal to my chest."

"And I looked up and saw George's flags," Richard said. "Something clicked, and I said, 'Katrina, I want to call George.' And thank God I did. He really saved us."

Just then the other guests started arriving – Annika Jespersen, and Hans came. He's been very kind to me, ever since that day at the marina...

I sat across from him, and in between my son and my son-in-law. Richard has turned out to be a better man than I expected – he spoke Danish throughout the meal, and I was impressed with how he handled himself in a crisis situation. He had asked for help, admitted weakness, reached out to an older man. And in the aftermath, he's taken a new role in his firm so he doesn't have to travel so much. He's paying less attention to his clients and more attention to my daughter.

Over the traditional Christmas foods – smoked herring, *gravad lax,* pig cheeks, and so on – we continued to talk about the swindle. Claus, being a lawyer, told us about famous cases, like the older woman who was led to believe that her jewelry was cursed or haunted or some such nonsense. The psychic had to 'cleanse' it.

"… and of course once the psychic took the jewelry, the old lady never heard from her again," Claus said, shaking his head.

"Imagine, believing a piece of jewelry could be haunted," Hans said. "Why do the authorities allow them to continue operating when it's obvious they're all frauds? Fraud is illegal, isn't it?"

"Yes, fraud is illegal, but few victims ever come forward," Claus explained. "Most are too embarrassed to admit they've been fooled. And then it's hard to prove fraud – after all, the psychic has spent time with you, used supplies – crystals, incense, roses, and so on. So they claim any money they received was just payment for services rendered."

"What if the victim has been drugged? Surely it's illegal to drug someone without their knowledge," Richard said.

But Claus said, "Oh, that's even harder to prove. First you have to pay for the blood tests yourself. They're very expensive, and how do you know which drug to test for? And even in the one case in a hundred where the victim gets a positive test result, in court it's difficult to prove you didn't just take the drugs yourself. You may end up incriminating yourself for possession of illegal substances."

When it was time for dessert, the men went off to the solarium, talking about tax schemes, insurance coverage and real estate; Annika, Katrina and I sat by the fire in the winter parlor with our teacups.

*"Det er så dejligt herinde!* So nice and warm in here today – thanks for doing this, Mor," Katrina said.

"It's my pleasure," I said with a smile.

"Everything was lovely," Annika said.

"I hope you enjoyed the meal, Annika," I remarked. "You only ate the vegetables."

"Oh, yes. I finally took the step of becoming a vegetarian."

"You did? Good for you, Annika!" Katrina said.

"Do you get enough protein that way?" I asked.

"One has to be well-educated to be a vegetarian and stay healthy – it's important to get enough beans, especially soybeans – but if you pay attention, it's easy enough. And I feel so much better, so much lighter."

Katrina shuddered.

"What's wrong, Katrina?" I asked.

"Oh, it's just an echo," she replied.

"Echo of what?" Annika asked.

"The psychic told us that eating lightly made us fade, put us more in touch with the spirit world. I know it's nonsense, but I still flinch when I hear something that reminds me of her."

I said, "Oh, that's too bad," and I expected Annika to say something of the same, but instead she said, "That might be true."

"What are you saying?" I asked.

"It might be true that eating lightly, especially avoiding animal protein, helps a person get in touch with the spiritual realm. Mette is always lecturing on the evils of animal protein, Katrina. And think of the gurus in India who never eat anything but raw fruits and vegetables. There's a huge 'raw food' movement nowadays. The fiber cleanses the body of toxins…"

A country girl from Jelling at heart, I get annoyed at this kind of New Age nonsense.

"Annika, I have nothing against raw fruits and vegetables," I said. "But eating meat is hardly new – human beings have been eating meat for millions of years. One would think we'd be used to it by now."

"I've eaten meat most of my life," Annika admitted. "But when I realized how the antibiotics and hormones get into the meat, and saw how the animals are penned up in inhumane conditions, I realized that chemically and karmically, it was wrong for me."

"Annika is trying to get me to become a vegetarian," Katrina said.

"And stop drinking alcohol, and no more smoking," Annika added. "You see, I think all these things poisoned your body and mind until you couldn't think clearly."

"Well, it's true that something was yellowing my teeth – perhaps you noticed – I was starting to look like the Queen—"

"Katrina!" I said, running my tongue along my own smoker's teeth. "That's not a nice thing to say!"

"Not nice, but true," Annika pointed out.

"Anyway, it's gone away now, see?" she said, baring her teeth. "I've been using a special toothpaste."

"Were you smoking again, Katrina?" I asked.

"No, not for years now!" she proclaimed – but I noticed she blushed and looked away as she said it, so I wasn't quite convinced.

"So you think it was the toxins?" Annika asked.

"Perhaps it was the Pushkin Earl Grey I've been getting down at Perch's. The combination of citrus and tannin, and then we were drinking a lot of wine and eating a lot of rich and spicy foods. Søren would..." Katrina trailed off.

A silent moment emerged, grew round, and finally ebbed when I said, "Ah, poor Søren. What happened there, do you think?"

"He was a dear man," Katrina said. "But disturbed, I think. Richard heard that Søren's mother was deranged and committed suicide herself, amidst charges that she intentionally harmed her children."

"Oh, my. Well, he did seem a bit – eccentric," I said.

"But why would he hang himself from *your* rafter?" Annika asked.

"And how did the fire start?" I followed up.

Katrina hesitated.

"It seems that Søren was obsessed with me," she said. "He – did what he did as an expression of his desperation. He left me a note."

"You never told me," I said.

"No, well, it's embarrassing," Katrina responded.

"You weren't having an affair with him, were you?" Annika asked bluntly.

"No, nothing like that," Katrina said, turning scarlet once more.

"But you were aware of his feelings," I surmised.

"Yes," Katrina admitted, swallowing hard.

"He hung himself there so everyone could see his unrequited love," Annika said. "And then what I heard was that he knocked over a candle. Is that right, Katrina?"

"Yes," Katrina said. "The firemen said the sofa in the front bedroom contained something called 'accelerants' that made the fire spread quickly. We should never have left the candles burning, but we were in such a hurry that night! I never thought to check the upstairs."

"Well, it's a terrible thing, but it's over," I said. "No one was hurt seriously. The house can be replaced. Speaking of which, how are you settling in to your new home? I am so glad you were able to find a place so close by..."

And the conversation turned to brighter topics.

Later on, in the winter parlor, Hans and Richard sat in the easy chairs drinking vintage port, sipping it, coughing, and then holding it up to the light as if they expected it to change color or something, all the while telling each other how smooth it was. Agnete played a card game on the floor with the children.

Meanwhile, I sat with *my* children in the garden-parlor, sipping coffee as the last hint of color drained from the sky.

"*Hvad er klokken?* Huh, quarter-to-four," I said. "Funny, it feels much later than that."

"Yes, it's always later than you think," Claus said with a wry grin.

"Or at least it seems like that when you're *thirtysomething,*" Katrina teased.

Claus laughed. It seemed as if the sun was just coming back into his face after many years' absence.

"You'll be thirty in no time, Skat – isn't it your birthday this month? You'll be twenty-eight, yes?" he pointed out.

"Yes, but I'll always be younger than you!" she replied.

"And prettier," he added.

"Well, I can't disagree with you there," she said, and they both laughed.

It was good to see the two of them together like this.

"When are you putting up the tree, Mor?" Claus asked.

"I thought about putting it up for today, but it was too much work, and there's still three weeks till Christmas," I said.

"Shall we put it up this evening?" Claus asked.

"Oh, well, I don't know..."

"Yes, the children will love it!" Katrina chimed in.

"Just tell me where the box of ornaments is," Claus said, getting carried away with the moment.

"It won't do any good to tell you," I said, slyly.

"Why not, don't you think I can find them in that garage of yours?" Claus asked.

"I don't have a tree to put them on yet," I said.

"That's not a problem," Hans said as he and Richard wandered into the room, bringing the bottle with them.

"Why not?" I asked. "We can't very well hang the ornaments from the ceiling."

"They're selling trees on the quay already. I could be back with a tree in no time," he explained.

"And the kids would love it," Claus repeated.

"Very well," I said, and there was a chorus of cheers and "Can we go too?" from the children, who had overheard the conversation and were streaming into the room, followed by their mother.

"No," I said. "You little ones need to stay here and help the grown-ups with the decorations."

Claus got down the boxes of Christmas lights, handicraft elves, and decorations for the tree – candles, tinsel, glass spheres, and a five-pointed star for the top. There was one small box of ornaments that I had forgotten about: eggshells that had been hollowed out and decorated in the seventies, with photographs in them. There were shells of blue and green and silver; and inside a gold one, I found a picture of Per.

It made me pause. It was a younger, happier Per than I recalled, and I felt the corners of my mouth droop.

"Look at this one, Mor," Katrina said, showing me an egg that contained all four of us.

Suddenly, I heard an explosion and I gave out a little high-pitched scream. A large glass ornament had fallen and shattered on the carpet. I heard the cries of the children, and I saw Katrina and Claus comforting them, but made no movement myself.

It was the day Per died. After he was gone, after the white noise of the hospital and the horror of identifying the body in the basement, we came back here. The day was bright, but in this room, it was dark. The shards of emotional broken glass lay thick on the living room rug.

*The globe of our little family had exploded, sending fragments of eggshell-thin glass deep into our hearts like the shattered mirror in The Snow Queen. The unseen cutlass of ice froze us, froze us in that moment of time. And it's only now, so many years later that the shards of ice have melted and our hearts are whole once more.*

Katrina was not the only one who was haunted. We all had our ghosts. Perhaps she felt guilty for running away, for leaving me alone like that. But she was just a girl. I should never have let her go to New York, not right after Per's death.

I looked again at the photo of Per in the golden egg, and thought of the picture Katrina had hung over the sideboard. It must have been like seeing her own father's image, a brooding portrait of her father. The whole fiasco grew out of unresolved feelings of grief and guilt.

Just then Richard and Hans came in, carrying the tree.

Katrina had already swept up the glass, and the children clamored happily to help set up the tree – the minor catastrophe with the ornament already forgotten. Claus and Richard worked together to put the tree in its stand. Katrina sat at the piano and played "Silent Night."

Losing people is different from losing things. There is no quick cleanup of emotional messes, no way to avoid the morass of grief. We all shall love and we all shall lose.

We lose mothers, fathers, all – and the world marks it not. We can do nothing to change this fate. All we can do, in the space of time allotted to us, is live.

Hans poured out several glasses of port wine and brought over the tray. "Would you care for a port, my dear?"

"Yes. Yes, I would," I said, smiling and thanking him. We toasted the season, and I felt the warmth invade my chest.

# 46. Katrina

The snow swirled around the black and white checked taxicab that stood outside our new Hellerup home. All color seemed to have drained from the world. The whorl of wet snowflakes was so thick that I could barely see the driver, who stood calmly by the open trunk, wrapped in layers of white garments from top to toe, seemingly immune to the weather. Something about him seemed familiar as he took our bags.

"Flying south for the winter?" he asked amiably, his tropical face radiant.

"No," I said, settling in to the back seat. "We're flying to New York for New Year's."

"Yeah, and it's snowing there too," Richard grumbled.

"Well, you'll have no trouble getting out, Mister Hans. Kastrup is used to this kind of weather," he said in an assuring lilt.

"My name is Richard – what made you say Hans?"

"Oh, pardon me! I thought I heard Mahm say *Hans* at the door," the driver said.

"I did," I replied. "Hans is the man who will keep an eye on things while we're gone. He's just my mother's, uh, friend."

"You mean *boyfriend*, don't you?" Richard said with a twinkle in the eye.

"Well..." I said, making a wry face, but I knew it was true.

"Go on, admit it! It's great for her; she looks wonderful, ten years younger!"

"You're right."

The cab made slow progress toward Copenhagen through the thick blanket of snow.

"Gee, look at it come down! Maybe we should call the airport. I left my cell phone at home, since I knew it wouldn't work in New York anyway," Richard said. "Excuse me, Driver, do you have a cell phone? I'll be happy to pay extra for the call."

"No, I'm sorry, but I don't," he said, and it was true, I didn't see any electronics at all. No mobile phone, no radio, not even a meter.

"Snow, you don't like it?" the driver asked.

"Nah, never did," Richard admitted.

"You must be a real flatlander, then. In the high country where I come from, we are used to it. Snow is considered to be very beautiful, even magic. Mountain air is also very healthy – sick people go there to get well."

As I listened to the music of our driver's voice, I realized that I had met him before.

"Excuse me," I said. "But haven't you driven me before?"

"Oh, yes, I expect so," he said and flashed a beatific smile. "I am Jibril. It is my pleasure to guide you on your way in these slippery times."

"The worst isn't the ice or the snow," Richard said. "It's the darkness. I just can't get used to having so little daylight. So many clouds."

"Yes, I too miss the sunlight," Jibril said, "but I thank God for the clouds! They protect us, too."

"Protect us from what?" I asked.

Just then we passed by our old street, and I shuddered.

"Shadows, Mahm," the driver said.

Richard gave a nervous laugh and said, "What do you mean by that?"

"In my country, we have an expression, 'For every man who walks in sunlight, there is another, just behind.' You see, our shadows are always with us. When it is cloudy, they are hiding; in summertime, the shadows strengthen and show themselves, sharp on the sand."

It had never occurred to me before, but our taxicab-philosopher was right: the more intense the light, the darker the shadows will be.

And as if he'd read my thoughts, Jibril said, "Yes, the darkest by far are the shadows in summer."


When we got to the Gold desk at SAS, we found out that there was a problem – the flight was delayed.

"Five hours!" Richard said so loudly that heads turned.

"Yes, the weather, you know," the agent said. "But you may wait in the Gold lounge, and keep an eye on the screens. Maybe you'll be lucky and get out earlier."

"All right," Richard said, and then under his breath, "Aw, I knew we should've called."

So we went through security and found our way to the Club on the upper level, where the drinks were free and so were the drinkers. Despite the fact that it a Monday afternoon, the main room looked like a frat party – American football on a big screen television showing some kind of sporting event; a pack of open-collared, half-drooling businessmen chugging beer and cheering as they padded around their plush savannah of sofas and easy chairs.

I told Richard it would be fine if he wanted to watch the game; I had some reading I wanted to get done anyway. I watched him approach the herd, easing up to a large male who seemed like the Alpha. I held back, in the cover of a large ficus, not wanting to be drawn into the den of testosterone. I caught only snippets of the interchange as the males sniffed each other verbally: "What a great screen!" and "Who's playin'?" and "Oh my God, it's the Enevsea Title Game?"

Richard's voice rang out above the rest. "So you guys are from Tampa Bay, how'd TB make out this year.... Oh, you said *Green* Bay – 'Farve' is havin' a great year!"

Praising the "Farve" must have been some kind of password, because then I heard Alpha say, "Hey Richie, have a brewski." I knew then that he had been accepted into their ranks; he was lost to me, and I went to find a quiet spot in which to crawl into my book.

Near the entrance of the Club, there was a sparsely-populated lounge. A handful of scraggly patrons huddled in the booths along the wall on the right-hand side; one or two wiped-out businessmen slumped at a bar with four or five barstools. The best light was at the bar, so I claimed the stool on the far left. As the only woman in the room, I felt like I was on display, on a pedestal sitting up there.

Behind the bar was a swinging iron door that led to the kitchen. The Club provided food as well as beverages; the young bartender seemed to run the whole show, overseeing several white-clad women chugging back and forth bearing pitchers and platters for him. The barman had the efficiency of a timepiece and a wispy moustache that didn't suit him. His puppy-dog eyes looked out from over pillow puffs that made him look sad or tired, and entirely too old for his years.

I went to open my paperback, a Danish translation of a German classic, but I had not read far before I heard the bartender's clipped tones. "And what can I get for you, Madam?"

"Please don't call me that, it makes me feel so old!" I said. His nametag said *Dave O.* "If I can call you Dave, you may call me Katrina."

"As you wish, Miss Katrina. What can I get for you?"

"Well, what do you recommend?"

"Miss Katrina," he said, inhaling, "it hardly matters what I think, as you are the one who will be drinking it."

"Yes, but you're the expert. I'm asking for your recommendation."

"Well then, since you ask, for this kind of weather – ach, it reminds me of home! – *glühwein,* of course."

"*Glühwein!* How wonderful, did you make it yourself?"

"My mother's recipe," he said.

"So you're German?"

"Swiss-German," he said. "From the mountainous canton of Graubünden."

"Well then, since it's so authentic, I'll take a cup," I told him. Dave ladled out the hot wine into a large mug, adding a lemon slice with a practiced flourish. The smell of cinnamon and cloves reminded me of my mother's kitchen, and I started to feel warm inside even before I took a sip.

"This is delicious," I said. Dave just nodded. "Snow is not new for you?"

"*Ach,* we get tons of it!" he said, brightening. "Back home at this time of year, one can hardly get through the city-streets, let alone the roads. The snow piles up by the meter, so high that driving through a mountain pass is like walking down a narrow corridor that grows and grows until the towering snow banks on both sides leave just a tiny strip of blue – or more likely grey – for a ceiling."

"Oh my. That doesn't sound at all inviting."

"Oh, but it is – the clouds can roll in for weeks at a time, but then one day, suddenly one sees the high Alps all around! They've been there the whole time, of course, but hidden, in the mist and fog. Then the heavenly blue returns – it's quite a shock, it really is," he said with enthusiasm, and his face lit up like a Christmas tree.

Just then one of the underlings came in and led him away to duties in the kitchen, leaving me alone in the empty bar, and I didn't see him again. I glanced at the board and saw that there were still several hours before our flight. From the various cheers and shouts in the next room, I could hear that Richard's game was still on. So I poured myself some more wine from the carafe that Dave had left on the counter, and felt the sweet, hot wine begin to work its magic, subduing my senses.

There I was, leaden-eyed in the mirror behind the bar, sitting and staring at my cup like a faded barmaid in an Impressionist painting.

Twenty-eight today. Somehow the fact that it was my birthday made me uncomfortable. Was it the idea of approaching thirty? It had been a rough year.

It had been nearly three months since... since everything. Afterwards, I had blamed myself for Søren's death. If I hadn't taken that Luminal; if I hadn't purchased that scarf; if I had arrived earlier... but it wouldn't have mattered. After what Søren had gone through as a child – first losing his brother, then finding his mother like that. I wished I could've understood him, comforted him somehow. But there was nothing I could have done for him, no more than there was anything I could have done for Fa' – he had made his choices, and no matter how good a girl I'd been or not been, it wouldn't have made any difference. Nothing I could have done would have made Søren content, short of leaving Richard. In his dramatic death he had followed the same script he had in life – anything for attention.

Still, I felt there was something unfinished, as there had been with Fa'. Perhaps it was because there were so many things we never really got to know for sure: Were we imagining the sounds of walking on the stairs and floorboards? Was the ghostly man in the window a trick of the light – was it Søren standing there in the garden that night? How did the books move across the room? Was I pushed down the stairs or did I just trip on the door saddle? How did I play *Le Gibet* on first sight?

I looked at myself in the mirror and wondered where I'd gone wrong. There was no shortage of opinions. Annika was still hounding me about animal protein and toxins in my system. Feng shui was the first thing we tried – wouldn't it be ironic if it was the right path all along? What if the truth lay in the East the whole time? What if the suicide and fire were just further proof of the imbalance of Qi? That's what Mette said.

Snatching a cocktail napkin and ballpoint pen that were lying on the bar, I wrote *Mette,* making the *M* very large, in my best hand. She predicted we would move in the end. She also told me to call in a dowser. Why hadn't I? My mother convinced me that dowsing was just so much hogwash.

I inscribed her name, *Ingrid,* on the serviette, just below *Mette.* My mother saw my flirtation with Eastern ideas as superstitious, preferring to take a pragmatic view that the haunting was symbolic, a family problem. She said I was feeling guilty about abandoning her and Claus. Coming home forced me to confront my father's death and my unresolved feelings of guilt and grief. The ghost that was haunting me was not Karl Damsgaard but my own father who, like Hamlet's Ghost, cried out, "Remember me!"

But as my husband pointed out, the "Freudian" theory does nothing to explain why *he* had many of the same experiences I did. I wrote *Richard* on the napkin. He blamed Søren. It's hard to know how much of what he told us was true. Was Karl Damsgaard really a monster? Did he fall down the steps to his death? Or were these fabrications, designed to make us vulnerable?

Richard seemed to think that Søren was poisoning us, slipping barbiturates in the bouillabaisse. I didn't believe it. For goodness' sake, he was in love with me, wouldn't harm me for the world. Even the suicide note said as much. Sure, there were plenty of unusual plants in his yard, but that was not odd if one understood homeopathy, whose first principle was "Like cures like." Many of the cures included tiny amounts of substances that in larger doses would be deadly – belladonna, lobelia, aconite, even strychnine. It wasn't not such a crazy idea – after all, vaccinations work much the same way. Besides, even if Søren did exaggerate some of his stories to gain attention, he couldn't have infiltrated my mother-in-law's dreams or enabled me to play *Le Gibet.*

I wrote *Angelina.* She insisted that there had never been a ghost, that she never thought there was. But at the time, she was the one who kept wanting us to get a priest. She said our troubles started when we veered from Christianity and brought in superstitions like feng shui. What saved us, she believed, was the power of prayer, and especially the Rosary; and she points out that it was the "rosy" cross on the English flag that broke the spell we were under.

It was our neighbor who saved us, and I wrote *George* next. He introduced us to the idea of ley lines – I've often wondered if the surveyor's transit in the front bedroom had been used to find the best site for the house, perhaps even a ley line – but he insisted that they were never more than a parlor game for him, no more than fun for weekend strolls in Cambridgeshire. But I got a letter from the ley hunters. It turned out that there *is* a Benedictine monastery from the Middle

Ages right in the middle of the Swedish lake, Ringsjön. So I was right after all! But the coordinates of the proposed extension of the Danish Main Line ran several kilometers north of Svanemølle, so they thanked us for our input, but had no further interest in our case.

George and Una have been incredibly kind to us, inviting us out to tea on several occasions. We went with them to their church one time, too. They'd love to see us go more regularly. Was religion the answer? Was it all about angels and demons in the end? Some see Religion as just one more name for Superstition. I wrote one final name on the napkin, *Edvard.*

Our skeptical friend told us that once a group started to hold an opinion, even a demonstrably false opinion, it became almost impossible for an individual to dissent. False beliefs held by large numbers of people can lead to mass hysteria – like the witch trials at Salem or the extermination camps of the Third Reich.

Edvard, obsessive about such things, compiled a list of 18 separate misunderstandings, and dedicated himself to the task of refuting them one at a time:

an article reported that wineglasses from Poland will explode spontaneously if you put them in the dishwasher;

if one types *ADD*, but holds *Control* instead of *Shift*, this deletes all the text in a document and replaces it with the letter *D* – appearing to be Damsgaard's calling card;

"post-hypnotic suggestion" could explain other phenomena – Rowena could have given us coded instructions that, in our highly suggestible state, made us see things like the hairy legs in the bath. Before she came along, he claims we unwittingly gave *each other* suggestions like "I heard running on the stairs. Let me know if you hear anything like that."

But many of the incidents still remained unexplained.

Edvard's recommendation was psychotropic medication. Like most Danes, I was wary of taking drugs; luckily, Dr. Schroeder, whom I see once a week, was very understanding. The main thing was that I wasn't hallucinating any more. The flashbacks were tapering off, and I was sleeping well. No more unexplained phenomena. I didn't *need* medication.

Whatever they were, it seemed my ghosts were buried. And soon it would be New Year's, time for a fresh start.

I looked down at what I'd written on the napkin.

METTE

INGRID

RICHARD

ANGELINA

GEORGE

EDVARD


I startled. The letters spelled out *MIRAGE*, what we call in Danish *fata morgana*. Another coincidence? Or was the Universe arranging itself to tell me that all these explanations were just comforting illusions, like when the dying imagine water in the desert?

The Psychic was a fake, a mirage, but the abnormal activity predated her. What if the charlatan walked in on the real thing?

In the dream, was Fa' scraping the letters of his name off the door? Or could the Scraping Man have been Karl Damsgaard, attacking my family name?

*Damsgaard,* whom I saw with an empty chest because he was heartless;

*Damsgaard,* the collaborator who met with Nazis at the D'Angleterre and watched the coast from his study through the brass transit;

*Damsgaard,* co-founder of the Firm who left on condition that the name never be changed, and appeared to Fa' in the conference room that day, causing his heart failure;

*Damsgaard,* who used his connection to me via the pocket watch to start appearing in my dreams a year ago, about the time when his son Peder left for the nursing home;

*Damsgaard,* who lured me to the house, then started entering me for his own pleasure. This would explain the cigarettes I would find now and then hidden in unexpected places – the arm of the sofa, an old shoebox in the armoire, the bottom of my underwear drawer. It would account for the yellow stains on my teeth, "lost time," sexual fantasies. And how I was able to play *Le Gibet!*

The con artist must have been scared out of her mind running into a real ghost – was that why Rowena left us alone with the crystal in the front room? Was she in over her head and needed counsel or reinforcements?

She had said something about my birthday. Oh, what was it? Then I remembered, and my face and blood froze. Rowena had said:

"If we do nothing, the entity will take over by degrees and finally seize complete control. At that point, there is nothing anyone can do: you will be lost to us. On your next birthday, December 30th."

Today!

I downed the rest of my drink and was about to go run into the frat party and tell Richard everything, when I heard a loud voice say, "Bartender!"

It was Niels Dahl's voice. *What was he doing here?*

Well, it wasn't surprising to see him in a bar.

He sat on the stool next to me and said to the air, "What does a man have to do to get a drink in this place?" Then he looked in my direction and said, "Oh, my goodness, Katrina!"

"Niels, good to see you. *Længe siden.*" His firm had acted as broker for us, but we hadn't seen him since the fire. He looked awful. His eyes were blood red, his face shrunken, and much of his hair was gone, though there seemed like more than ever in his eyebrows and nose and ears.

"Yes, well. A lot has happened. You see, my wife passed away. Six weeks ago."

"Oh, I'm so sorry, Niels."

"Ah, well, nothing to be done about it. Fifty years, we were together. It's a long time. But at least she didn't suffer. Heart attack, *saa.* We were going to spend New Year's Eve in Puerto Banús. Nonrefundable. The bastards at the airline wouldn't give me a refund, not even for her ticket. So at least I'm using one of them. Goddammit, where's there a drink?" He slipped behind the bar and poured himself a large tumbler full of aquavit. He drank it down quickly, not pausing to say *skål,* and it seemed to revive him.

He smiled at me and said, "Oh, I'm sorry, my dear. Where are my manners? What are you drinking?"

"*Glühwein,* German mulled wine."

He poured us both another round. His face became grave and he said, "You know, I told Richard—"

"About Søren, yes, I know."

"About *Berlin.*"

"He told me. That's where you got the items," I said. "My father's pocket watch." Just then, I heard a chime. His hand went automatically to his waistcoat pocket. "You have one too?"

"I have the other one. Only two were ever made."

He pulled it out and opened the golden case. It was identical. The dull white face like soap film, the faint, ghostly hands, the jet black numbering, the dark clouds and crescent moon indicating night. Perpetual night.

"How did you come to have this watch?" I asked.

"It was my payment as executor. It was just luck that gave one watch to your father as the juniormost partner and the other to me. I think that's how we got to be such close friends."

"Such a watch must be worth a lot of money."

"You have no idea. If you sold this to the right person? A fortune."

"Niels, I don't understand. Why did Karl Damsgaard give these valuable possessions to the partners of the firm he'd been kicked out of?"

"The *will* stated that he felt remorse for having brought them into the scandal."

"What scandal?"

"Denmark was neutral during the first world war. Profiteers made millions, including Karl Damsgaard and his partners. But Karl got a little too close to the Kaiser, and he was pushed out."

"So he felt remorse and gave them such rich presents, even partners like my father, whom he never knew?"

"The testament says that, yes."

"But you think otherwise."

"Yeah, I think he wanted to keep some kind of connection, a chain of gold, to the partners, to the Firm. To the living."

He chuckled, smirked, and poured himself another one.

*The bylaws.*

"Niels, the firm's name was supposed to remain Justesen & Svindborg *in perpetuity.*"

"Damsgaard didn't want anyone to take his place, that's right."

"So when the partners voted to add Nielsen…" I leaned closer. I was just inches from his wrinkled face, etched as it was with thousands of tiny *x*'s, like scrimshaw. "Niels, do you think Damsgaard killed my father?"

He laughed, but with no mirth in his eyes. "How could that be? Damsgaard died, *jo,* more than twenty years before your father."

I kept staring at him, at the blue-and-purple spider veins in his alcoholic cheeks and nose. He knew what I was thinking, couldn't hold my gaze.

"You were in the conference room that day—"

"How do you know—"

"And Damsgaard was there too, I don't know how…"

"Do you even know what you're saying?"

"… but he came into the Wannsee Conference Room—"

"*Wannsee!* Of course it would be." He covered his face in his hands. *"For Fanden,* it's time I told somebody. No one knew, not even Helle, my own dear Helle."

"Tell me what?"

"The items. You see, those things weren't just…" He hesitated, looked around. "They weren't natural."

"What do you mean?" I asked, a frisson of fear going through me.

"Oh, at first glance, everything was nice and shiny and attractive. But when you examined them, each one was more of a curiosity than a work of art or handicraft."

"My mother said there was a painting, by Eckersberg."

"Yes, but did she tell you it was his last painting, done while his eyesight was failing and he was dying in a cholera epidemic? It was dark and festered, a cry of pain. No one would exhibit such a work at the time. It was kept hidden. Though I heard that Edvard Munch viewed the painting once while in the psychiatric ward in Taarbæk, and it inspired his famous *Scream.*"

The sweet smell of tobacco, languid and alluring, reached my nostrils. I looked around, but the bar seemed deserted.

"The other paintings were even worse. One called *Island of the Dead,* showed the ferryman of Hades in his boat. Another was the most dreadful thing I've ever seen. Called *Buch. 1942,* it took up most of one wall. It was in the cubist style, what do they call that, 'montage' technique?"

"Collage?" I tried.

"That's it. There were bits and pieces of a lot of different things – eyeglasses, hearing aids, patches of fabric, and what looked like three or four ink representations of stories on parchment – Hansel and Gretel, St. George and the Dragon. When I first saw them, I said, 'Huh, looks like a tattoo.' Well, I had everything appraised, of course. Turns out they *were* tattoos. The swatches were made of *human skin.*"

Just then he looked up, his eyes wide and said, "Oh, no!"

I turned and saw an older gentleman – once dashing but now in decline – surrounded by a little cloud of smoke at a booth against the wall. Apparently a man of business, his hair was slicked jet-black and he wore a dark jacket with paisley cravat. The flashy moustache, slightly open mouth and vacant stare were reminiscent of the painter Salvador Dali in his later years. The man appeared to have drunk more than his share, as several open bottles standing on the table in front of him testified.

Was this the man that made Niels cry out?

When I turned to ask him, his chair was empty. He'd left his jacket, perhaps he would return.

What was he saying just before he left? I couldn't remember.

*Ah well, no matter. My, that smoke smelled good.*

I smiled at the old man. *"Det dufter dejligt,"* I said. "but I don't think you're allowed to smoke in here."

At this he smiled back, a weak smile as if the muscles had not been used in a long time, as if the ends of the mouth had to be raised on wires. He made no reply other than to roll his eyes and cock his head imperceptibly upward and to the right, as if to indicate the brass placard on the wall stating, *Prince of Denmark Gold Lounge – Smoking Permitted.*

Smoking men still had one refuge left in Kastrup.

"Oh, I see," I said, nodding.

The man said nothing, just kept staring at me, or rather at a spot just over my head. It was off-putting, and I fumbled with my napkin, my purse, my cup. I filled it and drained it again. An ancient, familiar desire rose up in my blood. It was a ridiculous idea that came into my head, yet once there, I could not get rid of it.

It was the idea of asking him for a cigarette. I wrestled with myself. Surely I couldn't. I hadn't smoked in years.

I turned toward him, and started to say, "Do you have…"

But I was talking to the yellowed walls. He was gone; the room was empty. I looked up and could just discern a faint cloud of smoke still visible in the wan light.

By this point, my head was pounding – no doubt the hot wine had gone to it. I left some money on the bar, ran out of the cave-like lounge and down the plush stairs. All I could think of was buying a bottle of aspirin. I passed through the double doors and tripped out onto the busy concourse. I spied a tobacconist shop not twenty meters away on my left-hand side, and made straight for it.

Despite its small size, the store offered a wide assortment of over-the-counter remedies, alternative medicines and tobacco products. I approached the counter where a rack of pipes stood on one side and on the other, a stack of cigar boxes with exotic-sounding names like Montecristo, Perdomo, Diablo and Trichinopoly Black Tiger. From in-between, a small mustachioed tobacconist peeped out and said in a French accent, "Can I 'elp you?"

"I have a splitting headache," I said, holding my temples with my fingers.

"I'm so sorry to hear zat," he said with a broad grin.

The witty posters behind him were French. One showed the image of a large pipe above the caption *"Ceci n'est pas une pipe."* Another showed a horned red devil, a curvaceous blonde on his arm, smoking a cigar over the phrase *"Il n'y a pas de Feu sans Fumee."*

"Would you like to try something 'erbal? Or 'omeopathique, perhaps?"

"No, just some aspirin, please."

As the cheerful Frenchman rang me up, I had an impulse.

"Oh, and let me have a pack of cigarettes," I heard myself say.

"Which brand?"

Inspired by the poster of a triumphant blue package with a winged helmet, I said, *"Gauloises – blondes."*

The tobacconist raised an eyebrow, and said with a smile, *"Oui, Gauloises –* like the Queen."

# Author's Note

This novel is a work of fiction; the characters are creatures of my imagination. But like many works of fiction, the story has been inspired by actual events.

All of us experience odd occurrences, coincidences let's call them, from time to time. During a two-year period, I was exposed to a baffling run of them: all but two of the events on Edvard's list are taken directly from real life.

Given such a set of experiences, one may assume various intellectual postures: Skeptic (it's all a fluke), Believer (it's a ghost or "energy"), Detective (someone is manipulating you), Religious (angels and demons at work), Psychiatrist (you need medication), Agnostic ("there are stranger things...").

I emerged from the years of strangeness with the desire to explore such a "haunting" in fiction. I wanted to show the reader each point of view, and enable each character to tell the story, like kids around a campfire. The result is *Shadows in Summer: A Novel in Six Voices*.

My aim has been to entertain, but beyond this, I hope the story has given you the chance to consider what *you* think about the soul, the paranormal, and what happens to us when we finally doff this robe of flesh.

– Crescent Varrone
Risskov, Denmark
September 5, 2009

A.M.D.G.